WHITE KING AND THE BATTLE OF AMERICA

The Endgame

WHITE KING AND THE BATTLE OF AMERICA

The Endgame

A SUSPENSE NOVEL
BY
LEE KESSLER

Printed in the United States of America

ISBN: 978-0-9888408-0-5

Library of Congress Control Number: 2013900355

Brunnen
PUBLISHING

"Skillfully woven, *White King and the Battle of America* is a thought-provoking thriller that goes beyond targeting the obvious enemies of liberty and addresses the true puppet masters and their unwitting marionettes. Kessler's insight and brilliant combination of fiction and fact will lead you through a remarkable journey; and the spine-tingling conclusion is exactly the sort of awakening our society needs to shake us of our complacency. Despite the fearsome truths Kessler unveils, she offers the reader hope within the maelstrom—that even in the darkest hour, it is never too late for the people to triumph."

—Jess Phillips, Writer and Writing Consultant
Sherman Oaks, CA

"*White King and the Battle of America* is a timely, well-written, and well-researched novel that will open the readers' eyes to the issues our world is facing today. Lee Kessler has crafted a story that shows readers the 'why' behind some of today's largest global issues. By taking these complex topics and putting them in story form, Kessler challenges her readers to think outside the box for ways to help their own communities. Following in the footsteps of the first two *White King* books, *White King and the Battle of America* will incite hope in the reader, with its dramatic storyline that has you cheering on the underdogs from the first page. I absolutely loved this book. I was sad to see the series end, but I enjoyed every minute of seeing how the journey unfolded."

—Tara McCleskey, Stage Manager, Field of
Dreams Performing Arts Conservatory
Raleigh, NC

"Ms Kessler has done it again with *White King and The Battle of America*. What a fun, fine read. In addition to being a stand-alone thriller, this book brings an exciting and definitive climax to her unique trilogy. It is the proverbial page turner, with not only a story line very pertinent to the current political and economic climates with which the U.S. is now faced but, in addition, a very probable solution to those enigmas."

—"CJ" Johnson, Property Developer
Troy, MT

"I just finished reading *White King and the Battle of America*. Like each of Lee Kessler's previous installments in this action packed trilogy, I couldn't put it down once I started.

"The thing that has been so mesmerizing about parts one and two, were that they served as prophetic novels that were eventually played out in real life world events. What is most intriguing about the third and final installment is the eye opening realization that events about which Kessler began writing, more than a year ago, are now actually beginning to take place around the world in the financial markets.

"My greatest hope for this series and the future of our country is that this trilogy is eventually adapted by Hollywood to the big screen in an attempt to serve as a wakeup call for those of us who still believe in America and the principles upon which we were founded."

—Vincent Rush, President, Rush International
Cincinnati, Ohio

"With this book, Lee Kessler proves once again that she is a masterful suspense novelist. Her topics are a combination of intensive research and her futuristic visions. The result is always a *tour de force* that captures and delights every reader."

—Verna Sabelle, Editor and Publisher
New York, NY

This book is dedicated to one of the great Americans of our time, Mr. Rich DeVos. He is a giant in the world of Free Enterprise, a champion of freedom the world over, and a hero of mine.

Author's Note

*F*ollowing a speech I gave last year at a leadership conference for members of Generation Y, a college student read my first two books and posted a comment on Facebook. She said, "I've never liked history, but this is history in our time. I learned more from these books than I had in 23 years."

For those of you who have read the first two books in the trilogy, you know that in *White King Rising*, with the release of the computer game, we moved into a fictitious alternative history—one running parallel to actual events.

The third book begins in that "alternative history," in a world that *could be*—both the bad and the good. It is the story of what may yet happen, or may even *be* happening.

In these frustrating and dangerous times, I am reminded of several things I embraced along my journey in life. One: that the word "crisis" in Chinese means "opportunity riding a dangerous wind." Two: Mark Twain's ironic observation that, "It is easier to fool people than it is to convince them that they have been fooled." And three: something Robert F. Kennedy said. "There are those who look at things the way they are, and ask why…I dream of things that never were, and ask why not?"

As we finish the trilogy of the *White King*, it is my intention that we—no matter the crisis—see what could be and ask, "Why not?" The trilogy's young heroes inspire us to know that no matter what we have to face, something can always be done about it.

CHAPTER 1
THE ANALYST

*T*he small red flicker of the guard's cigarette silhouetted the man, causing James to crouch down into the tall pasture grass. He had assumed that Bud Walker would maintain a security guard presence at his ranch following the revelations throughout the world's news media that he had brought the propaganda chief of Al Qaeda himself into his inner circle. James Mikolas was nonetheless disappointed by this heightened danger tonight.

It was rumored that the billionaire media mogul and head of Walker News Group had slipped into a personal decline of drinking and depression following the infiltration of his media empire by a clandestine operative sent by the mastermind of Al Qaeda. The long arm of Al Qaeda had penetrated deep into America, reaching out from the TV screen itself into the homes and psyche of an unsuspecting public. Mikolas had no idea whether this rumor was true. He only knew the man had become very reclusive over the last three years.

WNG still existed, but many of its bureau chiefs had resigned, leaving only junior personnel to run what had once been perhaps the toughest and most competitive network in cable news. Why anyone remained was a mystery in their industry, given that the "magic" and driving force of the media empire had been devastated by the FBI's discoveries about his protégé. Bud Walker had trusted and admired Samir Taghavi, and now his life and business enterprises were in chaos.

Mikolas, however, had no sympathy for Walker and normally would never have even considered a face to face meeting with the man, let alone risked a breaking and entering charge to accomplish it. James Mikolas was a man on a mission that night. He, too, had walked through his own personal hell following the murder of Kelly Weir at the hands of an Al Qaeda-hired assassin. It was little comfort knowing that the assassin, known as "the Viper," had himself been assassinated by the Mossad.

No one could bring back his fiancé, and so the death of her attacker meant only one thing to James: There was one less bad guy roaming throughout South America and Europe. That was all.

Tonight, though, he had his attention on the living, and he had decided to do something he never would have risked otherwise. As he checked the magazine in his Glock to make sure he could handle any situation he might encounter, James slid forward on his stomach and cleared the bottom wire of an electrified cattle fence that protected the vast cattle range owned by Walker.

It was quiet—the only disturbance to the silence being the braying of cattle hundreds of acres away. An occasional hoot of an owl told James he wasn't the only creature of prey out that night. Having cleared the gate without arousing the guard, he headed toward the residence. From his vantage point, it looked deserted. *Perhaps he is not here after all,* James reflected. *Maybe this whole exercise is futile.*

But something told James that Walker was there. He could smell him. As he moved closer to the imposing stone and log lodge, his ability to see improved. Fear of the guard at the gate also dissipated when he realized there was no one else protecting the perimeter of the house. *Just one guard,* he thought. *Probably some $10/hour local security guy who gets paid to make the place look occupied. Shouldn't present a problem—if I move quickly.*

That thought alone propelled James across the manicured lawn, which formed an oasis in the sprawling pastureland, bringing him closer to the house. And there he saw it—one yellowish light in a room at the back, and the flickering of dying embers in a fireplace. *I got you, Bud Walker. Tonight we meet.*

James breathed in the cool Montana air, bracing himself for the encounter to come.

Walker was sprawled on an indecently large leather chair, seemingly unconscious. There was no one else in the room, and Walker seemed unaware of the dying embers. Only the near-empty bottle of Stolichnaya on the matching foot stool exposed the reality that the man was alive, and apparently burying himself in the bottle.

What a cliché, James thought, sneering.

He gently opened the French doors from the patio and walked into the room. Despite the fact that he had been stealthy, it proved unnecessary. It was unlikely Walker would have heard a fire alarm going off.

Selecting a chair opposite the man, he sat down and waited. *And to think, I've come for him!*

CHAPTER 2
THE GAMERS

"Brian, you got a minute?" Andy Weir interrupted his housemate as Brian was emptying the trash. It never ceased to amaze him that Brian still wanted to do the trash duty. Andy smiled as he watched his friend meticulously snap the lid back on the city-provided containers. *No critters going to get any vittles here,* he mused.

Although the computer game they had created in 2007 made each of them wealthy enough to have bought separate homes in the hills overlooking the Sunset Strip and the Los Angeles basin many times over, they'd been together so long now that they preferred each other's company, and trusted each other.

Perhaps it was the fact that they were both orphans now—their families casualties of the pharmaceutical-psychiatric cartels and the terrorists they facilitated—or perhaps it was the bond between two men who had turned that issue around for the United States and for the world as well. The popularity of the game "White King Rising" was such an international phenomenon that it swept the globe in just two years. Not only did it make Andy and Brian very wealthy, influential, young men, but it had also freed countless millions of young men and women from the ravages of street drugs and prescription pharmaceuticals. It had given both men the platform to address America's youth, anytime and anywhere of their choosing.

On the day Andy had scattered the ashes of his mother—a fallen hero in the War on Terror—he had met the stunning redhead with the glittering green eyes who had been his steady girl for the last three years. He'd made a decision recently, and he felt he needed to discuss it with Brian, even before he approached Reagan. She was engrossed in relentless research concerning the latest human rights atrocity to come on the radar screen, and she and the organization she supported were preparing their attack line.

Ironically, drugs, as a vital part of the economy, had waned—due largely to the enormous impact of Andy's game. But human trafficking now seemed to be the crime of choice of the cartels throughout Latin America. The increase in violence and kidnappings—especially in Mexico and Arizona—was causing the U.S. to reel. Reagan Lynch was in the thick of that. The game's victory over drugs had exacerbated Terrorism's need for a source of money, and so the slavery market had increased—propelling Reagan into the thick of the War on Terror as well. Since she'd be gone a few days, Andy decided it was time to talk to Brian.

"Okay, bro, what's up?" Brian ducked into the kitchen and washed his hands, leaving Andy to follow him.

"I want to talk to you about something," Andy said, as he sat at the table, motioning for Brian to join him.

"Sure."

Andy Weir had never been indecisive. By age eighteen, he had become a Grandmaster chess champion with a career ahead of him. Nor had he ever been reluctant to make changes when change was needed. But, as he looked at his partner, he experienced a slight tremor in his stomach. He knew Brian would be all right with this. It wasn't that. It was just the end of an era; that was all. Time to move on. Exhaling slightly, he said, "I wanted to let you know, before I even spoke to her, that I intend to ask Reagan to marry me."

Brian's reaction was immediate. "Man, that is fantastic! About time, is all I can say. I was about to have to tell you that if you didn't snap her up, I would," Brian joked.

Andy laughed. For a moment, it seemed like their high school days in Arlington, Va., where, before a football game, they'd occasionally talk about what girl they were hanging with at the time, offering each other teenage advice on love and love languages. He knew Brian would be happy about this. Now, for the next bit.

"So, Brian, as much as I love sharing the house with you…" He never got the sentence finished.

Brian interjected. "Say no more. I totally get it. Matter of fact, I've had my eye on a house out in the Palisades, and I couldn't figure out how to break the news to you. So, just buy me out of this one, and I'll snag the other one."

That was it. *All there is to it,* Andy thought. *You always could handle an incoming ball.* Andy just looked at Brian for a moment and smiled. Years earlier, they had been like that. Andy as the quarterback would look for his favorite wide receiver, and he'd toss it into the hands of Brian Washington Carver. It didn't seem to have mattered whether Brian was open or not—or even if he was set—Brian always seemed able to reach out, grab the ball, and complete the play. Today was no exception.

"Thanks, Brian."

"No problem, bro." Rising, Brian gently tackled Andy's shoulder and added, "You'd better hope she says yes, or you're going to be living here all by yourself!"

"Good point."

"Yeah, you let me know how that goes. For now, my lips are sealed." He'd stopped speaking, but he didn't leave. Rather he just stared at Andy.

"What?"

Brian hesitated for a moment, then answered, "I was just thinking your mom would have approved."

To his surprise, Andy teared up a bit and cleared his throat. "Yes, she would."

Still standing there, Brian ventured a question of his own. This one was awkward, and it revealed something still lingering with him. "Do you think age makes any difference to feeling like an orphan? Does it ache less because you're older?"

Andy shook his head, shrugged, and said, "Don't know, friend. I still miss her."

"Me, too." He stopped momentarily, finally adding, "I miss all of them." Then, as abruptly as he had entered into melancholy, he withdrew from it. "But Reagan will sure brighten up the place!"

CHAPTER 3
THE PROPAGANDA CHIEF

Samir's deep inhalations were his first breaths of free air in more than three years. He didn't really know how "free" he was, given that he was about to land in Pelotas, Brazil for transport into Colombia, and to a meeting scheduled with the FARC, which would determine the financial fate of Al Qaeda and the direction the organization would go in the years ahead.

I at least made it out of Pakistan alive, he thought, commending himself. Samir Taghavi had indeed been walking a tight rope between Bin Laden and the Doctor since his narrow escape from the United States. Knowing that the two Titans of the Al Qaeda movement were in a stand-off—certain that for one to kill the other would be an exercise in mutually assured destruction—he had convinced each that he was, and always had been, loyal to them.

That had not been an easy task, for their tiny quarters in Abbottabad reeked of betrayal. Bin Laden, aware now that his friend and trusted physician had drugged and sequestered him in Iran, was vulnerable. Yet he knew he needed the Doctor and access to the Doctor's connections—along with the money the Doctor had appropriated—if he were to resume control of an organization that had been decimated by relentless U.S. attacks on all fronts since 2001.

For Bin Laden, truth be told, had been stunned to learn of the death of almost all of his colleagues and highly trained personnel. From the moment he had been drugged just outside of Tora Bora in December of 2001 and transported to Iran for "safe keeping" by the Doctor, Bin Laden had no knowledge of the fate of Al Qaeda, its Jihad, or his friends. Now, the only colleague he would have regarded as his true friend was under suspicion.

Samir knew this, and knew that, whatever Zawahiri might have done, it was likely he would emerge the victor here. *Still, it's too dangerous to be in the crossfire if these two go at it,* he had told himself. So, no matter how distasteful a task he would be given, if it got him out of the range of those two, he was prepared to do it.

Moreover, the perceived shambles made the group vulnerable to the power plays of their region. Hezbollah, Hamas, all of them, had revved up their game in the apparent confusion of leadership. And, if that weren't bad enough, it was now clear that Iran had its own agenda and really could not be counted on in the Jihad. All Iran could be counted on to carry out, as far as Al Qaeda leadership could ascertain, was the annihilation of Israel.

Samir Taghavi was Al Qaeda's propaganda chief. He had presided over the near demise of the United States through the infiltration of their media at its highest levels, and through masterminding the implementation of mind control upon its people through the widespread use of deadly, but appealing, pharmaceuticals.

It had nearly worked until the United States had mysteriously rejected the pharmaceuticals, psychotropic drugs, and the psychiatrists who had promoted this way to sedate and anesthetize a population. The reversal was so sudden and swift that it had taken the mastermind of Al Qaeda, the Doctor, by complete surprise. At first, no one knew why America's youth were in open rebellion about something they had heartily embraced for thirty years.

Samir's investigation into it had exposed the likely culprit as the computer game, "White King Rising," created by a football-playing ghetto punk and his brainy chess-master friend. As unlikely as that seemed, Samir, nonetheless, had had to inform Al Qaeda's mastermind that two boys, barely out of their teens, had somehow trashed his plans.

To make matters worse, the young men and women who were typically easily influenced by his skillful public relations campaigns had also turned their backs, with a vengeance, on illegal street drugs. It seems America's youth were now leading the world in a wholesale reversal of the drug scene.

And that was bad for business. It was bad for terrorists who supplied the heroin to the drug cartels; it was bad for the cartels; it was bad for the governments who benefited legally and illegally from this entrenched commerce. No one benefited, except the *people* of countries once ravaged.

Knowing that a new game had to be created, Samir had sat in as Bin Laden and Zawahiri considered their options. Arms sales would continue, as would all of their money-laundering operations and Internet banking and telecommunications fraud. But they had decided upon another revenue source, hoping it could partially replace the lessening drug revenues. More important than the money even was the fact that they needed to retain influence.

To do that, they needed their Public Relations officer. His gruesome assignment was to strike a deal with the Colombian FARC regarding the sale of women into slavery. The FARC and their other partners in slavery would deliver the "slaves," and Samir would deliver the "buyers" from the Mid-East and Africa. With 27 million people already enslaved in the world, the appetite for sex slaves was escalating, and the "broker's fee" that Al Qaeda would acquire for arranging the transport of these women to men in the Mid-East and Africa would offset some of their losses, but, more importantly, it fit their definition of terror.

His own journey aboard ship had been a test run. Brought out through Pakistan to Yemen, and from there to Somalia, he had boarded a freighter as "cargo" and been conveyed into this Brazilian harbor. There had been little food, bad air, and horrible containment conditions. But he had made it. *And, so will the women, going the reverse direction,* he concluded.

Tugboat horns brought him out of his reverie and alerted him to the fact that he would soon disembark. The fresh air made him slightly dizzy, and the light rain falling made him feel almost cleansed of the putrid smells aboard the ship. Were it not for the oppressive humidity he was experiencing, it would have seemed a perfect welcome.

Samir caressed the documents he held firmly in his hand, telling himself that the forged papers would secure his safe passage into the city, and on through to the triangle of Brazil, Uruguay, and Argentina. Crossing the border in that sector made it possible to connect with the principle traffic lanes for terrorists in South America. Moving north through Bolivia and Peru, they could then access Colombia, where numerous safe houses and zones existed for harbor. Drug cartels and terror organizations were fraternal twins and shared a great deal.

At this moment, Al Qaeda was entering into human trafficking, and their propaganda chief, Samir Taghavi, was their advance man. In three days, he would meet with a man he knew only as "Hyena."

Disoriented by the trip, and having crossed numerous time zones, Samir pulled out his watch to check the date and time in this sector of the world. It was May 1, 2011. He would be expected to check in at an Internet café, intercepting any vital email traffic that Makkawi, whose real name was Saif Al-Adel, would have left for him. The email was to be used only in case of emergency.

For a number of years now, Makkawi had been the military commander of Al Qaeda. He had escaped death or capture through meticulous control of communication lines, and use of public computers in innocuous cafes was a frequent tactic.

Disembarking, Samir had no way of knowing that there was indeed a message waiting. No one on the docks paid any attention to the announcement that the President of the United States would address his people that evening, let alone the reason for a Sunday evening Presidential communication. Nor did Samir have any idea just how much his future had changed in a mere 24 hours.

CHAPTER 4

*H*e was more alert than he appeared. Bud Walker may have been a billionaire media mogul, invited guest of the President of France, and darling of the iconoclastic, self-made impresarios, but he was also a Montanan.

Decades of living on a ranch had taught him to be prepared for whatever the elements of Montana might present, and to be ready for any animal—two legged or four legged—that he might encounter. Clearly though, he was at a disadvantage as he roused himself from the stupor into which he had slipped.

He couldn't say what had woken him. Perhaps it was the chill in the room now that the fire had died. More likely, it was the armed man who was watching him.

Well, if he planned to kill me, he probably would have done so by now, Bud thought. *Or at least have it pointed at me.* Then suddenly he laughed at the irony. *Shit, he knows I'm too far gone to present any threat to him. Better find out what he wants.*

"I gather I ought to fire the son of a bitch at the front gate…"

"Seems like it, yes, Mr. Walker." James couldn't help but admire the man for his humor in the face of a man with a gun. *But then again, I don't have it pointed at him, so he knows he's safe—for now.*

Walker tried to sit up, but tipped backwards into the plush back cushions. Swinging his legs around to get a better angle, he pushed forward again until he was upright and eyeing the man opposite him. That is, until the dizziness caused him to lose focus. *Damn, how long have I been drinking, and where the hell is my gun when I need it?* He truly could not remember where he had put it, and an incipient surge of fear was starting to hit his sphincter muscle.

Suddenly, the intruder stood, grabbed him by the front of his shirt, and started marching him toward the sprawling master suite on the first floor. "I want you sobered up when we talk, and you need a shower. How in the hell did you turn yourself into riff-raff so quickly?"

"I've always been riff-raff, didn't you know?" Bud giggled. He was a happy drunk, always had been. That fact had gotten him out of a lot of scuffles in the past. He wondered if it would now.

The intruder did not respond; instead, he walked Bud into the six-foot-by-six-foot shower with its six shower heads, sat him on the stone seat in the center, and turned the water on full—soaking him, clothing and all. The temperature was enough to wake the dead, and Walker wished he had the footing to stand up and get the hell out of there. Knowing he didn't though, he meekly took the bar of WNG-branded oatmeal soap the man handed him.

"Who are you?"

No answer. Impaired or not, Bud Walker wasn't a man to ask a question and fail to have it answered.

"I asked you WHO you are, goddamn it!"

James Mikolas looked down at the man in the shower and said simply, "Not a friend."

Defiantly, Walker challenged him. "Well, if you are a god-damned enemy, you should have signed the guest book. I've got plenty of them."

"Not an enemy either."

"Well, then what…who…the gun…Jesus, I'm confused." He was beginning to be thankful for the sobering cold water, which was rousing him second by second. The stranger had him at an obvious disadvantage; the faster he could restore himself, the better.

"I'm a man you took something from, and I want you to fix it, that's all. So, take your clothes off, Mr. Walker, clean yourself up, and start acting like the confident son of a bitch we all had to listen to for the last decade."

Bud Walker, for some reason, found that funny, and he could not suppress a chuckle that grew into a loud guffaw. Though the man still held the gun, it was obvious he wasn't going to use it. *At least not right now.*

Shouting over the top of the shower, he eyed the man and asked, "So, once again, who are you, and why'd you bring a gun to meet with a drunk?"

"James Mikolas. And like the Boy Scouts, I like to 'be prepared.'"

The fog of drink was definitely clearing a bit now—enough for Walker to know something was about to change. "Are you a Boy Scout, Mr. Mikolas?"

"Absolutely," James responded without hesitation.

"So, what are you here for, Mr. Boy Scout? You gonna *redeem* my sorry ass?"

"No." James let that hover for a moment and then answered, "*You're* going to redeem your sorry ass. So, get your robe on, and we'll talk."

Walker had eaten well. He may have been drinking heavily, but James noticed the refrigerator was well stocked. James made him a mound of scrambled eggs, bacon, and toast—the only things he knew how to cook. That and tuna fish sandwiches were the staples upon which Mikolas had survived for thirty years. He didn't see any reason to experiment for this sorry sack.

Fortunately, Walker seemed to know how to operate his Espresso machine and made a double shot for himself. Graciously offering one to James, he shrugged it off with a, "Suit yourself," as James demurred.

Sliding his plate away and wiping his mouth, Bud Walker was grateful for the meal. It was definitely the capper after the shower, and he was starting to feel like his normal self again. Except for the fact that his head felt like a bowling ball, he was pretty stable. Bud had many faults, but ingratitude wasn't one of them. Looking up at Mikolas, he studied him for a moment and then said, "Thank you."

"You're welcome."

The two men sat silently, eyeing each other. James was holding a folded piece of paper in his right hand. He would occasionally tap the table rhythmically with it. In any kind of standoff, someone blinks first. This time it was Walker. "All right, what is it you want?"

"I want to talk to you about what you've done, and what you are going to do to fix it."

"Well, James, is it? I've done a lot of things it seems. So, enlighten me as to what you mean."

James spoke succinctly but painted a vivid picture for Walker. Bud knew he had unwittingly brought Al Qaeda's Propaganda Chief into the living rooms, dens, kitchens, and bedrooms of millions of American households. He knew further that he had let that man influence his own thinking, and therefore his company's direction and focus. He also knew he had weakened the people he honestly felt he was supposed to protect— the American citizens who relied upon his judgment and the reporting of his news agency in order to know the peril they might be in, to analyze choices they should make, and to figure out how to help their government fight an enemy that was brilliantly fighting not only militarily and economically, but also psychologically.

He was a stunning disappointment to himself, and to everyone around him, and he surely didn't think this man was going to bring anything new to the table. He was wrong. The content of that folded paper, and what James Mikolas relayed to him in the kitchen of a log ranch house nestled in the shadows of the Continental Divide, would change the course of history.

Mikolas revealed who he was, and how he and two young men had been chasing the Mastermind of Al Qaeda since 2001. He explained how his Grandmaster Chess Champion partner had concluded that "the Doctor" was running eight different chess games simultaneously, and that they were arranged in an order of importance.

The lowest level game was Religion and was being used to recruit disenfranchised youth around the world. The second was Military, and that had most of the governments of the world in turmoil. Then Intelligence and Public Relations, which had eventually tipped off James and his partners to the fact that the enemy was using our own media to propagandize and exert mind-control inside the United States. Since WNG was dominant as a result of "help" supplied by one Samir Taghavi, they were the rooster crowing—the news agency CNN, Fox, and all the others had copied.

That left the American citizen surrounded by a pervasive media presence that had pummeled him with skillfully planted false information, and had influenced elections, government policy decisions, and just about everything else in America from 2001 to now.

Stunning to Walker was James' revelation that the Weapons game the enemy had deployed included Fear, and the main delivery mechanism of fear, and its attendant chaos and paralysis, was the Media itself. The next game was Sociology, and the resultant collapse of so many of America's institutions when those institutions were being driven and motivated by fear. And the poor American became anxious and depressed, leading him directly to slaughter in the game second from the top, Medical.

It was there, in one of the most stunning analyses ever done on behalf of the nation, that Andrew Weir had discovered the use of pharmaceuticals to anesthetize and subdue the American people by addicting them to psychiatric medications and prescription medications of all types. It was that discovery which located the likely "hide in plain sight" of "the Doctor" himself—as an investor in Decu-Hehiz, a major Swiss pharmaceutical company. This information unlocked the top game, the end game.

All roads led to Money. And that is why James Mikolas had risked a felony charge that night. He had come to find an unlikely partner.

"All right, Mikolas," Walker said. "I'm tracking with you so far. I'm sick to my stomach, but I'm tracking. And I don't get it."

"Don't get what?"

"Your boys, Carver and Weir?"

"Yeah, what about them?" James was testy about any reference to the two young men he loved more than anyone else. They were family to him, and he rankled at even an inflection of criticism of either one of them.

"They invented that game..." He was grasping for the name. "Yeah, that game 'White King Rising.'"

James nodded.

"Well, Jesus, that game ended the whole drug scene! My God, even my wife's nephew was playing it and got himself off the cocktail of drugs he was on. Now *he's* like a Crusader." He paused, looking the scene over, and continued. "My God, the demand for drugs is drying up all over the country, and the pharmaceutical companies are crashing and burning. I ought to know, goddamn it; they were my advertisers. When they collapsed, we had no advertisers. No advertisers, no shows."

He stopped just long enough to see James smiling. Looking at him challengingly, he said, "Well, what are you complaining about, Mikolas? You WON, you bastard. You WON! Between the dry up of the market for my network's sponsors, and the disgrace of my being a mouthpiece for Al Qaeda, you WON."

Letting him seethe for a minute, James knew they were heading in the right direction because Bud Walker was getting mad. And mad was better than the near-death apathy of a liquor state. Finally, Bud was breathing better, settling down a bit, so James spoke. "Not quite."

He could see the question mark on Walker's face. "Walker, that area is improved. You're right. In fact, it reversed so damned fast it must have taken every drug cartel and legal drug manufacturer in the world by surprise. But, there's one thing more."

Explaining the "Trojan Horse" that had been brought into our society, whose agents had dropped out of the belly of the horse, like their counterparts in Greek legend, and who had penetrated Education, Military, Justice, Family, Religion, Business—basically every foundational institution of the United States—James acknowledged readily that the Trojan

Horse had been destroyed, and the agents who pushed those meds were being economically starved out of business.

It was then that he dropped the bombshell. "But, Walker, this is why I need you. There's one unanswered question. Who sent the Trojan Horse in the first place? Who masterminded the Medical, Military, Public Relations, Weapons, and Religion games that are ravaging every sector of this planet? Sure, we won on drugs, psychiatry, and greedy quacks. But, who sent them to be the Fifth Column, and who has unleashed the other columns attacking at will?"

"How the hell would I know? I'm just a dumb rancher from Montana who built something and had a few lucky breaks." Walker seemed genuinely clueless, and was squirming now in the hand-hewn oak chair. He was wishing he hadn't eaten quite so much. His stomach was trying to bring it back up on him, as if trying to resist everything that was being "fed" to him.

"Look, just *look*. The top game, Walker, is Money. Who financed the pharmaceutical giants at will? Who finances governments so they can wage war? And what's the pound of flesh?"

James let that sink in; then added, "And who finances Terror groups? Where *are* they getting their money?"

"And you think I know the answer to this?" Getting his stomach's reactions under control, Bud challenged him defiantly. "You're crazy, Mikolas. You should talk to Oliver Stone; he'd be more able to ferret out that conspiracy than me!"

Starting to rise in order to end the conversation, James stopped him with, "Not really, Walker, not really. I think *you* can figure it out. And moreover I think you *want* to."

Bud Walker scoffed, picked up his plate, and set it down in the sink, snatching and eating the last piece of bacon. Leaning on the polished river rock counter, he said, "Because it will be my final good deed? Is that what you think?"

He was not prepared for what James said next. Nor was a man 6,000 miles away who had indeed sent Bud Walker to unwittingly promote the "Trojan Horse."

"No. Because I have come to believe you are an American, first and foremost, and somehow I think you know you were played for a fool, and you want your payback."

James carefully unfolded the paper he'd held secret. Placing it in front of Walker, he explained. "This was given to me by Mossad. They found it in the data banks of Samir Taghavi when they raided his Paris office, which turned out to be an Al Qaeda propaganda cell." Pausing for effect, he added, "You see it is a list of names—two lists actually."

"Yeah." Walker was scanning the second column and then stopped, his eyes frozen to a point in the right hand column. He said nothing, his breathing suspended momentarily.

"That's right, Walker, your name. This is a list of people Al Qaeda uses to accomplish its goals. The left side, short list, is the Witting list, meaning those who know they are complicit and willingly engaging on Al Qaeda's behalf. The list on the right is the Unwitting."

Walker remained silent. He resumed breathing, however, and he was swallowing hard. Not only did he know many of the names on that list but he was also staring at his own name—prominently near the top.

"So, as you see, you were selected early by Samir and Zawahiri to play an unwitting part in their plans. You were never to know. But, make no mistake; you were to play your part."

Walker said nothing for almost a minute. The only sound in the area was the ticking of the clock over the sink. His head was down, and he seemed to be looking at his boots. Finally, he whispered, "You think so, huh? That I want my revenge?"

"Yeah, and I came to help you get it. I'm not really a revenge type of guy. Too messy, leads to more screw-ups. Never works well in Intelligence or government. But, I do have a sense that you are going to want to make this right. And if you're smart—very smart—you *might* just have a shot."

"Well, Mikolas, how do you suggest I'm going to accomplish this— whatever we call it?"

"By doing what you do best." James stopped, took possession of the paper again, folded it, and slipped it into his vest pocket. "And, by the way, I didn't buy that 'drunken mess, dropped off the deep end' propaganda the media's been pushing about you. My hunch, Walker, is that tonight was the exception, not the rule."

Bud snorted and thought, *This guy's good!*

"You're right, Mikolas," he said. "Like any injured animal I've been licking my wounds. But I'm no drunk. And I sure as hell am not *depressed.*" He dragged the word out to emphasize his distaste.

"So, you ready then?"

"Don't know about ready, but I am willing. Will that do?"

James nodded, satisfied. "Yes, it will."

CHAPTER 5
THE HUMAN RIGHTS ACTIVIST

"What's up, girl? You look excited." Andy could see Reagan was into something. She normally bounded through his door with enthusiasm, but today, she burst in with such energy it rocked the house. *Or was that a tremor?* Certain that it was her and not some seismic phenomena, which residents of Los Angeles regularly experienced, he joked, "Maybe I should call Cal Tech and get the magnitude of the quake you just caused."

"Very funny!" She dropped her purse on the side table and cuffed Andy on the head as she headed for the fridge.

"Ouch!"

"That didn't hurt!"

"How do you know?" he defended.

Pulling out a can of vegetable juice, she opened it and triumphantly said, "'Cause if I had wanted to hurt you, believe me, you would know it, Mr. Andrew Weir."

She had him; he knew it. He raised his arms in a position of surrender.

"Okay. That's good that you know when you're defeated."

She leaned in and kissed him gently on the mouth, then sat down next to him at the table. For a moment, they just looked at each other. Reagan really loved this guy, and the totally sane, genuine demeanor he displayed. She wished she'd known his mom, Kelly, because only a really special woman could have created someone this bright, strong, and decent. *I hope he proposes soon,* was what she was thinking. *Even if I don't get a mother-in-law, I'd be honored to have the son.*

Not wanting to reflect on that too long, she reminded herself that she had a message to convey. "I am excited, Andy. But there's a change of plans, and I wanted to let you know I can't go with you to the Hollywood Bowl next month."

Andy was fine with that but a little perplexed as to why she'd come all the way over from Hollywood to tell him in person. Not that he didn't always look forward to her presence in the house, but her drop-in was unexpected, catching him right in the middle of an afternoon snack and his ritual of reading *Business 2.0*.

After all, it was just a concert—and a ways away at that—not an anniversary of any kind. Or was it? *Did I forget something?* he asked himself.

He must have flinched, because she picked up on it right away. Those green eyes of hers missed nothing. "What?"

"Nothing." He dismissed it, leading her out onto the shaded patio on the north side of the home. He hadn't decided when he was going to pop the question, and somehow he felt that the kitchen, with him in shorts and a T-shirt, was probably not the most romantic thing he could create. So, he did what he'd had players do many times in the past in his football days. He punted.

"So, what are you doing instead?"

"Going to El Paso. We got her, Andy, we got her!"

Andy figured he'd missed something here, so he waited for Reagan to continue. She saw he needed help and quickly added, "Remember I told you Edith and I were reaching out to that disgraced journalist from WNG, to see if she would consider a story on human trafficking across the border?"

He did remember that Reagan's senior partner at the human rights organization was hell-bent on finding this woman, and he knew Edith was a woman who could not be deterred, "Oh, yeah, of course, but I thought your partner was handling that."

"Edith *was* handling it. In fact, so well, she managed to find her, and persuade her that she could do a lot of good if she helped us determine who was grabbing and funneling women across that border. It's been hell for Hispanic women, Andy. Legal, illegal, it doesn't seem to matter. The number of missing is rising; it's too high."

Andy nodded understanding but didn't quite see how this related to Reagan. She continued. "Well, she agreed to help, and we start the investigation next month!" She was beaming now, having pulled off quite a coup in her estimation.

"We? You said we?"

"Yeah, that's the thing. Edith feels it's too big a job for her by herself, so I'm going in as her partner. You know, to make the work load lighter."

Before Andy could respond, Brian interrupted them, making an exaggerated entrance from the kitchen. Feigning fear, he croaked, "Is everything all right here? Are we having an earthquake? A tornado? The whole house shook!"

Reagan tried to cuff him, too, but Brian had been a wide receiver before he'd become a famous computer game designer and entrepreneur. He swiveled his hips, pivoted, and escaped easily. Then he sashayed toward her with a mock taunt.

Then he pretended to be sober and asked, "What work load?" Andy couldn't help but suppress a laugh. Brian didn't seem to feel squeamish at all about joining other people's conversations. He never had—and especially not these two. Andy and Reagan were a natural, comfortable team, and, frankly, they were his family. So, he expected to be included in all family-type discussions and was eager to hear more.

"Well, Edith and I will be working up an investigation, which we can use in Washington next year at hearings two Senators in our camp will be commencing. And, of course, it's a coup for her, too."

"Who?" Brian was missing something here.

"Alicia Quixote," Andy and Reagan answered simultaneously.

"She's a hottie!" That was all Brian said, standing there not really understanding the connection.

Reagan must have looked stunned at that non-sequitur, because Andy felt the need to explain. "Reagan, Brian has had a 'thing' for Alicia Quixote from the moment he saw her on WNG, Los Angeles."

"That's not true, Andy, that is NOT true!" Brian protested. "I've had a 'thing' for her since you and I used to see her at Ugo's Restaurant with that guy—the one who turned out to be the terrorist…" He didn't get the word out. Andy finished his sentence for him.

"Right. Samir Taghavi. The guy she was sleeping with, who appears to have been Al Qaeda's propaganda chief." There was enough disdain in Andy's voice that Brian defended Alicia.

"Well, yeah, but she didn't know that. Jesus, Andy, it wrecked her career! And she was Walker's up and coming star anchor." He snorted and added, "Bet she was pissed when she found out."

Not wanting to get into this any further, Reagan interjected lightly, "That's right, Brian, she was. And she's been in hiding. That's what's so great about what we are doing."

Both men were looking at her now. "Yeah, she's a great journalist. And getting her back in the game—on an issue this important—it's a chance for her, too, don't you see?"

They did. Both had had their second chances, too. No one had come out of 9/11 unscarred if they had been involved in it at all. Andy had lost his beloved mom, Kelly, and delayed his life for years chasing vermin. Joining Andy following the death of his entire family to a pharmaceutical-induced murder/suicide, Brian had lost his way as well.

That was, until James Mikolas had helped each of them engage, and find a way to defeat the drug lords and their terrorist partners. They had been redeemed, and their purposes in life had flowed parallel ever since.

Mikolas had lost his beloved Kelly, too, before he could even marry her. The years following that had been grim for him as well. So Andy and Brian stopped for a moment; looked at Reagan; and realized she was exactly right. There was still a war to win, and Reagan's group was on the front lines in the newest commerce to which Al Qaeda, Hezbollah, and the rest of the world's riff raff were converting—the enslaving of human beings, and the selling of them to equally disgusting "buyers."

Brian broke the silence. "Well, if she can redeem herself, and get back on track again, I'm all for it, Reagan."

Andy was in a conciliatory mood and nodded his agreement, reaching out and stroking her copper-red hair. "Me, too." He looked into those amazing eyes remembering how this vibrant young woman had brought him around following his mom's death, and how she had sparked in him the desire to do battle again. She had helped him, and had befriended James in his loneliness, and that was enough for Andy to care for her forever. *She's definitely the one.*

Instead of proposing though, with the ubiquitous Brian around, he simply added, "And if anyone can instill purpose in that woman again, it is you…and your friend, Edith."

Brian nodded, grinned, and said, "You two hungry? I'm buying."

Samir sat back, staring at the screen in front of him, his mouth slightly open. Looking right and left, he saw a variety of young people and business types working at computers, handling emails, and sipping their beverage of choice. No one paid attention to him.

Apparently, no one had heard the slight guttural intake of air that occurred when he read Makkawi's urgent message, addressed to him. Though still hours away from the President of the United States making the formal announcement of the death of Usama Bin Laden in Abbottabad, Pakistan, Makkawi had prayed his Public Relations chief would intercept the message.

Whether it timed on the actual day of the announcement was really immaterial. What was vitally material to Samir's mission, however, was the content of the message. It seems there was a change by way of an addition to the mission.

Samir instantly recognized the inherent dangers of such a move, but he knew also that the instructions were authentic, and that Zawahiri himself had made the order. It would be weeks before the Western Media would know who was actually in command of Al Qaeda, temporarily and permanently, but Samir had known since his return to Pakistan, and the awkward meeting between Bin Laden and Zawahiri, that, if Bin Laden were to die, the power would remain where it factually had since 2001. It would remain with the Doctor. *Those fools can delude themselves all they want into thinking Bin Laden was in control,* he sneered.

He knew that the addendum to the mission, done to "avenge the death of our beloved leader and brother," was ill-conceived and rash. He had seen it before with the appointment of Zarqawi, and the unleashing of his heinous violence on Westerners and Muslims alike. It had taken all of his propaganda skill to offset in the American media the blunders and sheer butchery of that mad dog.

Whether Zawahiri had him killed, or whether Abou al-Zarqawi had just run his "ninth life," had been of no concern to Samir. He had simply been profoundly relieved to be rid of having to handle the PR flaps that cropped up due to that man's unique way of waging Jihad.

And now, here Samir was again, staring at a direct order from the "new" commander of Al Qaeda, Ayman al-Zawahiri. He had no choice but to obey it, for he would have to return to Pakistan once the mission was accomplished in Colombia—at the very least, he would have to return to Yemen. And that would most assuredly put him in jeopardy at the hands of Zawahiri if he had failed to comply.

His dry mouth told him this rash, retaliatory reaction would be as dangerous as the assassination the Doctor had ordered following the destruction of his pharmaceutical empire and investments by a computer game called "White King Rising." He had heard that the assassin, known as the "Viper," had been killed by the Mossad. He knew that Brian Washington Carver and his partner Andrew Weir were still alive, given the amount of publicity the young duo got throughout the world, and he suspected that their mysterious side-kick, James Mikolas, was as well.

He had no idea whether the "Viper" had succeeded in an assassination, or who the target might have been, if he had. But he had an uneasy feeling that something had backfired. What Samir did not know was that Zawahiri had targeted and killed, at the "Viper's" hands, Kelly Weir—mother of Andrew Weir, and fiancé of James Mikolas.

Nor did he know that, as he read his next set of orders, James Mikolas was about to summon Washington and Weir into another mission—a retaliatory one as well.

It was just as well. He had his work cut out for him as it was. His orders read:

> Addendum:
>
> 1. Expand the abduction of women into the United States population, to include not just Hispanic women of Mexico and Central America, as we have been doing, but women of all races and ages of America itself. They have taken what we held most dear and holy, and now we will avenge his death by defiling what they hold dear and sacred.
>
> 2. Inform our Colombian partners that we will pay double for American women successfully kidnapped, brought to us, and sold by us. Make certain they understand that "damaged goods" will not serve the needs and demands of our clients here, and that we will hold them personally accountable for actions taken against these particular captives. The fate that awaits these women is for us to render, and no one else.
>
> 3. All other nationalities are to be kidnapped as per the original instructions, and will be transported and sold throughout Africa, India, and the Mid-East.

Samir deleted the email, sitting calmly as he verified that the session was ended and the data, gone. A smile crept onto his face, revealing a malevolence few would see. True, he found the whole assignment repugnant, but not because he found the actions repugnant. He well understood the stunning Public Relations impact this would have on every American citizen. Their own media would be guaranteed to cover this; every civic organization would engage to protect the women of the United States; and every government agency would as well. All he could think of was what Lenin had said about terror: "The purpose of terror is to terrify."

Calmly sipping his own latte, Samir Taghavi knew exactly what his job was. He was the modern day purveyor of terror—and he was very good at it. *Let's see just how deep we can reach into America this time,* he thought, as he added another cube of sugar to his cup.

CHAPTER 6

"*O*kay, Boy Scout, what is it you'd have me do?" Walker squared up opposite James at the kitchen table and sat expectantly.

James laughed lightly at the nickname Walker had chosen for him. What made him laugh was the fact that he'd called Andy, "Kid" from the first days of their working together, and later he'd dubbed Brian, "Pal," when he came on the scene. For some reason he found it ironic that Walker, too, appeared to give people nicknames. *Maybe he's not so bad,* he thought.

"Bud…" James remembered his manners, "May I call you that?"

Walker nodded.

"Here's my thinking." He pulled out his small notepad from his breast pocket and began to make a few notes and sketches for Walker. "The pharmaceuticals and drugs were not just killing people. They were anesthetizing or sedating all of us Americans. That's an act of war, which, thank God, the people are waking up to with the 'White King Rising' game. It looks like we've got a chance to salvage that generation at least, and we'll all be better off—getting saner by the minute."

Walker was looking at him blankly, as if he couldn't connect with this, or understand its relevance to him. James continued. "Are you a military man, Bud?"

"Uh, no." Walker stuttered a bit, caught off guard by the question. "No," he responded, a little defensively.

"No problem, Bud, but you need to know some things here. Our enemies *are,* and they think like military people, and wage war as such— using any and all means to compromise us and defeat us."

"You think?" Bud spat it out, not even attempting to mask the sarcasm. Reconsidering, he did an about face. "Okay, I got that, but what does that have to do with me?"

James paused for a moment, looking something over in his mind, and answered, "The drugs and those who promoted them were a Fifth Column—the force inside the U.S. designed to weaken it from within, so the external forces could take us down more easily at will."

Walker was silent, but keenly listening now.

"So Bud, it's implicit that someone sent the Trojan Horse, you know, created and nurtured the Fifth Column. And if we don't figure out who that is, and more importantly, take them down, it won't matter that we have handled the drug influence in our country. We still go down."

Bud Walker exhaled to compensate for a growing sense of apprehension. He had looked this over time and time again since the revelation that Al Qaeda's PR man was a friend; a lover of Walker's LA Anchorwoman, Alicia Quixote; and an "expert" who had given direct input to major talk radio personalities, who then turned and injected some implanted garbage into their own audiences. *Christ, Samir was a walking Fifth Column all on his own!*

Deep inside though, he knew that he was responsible for even more than letting that vermin into the American households, and into the editorial viewpoint of his networks. There was a haunting feeling that there was yet more, something even more dangerous that he had done. But what had him at the edge of grief was the fact that he could not discover what it was. It was just a pervasive and relentless anxiety. Looking at Mikolas, he now realized there could be only one reason Mikolas had sought him out. And he was terrified.

Face it, man, just ask the question, he said to himself. Daring to, he asked, "Am I involved?"

"Well, now, that's why I came to see you. You see, I have this theory that whoever sent the pharmaceutical and drug pushers, who sent the army of psychiatrists into every nook and cranny of our lives, had to have accomplices who would soften up the target—you know—make them want what the pushers were peddling."

"Yeah."

"Yeah, and looking over the scene, it became obvious to my boy Andy that the American media was being used as a tool—wittingly or unwittingly." He thumped the list he had shown Walker earlier to remind him of the two columns. "The Media peddles fear and confusion, and it seems to me that fear eats away at folks, causing a whole host of sociological reactions and problems, which then require the 'help' of the Psychiatric/

Pharmaceutical cartels to sedate us." He paused and then continued. "Notice it's never to 'cure,' just to subdue and make us pliable."

James smiled now in admiration of Andy Weir. "You see, Walker, that young man Andy Weir, whom you blame for ruining your networks, had the guts to look evil right in the eye and attack. He figured out that our enemies are playing multiple games simultaneously, using the same personnel in different games, with different responsibilities."

"Well, what was I doing in this?" Bud asked, almost afraid to know.

"You? You were a major chess piece in the Public Relations game and the Weapons game as you spread fear, but a pawn in the Sociology game, Medical game and, this is the sweet one, the Money game. You and your competitors were just caught up in your own game, and didn't realize someone had turned you into pawns, that's all."

Walker was not happy with this indictment, but oddly enough he could feel the anxiety abating. The dread he had experienced was lessening as well. So, he sat there, and he took it.

"You made an awful lot of money for some people. The question is who?"

"The pharmaceutical companies, I know that," Walker retorted.

"No, no, Bud, not according to my analysis. They were just the Fifth Column. Who sent them? Who is the attacking outside force, and what are they planning? That's the question."

"I just don't get how you think I would know this." Walker was becoming more belligerent and combative with each word. James realized he needed to change the tempo and tone a bit, or he risked Walker digging in and refusing to really look, or cooperate.

"Did I tell you my job was analysis at the CIA? And that I was damned good at it?" James was setting it up now, coming through another door.

"No, you did not, but I repeat, how would I know this?"

"Well, one of the things I learned long ago is that when one faces two possibilities—and one is complex and one is simple—it is better to explore the simple if you want to find truth. It's simple I think. If you and your ilk were responsible for making it possible for the Fifth Column to undermine us, you were then doing what the primary attackers wanted done. They sent you to prepare the field. So, all we have to know now is 'who sent *you*?'"

Bud was confused, or stonewalling. "Me personally, or all of us media moguls?"

"All of you." James needed to clarify something for him. "Someone made it possible for every one of you to rise to power, to create wealth and influence. Someone—or several someones—did that for all of you."

The agitation was back now, and anxiety was mounting again. It rose in his GI tract and seemed to be swamping his lungs. Bud was starting to wish Mikolas would just come right out and shoot him, or put him out of this mystery somehow. Walker was not a man to be toyed with, and he did not like the feeling of being left out. "Well, if that's the case, what the hell are you doing on my ranch in Ovando, Montana talking to a has-been, rather than indicting some other poor slob whose empire is still vibrant? They're your threat, man, not me anymore."

James nodded. He totally agreed that the Media was still a threat, largely because they didn't know they were being played and had been duped. But, for that very reason, he felt they were useless to anyone now to reverse this.

"Simple, Bud. However it happened, you're less of a player today than you were three years ago, and I pegged you to be more accessible to me than the others."

"Thanks!" Bud scoffed and sat there sneering. After a moment, he found some humor in that and added, "All right, Boy Scout. I can see you're not a stupid man. What made you think I would be the one to help?"

With no lag whatsoever, James responded earnestly, "Because you are the only SOB of the lot who showed any remorse. Yes, Samir Taghavi penetrated your trust and network. It happened to you. But not one of those other bastards even stopped to think maybe it had happened to them, too—maybe, just maybe, they were being played as well. And we have a saying in the Intelligence business: 'Don't play with someone too stupid to play.'"

Walker started to laugh. At first, it was small and somewhat stifled, but then the laughter escaped and grew. The absurd simplicity of it was stunningly obvious to him and raucously funny. It was some minutes before he regained his composure.

"All right, Boy Scout, all right. I can think with that. That's about the only smart thing I've had said to me in the last three years."

"Glad you think so." James waited for a minute. "So, Bud, who *sent* you? Who made it possible for Bud Walker to become *Bud Walker—Billionaire Media Mogul?* And why? What you need to discover, Bud, is why he did it, and did you, wittingly or unwittingly, pay him back."

If I wasn't sober before this, I sure as hell am now! Bud thought. He was eerily calm right then, though. All internal quivering had stopped. He wondered whether this calm he was experiencing was characteristic of one encountering truth—even if the truth was shocking and unexpected. For he knew indeed who it was that had given him his start, and who had "opened doors" for him—every step of the way. There *was* one man.

He must have looked sad and distant, because he heard James' voice calling him back. "Walker, stay with me. You'll make it."

"Yeah, I guess…" His voice trailed away into a whisper.

"Cheer up. I can see by the look on your face that you know *who*. Now all we have to do is figure out why. What is he planning?" Walker looked up somewhat hopefully, albeit painfully. With firm compassion, James added, "And once you figure that out, I'm going to have you meet a couple of guys who can help us stop him."

Walker nodded but remained silent. He didn't know whether to laugh or cry at the absurdity of this situation. All he knew was that, somehow, it felt right. Bud Walker had been an arrogant and ambitious man, true, but he had also been a very competent man. He was a pit bull if the situation demanded it. Mikolas had picked the right man.

CHAPTER 7
THE BANKER

"**Y**our car is ready, sir."

There was no immediate response from his employer, as Ashton Somers waited in the doorway to the lavish cherry wood and verdant green, silk-paneled office that Sir Harley Grantham-Jones used when at his estate northwest of London.

Grantham-Jones stood looking out the French doors into the formal gardens and fountains, which made his estate one of the most admired in its class. Every detail insured serenity, and some of the finest architectural landscaping in all of Great Britain graced the mixture of woodlands, pastures, and meticulously manicured lawns.

He was holding in his hand the summons he had received earlier that morning. *Couldn't it have waited until Tuesday when I returned to London,* he had protested silently, when the courier delivered the pouch. It was Sunday, and no one delivers a pouch on Sunday—let alone a diplomatic pouch from the Repository of International Transactions in Basel, Switzerland.

As the Director of one of the world's largest Central Banks, he was accustomed to pouches, but not on Sunday, and not from the private security force of the RIT. He was seventy-nine years old and had known since the late '70s that he would one day be summoned. As the decades had gone on, their plan had progressed, and he knew that probably in five years or so—if he still lived—he would fulfill the legendary mission of the ancient moneychangers and carry out the final plan, which had been put in place long ago.

Why now? Why so soon? Something must have happened to advance the target date... His thoughts were interrupted by Ashton clearing his throat and repeating, "Sir, your car is ready. And Geoffrey has the plane on the tarmac. They are ready when you are."

Turning and smiling, Harley Grantham-Jones acted as if nothing unusual was transpiring. "Thank you, Ashton. I packed more bags than usual this time, so I'm afraid you may need some assistance in loading it all."

"Yes, sir." Ashton turned and began carrying bags from the front vestibule to the awaiting Bentley. The journey to the airstrip would take less than five minutes, but he was nonetheless meticulous about how he placed the bags in the elegant silver/black vehicle.

Harley Grantham-Jones had decided not to leave a note for his wife. She was on a fox hunt, and planning their granddaughter's wedding after that, so he decided to inform her casually by phone that he had been called to Switzerland and that he'd let her know when to expect him.

That will let her down easily, he reassured himself. *It's best. Less drama this way.* For Grantham-Jones knew he would not be returning. He knew also that when his wife learned the true actions of her husband of fifty-two years, she would not want to see him again. He had lived a double life for a long time, and that charade was about to end.

He looked down at the note he had received. It was typed on elegant velum stationery. Very few, terse words, and yet they were harbingers of a change in the world—one of those apocalyptic moments that transcend all previous history and create a new order of things. The note said simply, "You are invited immediately to an important conclave... Arrive Zurich... Transport by ground to Basel... Do not use your personal staff... Check in at the Eifler—your usual suite... Disguise yourself; use only your first name; and arrive at Grey's Chocolate Shop by Monday, 1PM Basel time... Prepare for a prolonged stay."

Not trusting his memory as he used to, Harley Grantham-Jones pocketed the note; drew the curtains in his opulent office; closed the door separating the office from the rest of the quarters; and exited. As he had done for over forty years now, he graciously smiled at his staff. None of them would accompany him on this final journey.

"Phillip, my dear fellow, so very sorry to interrupt your quiet Sunday."

"It is not a problem, sir. Any time."

"Well, nonetheless, I have appreciated your loyal service. So, take me to Geoffrey, please."

"Sir, yes." Phillip was indeed a loyal and skilled driver—trained to meet any challenge or threat to one of Great Britain's pillars of society, economic giants, and media moguls—but he was also not a literary man. He did not notice his employer's use of the past tense. He would regret that in the months to come.

CHAPTER 8

That summer evening in 1969 was much the same as this one, down to his standing out on a veranda, smoking his favorite cigar, quietly reflecting on the fragrances of the countryside at twilight. Only that night held one difference.

It was the night he had first been introduced to the famous Partagas Lusitania cigar by Sir Harley Grantham-Jones at the Grantham-Jones estate. Bud was a young Oxford student, on a Rhodes scholarship from the United States, and he was experiencing the thrill of being introduced to some of England's most prominent businessmen. That night, the richness of the cigar seemed to mirror the company he was keeping. It was a heady environment by anyone's definition.

Given his natural self-confidence and the candor that often accompanies young men who grew up rural, Bud Walker had started to attract the attention of London's elite banking, law, and finance circles. He had not known at the time what they saw in someone who was pursuing journalism, but the Grantham-Jones family did own the *Sphere* newspaper, and a host of other related magazines. A roommate, who was three years his senior, had introduced him to a family friend—the head of that entire empire.

Grantham-Jones was himself a fairly young man, who had accomplished much in his thirty-five years. He carried himself with the maturity of one who was experienced in life, and firmly commanding his family's prodigious undertakings. He had taken a liking to the young American, despite the fact that his horsemanship left something to be desired. Certain that he would never invite Bud Walker into a polo match, he appreciated the audacity of the American to even attempt a fox hunt. At least Walker had kept up, even after taking a fall, and Harley had expressed his approval of "your cheekiness," as he had put it.

On the veranda, under a wisteria arbor on the edge of the stone complement to their historic home, Bud had been offered his first cigar. Reluctant to make a fool of himself, he contemplated refusing the offer, but had decided against it.

He smiled as he remembered reaching out gingerly for it, listening with appreciation and admiration to the history and qualities of the hand-made gem of Havana, and then taking the precise instructions Harley had provided on the snipping of the end, the right way to hold it, to light it, and, most importantly, the right way to smoke it. Tonight, on the veranda of his own estate, he could not actually say whether his famous taste in cigars, and his insistence on smoking them in all manner of company, had stemmed from the Partagas Lusitania itself that night, or the fact that a man of Grantham-Jones' stature had taken a liking to him.

Whatever the reason, Bud still relished his smokes, and was still re-garded as the protégé of that wing of British commercial royalty.

Bud Walker had always known his own worth, had always been cou-rageously ambitious, and had never once stopped to doubt the authentic-ity of his mentor's generosity—or his motives. As far as Bud Walker had been concerned, it was all deserved, and the fact that a man of Harley's stature had noticed it was just further confirmation to Bud of his own specialness, and destiny.

So, throughout the years, he had happily accepted every soiree invita-tion, every offer of financial connections, including the legal assistance needed when the family ultimately allowed him years later to assume the helm of the newspaper chain, and its burgeoning TV networks as well. Truth be told, if it had not been for Harley Grantham-Jones and the vig-orous defense and promotion of Walker that he mounted, Walker would never have been able to pull off the takeover of what was now known as Walker News Group.

A chill suddenly ran the entirety of Bud Walker's body as he stood on his Montana veranda, and he knew it had nothing to do with the summer evening. James Mikolas had said he needed to know who had sent Bud Walker and why. And Bud *knew* in his spirit, as soon as the question was asked, that he had been "sent"—hand-picked, groomed, and then sent.

He snorted as he looked at the possibility that, despite the fact that he had decades of track record of his own, and had implemented a principled but ruthless expansion of his global network, challenging every other me-dia mogul from Murdock to Turner, this had all been designed. *If that is the case, what was it Harley saw that made him select me?* He thought about it for a moment, almost unwilling to look at the answer his own common sense offered up. *It would have to be a flaw. What flaw?* That question alone was sobering.

Even more disturbing was the fact that he was actually looking with suspicion now at someone he revered, loved as an uncle, and had taken counsel from throughout his career. This man was the Director of the Bank of the United Kingdom; a man who, for a long time, had been a director with the World Health Organization, expediting, through his media and banking connections, any activity that organization had prioritized. He had been a consultant and advisor to Prime Ministers for decades.

My God, he's regarded as one of Europe's great humanitarians and public servants! Grantham-Jones had flourished in finance and banking, and had devoted his time to these charitable activities after relinquishing control of his media empire—not to family, or the other British challenger—but to Walker, an American.

The direction in which Bud's mind was going almost made him nauseous. To find himself doubting his humorous, kindly benefactor seemed almost treasonous, and he did not know if he could truly explore this. Try as he would though, he couldn't turn the idea off. After all, he was a newspaperman, and he had sniffed out many a story, scooped many a competitor. *God only knows if he is also involved in pharmaceuticals,* Walker wailed silently. *Just how many dots are going to connect here?*

That small voice within would not shut up. *What did he want with me?* That was the question that wouldn't go away. He continued to resist the idea, partly because to answer it would be a further indictment of Walker's gullibility, arrogance, and complicity in the global struggle that was currently unfolding, and partly because he just plain didn't believe his affable advisor could possibly be capable of—what was it that Mikolas had called it?—sending the Trojan Horse.

He didn't know how long he stood there with the battle raging between the voice of the loyal friend and the voice of the seasoned investigator. Neither did he truly admit which voice had won out. Carefully extinguishing his cigar, and inserting it into the humidor he'd had designed to fit into the Montana river rock patio in order to keep the moisture level perfect, he concluded, *It's not possible. He wouldn't knowingly participate in these mythical-type conspiracies. It's preposterous.*

"Nice night." Mikolas slid onto the veranda, looking out into the blue and lavender mountains in the distance.

"Yeah."

The next thing Walker knew, Mikolas was standing beside him, still keeping his gaze outward.

"Would you care for a cigar, Boy Scout?" he offered, tapping the humidor. "It's the finest brand on earth, I do believe."

"Who told you that?"

"An old friend." He hesitated; then added, "A man I trust."

James paused for only a second before jumping in. "No thank you, Walker. I've never been a cigar man myself. That's for more important men than me." Risking it, the analyst advanced his theory. "That's the 'button,' you know, the marketing button they got you with. 'Importance.' Make Bud Walker important, and you will have his attention."

Walker immediately stiffened, thrust his jaw out, and stepped to the side to widen the distance between himself and Mikolas. As he did so, James calmly turned to face him. Silhouetted in the stand-off, James finished with, "It wasn't your ambition, Walker; or your conceit; or your brilliance. You have all that. It was your need to feel important."

Bud cut him off. "What are you, my shrink?"

"No, but you should ask yourself who recommended the one you do have."

That stopped Walker cold. He did, indeed, have a psychiatrist. A sharp exhale accompanied his sudden awareness that it was Harley who had recommended his doctor to him, during the brutal divorce from his first wife. Despondent, and shaken by the visceral nature of their breakup, and its fallout relevant to Bud's position in British society, the ever-helpful Grantham-Jones had come to his rescue with his own recommendation— a personal friend and highly recommended psychiatrist.

Bud heaved as if in pain. James said nothing. He allowed Walker to handle this. *Given the response, I'd say I hit that one on the head.* James waited. There was no hurry.

It seemed like an eternity to Bud. He had nothing further he wanted to say to this man. Yet he knew by the churning in his gut that he was not going to be able to dodge this one. So, he, too, stood in silence.

James broke the stalemate. "Your plan?"

"My plan, Boy Scout, is to go see him." Bud's tone was surly, but resigned. "I owe him that at least. But more importantly, because I think you're full of it, and that he can clear this up for me."

"Fine. When do we leave?"

Walker laughed. "No, you're not going. This is something I can take care of on my own. We've known each other for forty-two years!"

"All the more reason for me to go. Maybe he isn't involved. But someone he knows is. And they are planning something, Walker—and it's big enough that you need me shadowing you. Don't forget who you are, Bud, and the power you still have in your industry. Maybe not to him, but to someone, you could be a threat."

Bud chewed on that for a moment; then challenged, "Shadow only?" James nodded.

"So, what do I call you? Boy Scout? Or Shadow?" Walker turned and walked back into his home.

He is a charmer! They must have known it would carry him far...

Bud didn't seem to mind James walking into his study, as he was already into the phone call. There was no appearance of secrecy. If he had any trepidation or butterflies about the call, none were visible to James. To a casual observer, it would have seemed like any ordinary call. *He doesn't really believe this*, James noted. *Whoever he's calling, he doesn't really believe it yet.*

Walker may have had doubts about the theory, but James did not. From the moment the Mossad had revealed the list with unwitting participants in the erosion of America, and Bud Walker's name jumped out, James knew that whoever was pulling Walker's strings had to be someone he trusted implicitly—someone who would have made him feel so special that it would be inconceivable to Bud Walker that he could be manipulated to the degree that he would be incapable of spotting the strings that were causing him and the entire Walker News Group to dance.

There it was—that familiar, skipped beat of the heart and sudden rush of adrenalin. James was eager now, as he felt he was closing in on his prey.

"Sylvia, hello there, gal!" Walker was smiling, apparently happy to have her answer the call. Whatever repartee with which she responded was not within James' hearing. He sat down in one of the two red leather chairs that embraced an oddly rough-hewn desk. He made a note to ask Bud about that desk. One day he hoped to do a little wood working himself, using some of the indigenous timber of North Carolina. Quickly though, he returned his attention to Bud's conversation.

Laughing comfortably with his old friend, Bud said, "Is he there? I need to get with him." The smile evaporated slightly with her response.

"No, Bud, he left very abruptly this afternoon while I was out riding. Told the staff he'd call me later."

"I see…"

James was sitting forward now, hoping to hear the voice himself.

"Fine." Bud exhaled with a look of disappointment. He hesitated for a moment, then decided to press it. "You don't happen to know where he was headed, do you?"

"Basel, I presume, Bud. What's odd is it's not the week he normally goes there for his meeting. I'm in a bit of a mystery about this myself. "

"I see. Do you know the hotel in Basel where he normally stays? I'll ring him up there."

Walker scrambled to pull the notepad around and write down her answer. Scribbling, he jotted down "Hotel Eifler." He was placing the cap back on the pen when Harley's wife apparently added something else. "Across from the railroad station."

"Thank you, Sylvia. I'll reach him a little later. And please tell your lovely granddaughter I'm eager to see her come down that aisle. Don't know why she didn't want to do this in Montana, but I'll get over it."

He and Sylvia both laughed, enjoying what was an inside joke. James surmised Bud had offered his ranch for the ceremony, and that the girl— whoever she was—had chosen something a bit more conventional. *Come on, Walker. Come on.*

Walker hung up. "We'll have to wait some hours, Boy Scout. It appears he is en route to Basel, Switzerland. I'll give him time to get there, and ring him up."

James smiled inwardly at the decidedly British turn of phrase. He couldn't tell whether Walker was affecting it, or whether he routinely slipped into it when in the company of his British friends. He guessed the latter. Whatever Bud Walker might seem to be, he did not seem pretentious—just cocky.

James still had no idea yet to whom they were referring—only that he had a wife named Sylvia, and a granddaughter about to get married. That mystery would not alter James' game plan, however. "Don't call him first. Confirm his arrival with the hotel. Then go to him." It was said with such authority that Walker almost felt he had been given a direct order, and that he was in some kind of covert ops briefing. Looking it over though, he knew it *was* the better course of action. A phone call was completely inappropriate, and would not reveal what he needed to *see*, not just *hear*.

Bud Walker trusted his ability to "read" a man—Samir Taghavi notwithstanding. He had, for the greater part of his career, succeeded because he knew men and their motives, and was generally not deceived or distracted by any kind of charade. He had risen to the top in an industry where one had to routinely take the measure of men and governments, and make snap decisions regarding them. Even if Harley Grantham-Jones had furthered his career deliberately, with an ulterior motive, Bud Walker still knew he had achieved a great deal on his own. Not all confidence had been drained from him, and that amount which still remained would make all the difference.

"Fine. We'll take my jet. With tail winds, we can be there by noon tomorrow."

James nodded, and Bud added, "I gather I'm going to have to wardrobe you?"

"That depends. Where are we going? Who are we meeting?"

"Basel, Switzerland. Sir Harley Grantham-Jones, Director of the Bank of the United Kingdom."

James showed no emotion, but his stomach literally turned over. The BUK was one of the four largest Central Banks in the world, holding enormous power and influence amongst the world's twenty major Central Banks. Fifty-five in all, those in the top twenty exerted the most influence. Though neither an economist nor financier, James had studied and tracked banking systems and operations as part of his analysis work for the CIA.

Aware that numerous international commercial banks were knowingly financing Al Qaeda, Hezbollah—the lot—another surge of adrenalin reassured Mikolas he was indeed coming up on a legitimate target.

Financial counter terrorist analysts were trying to make the link between terrorism, commercial banks, and the Central Banks that controlled their financial policy and monetary supply. To date, nothing concrete had surfaced except proof of complicity with terror organizations of certain commercial banks like the Dubai-headquartered Al-Bakarat Bank and the Bahama-based Al-Tuqwa Bank. Rumors abounded. But was there in fact a link between the Central Banks and the terror-sponsoring commercial banks throughout the world? Were the Italian banks and the Zurich bank, which had been caught and closed, linked to a larger conspiracy?

In some intelligence circles, it was viewed as sheer "conspiracy theory" stuff to go anywhere near the idea of Central Banks themselves willingly fomenting terror. In other circles, it seemed like a logical, albeit evil, connection to make.

Today, James Mikolas felt he was on the verge of resolving that debate and discovering some truth. He had told Bud Walker to answer the question about who had sent him, and Walker had done just that. Now, they were headed to Basel.

Walker was still waiting for an answer on the wardrobe, so James pulled himself back to the question at hand. "Yes. You will have to wardrobe me a bit. I have nothing suitable for meetings at that level of hotel, or with that level of—" He almost said "mark" but caught himself and changed it to something milder: "—player."

"Fine!" Walker barked. Mysteriously, as the two hustled to gather briefcases, computer bags, and wardrobe, Walker made another call. James heard only the last part.

"All of them. I want to know who is responsible for all of them…"

CHAPTER 9

*T*he city lights were just coming on, almost causing a pulse in the haze that was still hovering over Los Angeles. The inversion layer Los Angelinos referred to as "June Gloom" had started early this year. The result was subdued sunsets and chillier evenings.

For now, though, it was warm, and Andy was enjoying the slight breeze that his amazing patio always seemed to attract. Leaning forward, elbows on knees, he was fingering the gold pendant he'd inherited from his mother. The leaf pin had originally been worn by his father, who had been a guard at the Tomb of the Unknown Soldier. A special insignia marked their duty and was recognized by every military man who wore a United States uniform. It was a badge of honor to be selected, and Greg Weir had worn it well.

Following his death before Andy had even entered his teens, Kelly Weir had placed it on a gold chain and worn it every day of her life. Interpol had returned it to Andy after his mother's assassination while on holiday in Venice, Italy. He, Brian, and James had scattered her ashes in Arlington Cemetery at her husband's grave. Andy retained the pendant, as the only material keepsake he wanted.

He had offered it to James, knowing that Kelly Weir had been a lifelong, almost unexpected, dream for James, and he knew that, had she lived, they would have made a wonderful life together. James had demurred. *Kid, you keep it. I have my memories, which are in my mind, and always will be. One day you'll find a girl, have a family, and you'll want them to have this family treasure.*

Well, James was right. He had found the girl. In fact, he could hear her coming in the front door and calling for him. "Out here," he called back, hastily placing the necklace in an elegant satin box.

Reagan came out onto the patio, breezed over to him, and kissed him gently. He pulled up one of the awkward wrought iron chairs that punctuated the stone patio. *Geez, these are heavy! Why on earth did I get these?* Then he remembered he hadn't. The patio décor had been Brian's choice. *Last time I leave choice of furniture to a football player who can bench press three hundred pounds,* Andy admonished himself.

"Hey, girl, you look smashing!"

Reagan flashed that dazzling smile at him, and cocked her head to let him know she appreciated the compliment.

He decided to do it right then. There were myriad restaurants and romantic ocean viewpoints that he could have selected. But, he knew Reagan, and knew that she was not overly impressed with fancy meals and pretentious atmospheres. She seemed to just like to hang out with him—and with Brian.

Funny how it never seemed odd—the four of them. Reagan had embraced Brian and James as if she were getting them as part of the package. The fact that she could make him feel like the only one in the room, yet graciously befriend and welcome his two best friends in life at the same time, he felt was a sign of her genuine ease and appreciation of people. *And her unselfishness,* he reflected.

So, he knew she'd probably find this "romantic" and not the least bit of a cliché. He had just started the proposal with, "Reagan, I've got something really important to ask you, and I don't want to put it off..." when he was interrupted by Brian bursting onto the deck in his swimsuit. Once again, he just appeared out of nowhere and inserted himself into the conversation. It was almost as if Brian thought that anything Andy was doing, he should do, too.

"Ask her what?" Brian said, as he pulled one of the wrought iron chairs over with such ease one would have thought it was a feather.

Oh, brother, I can't believe this! Andy had to decide whether to hold or go ahead.

Not to be deterred, he shot Brian a glance, and Brian, as usual, was oblivious to it. He seemed to have forgotten their earlier conversation altogether. It was obvious Brian was going to stay, so Andy just plunged ahead. Holding out the satin box, he silently offered it to Reagan. He did have to admit, she looked a bit apprehensive, or stunned. He couldn't tell which.

Opening it, she pulled out the pendant, dangling it in front of her as she admired it. Reagan knew it was his mother's, as she had seen it prominently worn around Kelly's neck in a family photo. By now, she had guessed what Andy wanted to ask, but didn't know what to say or do, since he hadn't actually spoken. So, she wetted her lips and very sincerely said, "Thank you so much, Andy. It is truly beautiful, and I will cherish it always."

Andy was trying to recover now, as if he had fumbled the ball. Now he understood how James must have felt when he'd tried to get advice from Andy on dating Kelly. Brian was no help. He was just grinning. *He knows how I'm fumbling here, and he's not helping me at all!*

Andy Weir, however, was in fact a very poised, determined man who had outwitted Al Qaeda's mastermind. Their duel of wits over the years had saved many lives, and the game that was born out of that struggle would have ramifications for generations to come. So, although he had had an awkward moment, and though his timing was somewhat off, he recovered immediately.

"Reagan, it looks like we have a witness to this," he commented, nodding in Brian's direction. By now, Reagan was laughing. Her head was going up and down, and he knew she understood. "I love you very much, and would like to ask you to marry me. You can have any ring you want—as long as you and I pick it out together—but the official expression of my love for you is in your hand right now. It represents the heritage of the Weir family, and I would be proud if you would wear it."

For a moment, Reagan said nothing. She had prayed he would ask her to marry him. When he started, she knew that time had come. And yet, she was having trouble framing a word. Somehow, the moment and its total sincerity had taken her by surprise. Suddenly, she blurted out, "I would be honored." Her voice broke as she said it.

Andy grinned, and Brian looked down, wishing now that he could hide under a chair, or slither under one of those rocks in their garden waterfall. *Too late now,* he told himself. *I'll catch hell from Andy later.* But, his enthusiasm for this pairing, and his relief that Andy had just gone ahead and done it—and that she had accepted—surpassed any momentary embarrassment.

"Man, that rocks! Truly rocks!"

Andy and Reagan turned and looked at him. For a moment, it was like a three-way Mexican stand-off, and then, very spontaneously, all three started to laugh.

It was pitch black out there now, and the pool light was the only thing illuminating the three of them. Although the patio lights nearest the house entrance were on, it was the light of the pool and sensation of moving water that gave such a sense of calm.

Following Andy's unconventional proposal, they'd opened a bottle of champagne and scarfed down some chips and salsa. It was the one thing Andy knew Reagan could cook. She would often make up a batch of hot salsa, leaving it in the refrigerator for both guys to find when they got home. As luck would have it, there was still some from her last foray into the kitchen.

"It's a huge problem, guys, much bigger than I had imagined." She was explaining to them the rise in human trafficking in the last decade, and her discoveries regarding the amount of commerce being created by the illicit securing of men, women, and children, and the transportation of these unfortunate people throughout the world.

The human rights organization, of which she was vice-president, was funding investigations into the extent of it inside the United States as well—most specifically as it pertained to women. Her boss, Edith, was in fact in Texas, preparing the first parts of an undercover operation to follow not only the money but also the routes and destinations the captives would take. Everyone had theories as to just who were the human traffickers, and who was funding them. But this group hoped to discover the reality of it.

"There are so many women—Hispanic women—disappearing in Texas right now. We're sure they are being trafficked across the border, and for some reason."

"You mean slaves, don't you, Reagan?" Brian had suddenly interrupted her. There was an edge to his voice.

Reagan wasn't sure just what he meant by that, so she hesitated. Brian continued, "I'm a brother, and where I come from, you white people can call it 'human trafficking' if you want. But laundering it up isn't going to change the fact that you are talking about these people becoming slaves!"

Andy looked at Reagan and shrugged. He had no intention of trying to reprimand Brian. Every now and again, the boy from the hood appeared—language and all. Now that he looked at it, the term *was* whitewashed.

"Reagan, girl, I love you. But until you persuade those bozos in Washington not to sanitize what this is, you'll never get the support you need. A slave is a slave, and a slave trader is a slave trader. Remember, my field is marketing, and somebody has pulled off a nice marketing con, right Andy?"

Andy whistled, looked into the distance for a moment, and nodded his agreement. "Yeah, now that you put it that way, I would have to agree, Brian. Some Public Relations fool on the 'Hill' must have thought people would relate better."

"Well, they won't. You can dress slavery up any way you want, and you can call the scum who steal people, and sell them, anything you want. But, no matter how you cut it, they are slave-traders. And the United States is going to have to ante up on this one."

Reagan agreed. "Yes, Brian, I see." She did see. She had been startled by his outburst, but not even remotely offended at the severity of his viewpoint.

"Unless, of course, we're in on it, making money from it," he added.

"Well," she reached across and patted his forearm gently, but not patronizingly, "that's exactly what Edith and I, and Alicia Quixote, are going to find out. Who benefits?"

Raising his now empty glass, he flashed his winning smile and said, "Well, more power to you, honey! I'm proud of you." Then, wanting to be sure she got it, he added, "Just remember to call a spade a spade, girl. This is slavery you are talking about, and those women are now slaves."

Samir was appalled at the smell of the place. *Jesus, do these people never bathe?* Try as he could to change his feelings, the hygiene of their allies and partners in Central and South America offended him. He wasn't wearing the preppy attire he had while running his PR firms, but no matter how he was traveling, Samir had kept himself clean.

Being generous, however, he did have to admit, the camp had limited access to water, and most of its inhabitants were purposely being kept out of sight under jungle canopies, so as to avoid detection. Trips to the stream were quick, and purposeful. Bathing was not a luxury in which the Hyena, or his men, indulged.

He had expected to find the camp in Colombia, but when he was transported north through South America by his handler, they had continued on, just across the border into Venezuela.

I wonder if Ayman knows we're operating out of Venezuela now? Samir asked himself. To be sure, he was not going to speak to any of this crew about it. If Ayman al-Zawahiri, known as the Doctor in Al Qaeda circles, wasn't aware of the move across the border, Samir would inform him when he returned with the "first shipment."

Hyena showed him the layout proudly. Three separate quarters were set up, based upon the newest instructions from the Doctor. One hut, with latrine outside in the rear, held about a dozen men. Most were relatively young, and it was obvious they had been drugged to keep them subdued. Believing they were hiring onto a crew to work and feed their families, the shock of being taken hostage and not allowed to leave would have driven most of them to desperate action. Young, and still strong, their captors knew to chemically restrain them.

Hyena had learned long ago of the sedative effect of drugs. So, a small amount of their drug trade was siphoned off and used on the men. He would exact the amount due for the reduction of his drug inventory by demanding Al Qaeda add in an additional quantity to the heroin they were smuggling to the FARC. The weapons the FARC would exchange for the heroin made the additional operational expense of the human trafficking business worthwhile. To him it was just a cost of business.

The second, somewhat larger hut, held almost thirty women. They had been collected from Mexico, Guatemala, Honduras, and about ten of them were from the United States. All were Hispanic, and had been violently kidnapped—snatched from their lives as they lived them. All were scheduled to be sold into prostitution.

Samir heard weeping and sobbing and knew it was coming from this facility. He did not even want to know what was being done to these women as they awaited transport. He was, however, keenly interested in the third hut, set farther up the hill, and isolated from the rest of the camp.

"This, my friend, is where we will house the Americans," Hyena bragged, letting loose the laugh that had earned him his nickname. Samir felt it was not only unnerving in its character but also in its volume, and he could not wait to get away from this man. He reminded himself to check the magazine in his concealed weapon later, for he was taking no chances with this "comrade."

"Per your demand, when these women arrive they will be kept here—away from the men and from the rest of the detainees. As you can see, we will be posting a 24-hour guard on the building itself. These guards are not to guard the perimeter or the camp, but only these women."

Samir nodded his approval. "You understand the penalty if any of them are harmed here?"

"I do. And you understand I cannot guarantee their condition arriving here. Transporting them from the United States to our camp is difficult, and there could be some damage. But, once they arrive here, this will be your 'prime product.' They should command a very great price. We will feed them and keep them away from the men. All guards are on orders to kill anyone who tries to tamper with the merchandise."

Once again, Hyena laughed and slapped Samir on the back. "Okay with you, amigo?" He breathed into Samir's face. Samir wondered whether this man had any idea who he was really dealing with. Neither the Doctor nor Samir took kindly to being played with, and he concluded Hyena was only bold enough to risk such insubordination and familiarity because of the devastating news of the death of Bin Laden, and the temporary marginalization of Al Qaeda.

He'd better not push me! Samir knew that fulfilling the mission was vital to his own survival, and he was not going to let this drug-addicted, foul-smelling gang leader toy with him. Deciding not to escalate the situation, he nodded his agreement.

"You realize, of course, that this kind of extra handling represents an increase in our cost of doing business, and that these women will command a higher price. They are 'top of the line,' so to speak." He grinned, knowing he had Samir where he wanted him.

"Understood." Samir paused deliberately, tapped Hyena lightly with a stick, and just as he had been taught by Ayman Al-Zawahiri to do, he wrote in the earth the amount Al Qaeda was willing to pay per woman. A few years earlier, in 2005, the Doctor himself had negotiated with Hyena the price for the FARC to provide a permanent location and training area for the terrorist group, as they moved their men out of the Middle East and into their new home on the doorstep of their enemy. That amount had been written in the earth as well. Once agreed upon, it was wiped away with the motion of a foot.

Tonight was no different. It was agreed, and quickly erased in the soil with the motion of Samir's left foot. For the first time, ordinary American women had a price on their heads—not because they were a soldier, not because they were a diplomat, not because they were a wealthy capitalist, or from a wealthy family—simply because they were American.

"I'll start with eleven." Samir placed his first order.

Across the equator, Americans were preparing their Memorial Day celebrations and family barbeques. No one knew what was coming. It was just as well.

CHAPTER 10

Walker's Gulfstream was cleared for landing amidst an unusually heavy bank of clouds. Though it was not raining in Basel, James knew they weren't going to be seeing much blue sky from the ground vantage point once they landed. He was glad he at least had his own jacket with him, and wasn't going to have to rely solely on Bud Walker's wardrobe choices.

He had no idea what was waiting for them in Basel, or even if the trip would prove fruitful. That made him eager to get on the ground and get into the game. Unaccustomed to flying in a private jet, James looked around almost habitually for the flight attendant who would mandatorily seize his glass and insist upon his handing over all trash.

Smiling, he remembered there was a hostess aboard, but she had spent most of the overnight flight reading in the galley. Frankly, the passengers could hold onto anything they wanted to when flying in a private plane with the owner aboard. Walker would have set the policies aboard his aircraft, and it appeared he lived aboard his plane pretty much as he lived in Montana—alone, free, and unrestricted.

It was noon, Basel time, on a cool late spring Monday when they rolled to a stop and the blocks were placed in front of the wheels to secure the aircraft. Swiss Customs boarded the plane immediately, knowing full well that a prominent American was aboard. There was no way such a dignitary would have to go into a line with other arriving passengers. So this was a courtesy of the Swiss Government.

Handing back the passports, the agent said, "Welcome to Switzerland, Monsieurs," and without expecting even an acknowledgement from them, he turned and exited.

It seemed a mere five minutes from their landing to entering the cab just outside the chain link fence. "Hotel Eifler," Walker directed, as he turned on his smart phone. Then, as if the driver might not know the hotel, he added, "across from the railroad station."

They had to circle the hotel one full time, as the driver was not in fact familiar with the hotel's automobile entrance. He would have missed the hotel altogether if Walker had not spotted Grey's Chocolate Shop across the street, realized they were there, and pointed to the hotel's entrance just as they were driving past their turn in. It took longer than expected to navigate around the city block, as the persistent drizzle was causing pedestrians to dart out between parked cars rather than to cross at the meticulously marked cross-walks. The driver had to put on his brakes more than once as they rounded each turn. Walker said nothing. He merely peered out of the slightly-fogged rear window and stared expressionless into the grey mist.

Once at the hotel, the cabbie was unnecessarily apologetic for missing the turn and delaying their arrival, and he was unctuous in his desire to please Walker. Afraid he might not get a good tip for having lost his bearings momentarily, he was especially insistent about carrying the bags into the hotel himself.

Walker was willing to let him handle their overnight bags but not the attaché case, which housed his primary laptop, with its encryption. As head of one of the world's largest media corporations, there were often transmissions coming to him from department heads, editors, and journalists, which had to remain confidential. Normal email traffic would have placed scoop stories at risk if someone got information prematurely.

In some cases, the information was so sensitive that it could jeopardize the sender. Bud politely signaled that he would retain possession of the attaché case, and looked to James to see if he needed any additional help. He did not.

Bud paid the cabbie generously for the ride, and for the additional service. Smiling appreciatively, the man pulled the vehicle away from the entrance while Walker and James started into the hotel. An elegantly dressed doorman opened the door with its etched glass logo, and James and Bud were just entering when they nearly collided with a man who was hastily exiting.

He was an elderly gentleman, somewhat portly, with dark hair and a silver-peppered mustache. Dressed in a dark grey raincoat and fedora, the man had tilted the brim of the hat forward to cover his eyes and brow. It appeared he was expecting rain. He held an expensive, but much-used, attaché case and was looking down at his watch when he narrowly missed colliding with Bud Walker.

"Pardon." He mumbled his apology without even looking up; then quickened his pace, as if running late for an appointment. Walker stopped for a moment, watching the man as he crossed the street almost without looking for traffic, and disappeared into the chocolate shop.

Though he had not really gotten a good luck at the gentleman—given the brevity of the encounter and the fact that the man had been distracted and looking down—Bud had an odd sense that he had met this man before. Not being able to place him though, he dismissed it. *Don't know...*

Then he caught up with James, who had already entered the immaculate, old-world men's club lobby area. It was 1PM, Basel, Switzerland time.

Four men awaited Harley Grantham-Jones as he entered the abandoned Waldstetter Hotel Annex, situated just above Grey's Chocolate Shop. A back stairway, sealed for almost thirty-five years, had been opened just hours before, as each of the men made their way from the old hotel into the upstairs annex.

The musty, cobweb-filled space had a history that would make ordinary men faint. These wood-paneled rooms held secrets and intrigue dating as far back as the 1930s. Deals had been made and plans had been laid long ago for an apocalyptic future moment. A group had waited patiently, year by year, decade by decade—setting the stage for what they knew would be world domination. With the goal in sight now, the men—some of whom were heirs to the original planners—knew that there was not one government in the world that could, or would, withstand their next actions.

For a very long time, they had been manipulating the financial markets so successfully that well-intentioned heads of state and their finance ministries had unwittingly played right into their hands as those men and women strove to stabilize their nations' currencies, manage their debts and credit ratings, and control interest rates. One would have had to connect dots across six decades, through three generations of international financiers, and through a massively fluid and ever-changing mishmash of global currencies, monetary policies, and indebtedness, to even get a hint of the picture.

These men, however, knew the picture in advance, so they never lost sight of it. All they monitored was how close the real world situation was coming to the financial Armageddon they envisioned. And, for their own reasons, they had concluded that the time was now.

Harley Grantham-Jones first removed his fedora, then the grey raincoat, and stood before his colleagues. They all laughed, appreciating the startling change of appearance his black-dyed hair and full mustache created.

"You look at least twenty years younger, Harley! And I have to say you look Italian. Thank goodness we have left the Italians out of this meeting," the small red-haired man from the Swiss Central Bank quipped. "Braghelli here is not really Italian. Too much time in the United States you know. If he were, he might take offense at your mimicry—even if just for national pride." Grantham-Jones and Antonio Braghelli appreciated the ribbing, seeming to take it in stride.

Shaking hands, the meeting immediately turned in a more solemn direction. The four who had preceded Grantham-Jones into the hidden chamber were the Directors of the Central Banks of the United States, Germany, Switzerland, and the former head of the Central Bank of Italy. Including Grantham-Jones, who was the current Director of the Bank of the United Kingdom, they represented half of the G8. The remaining four of the world's largest economies regularly included in the G8—Japan, Canada, Russia, and France—had been deliberately excluded. These five men—from the United States, Great Britain, Germany, Italy, and a tag-along Switzerland—were about to change the course of world history.

CHAPTER 11

"*A*ntonio, could you not have had the place at least dusted!" Harley scolded with mock sarcasm. Five of the most powerful men in the world were convening in these quarters, and it looked as if the room had not been used, let alone serviced, in decades.

Antonio Braghelli was the newly-elected Director of the Repository of International Transactions, following a meteoric career climb in the United States investment banking business. As that field began its collapse, he had returned to his native Italy where he had promptly been placed in charge of Italy's Central Bank. Then, in a surprise move, Sir Harley Grantham-Jones—arguably the most significant member of the group—had endorsed Braghelli to be elected the new Director of the Repository of International Transactions.

The job suited Braghelli well. In his late forties, he resembled a young Mussolini, though nowhere near as stout. But his carriage suggested a real disdain for anyone beneath him. Known for a notorious temper, he camouflaged it impeccably with a smooth and menacingly measured style of speech. Antonio Braghelli chose to say very few words, but his strategies were respected in the world of commercial warfare.

And that was how he viewed every choice he had made in investment banking, finance, and management—an act of war. Looking always for the advantage it would gain him and his company, only someone truly naïve would even consider that he would do anything that had an "unintended consequence." Yet that is exactly how the recent financial crises—whose steering and oversight he was responsible for—were viewed by the United States government, and by the media who, robot-like, reported what they were fed by the Public Relations department of each of the Central Banks. For all intents and purposes, Antonio Braghelli had been "given a pass."

Americans, mesmerized by ignorant media propaganda, had overlooked a glaring out-point in the entire collapse of the mortgage banking and mortgage insurance industries. The "party line" was that all the finance experts who controlled U.S. monetary policy, and the printing of money itself, had done the best they could with what they had and knew. And that these collapses were just "unfortunate consequences." No one had asked, "How do you get to the pinnacle of your field, in control of the United States currency and money supply, and not know basic banking policy, and the certain ramifications of specific actions?"

Trust had always been one of the great strengths of the Americans. It had been turned into a weakness that was set to devour an entire economy, and enslave the nation. That plan was beginning right now, in this musty, ill-maintained room above a candy shop.

"No complaints, any of you!" Braghelli barked. "It's precisely because this has remained abandoned that we are using it. To have it 'spiffed' up for you, Harley, would have signaled something was going on." He paused to make certain he had everyone's attention, and then continued. "We are not ready for the other four to know—let alone the fifty-five members. We are going to provide plausible deniability to our four colleagues from Canada, France, Japan, and Russia. They will accept everything we teach them as necessary courses of action intended to help the nations of Earth.

"They, in turn, will sell it very persuasively to the rest of the fifty-five members, and they *all* will sell it to their governments. And the media, my friends, will sell the fear and chaos. For now, though, no one but us may know we are here."

Harley nodded his concurrence. Ceremoniously dusting off a chair with his handkerchief, he sat down—straight-backed, as was his habit—and waited. The others, impatient to know exactly why they had been called here, almost five years ahead of when they'd expected to launch, were almost a chorus: "Yes, Antonio, why are we here *now?* What is the urgency? We thought things were going according to our plan for 2016."

"They were, friends, until recently. But that change in the world picture could jeopardize the whole plan and our ascendancy. We will stay here for a few hours while I review with you what has been accomplished, what yet has to be done, and what our initial strike will be."

Seeing that he had ruffled some egos by assuming these men would not have input on the direction of their attack, he quickly recovered. "I mean, of course, we will discuss all this, and come to agreement on the course of action, once you have the most current information. But our actions must be decisive and merciless. There is no turning back now." It seemed to work as, one by one, they each found a kerchief, either dusting off the chair and disposing of it, or placing it gingerly on the seat and then settling on the kerchief. They then pulled the chairs into a semi-circle in the center of an otherwise empty room.

No one spoke. The only sound heard for the better part of a minute was the chime of the bell hanging over the entrance to the candy store below. Someone had just entered, looking for a confectionary delight. Not wanting to draw attention to their presence in this otherwise unused portion of the building, they muffled their voices and restrained their movements.

Those amongst them who had fought in wars knew the kind of tension and pitch combat forces arrive at just before being unleashed in a stealth attack. Braghelli had that look, and there was tension in his voice when he resumed his train of thought.

"Be assured though, my friends, when we finish here, you will return to your hotel and enjoy a normal meal, a normal night's rest. But tomorrow you will report to headquarters, where your life in our facility commences. None of you will be returning home. Within months, you will be in control of every government and economy in the world. During the turbulent transition, you will be safe inside our facility, and can work without distractions."

"And you?" the Central Bank Director of Switzerland challenged, peering over his ridiculous horn-rimmed glasses. The man looked like a nerdy Elton John.

"I will be joining you. The world did not know we existed—at least not as a group with the goal that is about to become apparent even to the dullest of them—and if they do realize that what they'd assumed was just a conspiracy theory or the ranting of some fool is a reality, and that they themselves chose us, handing us the power and authority we now have, well, we will all live cloistered lives."

He took a sip of water and added, "We will call all the directors in, and thereby remain camouflaged amongst the fifty-five. All can be sequestered—ostensibly to keep the fifty-five top finance ministers safe and working on the 'catastrophe' in a distraction-free environment." He paused to make sure they agreed; then continued smugly. "People will accept that, I think."

This moment had been planned for almost four decades, yet as it was arriving and delivering to them the peoples of Earth, each man was nonetheless sobered by the reality. Braghelli could read it on their faces, see it in their frowns. More gently, he reassured them, "For a short time… only a short time. It will be over quickly. They will not see it coming."

Each nodded. Then the head of the United States' largest central bank asked, "All right. So what is this 'change in the world picture?'"

Braghelli frowned. The shafts of afternoon light, penetrating through splotches of grime on the windows, cast an almost ghoulish shadow across his face. "The Americans have started to wake up. We spent decades sedating them, but the sedatives are wearing off."

"Really?" Harley seemed a bit skeptical.

"Yes." Pausing for effect, he added, "It started with 'White King Rising.'"

Hours later, the blackout curtains had been pulled to suppress any light escaping from the room. Despite the deplorable condition of the room, a sumptuous meal had been brought to them in secrecy, using the old dumb waiter, which was a fixture in old, grand hotels, and in the mansions of Europe. Well-fed and saturated with information, each man had concluded that indeed the nation their Central Bank controlled was ready.

The primary vulnerability for every country was the weakening value of its currency. Only one or two were considered even remotely strong. And the debtor nation status of nearly everyone made each country vulnerable. Most endangered of all were the U.S. and Great Britain—particularly the United States. Having assumed the primary burden of warring against the nations and groups that initiated the attack on American soil on 9/11/01, and not knowing the attackers were financed by banking entities authorized to loan money to them by the men in that room, the United States had done what every nation in history had done when waging war—it had gone further into debt. With a debt now exceeding what it produced, any ordinary person would have recognized that, if this were the case of their personal finances, they were "cooked."

Unexpectedly, the Director from Germany asked, "Do you think they know?"

"Know what?"

"That 9/11 was just the bait, and that borrowing to eliminate that threat was what sprung the trap?"

Braghelli inhaled deeply, held it an almost frighteningly long time, and then exhaled. It was a question, however, that he had expected to answer. "Yes. They are not dumb men and women in Washington." Chewing over his next statement, however, he paused again; then continued. "And, by now, the White House has recognized it has precious few options."

"What do you think they will do?"

"Try to raise the debt ceiling, as usual." He responded without hesitation.

At this point Harley Grantham-Jones cleared his throat, signaling he wanted to add something. His protégé responded respectfully. "Harley?"

"Just know, gentlemen, that any option they select is onerous. To raise the debt ceiling will seem like the least of the evils, and it will buy them time according to their viewpoint. And if there is one thing I know about American politicians, it is that they like to buy time." He laughed.

The head of the Bank of the United States was normally a quiet man. Middle-aged now, with thinning hair and a bald spot in the center back, he looked like the quintessential accountant. He exerted enormous power in Washington, however, and on Wall Street, and was accustomed to being listened to. He interrupted his counterpart from Great Britain. "In an emergency why would my government not take the other options of perhaps seizing private property and taxing corporations to raise revenue, or raiding the Social Security program much like Argentina did when they took over private pensions in 2008? It seems to me the Administration is pre-disposed toward that."

"No, they will behave like politicians, and try to buy time. I am certain of it," Harley retorted unequivocally.

That prompted a virtual chorus of questions from the remaining executives. The questions simmered down when Grantham-Jones suddenly stamped his foot. "Gentlemen, to answer your *real* question as to why that won't work for them, in a nutshell, it will not work because *this* time we will not extend them any additional credit. No more money manufactured or transferred electronically. This time, we say *no*."

Braghelli was smiling now, as the main part of the plot became visible. "Harley is telling you the first step, gentlemen. This time we say no. Now, here's what happens next, even before they start to default on other countries to whom they owe money. This will bring those presumptuous bastards in China down with them by the way. The RIT is prepared to call in the debt—Treasury notes, Bonds, all of it—every nation, all debts due."

None of the conspirators were shocked by this. Each had an almost sociopathic calm visage. Rather they looked inward, calculating the untold and immediate chaos and destruction such a move would cause. Had they even a sliver of conscience, each would have felt a twinge of remorse at the devastation, and descent into barbarism, that would ensue. But, each had been carefully selected and groomed by Harley Grantham-Jones for some time now. He knew their souls and knew they could be counted on.

Grantham-Jones broke their introspection. "Gentlemen, you are about to see the fabric of society unravel. Hummph. Should be fascinating. Civilized men behave in a very unusual and unseemly fashion when threatened with starvation."

Showing no concern for the human suffering aspect whatsoever, Braghelli resumed with, "So, first our refusal to extend credit, followed by our calling up all notes, and then, as economies are tumbling and countries writhing with fear and recrimination, we step in with our solution. They already agreed to it in 2009, though I doubt any one of them thought it was anything more than what we promoted it to be—a humane gesture to make sure such criminal and incompetent financial activities they experienced in the 1990s and early 2000s could not happen again. And, in their conceit, I doubt they created any hypothetical examples of the terms of the Financial Responsibility Board's document when they signed it. They just signed it. It was politically correct to do so."

The other four nodded their agreement with that assertion. Below them, they could hear the shopkeeper closing his business for the day, locking up, and going home. For a moment, they sat quietly, then the discussion resumed, albeit much less restrained vocally.

"There are twelve points in the Financial Responsibility Board's document," the Director from Switzerland queried. "Which do we implement first?"

"Three, simultaneously." Braghelli paused, knowing the others were now engaging the databases in their smart phones and notebooks to highlight, each in his own way, the attack line. "Point number one will be the very structure of their government. We need to disband some of these republics and democracies. Second will be oversight and possible appropriation of their retirement assets. Third will be oversight on our part of their medical records and programs."

"And don't forget, Antonio," the Swiss Director added, "that the credit lines are to remain open for Al Qaeda, and our other terrorist friends, at the Swiss banks. We must not forget to inform them through channels to move their accounts to Switzerland. And credit lines of course remain open for all Swiss pharmaceutical companies." The man never missed a chance to promote the clandestine activities of his country, and was always looking for self-serving ways for the Swiss to survive.

He suppressed a smile, as he didn't want to appear overly confident or greedy, knowing that once again, Switzerland would come out a major winner in these 21st century war games. Long ago, he realized that the resurgence of the psychiatric/pharmaceutical cartels would be necessary to sedate and handle any truly ornery or dissident citizens in any nation. *"White King Rising" be damned! Those pathetic, young, and undereducated youth in America can dream all they want about the reversal of the drug society, but when they are staring at guns drawn by their neighbors, they will be begging for something to render those neighbors controllable. They'll fall in line, the wimps!*

"Did you want to say something else, Fritz?" Braghelli's question brought the Swiss Director back from his personal soapbox.

"No, no. I was just thinking how ready Switzerland is to deliver in this area. That is all."

"Good, my friend, because I will control the timing on that," Grantham-Jones stated emphatically. "Let me explain why."

They all were listening, giving Braghelli a moment to stretch and then lean back in his chair. Once again, he was paying homage to his mentor.

"Our greatest threat is the United States. I think we all know that." Each man nodded. "But unless the entire country is able to go through a national drug withdrawal, and comes out of the sedation and anesthesia, that population will explode like other nations' populations. And we want it to...to the degree that it forces the U.S. government to yield to and accept those first three demands. Are you following?" They were. "The Americans *may* be more alert now than three years ago, and they are innately smart. We cannot afford for them to be alert *and* smart."

"Hear, hear."

"What has to happen, and gentlemen, I do mean *has* to happen, is for the American President to be persuaded to declare martial law. He would have the authority in the event of pervasive civil unrest to do so. That unrest will be created; and the President will take the first step in what will eventually be the dismantling of what America thinks is its greatest weapon—its Constitution. My grandfather taught me long ago—and I have taught every one of my protégés the same since—that the average man is pretty trashy. People cannot govern themselves, and a three-branch government is too rigid and slow for these times. Eventually the President of the United States will change the form of his government to a dictatorship in order to save the rabble he represents. But...it must be done slowly, like you would cook a frog."

Harley relished the somewhat quizzical looks on the faces of his colleagues. And, at his age and experience, he truly enjoyed the Financier Emeritus status he held with this group. "We Brits learned long ago that you cannot poke the American in the face to the degree he realizes he is threatened. Drugged or not, he has always managed to somehow rise up right then and there and strike back. No, the only way to take America down is to simmer the frog in a cool pan, gradually raising the temperature so that he becomes de-energized and soporific. When he's too sluggish to jump out, he is cooked. Drop an American in hot water and he's quick—he'll jump out. And a powerful, angry America is not something any of us wants to experience. It's counter-productive and unnecessary."

Just as he was about to continue, the harsh World War II-like siren of an ambulance shattered the calm of the small city transitioning into night. Waiting for it to pass, he took a sip of water. "No, let the Americans choose the martial law themselves; let them think they are in control and that martial law will hold the barbarians at the gate. It will be some time before they realize they stepped into the trap."

"Surrender?" Germany's youthful director asked.

"In a manner of speaking, son, yes. Once you have martial law, and people become accustomed to it, it is not such a long leap to change your form of government to one controlled more by the executive than by the legislative branches, which are controlled by citizenry. History teaches us that people will accept dictators and peacefully surrender republics if they can justify it. They may even welcome the cessation of their freedom if they are oblivious to the reality of that freedom. And we are about to create a situation where the people of the United States on their own— with no help from us thank God, since we have no military sufficient to accomplish that by force—will step their government down to one controlled by one man or woman. And at that moment, this obnoxious blip in history will have gone the way of the other attempts at republics."

That sobering reality sunk in, and Grantham-Jones finished very disparagingly with, "There never has been a mass of people really capable of running their own show. It has always been necessary for men like us to ultimately stop the games, and just assume control." He wrinkled his nose, as if there were some repugnant smell in the room that had come in with his contemplation of the common man.

"You see, my dear fellows, there are some very smart people on this planet, and there are some very conceited men as well. And in the coming months those conceited ones are about to discover just who is subordinate to whom! We are senior, and if we say they can have money, they can have it. If we say they can live, they can live. Basically, they belong to us.

"And we are going to disabuse them of any other delusions they may have of their independence and autonomy. It's time they knew the true score here. Their heads have gotten too big." Stopping his harangue long enough to catch his breath, Sir Harley turned to Braghelli and said, "The more I speak about this, the more I see how right you are in selecting this time. Without the drugs to sedate them, these Americans could very well slip out of their chemical straightjacket and become unmanageable once again. It is time to put them in their place. My family dates back a thousand years and has always held itself accountable for the order of things. Now, this mission is falling to me—and to you."

Sir Harley Grantham-Jones intended to control the people of Earth, and had nothing but disdain for them. It was this disdain that would open a door—a tiny vulnerability, if only a defender could exploit it.

Not more than an hour later, every one of the others had concluded exactly what Braghelli and Grantham-Jones knew they would. The plan was to their liking, and they had accepted the necessity of implementing it now. The world was theirs, providing that the United States remained weakened. If it gained strength, it would likely regain its innovative approach to crises, and to the men who fostered them. To win, the United States had to remain "just a little bit groggy," as Grantham-Jones had so superlatively put it.

Donning their disguises once again, they said good evening and left one at a time. For Sir Harley, it was a short walk past the railroad station and back to the Hotel Eifler. Politely asking the doorman for the time, he decided it was still early enough. A nice sherry would be an excellent way to end a truly exhilarating day. *Braghelli has done a superlative job,* he thought, congratulating himself. *This is the time. He called it correctly. Let the games begin!*

CHAPTER 12

" *E*in anderes bier?" The bartender broke Bud Walker's reverie.
"Nein, nein." Walker recovered, shook off his distraction, and
politely answered the man who had already served him two of Switzerland's best dark beers.

He was about to pay up and leave the bar at the Hotel Eifler where he
had been hanging out, hoping to spot Sir Harley. He was still disturbed
by the close and brief encounter earlier with the man in the fedora. Something kept nagging at him, bringing his attention back to the incident.
He'd easily left James Mikolas behind, as James appeared to be suffering
from jet lag. No matter whether traveling on a private jet or commercial
one, when one traversed as many time zones as they had in one day, body
jet lag can set in.

Bud was more used to it, as he and his ex-wife were prone to flying
regularly from Montana to London, or Paris. Over time, he had accustomed himself to rest aboard the plane. That, coupled with a trick he
had learned about staying up, no matter what, until the time one would
normally sleep in the new time zone, enabled him now to still be awake—
even if he was starting to drowse after the two beers and several handfuls
of nuts and pretzels he had enjoyed.

Bud didn't know how long he'd been at the bar, and he had not engaged in conversation with anyone. He was also deeply disturbed by the
last email transmission from his staff. Before leaving Montana, he had
asked them to research every media mogul in the world and identify, if
they could, who had sponsored them, who had been an "angel" in their
career, or who had taken them on as a protégé.

It had taken the duration of their flight for his staff to gather it, but
when he looked at the list of names, he was sickened. Each media mogul was indebted to the beneficence of a prominent citizen, and, more
importantly, to a prominent citizen who was a major player in the world

of International Finance. Most were Finance Ministers, Directors of, or Advisors to the Central Banks.

Lost in his own thoughts, trying to deny the ever-looming link between the Central Banks and the world's major media, he became slowly aware that he had escaped into a bar where discretion was definitely the better part of valor. There was no telling what types of deals had been struck here, or what types of orders given. The Hotel Eifler dated back to pre-World War II. Switzerland had maintained a famous neutrality during the great war, but it was generally known that Nazis frequently crossed into this sector—unharmed and uninterrupted. He could only guess what conspiracies had been hatched here.

And "Hitler's Bank," as it was dubbed for posterity, was in Basel, snuggled conveniently into the corner of Switzerland, France, and Germany. It was reported that one could see all three countries from the restaurant atop its tower. Of course, no ordinary citizen had ever been permitted to enter it, but rumor had it...

And it was those rumors, and others, that were haunting Walker. *It couldn't be true, could it?* He almost feared asking himself. That bank still existed—under a new name, and in new headquarters. The Repository of International Transactions—known as the RIT—was only about a mile away. Walker was disturbed by the very appearance of the tower, even at the distance of a mile. He had never paid any attention to this before today. But *today* he was.

A mile away were two structures. One looked like a nuclear power plant. The other, though modern and glass, was a round tower resembling a modern version of a Medieval turret. Tonight, after two beers, as his mind's eye looked them over, both of those shapes seemed menacing. Something else was bothering Bud Walker, something he could not shake. It felt as if a time machine had dropped a Feudal tower into the 21st century, and that anomaly was agitating him.

In all the years of journalism, in all the news stories in his country, and others, about banking and international finance, he had never seen pictures of these structures. Yet, there they were in the near distance, dominating this otherwise small and insignificant city. *Why would no one have ever spoken of those foreboding monstrosities? Why does no one know of them? Or speak of them really?*

He chuckled at the irony of the obvious answer. He had not looked at them; why would any other news media look? If the news didn't talk about it, it was not true or real for the average guy. Absent media attention, *it* did not exist—whatever *it* was. Again, he felt a wave of nauseous guilt wash over him, even though he couldn't quite pinpoint what he should feel guilty about. All he could ask himself was, *If the media doesn't cover it, does it exist? Do we determine what exists?*

That question was crowded out by another, more relentless thought. Walker hated conspiracy theorists—thought of them as nothing more than tabloid journalists. Yet, his own mind was nurturing an equally repugnant thought. It had to do with a question Mikolas had asked him back at the ranch. Looking back on it now, he didn't know whether it was just an innocuous attempt by Mikolas to keep the awkward conversation going, or if he had asked the question deliberately, hoping to come through a back door regarding whoever it was that had *sent* Bud Walker. He suspected the latter, since Mikolas didn't strike him as a guy who threw anything out casually. *He's trying to get me to turn on my friend, is all.* Bud justified this through the slight fog of the strong Swiss beer.

Back on the stone veranda, Mikolas had asked Bud how he had met Samir Taghavi in the first place.

"I met him at a party the President of France threw at his Paris apartment," Bud had answered easily. James had paused and then said, "Wow, that's impressive. His Paris apartment. The President of France invited you?" Bud had answered, just as easily as before, "No, my wife and I were invited by Harley and Sylvia."

Mikolas had said nothing else. But the possibility of that all being a set up to introduce Samir to Bud was sickening. It reeked of conspiracy theory and flimsy evidence of malfeasance, anchoring the supposition on what may have been nothing more than sheer coincidence. Yet, he could not shake it. That night on the balcony, and the conversation he had had with Samir Taghavi, had turned the direction of his news agency, and subsequently turned the direction of all his competitors when they followed his lead.

It was a moment he wished he could un-live. But now, it was sticking even more persistently because of the possible association with Sir Harley.

Deciding to tackle this whole mishmash in the morning when he could confront Harley face to face, he was pulling cash out when he saw a man enter the bar. The man was oblivious to anyone else in the room, and walked straight to a corner booth, cozy and softly lit, and settled in. He was carrying a fedora.

Walker instinctively pocketed his money instead, signaling the bartender, Horst, that he had changed his mind and would take another.

Cautiously eyeing the man through the mirror that decorated the bar and reflected the room, encompassing the total area, at first he questioned whether or not it could be Harley. But, without the fedora, and despite the mustache and dark hair color, he had to admit the resemblance was striking. Still not wanting to walk up and accuse a great friend of perpetrating some bazaar charade, he sipped his drink and waited.

Not more than a minute later, the man executed a gesture that Harley regularly used when he was impatient. He thumped his index and middle finger loudly twice, and then repeated it. Invariably it caught the attention of some servant who was lagging, and they would rush to his attention.

Tonight was no different. His waiter immediately came to his side, apologized quickly for letting himself get distracted, and inquired into what he needed. "Another."

Walker picked up his drink and walked directly to his friend. "You'd be interested in a conversation I had recently with a CIA analyst, Harley." He slid into the booth, uninvited. Bud Walker's empire might be under attack, but he had not lost "the nose." He knew that when you present something unexpected to someone, you surface their true colors, and a more accurate emotion.

At first, Harley was startled that he had been recognized, but his recovery was almost immediate. Playfully, he tried to con his friend by waiving his right hand at him, laughing and saying, "You caught me, my dear boy. You always were the best."

Walker, however, barely smiled. Sir Harley Grantham-Jones sobered a bit, scrutinized his protégé, and asked, "But what are *you* doing here?"

"Sylvia told me you were here. But the better question is, what are you doing here at this irregular time of the month, and more importantly, wearing a disguise?" Bud asked a bit too loudly.

Knowing that the jig was up, and that he had to think fast, Grantham-Jones quickly responded, "Well, if you promise to keep your voice down, I'll tell you why I'm in this Halloween costume." Bud nodded. "But first, I'm most interested in what your conversation with the CIA was about."

"Fair enough," Bud responded. "You know I've had a fair amount of trouble and scrutiny in the last three years regarding Al Qaeda, my networks, my associations—that whole mess."

"Yes, of course, but I've told you before, Bud, you are one of the best. You'll weather that, if you haven't already, and you'll remain the star I always knew you were."

"Thank you. I appreciate that Harley. Your confidence in me has kept me going through many a firefight."

Each man paused to take a drink. Bud took a swig of his beer; Harley, a sip of the Bristol Cream he had ordered. Just then the waiter returned with his second round, and Grantham-Jones offered a toast. Bud took it.

"To better times."

Walker looked away for a moment to make sure no one was within earshot. He leaned in then to his friend and quietly offered, "He asked me an interesting question, this CIA man."

"Does he have a name, this man?"

"Yes. James Mikolas—formerly with the CIA."

"And, currently with…?" Harley tried to conceal his intense curiosity.

"Bit of a lone ranger, Harley. Friend of Carver and Weir." There, he had dropped it onto the table. Walker honestly had no idea whether his friend was in fact a villain. He prayed he was not, but there was something sinister in this almost silly disguise and charade in this time warp of a room. Bud Walker was a simple man, with good instincts. If this were occurring in Montana, he would have no doubt someone was putting something over on someone. Tonight he decided to be American, and not faux-British. That one choice would open another window for a nation—still unaware that checkmate moves had been set in motion against it—to escape the trap.

Sir Harley feigned confusion. "Carver and Weir?"

"The young men who created the phenomenon in computer gaming, 'White King Rising.' You know, the game that has taken America pretty much off drugs."

"Ahh, yes, Carver and Weir. I do know about their magnificent contribution to sanity. And you say this…what did you say his name was?"

"Mikolas."

"Yes, this Mikolas, he works for them?"

"No, some kind of friend I think. Smart guy though."

"How so, Bud?"

"Well, he and Andy Weir ran an analysis that identified a series of chess games that are being played simultaneously in this post 9/11 world, which concluded that the game second from the top was Medical—dominated by the psychiatric/pharmaceutical cartels to subdue populations. Brian Washington Carver designed a computer game to reverse the demand for drugs of all kinds, and they proved to be a formidable trio."

Harley's hand quivered momentarily as he raised the sherry glass once again. To avoid Bud noticing, he asked, "You said second from the top?"

"Yes, I did."

"Well, I'm curious, what was the top game?"

"Money." Walker tossed it away, deliberately choosing not to engage or accuse.

Grantham-Jones took the bait, and missed it as well. At that moment, he concluded that his friend was not covertly inquiring into "Money" being Finance or International Banking but rather who stood to gain wealth by pushing drugs. *Seems safe enough,* Harley concluded, and he relaxed noticeably.

"Anyway, Mikolas asked me an interesting question."

"And that was?"

"He said the psychiatric medications and the profession that had infiltrated all the American institutions, weakening them by bringing drugs in as the solution, were sent by someone—that they were a Trojan Horse, if you will. And he asked if I knew who had sent the Trojan Horse. Mikolas said that was a lingering question with him."

Harley looked at this, as if sincerely trying to help his friend. "Well, that *is* an excellent question. Knowing you, you probably had an answer for him."

"Beats me, Harley. That's why I called you. I thought you might know. You're the one with all the money, remember?" Bud laughed, teasing his friend.

Both men laughed, neither wanting to expose his hand.

Having had enough, Bud switched gears. "So, what's with the Charlie Chaplin get-up?" Sir Harley looked as if he were going to try to sidestep this, so Bud blocked him. "You are the Director of the Central Bank of the United Kingdom, and you are in Basel, Switzerland weeks before your monthly meeting, and you are in disguise—a poor one—but a disguise nonetheless. What's up?"

"You know I can't tell you anything, Bud," Grantham-Jones retorted with a hint of resentment. Then softening, he asked, "Is this conversation off the record?"

"Absolutely."

In his best confessional mode, Harley motioned for his friend to lean in. Whispering confidentially, he said, "There is a real crisis, Bud. Not a drill or *potential* one. A real one. And it required an emergency meeting. If the press got wind of all of us showing up earlier than usual, there would be too much speculation."

"I see. Speculation, panic, those are your concerns?"

"Precisely. The global economy is precarious enough right now. We have a good plan to forestall and mitigate the crisis, but not if there is a spotlight on us. So, we're buying some time with this ruse."

"I see."

"Make sure you do, son, make sure you do." Despite the term of endearment, his tone was a bit castigating. "The hopes and dreams of people and nations are nothing to be tampered with. We will provide a solution, and a way to make sure this never happens again."

"And you are not going to hint at what this *crisis* is, are you?"

Grantham-Jones smiled, hoping he did not appear condescending, "Correct. I cannot—even off the record."

The two sat silently, staring into their drinks for a moment. Sir Harley broke the silence with, "But, what I can promise you, Bud, is that when I *can* reveal information, I will call you, rather than the others. I trust you completely—and WNG—to walk point on this. I have no doubt but that you will handle this *responsibly*." He sat back against the booth's cushion to signal he was comfortable with all of this.

"Thank you for that vote of confidence. I won't let you down, Harley."

"I know you won't, my boy. You'll learn what's happened soon enough. For now, just do your job."

Just do my job! It had sounded almost like a menacing order. It most definitely had the tone of someone ordering an underling. Then, Sir Harley's tone had turned condescending, which made Bud's spine tingle. The sobering, inescapable reality was hitting him. *You mean do the job you want me to, don't you?*

Like a chameleon, Sir Harley had changed colors and all hint of menace evaporated. "I wish I could tell you more, but you know I will be good for my word. When I have details for you, I will get you the most accurate information available, so that you can properly educate the people."

For a moment, Bud thought he was going to faint. He was prepared to accept a confirmation that it was the International Banking Community that had sent the Trojan Horse in the form of the agents of the psychiatric/pharmaceutical cartels. But not until that moment did he realize there had been a second Trojan Horse—also accepted as a cherished gift by unsuspecting citizens. That Trojan Horse had been sent by the same people. It was the American Media itself, men and women who were diligently and perhaps self-righteously trying to fulfill the promise of a free press, who unwittingly were delivering into every household on Earth the propaganda and spin these "credible" financial wizards were feeding them. Sent to educate, he knew now it was, in reality, to hypnotize and mislead.

Needing to escape, he smiled, patted Harley on the back in his customary salutation, and joked, "That's good enough for me, Harley. I'll wait to hear from you. Wouldn't want to misdirect people—especially during my 'comeback.'" He smiled and rose to leave, adding, "But, if you are going to be here awhile, you might want to rethink the disguise."

Harley chortled. "Fine. You have any recommendations?"

"Well, you could try an artist's smock. That might prove a better camouflage."

Bud started to pull some cash out, but Harley waived him off.

"Mikolas, wake up!"

James was confused by the urgency in Bud's voice. "We're leaving, Boy Scout, as soon as you can shake a leg."

"Why? And why now?"

"Because, Boy Scout, regrettably I think you may be right about your 'Trojan Horse.' And they are doing something right now. We had better figure out what that is, before they do it."

CHAPTER 13

James was especially grateful to be flying on a private aircraft for the
return flight. Given that he had barely had any sleep in two days, he
found it hard to believe it was only just now Tuesday. It seemed like an
eternity since he had arrived at Bud Walker's ranch on Saturday night.

No wonder Walker is doing a little better, James reflected. *He at least
slept through most of Saturday before I got him sobered up. Still he's a better
traveler than I am these days, given that we flew to Basel, stayed on the ground
nine hours, and are turning around.*

He wondered whether the ability to travel on a dime's notice of time,
cross multiple time zones, coupled with failing to get adequate sleep was
a skill one developed and which would atrophy if not used. Or perhaps
it was just a function of body age. *Yep, that's what I think it is, in my case.
I'm a little too old for a regular dose of this.*

However, they were headed west to Montana, and James sensed he
was going to be in for a pretty long haul on the ground once they landed.
For the flight home though, he had purposely sat in a leather swivel chair
close enough to Walker that he could watch him, but not so close as to
intrude. Walker had said not one word after barking the orders to get up;
they were heading home.

As their jet lifted off into the night and the pilot leveled it off at
37,000 feet, Bud just sat, his jaw protruded and set. He would occasionally look out the window, but for the most part, he merely stared straight
ahead, as if looking at some kind of disturbing image—his body language
and facial expression suggesting he was preparing for a fight.

James said nothing. He'd seen this demeanor often with men who had
just discovered that the world they thought they had inhabited was not
the one in which they were actually living. As a field operator in intelligence, he had seen many a man and woman have to come to grips with

betrayal. It was not a pretty sight. So, he sat back, resting his head on the mercifully high and soft headrest.

Suddenly, and quietly, Walker reached for the phone in the armrest of his own double-sized chair. First pressing a button on the console of his chair, he asked his pilot if he would turn on the secure channel. Once done, Walker dialed a number and waited, his jaw still set, but his complexion showed a little less pallor.

"It's me," he said quietly to someone who would obviously recognize his voice. James had no idea who he was calling now. Bud listened, nodded, and said, "Yes, I got the report. Thank you."

He looked out the window for a moment into the blackness that accompanies lonely planes at that altitude, then turned his attention back to the person he had just acknowledged. "Sorry to interrupt your dinner plans, but I need you to reach some people for me. It's urgent."

Whatever the other person said, Walker continued. "First, get Ray and tell him I need him at the ranch by noon tomorrow. Use whatever jet is available, and don't let him squawk. And be sure to tell him he is not to tell anyone where he is going. Understood?"

It appeared to be. "Next. Get Simon Atwater and tell him to be there as well—same time, same secrecy." Waiting for a moment, he added, "And, I need you as well, Edward. Make sure your cover story is a good one. I don't want the rest of the executive floor to know my Chief of Staff has left New York."

He hung up, signaled his pilot to disengage the encrypted channel, heaved a big sigh, and leaned back. His chair swiveled as well, and he smoothly turned it to face James. "Well, Boy Scout, you say you are always prepared?"

"Try to be…" James didn't finish the sentence, not sure where this was going. But he knew enough to let Walker do the talking. It seemed he was ready now.

"Good. 'Cause you're going to need your wits for this one. And I'm going to need you to have your 'analyst hat' back on, because we have some serious research to do."

"I can do that. You care to tell me what we're dealing with here?"

Bud took a sip of the ice water he kept nearby at all times on a flight. "You were right, Mikolas. Someone did *send me*. It's hard to believe, but he did. He's working on something, right now. And we're going to find out what he is up to."

James waited, saying nothing. After a few moments, Bud added, "Something is going on in Basel, Switzerland, and my gut tells me we had better find out what."

James had that same feeling of a pervasive menace. Though Bud assumed James had been asleep while he was reviewing the report his Chief of Staff had forwarded, and later while spending time in the bar of the hotel, James had in fact taken a side trip to the Repository of International Transactions. Knowing it was the only financial institution of any consequence in Basel, he'd heard of it, but never seen it.

What he saw there had unnerved him—truly unnerved him. He could not help but wonder whether this strange flight home, and the cloak and dagger conference Walker was convening on his ranch, had anything to do with a building surrounded by elaborate fencing and protected by a paramilitary force that wore no international insignia that James recognized. It was almost as if an autonomous structure from another world had been planted in an unlikely spot, and from that spot was extending energy into every sector of the planet.

James Mikolas had spent thirty years dealing with secrets, and the men who kept them. This one place was the most foreboding place he had ever come upon. He was ready for whatever Walker needed him to do.

"Is 'Ray' the Vice Chairman of the Board of WNG, Ray Elkins?"

Bud nodded.

"And who is Simon Atwater? I remember hearing the name, but I can't place him."

"A bureau chief…he heads up all reporting relevant to finance, economies, IMF, World Bank, investments…if it has to do with money, he's got it." Then he added a resounding endorsement. "Good man…studied with Milton Friedman. He worked with him on the Chile turn-around project."

"I see." James did in fact see.

"So, all I want to say right now, James, is that it seems Sir Harley Grantham-Jones, my friend, is expecting me to 'do my job.'" He waited for a moment, set his jaw again, squinted his eyes somewhat and added, "I'm gonna do just that. In 24 hours, I will turn over WNG to the very capable Ray Elkins and let him run the empire. I will then resume my very first job in the industry." For the first time since take-off, Walker flashed an almost ironic smile. Dominated by all his later accomplishments, Bud Walker's Wikipedia bio nonetheless clearly stated that he had gotten his start in the media as an investigative journalist.

_____

When Walker's jet landed in the dead of night on his ranch in Montana, it was pre-dawn in Washington, D.C. A gloomy drizzle shrouded the Mall and its monuments. A light came on in the bedroom of the occupant of the White House Residence. His Chief of Staff had personally decided it was time to wake him and escort the President of the United States to the Situation Room.

It seemed odd and menacing phenomena were occurring in financial markets around the world, and the President was receiving urgent phone calls from the Heads of State of the twenty most industrialized nations, known as the G20.

CHAPTER 14

*T*he first shipment of women was being off-loaded in the Somali port. Samir had the luxury of needing no disguise or subterfuge in this part of the world. In recent years, Somalia had become the Renaissance of pirating, and all that went with that.

The pirates used "child soldiers" whose brutality was shocking, even to those who had grown up with genocide and violence as part of ordinary existence, and who were controlled by the drugs they were administered. In that environment, the presence of female slaves drew no attention whatsoever. A casual observance would have noted that the women had been sedated by some kind of narcotic, but in Somalia, the bulk of the population was in a narcotic trance, or had been trained to look another direction.

Between terror training camps, kidnapping and creating the child soldiers, drug trafficking, arms dealing, civil insurrection, and slave trading, Somalia was a hub of all that was festering in the criminal world, and bleeding from the eastern side of Africa into the Mid-East.

As he looked at the fifteen women with whom he had just crossed the ocean, they were but a product to Samir, and he disciplined himself not to think of them as women. Once, on the journey, when they had allowed each girl to come to the deck for some air, and a brief walk, he had observed the uniform of a Catholic school girl. Upon inquiring, he learned she had become infatuated with a young man, who promised to take her away from her parochial life in Mexico City, where she attended an elite, but nun-dominated academy. She had planned to be a nurse.

But, her taboo lover had encouraged her to come with him to Bogota, where he claimed to have a home and business. Further, he promised she could become the nanny for some friends of his, who had two young children. Enticed by the prospect of an adventure, and working with children, and intoxicated by the prospect of a breath of freedom from the repressive academy environment, she had agreed to go.

Properly, he had secured a ticket for her, after she had done a phone interview with the "family" she was to serve. Happily she had snuck out of the dormitory and caught a plane to Bogota. Her lover was there, for sure, but when she met the "family," she had been incarcerated, drugged, and transported to the camp. Mercifully, the drugs kept her just soporific enough that, though she was completely aware that she had been betrayed, and was being held against her will, she had neither the strength nor mental power to escape.

He had heard of this type of thing. In his travels for Al Qaeda throughout Russia, Chechnya, and most especially Moldova, he had collided with the sex slave trading industry, and that is where he had first surmised how lucrative it could be, when he learned how much the women who were transported to the Netherlands were fetching in the marketplace.

Hearing that the FARC were successfully out-competing rival drug cartels by adding slave trading into their portfolio, he had broached the subject with Zawahiri, as a way of offsetting drug losses. Indeed, the Hyena was quite candid about the fact that slave trading was booming, and relatively danger-free, in contrast to the drug and arms running that was becoming increasingly competitive and more ferociously fought by the Americans.

So, though he understood the girl's plight, knowing she would soon either be sold to a brothel in Somalia, or moved into the Sudan for a worse fate, he finished smoking the cigar he favored and returned to his quarters aboard the freighter, dismissing her altogether.

The night before docking, he composed a letter to Zawahiri that would be delivered by courier once he reached Yemen. Samir had no intention of spending any time in Somalia. The pervasive desperation and chaos were repugnant to him. Gone were the glory days of Bin Laden and the "Doctor"—where every meeting was conducted more like a war council or a corporate board of directors meeting. They might have been in primitive quarters from time to time, but there never was a shortage of vision or professionalism.

Not so in Somalia and this whole sector. Chaos ruled like a living beast. He did not care whether the Buyers were too disorganized to properly run their human trafficking businesses. He had been paid handsomely, and he was out of there and headed for the bustling training camps of Yemen, and the protection of al-Awlaki.

Never having worked with the man, Samir enjoyed, however, the status of a senior executive who was visiting a franchise, if you will, of the larger corporate headquarters of Al Qaeda. With the death of Bin Laden, though, Samir had decided to extend his stay in Yemen.

It would be some time before Zawahiri announced himself as the new head of Al Qaeda, as he was following Samir's public relations strategy to keep the world's media focused on the death of Bin Laden, and on the mystery of who would succeed Usama. The Doctor was hidden, and for the moment, out of reach of the Americans; Makkawi released the press release Samir had created for him, remaining in Pakistan; and Samir, under orders from the Doctor, was to establish himself in a third location. The Doctor was insuring that no one American strike could decapitate Al Qaeda of its three remaining senior executives.

That was fine with Samir, at least until his ship landed. The courier pouch was on its way to the Doctor. The purchase order for eleven American women had been placed by satellite phone with Hyena, and the price—negotiated in the dirt—had been confirmed. As far as Hyena was concerned, he believed these women would be headed for the United Arab Emirates—where they would be sold to the wealthiest businessmen and government leaders in the area, as their personal sex slaves. A brothel was not in their future, like the fifteen Samir had just delivered, but rather perpetual slavery to the appetites of men who camouflaged their depravity under robes, turbans, and proclamations of the sanctity of their marriages.

While Hyena issued a "buy" order from slave traffickers he knew in Texas, deciding to avoid the more heavily monitored ports of California and Florida, Samir was thrust into the middle of the riots and violence that had erupted in Yemen. It seemed during his short absence to South America that all of the Middle East had erupted in flames, and he found himself covered in dust, dodging shrapnel and cartridges. The Western Media salivated over Egypt, Libya, and Syria, calling it "Arab Spring."

To Samir, it merely meant additional danger. He hastily completed the wire transfer of the money from the sale to the Somalis into the Swiss bank account Zawahiri had provided. Oddly, the Doctor's message instructed that from now forward, all transactions were to be done in one of three Swiss banks, and no others. One was in Zurich, one in Geneva, and one in Basel. *Why the restriction to just Swiss banks?* Dismissing it as just another of the Doctor's quirks, he decided to leave the finance matters of Al Qaeda in Zawahiri's hands.

But at that moment, having no intention of being caught in the middle of sniper fire and revolution in Yemen either, he sent another message to Zawahiri confirming the transfer of funds and advising that Yemen was not viable for the freedom of movement he needed. And, reassuring him of his complete loyalty and dedication to the mission, he stated he would leave al-Awlaki, and the movement in Yemen, in the capable hands of the Doctor, while he himself would return to South America to handpick the women.

Knowing the Doctor would approve on two counts—one, that the recent environment in Yemen was in fact too dangerous now for Samir, and he, like Makkawi and Zawahiri, would need to find more stable environments from which to command Al Qaeda's operations; and two, that these American women would not in fact be going to wealthy UAE businessmen, but rather to men in Pakistan who had a vengeance motive following the death of Bin Laden at the hands of the United States Seal Team Six—he purposely assured the Doctor in this latest message that he would inspect the merchandise on the ground in Hyena's Venezuelan sanctuary, and personally select the women whose loss would bring the greatest pain and humiliation to the United States.

That choice, made more out of cowardice and an absolute inability to get sullied by the sewers he created, would change the course of his life forever, and place him on a collision course with an American slave trader. For Samir Taghavi was still "green" in this new enterprise, and did not yet know that the biggest slave traders operating in the United States—particularly in Texas—were women.

CHAPTER 15

"Geez, man, where you been?" Brian shouted at Andy before Andy could even pocket his house keys.

Andy couldn't quite tell where Brian was until he turned in the direction of a loud thump at the top of the stairs. Brian dropped a "three-suiter," his computer bag and a roll-on—all of which he had apparently brought up the stairs in one trip. *Those amazing hands!* Andy mused.

Right behind the bags came Brian, who was still sounding somewhat accusative. "Didn't you get our texts?"

"Whose?" Andy hadn't been paying attention to his cell today. Having dropped Reagan off at the airport, he was a little distracted thinking about their wedding plans.

"James," and then, thinking it over, he added, "and mine. I must have texted you three times!"

Andy stood silent, in mystery about the urgency and the bags. Before he could speak, Brian barked an order. "You gotta pack, bro. James needs us!" There was an edge of agitation in Brian's voice, and Andy knew that could mean only one thing.

"Oh no, he's got another theory, doesn't he?"

"How the heck would I know? I just know he said he needs us in Montana as fast as we can get there. We're flying out of Santa Monica Airport, so shake a leg and get packed."

As close as the two were, Andy was a bit miffed that he was out of the loop here, and being pushed to travel somewhere to do something he probably wasn't going to want to do. Gritting his teeth, he insisted, "So that's where he's been. I wondered where he'd disappeared to this past week."

"Yeah, he's in Montana, near Butte, or Missoula, one of those two, I think."

Andy let out a huge sigh, looked out past the pool area for a moment, and then said, "Okay. Did he say why he needed us?"

"Nope. Just that Bud Walker had a plane for us, and he really needed us." Brian's tone signaled to Andy that this was serious, and not an invitation to go fly fishing in the famous Little Blackfoot River area of Montana.

"All right, all right," Andy shouted over his shoulder as he bounded down the stairs two at a time to his own master suite. "When do we need to catch the flight?"

"It's a private jet, Andy. Geez, man! They take off when we get there, not on a schedule."

Suddenly Andy laughed. Wealthy or not, neither he nor Brian had ever been overly impressed with all the trappings that went with their professional status. Truth be told, neither had ever even discussed needing a private jet. They were content to fly commercial to any of the speaking engagements and forums in which they participated—despite the Homeland Security inconveniences that impinged upon all Americans in the post 9/11 world.

Brian stood in the doorway, bouncing from right to left. That was characteristic of the dance he did to throw off defenders so they couldn't prevent him from catching the pass. If they couldn't anticipate the direction in which he was going to move, they were always a beat behind him. And if there was one thing Andy knew about his former football receiver, it was that you never want to be one beat behind Brian Washington Carver.

After five minutes, Andy had thrown together a bunch of underwear, two pair of jeans, a couple of sport shirts, one sport jacket, and his personal items. He was just about to close it up when Brian suggested he take some socks and maybe some shoes, and maybe think about a jacket. He laughed, yet was grateful for the supervision. There was something about the urgency of the packing that had him a little rattled—that, and the mystery.

"Brian, did he sound like he's in trouble?"

"He sounds like somebody sure as hell is, and he needs *us*. Sounds like Walker needs us, too, from what little I got. Something's going on, Andy, and I don't have a good feeling about it. James is working on something, but he apparently needs us to weigh in."

"Yeah, that's what I was afraid you were going to say." Andy stopped for a moment after dropping the bag to the side of the bed and extending the roll-away handle. "From the moment I first met that guy, every time he has a theory, my life is never the same. I was expecting it to be normal from here on in."

"Yeah, sure, Andy." Brian challenged him playfully, as they both started climbing the stairs to the front hall. "I can see you really are looking for *normal*, what with your fiancé chasing down slave traders, and every other type of abuser of human beings. Nothing out of the ordinary with that..." Andy smiled, getting the irony of what he had said.

Brian repeated, "Perfectly normal, you bet!"

Andy couldn't help but laugh at the truth of that statement. As his amusement settled down, he added, "Still, Brian, wherever James Mikolas is working, somebody dies."

He had said it lightly enough, but Brian immediately knew that Andy was dead serious about his long-time association with one of the CIA's most brilliant analysts. He felt a constriction in his stomach, as his association with James had brought him up close and personal with the dark world of terrorists and enslavers as well. He scolded himself for having been so curt with Andy. Truth be told, he, too, was apprehensive about what lay ahead. *What on earth could have happened?*

Trying to lighten the mood as they loaded up and jumped into Andy's BMW, Brian said deliberately and ever so politely, "So, Andy, where were you again? I was ragging on you so much, I didn't really hear your answer."

"I was dropping Reagan off at LAX. She's headed to El Paso, Texas."

CHAPTER 16

James was on the tarmac as Brian and Andy's plane landed into the sunset. A brisk breeze was blowing across the prairie end of the ranch, which held the hangars and airstrip. Evening now, James wore a light grey windbreaker and was hunched over, trying to disappear into it, to get away from the chilly early summer air. He barely waved at his friends as they skipped down the stairs to solid ground.

As they approached him, hoping to see the familiar James Mikolas smile, Brian was aware of other jets arriving and pulling up into the same area. An interesting collection of men stepped out of the planes—two were carrying attaché cases and had a real Brooks Brothers look, and the other two looked like they had been snatched from a workout at the gym—apparently as rattled and confused by their summons as Brian and Andy were with theirs.

James was no help as the three shook hands. He barely managed a smile, and looked grim. "Thanks for coming, boys. We have work to do."

Two Hummer limos and their drivers stood ready to carry all the arriving passengers. A ground crew rapidly loaded everyone's bags into the vehicles. Brian dropped back, allowing the four older, better-dressed men to climb aboard the first limo. He motioned to Andy to climb into the second. Then he went, "Psst, psst," to James.

"What, Pal?" James asked, stepping back to face Brian.

"I been lookin' around at the hired hands here, and the rest of the guest list we're traveling with, and I was wondering…"

"What?" James clearly wanted to get out of the wind and back to the ranch house.

"Kind of a strange bunch of house guests, don't you think?"

James just shook his head. "Pal, if it helps any, I can assure you this is not an Agatha Christie novel."

Having no idea what James meant by that, he allowed himself to be shoved into the limo.

There, to his surprise, he found Bud Walker and Andy, just sitting, staring at each other. Clearly Andy was waiting for James to join. Brian slid to his right, facing Walker and flanking his partner. James took the rear seat and immediately said, "Bud, these are the two guys I promised to introduce you to. Meet Andy Weir and Brian Washington Carver."

The tension was palpable as Walker responded tersely with, "I know who you are. Thank you for coming nonetheless."

They answered simultaneously. "You're welcome, sir."

"Of course, Mr. Walker."

At least they have manners, Walker thought. *Most kids today don't.* He decided to ease up on them, since James had insisted Walker was going to need a very special skill set these two possessed. He wondered.

"Just call me Bud. You might as well, since you almost single-handedly took down my network with that game of yours. Anybody works me over that good ought to be able to call me by my first name."

Whether he meant to or not, Walker had reintroduced a tension that was palpable. Neither Andy nor Brian had any idea how to respond to that combative welcome to his ranch. So, they just sat there and did nothing.

"Walker…" James took the lead, making certain he had Bud's attention. "You took yourself down when you got into bed with pharmaceutical companies and produced a product of fear and nausea every night. That product—your 'news'—sold America almost into drugged oblivion. These two did nothing more than solve a problem. And, Bud, you got an even bigger problem now, so you be nice to my boys. They saved your sorry ass once before, and we're going to need them to do it again. So watch it!"

With the tension escalated even further, Andy and Brian decided it was best to take the opportunity to inspect the inside of the Hummer limo. Other than the rawhide seats, and gun rack, it pretty much looked like any other limo—except it was big, really big. Neither Andy nor Brian, however, could figure out any polite conversation about the hides that had once been cattle, and the need for a Remington shot gun. So Brian decided to look outside and observe the countryside, while James and Walker glared at each other.

"Man, what is that?" Brian shouted, as the limo glided past a cowboy riding alongside the road. Looking as if he had just stepped out of a Charles Russell painting, the man wore chaps, a leather vest, and a weathered hat, which was tilted forward and down to protect his face from the elements. In his right hand, he held the reins of a horse he was leading.

The two animals and the lone man seemed in perfect harmony with each other, and with the high grassland and rolling hills, but in shocking contrast to the modern Hummer and private jet strip they were skirting. The boys were being introduced to Montana, a land of paradoxes. The juxtaposition of the frontier that Montana still represented and the 21st Century modernity that had overtaken it, were startling to almost any first-time visitor to the state.

Brian and Andy both had spent their lives in major city areas, and had never really experienced the space that defines Montana, let alone the natural beauty that nonetheless harbored danger. It was easier to gaze out the window than to face Walker, so both allowed themselves to be captivated and seduced by the scenery in all directions.

"It's so beautiful it's almost distracting," Andy commented, as he gazed at the sparkling waters of the North Fork of the Blackfoot River. Winding through the valley near Ovando, cutting in and out of ranch lands, one could expect to encounter all manner of wildlife as the animal inhabitants moved to the water at evening time. The sun, dropping toward the mountains west of them, caused the moving water to glisten.

Andy's reaction was so genuine and so enthusiastic that Walker was reminded of the first day he, too, had seen this valley. With the magnificent Swan Mountain range and its necklace of lakes on the west side, and with the Bob Marshall Wilderness north of the ranch still offering danger and thrills to those who entered it—generations after the first settlers had come here—Bud remembered almost sadly the time when he naively had felt he was on top of the world.

So much had changed in his world, in so short a time. *Thank God this hasn't,* he reflected gratefully.

No one spoke. Time suspended. All four men took in the splendor as the evening sun turned the hills and mountains into shades of lavender, blue, soft yellow, and purple in all directions. It was truly mesmerizing for the boys, and James, too, relaxed enough to really take a look. *Andy's right,* he thought. *It is almost distracting.*

Bud finally spoke, almost wistfully. "Yeah, that it is, Mr. Weir. So beautiful, yet a paradox." Andy turned to question what he meant by that. "No one should come here for security, Mr. Weir."

There was something mysterious in his voice. Brian turned to size him up a bit, wanting to see where Walker was going with this. "Montana can kill you in a heartbeat—and will." Once again, both boys just looked at him, having no response to that. "Remember that, you two. Just keep it in mind. If James here is right, I'm going to need you, and I don't want to see you become a casualty of this seductress." He patted the butt of the shotgun over his head, as if to punctuate the comment.

"Yes, sir. Thank you." A moment later, the limos turned into the main gate and the guard James had outwitted a few days earlier waived them in. No one in the vehicle that night had yet guessed that Montana, the beauty that could, and would, kill unskilled trespassers, was about to become the safest place in the United States—holding beneath her earth, and in the spirit of her inhabitants, a solution for all time. Like the gold treasure, hidden and untapped, within her hills, Montana held the potential to prevent slave masters from ever again rising to challenge the freedom and sovereignty of a people who had a heritage—even if they had long forgotten it.

But for now, she was just "so beautiful." And these men had work to do.

Just as Brian and Andy landed in Montana, SWA flight #1397 pulled up at Gate #5 in El Paso, Texas. A few minutes later, an excited Reagan Lynch exited the baggage claim area, looking for her boss, Edith. Hearing a horn honk, Reagan turned in time to see Edith Church climbing out of the driver's side, waving to get her friend's attention.

The two embraced, and it was obvious that they enjoyed each other. Edith Church was the head of a major human rights organization, a warrior who had battled injustice for more than forty years, and a woman whose osteoporosis had shrunk her from 5'6" to a mere 5'2" of pure piss and vinegar.

Size was no issue to Edith Church though. She was a titan in a small frame, who looked out from behind her wire-rimmed reading glasses to keenly observe people. Feisty, decisive, and yet fun, she adored her young protégé and was grateful Reagan had come.

"It's so good to see you, Edith. I have so much to tell you!" Reagan's enthusiasm was almost contagious.

"Likewise, my dear. I am glad you are here. We have work to do."

CHAPTER 17

Sir Harley Grantham-Jones had been the last to enter the monstrous tower that dominated the skyline of Basel. He'd been opposed to its construction. This was not because he did not appreciate the value of having a bunker that could sustain an assault—and which could house a virtual army of financial boards, committees, staff, communication and monitoring rooms, as well as an underground driving range for the golfers, and private suites for each of the Board of Directors of the Repository of International Settlements—but rather because in order to accomplish that, one had to build something resembling a medieval Keep.

He preferred anonymity, and had hoped they would remain below the radar of popular attention, but when this unusual piece of architecture was completed, and never opened its doors to a single visitor, it had caught the attention of tourists, but thankfully not the media. As a result, though it was photographed heavily, no one had set foot inside it other than those hired to work there. Had they done so, the sophistication of communication equipment and data transfer would have shocked them.

For the RIT "tentacles" extended into every financial market and sector, monitoring through Reuters, and digitally displaying to the second, all currency changes. Other boards tracked global stock markets and interest rates. And below this encased financial behemoth and its hundreds of employees lay an area known only to the Board of Directors. A large percentage of the mined, milled, and ingoted gold in the world was stored deep in vaults here and in the subterranean tunnel that connected the first tower with a second, shorter, but even more formidable, skyscraper.

He was in his new home—the second-largest and most grandiose of the suites. Knowing that he would be here possibly the remainder of his life, over the years, he had brought personal mementos to remind him of his life in England and of his family. *She will miss me I know, but soon it will seem as if I am dead to her, and she will be all right.* He tried to justify this, since he knew Sylvia would not be all right. If their plan worked, the economy of Great Britain would collapse, wiping out effectively all moneyed people in that country. Believing one must make sacrifices in order to achieve domination and to create a new world, he nonetheless preferred to shove thoughts of how Sylvia would end her days from his mind.

These thoughts were on his mind as he worked his way into the sequestered conference room he and the Directors from Germany, Italy, the United States, and Switzerland would use to finalize their attack strategy, and to implement the global takeover of governments. Harley calculated that people would act in self-serving ways. To survive, they would kill each other and behave as animals. His plan was to cause a certain amount of destruction and let fear and the people do the rest. Then, in order to restore order, the RIT and Financial Responsibility Board would step in and control the world's governments.

Laid out like a war room, they had decided to call this space, which looked like an underground bank vault, just that. For indeed it was war, and it was time to stop fooling around and win, as far as the main five were concerned.

Left out of the G8 group were France, Canada, Russia, and Japan in order to provide the planned "plausible deniability." The Directors of those Central Banks had been groomed by Harley personally through the years and totally believed they acted in the world's best interest. The conspirators knew that these four would thus be very effective at denying accusations that might come up. They had real PR value because their innocence had a genuine credibility.

Outside the facility, with its perpetual daylight, it was growing dusk, and only a few citizens were walking on the street, heading home from work. No one really paid any attention to the tower, with its brightly lit floors. Had they bothered to look to the top, they would have noticed that the top floor was completely dark—oddly so.

But they, like every other citizen on this planet who lived ordinary lives, were scurrying to get home to family and end of the day activities. None could have contemplated the underground fortress; none could conceive of the tower being but the tip of an architectural iceberg. How could they? No one had ever been allowed to enter.

Grantham-Jones and his crew were counting on that odd quirk of human nature. It is hard for people to spot oddities and things omitted. If someone had asked folks to stop and think about this building and its appearance and secrecy, protected by its own private security force, and whose inhabitants were accountable to no national government, they would have thought it odd. But no one had called it to the attention of the citizens of Basel, let alone the world. For decades it had been there, and no one really noticed its menacing façade. They would soon, but too late.

The Italian, Braghelli, gestured to Sir Harley that he would be honored to have him lay this out, and to lead the meeting. Sir Harley obliged, taking the chair farthest away from the vault door, and at the arc of the oval table.

"Gentlemen, this will be fairly simple. You are to be complimented, all of you, on the remarkable preparatory work you and your banks have done in bringing the world to this point. I believe all the necessary pieces are in place, and it is time now to implement the plan we discussed at the Waldstetter Annex."

Looking around to make sure each of them was with him, he thought he noticed an almost-imperceptible agitation on the part of the U.S. Director. Suddenly, with no warning, he challenged the man. "Are you with us, Thomas?"

The man snapped out of it, squared up to the table, looking Grantham-Jones straight in the eyes as he answered, "Absolutely. I'm all ears." The others laughed at the decidedly American slang their comrade was prone to using. The atmosphere relaxed, and Sir Harley continued.

"Think of this as chess, gentlemen. And that we are close now to the checkmate move. We'll allow a few more feints to keep the Heads of State and their Treasury Officers unaware of the final move, but each move we make now will bring them in deeper." The others nodded since this was nothing new. "These moves will be ones they are familiar with and which they are accustomed to, even if they don't like them. They will not arouse suspicion."

Hoping the ventilation could handle it, he lit one of his cigars. "But when we move, we are going to do this brutally—the way the Japanese do when they are downsizing." Chuckling at his own joke, he knew the others were well aware that the Japanese were famous for doing just one brutal cut, laying off everyone at once that they had to let go. The remaining ones then knew they would be keeping their jobs, and therefore settled down quickly, knowing there would be no uncertainty in their lives. They had survived the cut. Relieved to still have a game, they surrendered their anger and self-righteousness, and were grateful to put the whole thing behind them. "As the situation exacerbates, the global scene will predictably deteriorate rapidly," he calculated, and added, "people will act for their own self-preservation, making it necessary for us to save the day.

I can assure you that people will abandon their form of government in order to stay alive. After all, it is animal instinct." He paused, then said, "The people of all *your* countries will likely respond similarly. They will be grateful to eat, and they will surrender their autonomy."

Sipping some ice cold bottled water from the Swiss Mountain Lakes Region, he continued. "Our attack line will be simultaneous. As discussed, we will suddenly and inexplicably call in the notes. Whatever technical term the various nations call their IOUs—we're calling them in. Next, when nations come to us begging for help to pay what is owed, expecting us to extend more credit and transfer more money to them, we will refuse. No more credit extended anywhere, anytime, for any reason. Is that understood, gentlemen?"

Sobering as that thought was, none flinched. They were prepared to do this. "Last, we will dump the U.S. dollar and crash that government's currency. That should wipe out the wealth of the U.S. and anyone holding their currency, leading to chaos, rioting. The degree of civil unrest needs to be global and fierce." He paused to make sure each understood this. Most were taking notes. Continuing, he asked, "Are you confident your media contacts will take the information you give them, and report it to their public?" The other directors were quite certain of this, since they were directly and personally involved with the media giants of their respective countries. Confident that the heads of news organizations would not detect the deception, they would naively relay the data the RIT wanted fed to the public regarding blame and responsibility.

No one was expected to guess that this was all happening by design, and that their government leaders were just hapless dupes, exploited for decades by brighter men, with much greater ambition. Quite the opposite. Each of the directors understood propaganda warfare and were quite certain that ultimately the populations of each country would blame the leadership of their own country, and would turn with a vengeance upon their own governments.

And with that, Sir Harley Grantham-Jones revealed the final step in the takeover of the world by the men in that room. Under the twelve points of the Financial Responsibility Board, Braghelli would kindly offer help and assistance to the beleaguered governments, providing they adopted the twelve points—beginning with point number one, which demanded that RIT and its FRB assume jurisdiction and influence into the very structure of that country's government.

Combining this first point with the skillful salesmanship of the remaining central bank countries who were out of the loop, and with the media primed to "buy" the message, it was planned that the people themselves would overturn their own republican forms of government, their own democracies, and yield like dazed sheep to a more benign totalitarian form of government—controlled lock, stock, and barrel by the men in this war room.

Allowing them to digest these ideas, and providing time for the men to review the remaining eleven points, Grantham-Jones could see they were on top of this. He sensed complete agreement that this was a necessary step in man's evolution in that men had proved themselves incapable of governing themselves now for centuries, and the experiment of letting the "people" choose had led to depravity, instability, irrationality, and war. True, each of these men had made fortunes for the RIT by financing both sides of every war, but none had any doubts about the acceptability of that serendipity. They mutually gave themselves a pass on their own hypocrisy.

Believing themselves to be the world's true elite, capable of saving the stupid masses, they knew it was time. They desired everyone's money, goods, and real estate. At their core, they believed their fellow man to be nothing more than a stimulus-response machine, incapable of stewarding its wealth and property, requiring an operator to control it. Just as Sir Harley's family dated back one thousand years to the time an Islamic group, known as the Hashashin, ruled for 300 years, this group planned a financial Armageddon in order to insure *their* 300 years.

Before ending the evening, however, a question came into Sir Harley's mind. Deciding to broach the subject, he asked, "Before we adjourn, does anyone have any concerns about the reactions of any countries in particular?"

Immediately the Director from Germany said, "Yes, Harley, I do. I am concerned about two in particular."

Sir Harley smiled without showing his teeth, knowing what the man was thinking. "Go on."

"The United States and China. I just don't know if they will go down as easily as we expect, that is all."

Grantham-Jones decided to humor the youngest man on their team. At thirty-five, he was a babe in the woods in this finance game despite his wonder-boy credentials and meteoric career. He responded, "My dear fellow, I understand your concern completely. In fact, that is why Braghelli here decided we had to act now. At this moment, the U.S. is vulnerable—not just because of its financial precariousness but also its political divisiveness, and the fact that its people are, as we say in Great Britain, 'off their pins' due to a very successful drug campaign by our allies in the pharmaceutical industry. But, as they come off those medications, they become more dangerous by the day. Much less tractable…" Letting that sink in for a moment, he took another sip of water and added, "And as for the Chinese, you are worried they won't attempt to call in the U.S. Treasury Securities, am I correct? That they won't dump dollars or seize assets?"

Germany's Director nodded. Pouncing on it, Sir Harley almost joyfully exclaimed, "That is exactly why we must act now as well. We cannot allow China to consider itself to be a total ally and partner of the United States. If anything, we'll propagandize that their reckless acquisition of U.S. debt and holdings could destabilize their currency as well. Right now, they are a strong currency. We must persuade them to feel the need to keep it that way, by not allowing the U.S. bankruptcy—which we are engineering, dear fellow—to drag them down. They must be persuaded to pull back from their alliance with the U.S. That actually jeopardizes both countries more greatly, but if we do it right, China will not know we are playing them."

"And how will we do that?"

"By surprise attack, my friend, by surprise attack. We will attack the United States and China first. Immediately after them, the others in Europe. Call in the debt on both, simultaneously. And let us sit back and watch them spiral out of control, landing on our doorstep, as each goes looking for money. They will likely devour each other. China will go to the U.S. and ask them to pay up; the U.S. will come to us asking for money to pay China, and when we do not lend, we will have some fun watching them squirm, and the media will keep the pubic distracted by the disintegration of the European markets. But those two 'giants,' gentlemen," he sneered, "will walk into the checkmate move first. Are we clear now?"

Each man answered affirmatively, all talking over each other. Eager now to get out of the room, Sir Harley issued the order that would commence the attack. It would begin with a phone call to the Treasury Secretaries of the respective nations the following morning—placing the demand that loans be repaid.

Sir Harley felt unusually euphoric right then. Having made the decision, and having previously set up the U.S. with the imminent downgrade of its credit rating, he could easily justify calling in loans and refusing any further credit. But the momentary euphoria was coming from another area. He was sublimely happy about two things. First, that he had lived long enough to see his life's work come to fruition, and not be handed off into posterity without his direct involvement. Second, he was paradoxically relieved that he might not have to live too long though in this facility after all. Accustomed to a life of privilege and freedom, the confines of this place, which resembled the tombs of Pharaohs in its vault-like meeting rooms with impenetrable doors, brought home the certainty that this battle needed to be short.

What a delicious game this money game is, he ruminated. *In the end, it is an idea backed by confidence. And we are about to shake the world's confidence. What an interesting thing it will be to watch the world lose confidence in the almighty U.S. dollar, and in the foolish idea it represents.*

He was the last to leave the room. Not tired, he adjourned to the plush bar inside the tower and had the bartender serve him his favorite sherry.

Chapter 18

*B*rian was standing on the expansive wood deck outside the ranch hands' quarters at the north end of Walker's ranch. The area held not only the bunk buildings for the crew that ran his ranch but a myriad of outbuildings for equipment as well. Next to a small stream that snaked its way through the back of the property was a large guest quarters. It had at least thirteen bedrooms—each with its own bath—a great room, kitchen, saunas, laundry facility, and theatre room.

Each room faced out across the stream, a meadow, and into the trail-head into the Bob Marshall Wilderness and to the Scapegoat Wilderness on the Continental Divide to the east of the ranch. Tonight, Brian just stood marveling at the density of the forest in front of him, and the seemingly endless folds of mountain after mountain.

He had been told that in this wilderness was almost every carnivore on the North American continent, an abundance of lakes and streams, still primordial, and no limit to how he could disappear and never be heard from again. Wishing for a moment that he was here on a vacation with Andy where the boys would be engaging an outfitter to take them into the wilderness on horseback for a two- to three-week excursion, he dismissed it. One, he was uncomfortable yet attracted to the idea; but two, he was here because he had officially been summoned by James.

It had been a half hour since he had texted James to meet him here, and he was grateful to see the ranch's ATV pull up and James hop out. He turned once again to enjoy the evening quiet that was descending on the area.

"What's up, Pal?" James asked easily.

"They call this 'The Last Best Place,' James, did you know that?"

"Uh, huh, I did." James waited, not knowing what was on Brian's mind. He was hard enough to read in Los Angeles, but here, even though Brian had been here a few days, James had no idea what Brian was thinking.

"It sure is a beautiful place. Maybe the prettiest place I've ever seen."

James stepped up beside him and gazed into the wilderness twilight along with Brian.

"But, what's really meant by the 'last best place'?"

James thought about that for a moment before answering. "Pal, I think we're about to find out." Then, realizing Andy wasn't in on this, he asked, "Where's Andy?"

"He's on the phone with Reagan. They check in every night around this time—you know."

James did know, and he couldn't help but suppress a smile at Brian's response to his partner's new daily rituals.

"Yeah, well, I got to tell you there are more jets out at that runway and hangar than there are at the Santa Monica airport. Since we got here, James, somebody new has arrived every day, and by the looks of this bunk house and the guest house over there, they are planning on staying."

The mystery of the arriving guests held James' attention, too. But it was clear that Bud Walker was summoning a specific group of people. Since it was his party, James just figured he'd wait for Walker to reveal the details. He could see though that the whole thing was a mystery to Brian, and probably to Andy as well, and he didn't like keeping them in the dark.

Knowing that was about to change, he said, "Anyway, round up Andy and let's get back to the main house. Bud wants to see us."

The room they were using was very large. It could almost have held a round table. Tonight, fire blazing in the stone fireplace to ward off the cool Montana June evening, it was obvious a few additional people had indeed joined the group.

Bud's Finance Bureau Chief, Simon Atwater, was the latest to arrive. He'd been shuffling back and forth from New York repeatedly, and by the looks of his shirt, he'd had a long travel day, private jet or no private jet.

Walker had turned over WNG to the Vice-Chairman of the Board, Ray Elkins, and he too was streaking back and forth, as he assumed full responsibility for the day-to-day operations of Walker News Group. That left Bud Walker free to be a "civi," as he referred to himself. James didn't know exactly what that meant, but he guessed Walker was somehow releasing himself from the restraints of traditional journalism.

But in addition to the usual Bud and Simon, tonight the group included the Governor of Montana, Bruce Fitzerman. Walker had contributed heavily to getting this man elected, and whatever Walker was working on, it appeared now he needed to officially involve the State's government.

Notable also in today's new arrivals were Chester Riddle, a prominent oil man from Billings; the Chancellor of the state university system, Aaron Watkins; Stormy Helms, an industrialist employer from Flathead County with a name more like a character in some western pulp fiction; and the Sheriff of Lincoln County, Drew Peters. All of them were middle-aged, well-groomed, and were large in ego, if not in physical stature.

Brian entered ahead of Andy, quickly looking over the field of new attendees. *Man, oh man, what have you gotten us into, James?* he thought. Instead, he blurted out a little too loudly, "James, are there *any* black folk in Montana?"

If he hadn't called attention to himself walking into the room, that question did it, and the conversation stopped as each man turned to see who had asked it. James couldn't tell whether Brian was joking or truly a bit uncomfortable in this mix. Clearly, he and Andy were the youngest guys in the room, and clearly they represented a different world. In fact, looking around, he couldn't help but wonder just what kind of world this was that Walker was assembling.

"Walker?" James tipped his head, indicating he'd like a word.

Before he could speak to him though, Brian for some ungodly reason added insult to injury with, "What is this, Custer's Last Stand?" Even as he said it, he knew he was off base, but he couldn't retrieve it. Nor could he hide. Andy gracefully side-stepped him a foot or two to put some distance between himself and his partner.

He's just going to have to get out of this one himself, Andy mused, coughing slightly. *I'm not getting sacked over that remark.*

Thoughts hung suspended as each man sized up this bit of impertinence. Fortunately Walker broke the mood with, "No, Mr. Carver, that's east of here. You'd have to go past Billings if you wanted to see that memorial." He paused to allow Brian to regain his footing, remembering a time or two when he'd put his own proverbial foot in it. Then he laughed.

Andy's curiosity was up now. Being the chess player, he knew they were about to get a look at the scene, and the players. He knew it was game time. So did Brian, because he set his jaw just like he did every time he came up to the line for the next play on the football field. Both stood side by side. Then Andy simply asked, "Mr. Walker, is Montana the Last Best Place?"

Walker thought for a moment, fondled the cigar in his pocket as if he wished he could dart outside for a smoke, and then said, "I don't know, Andy. I feel it is. Certainly is why I chose to live here." The guys from New York were clearly out of their element, and unctuously tried to humor Bud with a "yeah, you bet." Those from Montana, however, just smiled.

Bud continued. "But, I'm pretty sure it's our Last Best Stand." He cleared his throat. "You boys mentioned Custer. Having lived here for a while now, I can tell you that fool had his last stand because he fell for a brilliant piece of divide and conquer strategy. And his ego got in the way; blinded him. Well, that isn't going to happen to us—no last stand here. Here we make our best stand. But we have a lot to figure out first."

Brian and Andy looked at each other quickly, in mutual understanding. Each was thinking, *Finally! We are game on!* Standing beside them, James couldn't help but feel a shift in the energy in the room. This was it. Whoever all these people were, apparently Bud had assembled his team.

"You ready, Boy Scout?" Walker challenged somewhat playfully.

"Yes, sir, Bud. I have my 'best analyst' mindset on—if we're all going to be into these 'last bests'…" He let it sink in. "I'm ready."

CHAPTER 19

*B*efore they could even begin, the game changed.

"Someone is dumping dollars," the flash traffic on Walker's secure line stated unemotionally. Bud Walker, however, had an emotional reaction and showed the communique immediately to James.

James asked calmly, "Confirmed?"

"Yes, by my source." Then, as an afterthought he added, "POTUS is in the situation Room."

James' next question had more insistence on it. "How long has the President of the United States been in the Situation Room?"

"According to my source, he's been in and out of there off and on since about the time we returned from Basel, but now, he's been there all night."

James knew what that meant. Handing the transmission back to Bud, he stated, "Then dumping dollars is an act of war."

Grabbing a chair and pulling it rather violently away from the table, Bud sat down. "Well, whatever it is and whoever is doing it, this has nothing to do with religion." Though said like a pronouncement, Bud was looking at James as if asking it as a question.

James took it as a question. "Yes, you're right. Andy says that Religion is the bottom game of the eight games enemies are playing simultaneously against the United States right now. It gets attention, draws recruits, and arouses emotions and violence. But, other than that, the top game—the one driving the rest—is Money."

"So, this..." he waved the paper, "this means it has started?"

James took a deep breath, looked at it a moment, and answered, "It would appear that way."

There was an interminable silence as Bud chewed on this. Looking it over from the angles he was familiar with, he knew this was truly beyond his expertise. Trusting that if Mikolas and the boys had been analyzing and chasing these attackers effectively so far, then he needed Mikolas to walk point on this. Firmly, he said, "Okay then, gentlemen. James, you are *in charge!*"

_____

The need for James to assume control of the analysis forced him to make a bold and, what would likely be, unpopular decision. Knowing that Walker would probably back him up, since he had placed him in charge in light of the new and alarming developments, he nonetheless wasn't looking forward to, and took no pleasure in the change-up he was about to orchestrate. *Well, it has to be done,* he told himself.

"Are you going to tell him, or am I?" James asked Bud Walker, motioning in the direction of Simon Atwater, WNG's veteran Economics and Finance Bureau Chief. Atwater had proven himself to Walker by staying on and remaining loyal following the Samir Taghavi debacle, and he was known to be a smart and discerning businessman—one of the few in TV news who actually understood the complex world of finance.

That is what had caused James to insist that he himself, and Andy, would be the ones to analyze the body of data they had sent Simon to collect, and not Simon. Atwater was just returning to the ranch with what Brian had jokingly referred to as a "bunch of junk," and his Harvard education shone through in his reaction to that remark. The idea of a football-playing, computer gamer—no matter how famous he was—just didn't sit right with Atwater when it came to analyzing and releasing information to the public.

It was that bias of the Ivy League clubs that had caused Simon Atwater to miss things in the first place. He had not deliberately set out to mislead investors and the public in the United States. But, in his ignorance and gullibility, he had done just that. So James knew that the same paradigms Atwater had used to evaluate this data before would still be in place. He fingered a hand-written note he had in his pocket. He hadn't shown it to anyone yet. It was an idea now turning into a theory. But to prove his theory, he had to have fresh eyes on the project.

Walker reluctantly said, "I'll tell him, after lunch." He paused to make sure James was in agreement with that and then continued. "Let the man turn over his work. If he did it the way we asked, he will have been very valuable to us."

"Agreed." For a moment, James felt he'd been too hard on Atwater a few days earlier. After all, he'd asked the man to bring him a very specific type of data, and had exhorted him "not to bring any Internet Wikipedia-level material, or anything laden with evaluation and interpretations, or God forbid, something already packaged by TV journalists and their marketing departments." Remembering how Atwater had braced as if being struck, James reminded himself that this was the man's job, and it was hard for Simon Atwater to accept the idea that he may have been duped by an enemy, let alone one that he trusted and whose information he had relied upon in his own reporting and in the reporting of those on his staff.

Specifically James had said to Simon Atwater, "I have a theory. But whether it is true or not can only be established by me and the Kid there," gesturing toward Andy though he was not within earshot. "To make this easier, you can discard all material from all sources except material involving a change of some kind, promoted by the banks themselves."

"Which banks?" Simon had queried.

"All Central banks, and all Investment banks. Remember Simon, I am specifically looking at changes in procedure, policy, purview promoted by the banks themselves in their own materials and websites—not marketing material. Look for anything that has been added in or taken away in the last thirty years—especially any changes subsequent to 9/11. If they changed a law or regulation to add something, I want to know. If they changed it to delete something, I want to know. No opinions, no evaluation, just the facts on *change*. Am I clear?"

James had known by Simon's stiffening that he was treading on thin ice with this guy, so he had turned it back over to the man's boss.

Before doing so, though, he had further instructed Atwater to pay special attention to anything the banks might have spun or propagandized to attract the media chiefs like himself. Seeing that Atwater didn't really know what that might look like, he explained he wanted anything that came from a bank showing how their action would be "helpful," how it would "assure, stabilize, or prevent misuse or abuse..." By then Atwater was getting it. He spotted almost immediately that his team would have picked up on that during their research, and would have started to promote it in their journalistic piece in order to serve their public—most likely citing the bank's source and verbiage. He had put Atwater on the jet giving him one last-minute instruction about locating anything that appeared to "save us all" from irresponsibility on the part of governments.

Today, seeing that Atwater looked tired, but satisfied, when he arrived at the ranch house, he assumed the man had found quite a "bunch of junk." Neither man knew at that moment just how important those last instructions, carried out almost on blind faith by a loyal employee, would prove to be.

James had asked Walker to send his guests back to Helena, Kalispell, and Billings once he realized an act of war had occurred. It had preempted any work they might do at this moment. The mystery remained, but the opening moves had already begun and that changed the timeline in which they were operating. James felt he needed to do the first analysis and then reassemble the team.

Those remaining were just finishing lunch and moving into the "War Room"—as Walker called it. The north wall was a command center of television units all on simultaneously to WNG and to its major competition. Fox and CNN were in the center, flanking WNG. Above and below those were the BBC, the CBC, and a variety of international networks. Basically, the world news was unfolding in real time in front of them. Every part of the planet was being covered and reported, and Walker could view any time zone, any country's news.

"Reminds me of the CIA," Andy said, leaning in to Brian. "Spooky."

Brian just shot him a look warning him not to pursue it any further.

Coming up through the center of yet another remarkable hand-crafted wooden conference table was the T4, secure line Walker used to stay in the moment, and on top of high security data. Land line phones encircled the room, each on separate stands that held pads and pens for anyone using them. Each table had its own Internet connection.

There were no windows in this room, since Walker wanted to be able to view the screens easily, and to be able to control the sound inside and outside the room.

Brian and Andy had been asked to join in, so each stepped inside after their momentary stop to take in the TV monitors. Andy flashed back to the windowless basement room he and James had used when they had begun their analysis that identified the White King. *It seems so long ago,* he thought. He had never liked rooms without windows, yet here he was again in a container-like space—a classy one for sure, but a container nonetheless.

"Sure beats the crude set up of monitors we had in that apartment when we tackled the 'White King Rising' analysis," Brian said admiringly. "This is pretty amazing. Wonder what encryption he's got on that pipe." Andy just shrugged. Characteristically, it never seemed to matter to Andy whether he was using low-tech or high-tech methodologies. A problem was a problem to him, so his demeanor was casual and unimpressed.

Walker, Simon, and James entered at the same time, with Walker slightly behind, ready to close the door and begin. A moment later, the material Atwater had collected was being uploaded from his flash drive to everyone's computer.

"Now that's better," Brian whispered to Andy. He had never gotten used to Andy having to do everything by hand during the excruciating process he, Andy, and James had used to select and enter the data, which, when crunched, had led to their discovery of the Trojan Horse responsible for the collapse of America's institutions. It was that discovery, done crudely but accurately, that had led to the creation of the game "White King Rising" and to the liberation of millions of people from the ravages of psychiatric medications and street drugs alike. Little did Brian know, however, that what they had created was actually responsible for what was about to happen globally, and for the speed and timing of the attack.

Before the men could even take their seats, and before Bud had had time to explain to Simon that he should finish uploading the material and then leave it in the unconventional, but capable, hands of a former CIA operative, the screens in the center of the wall caught their attention.

Something out of the ordinary had happened, and the first rumblings were reaching CNN, Fox, and the executive producer of WNG's daytime cable news show.

Less than an hour later, the shattering reality of some kind of cataclysmic economic phenomenon was apparent. Still standing, in that hour, five men had watched it roll across the screens. Beginning with more intense rioting in Greece, then the insanity spreading contagiously to Italy and Spain, at first they suspected this was an escalation of the already-troubled European economic situation that had been developing since 2008.

But when Israel's stock market plunged by 52%, plowing through all failsafe measures in a matter of minutes, Israel suspended trading and closed its exchange. They watched a type of panic and domino effect leap across the Atlantic and inundate the NY Stock Exchange. Fearing the worse, and in total confusion about what had happened—and why there was a crash—all NY stock exchanges shut down.

Before they did, Walker, who did have access to real time U.S. dollar data, saw what appeared to be a dumping of U.S. dollars. That confirmed the Intel they had received from Walker's source. Someone was surely selling them off, plunging their price. Then all went dark, and he assumed all currency trading would be suspended. It was, almost immediately. Reminiscent of 9/11, all five were aware that they were standing mesmerized and horrified at the sudden and mysterious chaos, which had apparently erupted globally. Just then, the red phone Walker used to connect directly to his executive producers lit up.

Walker dove for it, snatching it from its cradle with a tense, "Yeah, John, what's happening?"

Whatever John answered was not audible to the others, so finally they slid into a seat and waited. Walker listened without saying anything. His jaw tightened, and a muscle in the lower right jaw bulged and receded, rhythmically. Then, he appeared to shrink somehow, at least in James' estimation. It wasn't that he turned white; he just appeared smaller.

James had experienced this phenomenon before when a person of power is hit with something so suppressive and overriding—they actually appear to physically shrink. Attracting no one's attention, he slid his chair closer to Brian and Andy and said softly, "Get ready, boys. You are going to be needed."

Just then, Bud regained a measure of composure and hung up. Looking at the others, he simply answered the question they had not voiced. "He wanted to tell me the banks are closing—doors locked, no one allowed in. All banks nationwide are following suit, as near as he can tell. Closed, no transactions—no access even to safe deposit boxes."

Of all the men in the room that day, Simon Atwater, more than the others, knew the seriousness and possible ramifications to the holders of those boxes. He knew Federal regulations, and he knew what the Federal Government could and could not do in a time of national emergency. The law had been in place for decades, and the President of the United States held Executive Authority. Five minutes ago, the United States Government had taken actions only contemplated in a true national crisis.

"Bud, if I may, I feel I should return to NYC as soon as possible. As Bureau Chief, I do not want to leave this in the hands of the somewhat inexperienced team I recently recruited." Spoken like a seasoned professional, his tremulous voice momentarily exposed the underlying fear.

"Of course, Simon. I need you there. Take the Gulfstream. And open up your secure line to me immediately."

"Will do." He covered the waiver in his voice. "Bud, what do you want me to do with this, this…story?" He gestured toward the anarchy exploding on the TV monitors and on the frightening exclamations of the anchormen and women at his competing networks. Clearly they were scrambling.

"Ignore it."

"What did you just say?" Simon shook his head in disbelief.

"I said, ignore it." Then, feeling he needed to explain that startling order, he said, "With this much hysteria and confusion, there is nothing but fear coming from these networks. And whatever they start spouting in the next hours is likely to be suspect—*very suspect.* They will make the situation worse, and terrify the people more. No, WNG is going to take a different approach. We are going to keep our God-damned mouths shut until we know what the hell is going on here!"

Bud looked to James as if to ask, *Is this the right call?*

James nodded, impressed with a very savvy judgment call made by a guy who had never been in the military. *He's a cooler cucumber than I thought,* James noted.

"Just do your job, Simon. Get the facts, not the spin. Don't foster hysteria. We're going to figure this out, and by golly we are going to give the American people one damned network they can turn to that isn't spouting propaganda. So, don't repeat anything you hear on these other networks. They will be grabbing for any data they can get their hands on, and whoever has specifically caused whatever the hell this is will be right there to feed them some bullshit. Well, we are not going to be part of it!"

"Okay, man, I got it!" Simon shouted. "Right now we don't have any idea what *has* happened or *why,* so we are not going to speculate just to fill air time. I got it."

"Damn straight!"

Standing face-to-face, it suddenly dawned on Bud and Simon that they didn't need to be shouting at one another. They were in complete agreement. Simon ended the standoff with, "So, what exactly do you suggest I do? What should I be airing while we figure this out?"

"Beats me, Simon. I don't care if you air cooking shows all day."

He hadn't meant it to be funny, but the absurdity of the remark made all of them laugh. Seeing he'd become the old Bud Walker they were used to in the past, he punctuated it with, "Matter of fact, do just that. Might just alert our competition to the fact that they need to calm down, take a deep breath, make some pesto pasta, and wait to get some real facts before we are all in an abyss."

"Yeah, somehow I don't see that happening, Bud," Simon shouted over his shoulder, as he grabbed his briefcase and left.

While all that was going on, James had been scribbling something else on the small piece of paper he had in his pants pocket. Quite calm now, and without saying a word, he walked over to Andy and handed it to him.

Hesitating to read it, Andy looked to his partner Brian, who just rolled his eyes. They both knew what that little piece of paper meant. It meant James Mikolas had a theory, and he was ready to reveal it.

"Okay, James, let's see what you got this time…" Andy's voice trailed off as his eyes read the hastily-penned sentences. He lowered his head almost to his chest, exhaled, then looked up—staring slightly left and smiling.

"What?" The suspense was killing Brian.

James put him out of his misery with, "It means you kids got your work cut out for you!"

"We kids?" Brian challenged. "Who's this *we* you are talkin' about, my man James? Huh?"

"Well, better put, all three of us have our work cut out for us." That satisfied Brian, and he grabbed the note from Andy. Reading it, he merely shook his head.

CHAPTER 20

*T*he three women had hit it off extremely well, and it was clear that Alicia Quixote was slowly working herself back into the game. Still pretty, energetic, and smart, she seemed happy and relieved to be working directly on something of this magnitude.

True, it helped that Edith Church arrived with a considerable amount of data about the slave traders—as she now referred to them, in deference to a very valid point Reagan had made. Reagan's story of how strongly Brian had made the point about calling it slavery instead of human trafficking made sense to Edith, and she immediately adopted the stronger term. Now, all three women were hell bent on finding the "slave traders of the 21ˢᵗ century."

Rumor had it that the most successful slavers were women. For that reason, Edith and Reagan were excited about this afternoon's meeting with Alicia. She had texted Edith that she'd confirmed some information, and might be close to a meeting.

The narrow street in front of Alicia's apartment forced them to pull the car up on to the curb in order to park it. Reagan squeezed out, and they both stopped in front of the bougainvillea-covered building before going in.

"All right, Reagan. I have a feeling this is it."

"Me, too."

"Are you ready to meet these people face to face?" Edith looked a little apprehensive.

"Yes, because I know that if one of them does take a meeting with us, it is because they are experiencing remorse and are looking for some kind of amends."

Edith was old enough to admire the confidence of the young, but at the same time experienced enough to appreciate their vulnerability in dangerous environments. She told herself, *I hope so, Reagan. I hope so.*

As they climbed the front stoop, Alicia's cat Alley pounced out in a surprise attack from behind some potted geraniums. Attacking Reagan's bag, she landed all fours and clung to it as if it were an amusement ride. Fortunately, Alicia heard all this commotion and gingerly extricated Alley from the bag, checking it for damage.

"Come in, you two. I have an interesting development."

It didn't take her long to explain that an exploration she had made into the world of human trafficking, wherein she pretended to be a journalist working on a piece, and bound by journalists' codes for confidential informants, had led her to an export/import firm on the U.S./Mexico border, less than a mile from the Bridge of the Americas.

Crossing in and out of Juarez daily were thousands of people—college students, tourists, day workers, family members visiting relatives left behind in Mexico, and, regrettably, drug runners, gang bangers, and sex traffickers. It had become a hot and dangerous territory on the other side. Juarez was now a city whose murder rate resembled that of a war zone, earning it the name "Murder Capital of the World" for three years running—a city which had become suppressive and hostile to its own inhabitants who were just trying to live their lives.

Frankly, it was the gateway to Mexico's Civil War. Anyone crossing the Bridge of the Americas was placing themselves into harm's way. Gun battles left dozens dead on a daily basis—among them children and women, both the innocent and the guilty.

Alicia's source had told her that the primary human trafficker, especially for women, was a woman in Juarez. He felt that this woman, known as La Bella Casamentera, ironically nicknamed for her unique, if not sordid, matchmaking skills, would be willing to talk with someone, as long as she remained anonymous. She apparently ran a well-known brothel, and did not want her clientele to know the source of the women she offered—especially not the American clients who frequented her establishment.

Edith was particularly interested in this. She was quite familiar with a type of woman who had such disdain for men that she would take pride in degrading them inside her bordello, but would be willing to showcase her establishment to another woman, and only to a woman. Most people think of brothels as a place where the women prostitutes are degraded. But Edith knew the mentality of the female pimp, and whether the client knew it or not, he was being demeaned every moment he participated. Guessing that this was why the woman, La Bella Casamentera, had agreed to meet, and assuming she was expecting an American journalist, this appeared to be the real thing.

Alicia concurred. It was agreed that all three would cross the bridge once the meeting was set by Alicia's informant, and that Alicia would operate under the protection of her journalist credentials, pretending to introduce two Americans who were hoping to set up a human trafficking business of their own within the U.S. They hoped their attention and interest in this woman would flatter her enough that she would be forthcoming about the supply line and show them the routes the traffickers were using to transport their slaves.

It was now a matter of waiting for the call to go. Not knowing whether that would be days or weeks, they decided to just relax and take in a movie. As they stood in line to get their tickets, Alicia added something she had forgotten to mention. "Remember, we are looking to gain information for the supply side, not the demand side."

Reagan didn't appear to follow, so Alicia added, "She needs to know you wish to supply merchandise across that border and not purchase merchandise." For a moment, Reagan was confused. Her innocence showed in her question. "You mean people are bringing slaves *into* the United States?"

For a moment, Alicia flashed a quick and surly look to Edith as if to chastise her for bringing someone this unfamiliar with the scene into the project. As news anchor, she was renowned for that quick Latin temper and an expectation that everyone operate on her level. But having given up the game, she had mellowed enough so that today, it was only a blistering look rather than a tongue lashing.

Edith, diplomatic as always, settled it smoothly with, "Reagan's been looking at the global picture so long, and at the women who have gone missing in the U.S., I'm afraid she forgot there might be another side to this—that regrettably it is a two-way flow. But, to find the missing women, we have to find how they were taken out, and where they were headed. She is focused on that. That's why I love this girl. She is a pit bull. And find their trafficking route she will!"

Samir could not help but laugh robustly at the astonishing news Zawahiri had just given him. Talking live in one of the rare moments they had to use satellite phones, the Doctor had explained a courier pouch he had received recently.

Apparently, it had contained mail intercepted at the Post in Geneva, and in Paris. Knowing that Intelligence communities would be monitoring all known email accounts of Samir's Paris-based PR firm, ST and Associates, one thing was certain—Samir Taghavi would never check his emails. The Post Office box would also be watched, so a single Al Qaeda postal employee diligently monitored any incoming mail headed for Samir's firm, removed it from the postal system, and added it to the pouch for the Doctor.

Similarly, Zawahiri's alias and false identity, Phillipe Monet, was a revered citizen, businessman, and member of the Board of Directors of the pharmaceutical giant Decu-Hehiz—whose psychiatric medicine division was without question its most prosperous. Monet had abandoned his investment firm offices when Israel's Mossad was closing in. Like Samir, Phillipe Monet vanished into thin air. Monet's mail, too, was intercepted and sent by courier to Zawahiri's latest location.

What had the men laughing, but a tad regretful, was that each had received a letter from the Repository of International Transactions. The letter had come from one Harley Grantham-Jones, who had served on the Board of the World Health Organization, along with Phillipe Monet. He wanted to hire Samir to head up a specialized public relations campaign the Repository of International Transactions needed to launch immediately. And he had wanted someone who could explain the RIT's upcoming actions to the media and public.

At the same time, he wanted Phillipe Monet to make sure the funds that the Repository would continue to supply to pharmaceutical companies were properly used in the areas where they would provide the greatest benefit to a world population that would become increasingly anxious. The Doctor knew that was code for a resurgence of psychiatric drugging of populations.

"Pity we're not able to assist the gentleman," the Doctor exclaimed. "I met him once."

"Did you sense there was an ally there?"

"No, Samir, I did not. Regrettably, I'm sensing something more sinister now. Writes a good letter, though. One that Intelligence would assume was a logical reach from one businessman to another. They would never put it together."

"Do you think he knows who you are?" It was asked more out of curiosity than fear. Samir and the Doctor both were beyond the reach of international bankers now. Or so they thought.

"I expect he does." Zawahiri paused for a moment, as if looking at something. "And that's what seems sinister. I don't like it, Samir, when someone knows something about me I did not intend for them to know."

"I understand."

The Doctor shook off his feeling of uneasiness. "But, it's a moot point. As far as you and I are concerned, his letters never reached either of us. And neither were they intercepted by our enemies." Suddenly, he laughed.

"What?"

"I just found it ironic that we apparently had colleagues at the Repository of International Transactions. Swiss Commercial banks, of course. I've been dealing with them for years. But, RIT! Wonder what they are up to? Oh, well..." He dismissed it. "Where are you headed next?"

"In a few weeks, I will be headed back to South America to pick up the first shipment you asked for."

"Good. Those women will serve us well."

The core five were meeting once again in their own War Room. Known as the Directorate, it had taken all their negotiating skills to sell the actions RIT was taking to the members from France, Japan, Russia, and Canada. Once they did, however, these four became unwitting collaborators who effectively persuaded the remaining countries of the "Big 20," the largest industrialized hard currency economies in the world. Once those were all in alignment, it had been fairly simple to announce their decisions to the remaining members of the RIT.

Each of the heads of those banks was now preparing to "sell" the sudden and brutal actions of refusing to extend credit and calling in debt to their respective countries and their populations. Each had been briefed on the "nuclear option," which had been set in place back in 2009, and which the Directorate would soon "detonate."

Though Sir Harley, Braghelli, and the others from Switzerland, Germany, and the United States could barely tell night from day in their sequestered quarters underground, it was time for them to coalesce around a strategy that would cause the populations of the various countries to embrace the heinous terms, which the "nuclear option" would demand.

Since the Directorate had no army capable of enforcing this, Sir Harley Grantham-Jones knew that it would come down to mind control. Whoever could influence the minds of the populations the most would prevail. And to do that, they had to clear one predictably large hurdle.

"Gentlemen, tonight we are discussing how we are going to turn the populations of the United States, and Great Britain, against their own governments. The people must see our *solution* as the only viable option. So, now that the pain is beginning, we must insure they believe their own elected representatives caused it."

He stopped for a moment, enjoying this idea. "We will direct them to the wrong target. Delicious, actually, getting them to recalibrate and take aim at themselves." His colleagues smiled—all but one. Quietly getting himself cream for his tea at the beverage bar, the man's back was to Sir Harley, and Harley was unable to observe the U.S. member's reaction.

"Anyway, chaps, *we'll* be riding in on white chargers, saviors of them all, very shortly. Stoddard and Wipps will walk point and be the first credit agency to insert itself into a nation's political process. Given the degree of civil unrest out there—which will be increasing—I doubt anyone will notice that a private credit agency has never before had the authority to make financial decisions based upon its "opinion" of the political process of a sovereign nation. We will have bridged the gap. An external finance entity now will meddle with internal politics and be unchallenged by the people!"

He paused, enjoying the chess move he was implementing. Then, making sure they were all equally appreciative of this subtle but dramatic move, he asked, "Do you see?"

The question was rhetorical. They did, of course, see. Continuing, he quipped, "I would like to propose we begin with the United States. There will be time for the others later."

CHAPTER 21

"**W**hat in the hell is he doing?" Walker shouted, trying to rouse James and Andy from their immersion in the data analysis. Andy had hastily created a program that would allow them to input Atwater's research and align it all—no matter what the source—on a time line. After years in field work with the CIA, but more recently, after his time as an analyst with them, James knew that one of the ways to camouflage the truth so it could not be seen was to obscure the time line. Battle plans always had a sequence to them, but if you could scramble the events so the victim didn't recognize the sequence or the parts, you could effectively stage a coup.

His gut told him he was about to uncover perhaps one of the most elaborate plots created, and, though he was not a praying man much, he was praying that at its core, it would prove visible and simple. He needed Andy's genius not just to program it but also to evaluate it from the altitude of a Grandmaster Chess Champion—to filter out all the unnecessary noise and clutter, and get to the key elements. Time was so pressing with the civil unrest spreading dramatically over the last few days. Federal troops had been called into the major cities to contain any violence that might erupt, before a contagion of insurrection enveloped the United States. Europe was mostly in flames, with the unrest graduating into open insurrection in Greece, Italy, Portugal, and Spain. James knew it was only a matter of time.

For that reason, he did not hear Bud's urgent question, until Walker had apparently given up on him and went charging out of the room on some kind of mission. *Whatever it is, he'll have to handle it. I can't let myself be distracted,* James thought.

Brian was headed toward the trail head at the base of the Bob Marshall Wilderness. It would be some hours before Andy needed him to weigh in on whatever the research unearthed, and the suspense and anxiety of the economic implosion was frightening him. Brian Washington Carver did not lack for courage, but any man can be afraid when he does not know for sure who is attacking, why they are attacking, or what move he can make.

Remembering an exercise Andy had taught him when they were all struggling with the tragic loss of Brian's family, and his ensuing mood swings, he decided to "take a walk." *Yeah,* Brian thought. *James taught Andy to take a walk when he cramped up mentally. I need a walk, for sure!*

When one is unfamiliar with horses and merely out for a walk, the sound of a horse galloping toward you is an immediate attention grabber. Those who have experienced it know the sound and know the earth truly does shake. Brian didn't know what was about to overtake him, but something was. He stopped and turned just in time to see Bud Walker galloping up, dismounting before his horse had even come to a full stop.

"What the hell are you doing, Brian?" Walker sounded more afraid than angry. That confused Brian.

"Just taking a walk, Bud, just a walk. I'm not needed right now, and I thought a walk out here would clear my head, relax me so I'd be ready."

Walker relaxed some, softening his tone. "Brian, let me explain something. You don't take walks out here—not in the Bob Marshall; not by yourself and never unarmed." Seeing that Brian look confused, he explained. "This is wilderness. It's beautiful to look at from my porch and bunk quarters, but it is deadly territory unless you know what you are doing. And judging by the looks of you, you don't know what you are doing."

"What you mean?" Brian challenged, a little surly.

"I mean, son, you never come to Montana, and never bring anybody to Montana for them to be safe and secure. Montana can kill you in a minute—especially the Bob Marshall."

That appeared to be a popular thought with Bud.

Letting the warning sink in, he said, "This wilderness is a magnificent place, one of the most majestic in the world, and you could be gone for months in there. And that's just it, Brian, you—untrained and un-equipped—could be gone for months. All we'd find is your body."

That was a sobering thought. Growing up in Southeast Washington as a non-gang member, Brian knew he had to learn the street in order to stay safe on it. He realized now Montana had its own "street."

"First, you never go alone. There are cougar and bear out there that don't like interference in their territory—and remember, Brian, it is *their* territory. Hell, to a cougar, you could be lunch. There are creeks in there so cold even at this time of year that you'd have only minutes before you're gone to hypothermia if you fell in. And there are sudden cliffs and drop-offs, and absolutely no way for you to tell where the hell you are once you enter the dense forest, unless you have a compass, know expertly how to find trail markers, and are survival trained."

"So, you don't go in there?" Brian asked innocently.

"Sure, I do, son, but I am never alone, and I am always armed. So the first thing we are going to do is arm you; the second thing I am going to do is teach you how to shoot. You game?"

Brian couldn't help but laugh at the preposterous situation he was in. Here he was, a kid from the Inner City who had grown up around failure and violence, only to make his way out and into the world of considerable wealth, which he'd earned by using his mind. Now, he was hanging out with a media mogul who until recently had been in the enemy camp as far as the war on terror was concerned, whether he intended to be or not. *We have absolutely nothing in common,* he thought. *Yet it appears we need each other now.*

He cleared his throat, stifled a laugh, and graciously accepted Bud's invitation. "Mr. Walker, I'm going to take you up on that. No one ever allowed us to shoot in the Hood. You were a gang banger if you did. Up here…seems you are heartily endorsing it."

"Damn straight! It's not the two-legged animals I'm worried about up here. It's the four-legged ones. Let's head back, and we'll select a weapon for you."

Back at the house, Walker took Brian into a guest bedroom at the top of the suspended oak staircase and opened the closet. Brian's jaw dropped when he saw what was stored in this large walk-in. "Geez, this is an arsenal, Bud! In my neighborhood, we'd do twenty years for something like this…"

"Yeah, well, not here. Different weapons handle different situations. It's a matter of expertise." Then, more playfully, he added, "And intention."

Picking up a Glock 9mm from a shoe shelf full of handguns, he offered it to Brian, saying, "You just need something to protect yourself—a sweet handgun, is all. I am going to suggest my personal favorite." Brian took it gingerly. "Now, let's go teach you how to shoot it, without disturbing the wonder boys downstairs."

It was evening when Andy walked into the kitchen area. Kitchen areas in Montana homes always seemed to have what was called a "great room" attached. It was a large extension of the cooking area and might encompass dining table, sitting area, entertainment, all in one space. In Walker's home, that space occupied most of the first level.

James, Brian, Bud, and a recently returned, and terrified, Simon Atwater were sitting at the table where James and Bud sat the first night they'd met. It had been just a few short weeks since then, yet it seemed like a distant memory. Whether they wanted to be or not, whether they even liked each other or not, they were all bonded now.

Andy came in from the computer area in which he'd been hunkered down. He was holding a pad and pen. Standing in the doorway, he announced, "Well, I have good news and bad news."

Oh, no, Brian and James thought in unison. They knew what that meant.

"Okay, Kid, we're all ears. Want a sandwich?"

Andy waived him off, suggesting he'd eat later.

Taking the last seat, and placing the pad directly in front of him, he began. "First, you were right, James—this *is* definitely an enemy attack. It is not just some confluence of horrific financial decisions, flawed economic theories, poor government, poor timing, bad luck, or mismanagement. Basically, all the stuff you media guys have your attention on—*it's there*, but that is not what is causing this. Whoever it is, they are playing chess; they are very good at it; and they have been making moves luring us into bad economic and financial choices for more than twenty years. They know us very well, and their Public Relations is astounding. Brian, you will be impressed."

Brian retorted, "Yeah, I bet!"

"Jesus, Mary, and Joseph!" Bud exclaimed. "That's bad news!"

"Actually, that's the good news, Bud," Andy responded, grimacing.

Seeing a look of complete consternation on Bud's face, James jumped in. "Bud, Andy is perhaps the finest natural chess player on the planet, so, believe it or not, this is good news."

"Kid, can you beat them?" James asked the simple question. Brian looked down at the table, bracing himself for the bad news, which Andy had not yet articulated.

Not responding to the question immediately, Andy decided to finish his earlier thought. "The bad news is, they have set their checkmate move, and it's a game changer."

"Define 'game changer,'" Brian demanded softly.

"If they execute it successfully, the world as you know it is over. And a new world begins."

No one knew how long there was silence. It seemed long enough for the sun to set, rise, and set again. Each man was looking inward, pulling their own personal images of Armageddon up from their imaginations. Truth be told, every man in that room had pictured it would be something like a bomb or disease. This emerging scenario seemed almost surreal. Whatever it would turn out to be though, not one of them was going to hide from it.

James broke the almost hypnotic reverie first. Taking a deep breath, he simply asked his friend again, "Can you beat them?"

Brian was the first to look at Andy; then the others also turned hopefully to him. Andy looked slightly to his left, as if looking at something in the distance, and an ever so subtle smile appeared. Turning back, the smile broadened as he winked at Brian. "Absolutely."

That was a relief, but no one responded as such, given the gravity of the situation. Andy continued. "I am out in front of the checkmate move. It was set in place; it's hovering there, ready to be played. But I see it, and can forestall it. Guys, we are going to stop their move in its tracks, basically keep them stuck in an old game while we move into a new one. Brian will create that new game." Looking to Brian for some backup, Brian appeared supportive but dazed. He was clearly chewing on something.

Then Andy included the others. "I can theoretically pivot their chessboard 180 degrees and get them to checkmate themselves." He paused for emphasis, then said, "Theoretically, I can do that, but you are going to have to figure out how to do it in the real world." He remembered very well how accurate his theories had been right after 9/11, and how his recommendations, if taken, would have saved countless lives and billions of dollars. But he also bitterly remembered how the CIA, Defense Department, and White House—the entities who had the authority and know-how to implement the analysis in the real-world scenario—had dismissed it all, to their subsequent peril.

He could not risk that again. In his gut, he knew they were going to have only one shot at this, and that someone here had to figure a way to actually implement his solutions, as he and Brian created them. His next words placed the responsibility where it would truly lie. "Will *you* help me with that?"

Bud spoke for the others. "Absolutely."

CHAPTER 22

*E*dith and Reagan were each pulling a small overnight bag when they arrived at the El Paso airport. Accompanying them, but not scheduled to fly out until three hours later, was Alicia. The brothel owner, who operated out of Juarez due to increased pressure from American law enforcement, had apparently accepted their cover story that Alicia was a journalist doing a deep cover story about an American brothel owner who wanted to branch out, and who wanted to find an ally who could help her supply women to Latin America.

The hub of cocaine trafficking into the U.S. was Guadalajara, and Alicia was told the drug cartels there were the ones who had recently begun a second business in human trafficking—and that they specialized in the sale of women. Further, La Bella Casamentera had provided them with the name and address of someone in Guadalajara, who was willing to provide information on how to make contact with the cartels.

Originally, the three had planned to drive across the Bridge of the Americas and travel by car over to Guadalajara. But the situation had worsened dramatically in recent weeks. With Europe in flames due to rioting, and uprisings related to the economic collapse that was occurring, with U.S. law enforcement preoccupied with preventing looting and violence following the bank closings, and with the drug gangs seeing this as an opportunity to seize more territory and sell more drugs, any U.S. vehicle crossing the border was very vulnerable.

That change had forced the three to make air connections very rapidly, as they were due in Guadalajara on the next day. Unable to get all three booked on the same flight, Edith and Reagan were being routed from El Paso to Mexico City, whose airport was operating relatively normally despite the turbulence in Europe, and where there was visible police protection. Then from there they would connect to Guadalajara. Alicia, on the other hand, had a direct flight from El Paso to Guadalajara.

Anyone traveling through Mexico City knew its airport, which services 40 million people, was one of the largest and most sprawling of any of the international airports in the world. All on one level, it had been added onto so many times that it now resembled a scrabble game, with all the extensions that appear on a scrabble board as the players think of new words. Each concourse intersected with other concourses at odd points. There was no apparent symmetry, and long walks were required to make connections—sometimes as much as a mile.

For that reason, most U.S. carriers scheduled a long layover on the ground, in order to allow passengers to walk the maze. That fact alone would put Reagan and Edith in peril in the hours ahead.

While Alicia sipped her favorite Starbuck's coffee and browsed through a fashion magazine to keep her attention off the horrifying images on the TV screen, as rioting spread throughout Europe, leaving banks stormed or burning, challenging police and military, Reagan and Edith landed in Mexico City. For each it was their first time, and just flying in over the city had been startling. Knowing the metropolitan area of Los Angeles as she did, Reagan could hardly fathom the size of the city below her, and the pollution that hovered over it.

"Edith, my Spanish is decent, but this board is confusing." Reagan waived her friend over, standing in front of the Departures Board. Finally, Edith spotted their connecting flight, which appeared to be a commuter flight scheduled to depart from a section of the airport that handled the smaller, domestic flights in Mexico.

Asking directions, they headed off, expecting it to be relatively easy. That did not prove to be the case, as the signing along the way was either too abbreviated or non-existent. Several times they stopped to ask airline personnel for directions. Given the crowded conditions of the super-busy facility, and the thousands of passengers also looking for the right corridors, it was almost dizzying.

About 20 minutes into their walk, neither was concerned about time, but they were concerned that they were not headed to the terminal they needed. About forty feet in front of them was an information kiosk, and Edith headed directly for it.

"Perdona, señor…"

"Si, Signora," he acknowledged respectfully.

"I need to speak in English, if you can," Edith said apologetically.

"Yes, of course. What do you need?"

Explaining that she and Reagan had been walking for thirty minutes, and showing him her ticket so that he could confirm the terminal and gate, he reassured her that they were close, but the easiest route was for them to bear to their right about 100 yards ahead. Peering through the crowds of people, she confirmed she had the right corridor, thanked him, and motioned for Reagan to join her. She turned to smile and thank the man once again, but he had his back to her now. He appeared to be talking to someone on a walkie-talkie.

They worked their way through the human traffic, dodging carts and people with roll-on luggage, grateful to make the turn into the corridor the official had pointed out. Neither noticed that no one else made the turn with them. Happy to be walking without having to bob and weave around people, and chatting briefly about the meeting that would enable them to present data and hopefully secure an ally for their cause in Guadalajara, neither woman noticed that they were now completely alone.

The frenetic activity at the airport, and the sounds of all the people, were distant now. Suddenly, two men slid out from yet another side corridor, stepped quickly behind each woman, and grabbed them from behind, covering their mouths with a cloth soaked in Scopolamine. Using that powerful seasickness medication, they were unconscious immediately. In another moment, both women had vanished in the airport, which served the city known as the "Kidnap Capital of the World."

As they vanished, Alicia Quixote boarded her plane to meet her friends, eager to establish a confidential informant in the heart of the drug and human trafficking city of Guadalajara.

Only five of the top twenty nations on earth were continually sequestered. The remaining fifteen members would meet for their monthly clandestine meeting in a few weeks. But recent events in global finance had unnerved them, and they couldn't wait for the regular meeting. Nearly hysterical phone calls to Braghelli and Sir Harley from the normally calm

Directors of these Central Banks prompted Grantham-Jones to call an evening meeting in the restaurant atop the Tower.

Used only for special occasions when the monthly meetings were occurring within the walls, the entire top floor, from which one could see three countries, remained eerily empty and dark. Feeling in a celebratory mood, however, Grantham-Jones had ordered the entire circular top floor open for him and his few colleagues. They would dine handsomely tonight.

Braghelli had gracefully passed control of the meeting to the man whose master plan had been created decades ago. He was still on a learning curve and happy for the opportunity to observe and study Sir Harley. First, though, Sir Harley convened the meeting of the select five by merely tapping his index and middle finger on the table. That signaled the wait staff to exit the room, and demonstrated the action he would duplicate when he was ready for the repast.

"Gentlemen, before we enjoy this magnificent evening and the sunset appearing over France, I have a great announcement to make." His fatherly smile soothed the somewhat frayed nerves of his colleagues. For decades, they had worked with the remaining fifteen members of the RIT who held the most power. They had set financial policies, currency exchange rates, interest rates, approved the "printing" of money, and approved the financial transactions of the planet.

The men not in this room were respected for their brilliance, their commitment, and their service, not only to the RIT but also to their countries. Through years of Public Relations masterminded by Grantham-Jones himself, and through years of tutelage in financial ideology, technologies, and policies, they had convinced themselves that every action they took was in the best interest of the people of their country. They saw themselves as senior to the governments their people had chosen, and for the most part, saw themselves as the guarantors of financial prosperity. In their minds, they were the "white hats" who were protecting the people from the fiscal irresponsibility of their governments.

Every loan they approved or disapproved; every currency they devalued; every nation they assisted; and everyone they repressed, was justified, in their minds, under the task of helping people, and making certain bad things did not happen to them.

As such, they had been "programmed" and were predisposed to take authoritarian action against governments, if they felt that the financial policies of those governments had run amuck. Above the law, and certainly above the comprehension of the people and the representatives the people elected, they sat in the God's seat of world control. Each man dominated his government by his ability to control treasury loans, his ability to manipulate foreign exchanges and interest rates, thereby influencing the level of economic activity in his country, and, if need be, to bribe politicians with rewards after the politician left office.

Harley Grantham-Jones knew that, and he further knew that those members not in this room would accept what he would be selling them in the coming weeks. Dissention had been bred out of them, and a unilateral approach to superseding governments had been bred in. Like feudal lords, they would act in concert and in secret. Led by the unwitting delegates from the four "out of the loop" members of the G8, he knew all the others would fall in line.

But tonight he was meeting with the men who were in on the decades-old plot. All that was happening had been engineered by these five. It was a secret the group had kept since the 1970s and a secret they intended to keep. The fewer people "in the know" the better. He had created what politicians refer to as "plausible deniability" for the entire membership of the Central Banks, save for the four men with him now. Braghelli had evaluated the appropriate time to launch the attack. But now, Sir Harley was in charge. And he wanted to lay the time line in for these men.

"I want to keep this meeting brief, as I know we are all salivating over the succulent duck we will shortly be served." The others laughed and agreed, as each had been provided with a printed menu of the evening meal.

"First, I want to let you know that," he held up a printed document resembling a computer spread sheet, "it is confirmed that the aggregate debt of the world's nations has exceeded the net worth of all the movable goods and real estate on the planet."

He paused for the men to absorb the milestone they had reached. Each knew what came next. "That means, my friends, that we now own the entire planet. Every bit of collateral that would back up the loans we have given has now been exceeded. It is just a matter now of how and when we demand that real estate and material goods, or what we demand in return for letting them keep it." His smile at that moment was insidious as he thought, *That should satisfy them.*

"Now, before you point out the obvious that there are only five of us, and we really don't want all that real estate and property, in a matter of a few weeks—once the United States and China have started to rip apart at the seams—we will make the demands that each Head of State will accept, and which will put us in total political and social control of all the peoples of earth." He paused to observe their faces. "And that, my friends, ends this impossible attempt by these *'wannabes'* to govern themselves, and it ends the painful necessity we have endured of putting up with their ignorance and stupidity."

The first man to speak was the Director from Germany. "Ja, wohl!" The others joined in as well, raising their champagne glasses to toast their supremacy. No one noticed that the first round of endorsement came from the man most closely connected to Hitler's Bank. And none cared. There were many things in the philosophy of the Selection of the Fittest with which they wholeheartedly agreed.

Grantham-Jones then laid out once again for his colleagues the twelve demands that would be presented to the respective Heads of State by the Director of their Central Bank. That man would wholeheartedly believe he was acting in the best interest of his country, and the weight of his endorsement, and the persuasiveness of his argument, would, if things went as planned, persuade the politician.

Harley Grantham-Jones fancied himself a chess player, though his skill level was somewhat plebian. Nonetheless, he could not resist the analogy as he presented with a flourishing gesture, "Gentlemen, for each of you, the Checkmate move."

It was just one page, single-spaced. This list would usher in the new world these men dreamed of. The list of international standards for re-established relations with, and the support of, the RIT involved acceptance of a Board that would engage in:

"Clear specification of the structure and functions of government."

It was that first criteria that held the attention of one man in particular. He had seen it before and encouraged his government to sign onto it before. But, for the first time a sense of nausea was overtaking the Director from the United States. In one sweeping move, a private international clique was assuming control of, by reason of extortion, the functions of governments and the structure of governments. Though Sir Harley did not address it, each member reading it knew that two primary targets here were the three branches of the United States government, and the parliamentary system of Great Britain. The U.S. representative had nowhere to look. His counterpart from Great Britain was standing in front of him, imposing in every sense of that word. Knowing that a departure, even to the bathroom, would call attention to himself, he reached for the water in front of him, hoping no one would notice his trembling hands. Worse yet, he didn't know what nagging emotion was causing his hands to tremble.

Many of the activities listed on the sheet, into which the Financial Responsibility Board would insert itself, were totally acceptable to anyone in the international finance community. They had so long ago accepted this as necessary that no one would resist a third party taking over control. Including such things as risk management, foreign exchange settlement, and international standards of auditing, there was one that would arouse no disagreement anywhere—criminalizing the financing of terrorism.

More sinister, however, was the "statistical data gathering from the ministries of education, health, finance etc." and "corporate governance principles," "personal savings," and "secure retirement incomes…"

Those five "involvements" alone in the hands of someone with good intentions were dangerous enough. In the hands of someone whose goal was to "own the world," they would prove fatal to the culture of planet earth.

For the first time, someone in power in the United States recognized that he had not only created the monster that would bring a new order to his country, but also one that would devour the entire civilization as it existed in the 21st century. The sudden realization of the reality of his deeds produced a psychological claustrophobia.

His heart pounding and his breathing rate escalating, the man's blood pressure sky-rocketed, causing a heart episode. Their dinner was unceremoniously interrupted by the need to evacuate the man to the private hospital below ground, which had been set up for the extended stay and long term care of the men who planned to take over the world.

Pity, Harley thought, as he sat quietly in the lounge adjacent to the restaurant, sipping his sherry, *I needed him in top form for this. Oh well, it will be some weeks before we implement our "salvation offer." He'll be recovered by then I'm sure.*

CHAPTER 23

"James, I am telling you, I am not going to do this if it's just him, Atwater, and his Chief of Staff!" Andy was angrily and stubbornly standing his ground.

"Kid, I don't know what to say here. I've never seen you walk away from a fight." James knew as he said it that it was probably a mistake.

That was too much for Andy, and he pushed past James, thrusting one of the double doors open and exiting to the veranda. James just watched him for a moment, knowing that when Andy paced back and forth, as he was doing now on the outdoor deck, it was best to let him work through it before trying to talk to him.

The pacing slowed, and James ventured forth. "Okay. Tell me what's on your mind."

Andy seemed willing to talk, but he was still a little combative. He squared up on James and looked him straight in the eye to make sure his friend got the point. "The last time you had me do a 'briefing,' it was for one guy at the CIA. He had the authority and ability to do something about that invasion of Iraq, and he did nothing." James remembered well the burial of the discovery Andy had made about the WMD deception, and the ass covering that had followed all that. But, he didn't exactly see the connection.

Continuing, Andy said, "I want to tell this story once; and I want to tell it to someone who could actually implement a solution, that's all."

"And you don't think Walker can?" James was sincere.

"No, I don't. And I'll tell you why." Andy drew in a deep breath. "It's not that I don't like him, James, and it's not that I don't believe he sincerely understands the damage he did."

"So?"

"So, he is about to get a glimpse of the depth of his undermining, and I don't know if he can handle it. Even if he can, he's the media guy. He's not government—or finance. We're going to need government, finance, and media on this. I need the people who can *do* something in on this meeting—the ones who can receive the analysis and implement some kind of solution. If they are there, then I'll lay it all out. But, you have to let me call this 'audible,' James." Andy used a familiar football term, knowing that James would recognize that sometimes the coach just has to let the quarterback call the play from the field, especially if he sees something unusual in the opposing line. It's his judgment. James had watched Andy "call an audible" many a time during games in the first year they met.

Well, he did lead his team to a state championship... James reflected, remembering clearly a more innocent time.

"Yeah, sure, Kid. I get it. We do it your way."

That seemed to satisfy Andy. He nodded firmly twice, indicating his approval.

"So, who is going to tell Walker? You or me?"

"I'll tell him," James said, as he reentered the house.

This guy's starting to get the hang of this, James thought, with more than a bit of admiration.

Once Walker understood from James' perspective just how important this next briefing from Andy would likely be, he immediately grasped the necessity of moving quickly, and of getting reinforcements. Especially since he'd just been watching incoming news reports that the East Coast was starting to crumble in the major metropolitan areas.

Sporadic rioting and looting had broken out in Miami, Washington, D. C., and New York City. People were tense not having access to their money. Police presence seemed to be containing it, that and the fact the Administration was allowing people to withdraw small amounts of cash from ATMs. There was a daily limit, the lines were long, and no one knew what the next day would bring.

Worse yet were reports that the southern borders were being breached, leaving law enforcement unable to stop the exodus of people out of Mexico, seeking help and money in the United States. Law Enforcement was falling back to surround and defend the U.S. cities nearest the border.

With that reality screaming at him from the profusion of TV screens in his War Room, in what seemed like only a matter of minutes, Bud Walker had ordered all his planes fueled; called up all his pilots; and placed phone calls to people, leaving them no option but to be at his ranch by nightfall. Some of the people had been to the ranch a few weeks earlier, and had subsequently returned to work in Billings and Kalispell. Others were being summoned for the first time.

Ordering Atwater to stand by, and summoning Ray—who was running WNG for him in his absence—he had personally called the Governor of Montana telling him to return to the ranch. James overheard him add, "And bring the majority leaders of both the Senate and Assembly, and any staffers they need."

Given that the Montana Constitution mandated the Legislature meet no longer than ninety days every other odd-numbered year, that was a taller order than Bud realized. The Capital was in fact close to his ranch, but it was 2011, and they'd already met for their allotted "governing" time. The Governor informed Bud that it was going to take a while to "round everybody up," as he put it, but that he was willing to do so.

Next, Walker called his hunting and fishing buddy, Stormy Helms, the entrepreneur from Flathead County whose politics were the opposite of Bud's, but whose hunting excursions had been some of the most fun— and most successful—of Bud's career. Apparently, the man planned to bring someone with him, because Bud responded very affirmatively with, "Absolutely, I will be very interested in what Sheriff Peters has to offer. He's welcome back here anytime."

His next call was to the state head of the Chamber of Commerce, and to Chester Riddle, the oil man in Billings. Realizing he had forgotten something, he called the Governor back, saying, "Bruce, you'd better bring your Treasury Secretary, and the Attorney General. We are going to need legal advice." Whatever the Governor said in response, Bud quickly jotted a note to himself and added, "I'll call the University Chancellor and get him back here as well."

Knowing that it would be a few hours before the men began to arrive in the planes Bud had dispatched to pick them up, Andy and Brian were headed out the front door when they were intercepted by Walker.

"Whoa, whoa, where are you two going? I've convened quite a summit here, and they're coming to hear from you, Andy, at your insistence," he said, with an edge of criticism.

"Right, and we'll be back before they are even all here. Brian and I thought we'd better eat, and wanted to get out a bit, maybe get something local. We thought we'd try one of those Montana saloons we'd been hearing about."

"Which one were you headed to?"

"The Blue Sky in Avon."

Bud's reaction was immediate. "No, sirree! Let me 'hat' you boys up a bit on Montana saloons. There are two kinds—ones you go to, and ones you don't."

Seeing that they were listening respectfully, as usual, he instructed, "The typical saloon is like an English pub, where people go and hang out—whole families even."

"Yeah, we'd heard that. That's why we were headed there."

Undaunted, Bud continued. "Well, the second type of saloon is one you go to, expecting a fight."

"I see…" Brian did see. His years of dodging gangs and their various bars gave him a frame of reference. He asked, "And I gather the Blue Sky is one of those you go to for a fight, not a burger and fries?"

"Well, you can get the burger and fries, but it's the fight you want to miss," Walker said, laughing.

Not to be deterred from their mission, Andy asked, "So, for the *other* one, the one where families go—you know the kind of Montana saloon we thought Montana was famous for—where do you recommend?"

Bud decided not to explain to the boys that Montana was famous for both types of saloons. He was just grateful these kids took direction well. He looked at his watch, then tossed them the keys to his Hummer. "You have time to get to Garrison and back before we are assembling this crew you asked for, Andy." That suited Andy just fine. "So, try the Frontier Saloon. They have an especially good steak sandwich."

"Thanks, Bud. He thinks better on a full stomach!" Brian joked. "And, frankly, my partner here needs to 'take a walk.'" They were in the Hummer and gone before Bud could even ask why, if he needed a walk, they were driving all the way to Garrison to a saloon.

"Kids!"

Chapter 24

Six hours later, on one of those remarkable summer evenings in Montana where daylight lingers well past 10PM and Alpine Glow basks the mountain peaks, there had been a steady stream of cars from the airstrip to the main part of the ranch and its quarters. Given the pedigree of some of the guests, and the fact that they might be staying a while, Walker had also opened up the multiple guest suites in the main house. Normally they were reserved for the elite guests that billionaires sometimes entertain.

He'd told them all to shower, grab some food from the kitchen, bring their notepads, and be ready for a meeting at 10:30PM. The only one not quite there yet was Ray, who had had to fly out of JFK. Newark airport was nervous about flights, as there were reports of civil unrest beginning about five miles from the airport. His plane was thirty minutes out, but Bud decided to commence the meeting anyway.

"I'm going to introduce you, Kid," James whispered to Andy. "From there it is all yours. But I need to make sure these guys know exactly who they are dealing with so they don't undervalue your information. I've dealt with men like this my whole life, and we can't afford for them to turn self-important on us."

Andy nodded agreement, and James finished with, "I don't know what you've got, Kid, but I expect this is going to be one of those nights men like these write about in their memoirs."

"Let's hope so, James, let's hope so." Andy's voice faltered a bit.

"What's up?" James asked, trying to mask his concern.

Andy decided to write his answer and slide the note over to James, rather than risk being heard. It read simply, *"Fear. I know what's going on, but unless these men can help me solve it, none of us is going to be publishing our memoirs."* On that sobering thought, James turned to Bud, who was just informing his guests who James Mikolas was and how they had met.

- 124 -

That raised a few eyebrows and engendered a few smirks, but each of these men was well aware of the seriousness of recent world events, and each knew somehow that a fight was coming to them. So, they were prepared for anything, and secretly glad they were all together instead of sweating this out at home alone.

"Gentlemen," James began, "I'm about to introduce Andrew Weir. Behind you, in the chair near the rear door, is his partner Brian Washington Carver. When Andy talks to you tonight, I want you to understand just how much you should pay attention." He let the men look around to spot Brian and acknowledge him, and then to square up on Andy.

"This *Kid,* as I call him, is perhaps the finest chess player in the world today, and it was his analysis of data spanning decades that helped us figure out what Al Qaeda has been doing, where key leaders might be hiding, and how far their reach was into the United States. For those of you who may not know him, his analysis was shocking—and overlooked by almost everyone in authority. And that, gentlemen, must not happen here tonight! He and Brian figured out exactly how an enemy was undermining all of our institutions, and bringing us down from within—using psychiatric medications to sedate, weaken, and create addictions. Their game 'White King Rising' is almost single-handedly responsible for the United States winning the war on drugs, with the demand for street drugs and forced psychiatric medications dropping like a rock. Andy is a champion quarterback as well, and I believe you know Brian Washington Carver and his stunning career as a wide receiver with LA Western University."

James noted that the sheriff leaned in and looked toward Brian, smiling. He continued. "What Andy figured out was that our enemy has been playing chess, eight separate games to be exact, and that they have not been consecutive games but rather simultaneous games layered like a game of three-dimensional chess." The men were all ears, waiting for the pay off.

"It was the sequence of the games that, in my opinion, opened the door for us to prevail. 'White King Rising' was a brilliant counter attack upon game #7."

Bud Walker listened as if he were hearing this for the first time. He knew who Andy and Brian were in the world of business, but he had never been told the whole story. Not daring to interrupt James, he sat back and waited, sensing the enormity of the story.

James continued. "The first game Andy identified was Religion, used effectively by Al Qaeda to recruit and to stir up trouble everywhere.

The next game was Military, and I think all of us here know just how much activity has been expended into that game. Next up the line is Intelligence, leading straight to one of the most dangerous of the games, Public Relations. Not only did Andy discover that the same players were appearing in all the games—assuming different 'chess roles,' if you will, in different games—but that they were working in a masterful deception to use Public Relations and the American media in a plot to get Americans to turn on each other. Basically it is the Public Relations game that has torn America apart since 9/11."

Pausing for a moment, James took a sip of his black coffee. "Once the mind control was in effect, the next game up was Weapons, which includes fear. Fear affects the society, and the next game was Sociology. Following the old Soviet strategy of bringing us down from within, it was imperative to undermine our institutions. And of course, that type of activity—all going on simultaneously—led the entire United States into a near-fatal death grip of the Medical game. That game was driven and masterminded most especially by the field of Psychiatry. And those of you who know the now global phenomenon of Andy's game know that his, and Brian's, solution has decimated that game."

Frankly, this was new news to most of these men. Their faces manifested first shock, which then gave way to admiration and gratitude. James' introduction was intended to set Andy up as a man to be reckoned with. Though only twenty-eight years old, these two unlikely partners had deciphered and faced more than the finest minds in the world had been able to.

"So, gentlemen, the last game—at the top of the whole thing—is Money." There was an audible ahhah around the table." Each game leads to the next, and ultimately it is all about money. Whether you start with Money and move down the games in sequence, or whether you start with Religion and move up to Money, a victory in one game secures the next. And the same bad guys have been proven to be playing in all the games, connecting all these arenas under one global attack."

There was silence; the only sound being an overhead fan, which circulated air in Bud Walker's "War Room."

Finally, the Attorney General of Montana asked, "Mikolas, are you suggesting that Ayman Al-Zawahiri is masterminding the global financial crisis we are experiencing?"

Before answering that challenging question—both in its content and its tone—James looked to Andy, who signaled that the answer was "no" and that he would handle that. "Mr. Attorney General, no I am not. We stopped at the Trojan Horse, and created a game that destroyed the Medical game—which most definitely falls within the purview of someone like Zawahiri. But, the question of who sent that Trojan Horse falls under the top game, in my opinion. Someone sent the Trojan Horse for a reason, and I expect Andy is about to fill us in on how the money men did it. So, gentlemen, I'm just a thirty-year veteran of the CIA, and an analyst. Let me turn this over now to a young man who taught me more in a few short years than I had learned in a lifetime. Mr. Andrew Weir."

Oh, brother, I hope that wasn't too much, Andy thought, deciding to stand for his presentation. He looked at each man directly, eyeball to eyeball, wanting to establish a line to each as he began. Like a quarterback on the first day of pre-season training, looking over the new recruits who are joining his team, he was getting a measure of their confidence, and their ability to confront issues. To his pleasure, every single man stared him straight in the eyes, and seemed prepared to receive.

"James, thank you. Gentlemen, I wish we weren't here for this reason, but I am grateful you came on such short notice. In the next few minutes, I'll be able to lay out for you what I believe to be a deliberate and diabolical attack line designed to set up a financial dictatorship of planet Earth and to bring its entire population under the control of a few men. Basically, it is the beginning of a new kind of slave society, and, if I remember any history at all—" He was interrupted gently by the laughter of agreement from each man. Apparently, history hadn't been their strong suit either. Andy smiled and said, "—the beginning of a new Dark Ages. From the enemy's point of view, it's a new world order."

No one rolled their eyes; he had their attention as he explained that fundamentally the enemy was playing a kind of chess game where they would make a financial move, to which we would react. Our reaction each time was leading us deeper into a trap. Key to their understanding was Andy's insistence that, though the United States would always like to think it was in the lead, taking the initiative, in this game they were in the reactive mode—reacting to a carefully and thoughtfully engineered world financial move.

"Remember, James, when we discovered that the United States did not have the initiative in the Military game, that each move we initiated was actually a response to an enemy move? They were out in front, letting us think we were leading?"

James nodded almost sheepishly. He remembered well that moment. He also remembered how the CIA chiefs could not grasp the concept that our supposedly offensive moves were actually defensive and a reaction to something we didn't even know the enemy had done. He hoped these men were more open-minded than his CIA boss had been.

Andy restarted. "Just remember, as I go through a time line with you folks that nothing that is happening is accidental or the result of stupidity and bad luck. It is a cold and calculated coup d'etat. This enemy is very patient—like the terrorists they finance and whom they allow to do dirty work, stirring up wars and making them money—and for some reason they have decided to act egregiously right now, on our watch. I do not know why they are acting now. But I do know *what* they are doing, and *how*. It is a continuation of the Trojan Horse concept, whereby they are letting us take ourselves down, using the reasoning we used that got us into their trap in the first place. And you all will likely figure out who they are, more easily than I could. The *who* is not as important as the *how*—in my opinion—at this moment."

Oh, man, I was afraid of this. Not another Trojan Horse! Brian was thinking. Truth be told, he was frightened. He knew something about drugs, gangs, and coercion, coming from Southeast Washington, D. C., but he knew nothing about banking and finance. *Geez, I hope Andy is right that these guys can help!* He said nothing, however, and was grateful Andy had asked him to sit at the back, a bit separate from the rest.

"My analysis of the banking industry's policy changes and lobbying efforts, which resulted in new U.S. and international law, and the Public Relations efforts they initiated each time to paint themselves as the knights on white horses, revealed a number of moves they made, dating way back, and escalating since 9/11. What you have to pay attention to is the time line, gentlemen. The moves were done in different decades, by different people, handling different situations—each move seeming innocuous and palatable at the time, perhaps even desirous, or insignificant. I don't know. The point is, we missed it. Their Public Relations convinced us it was 'in our best interest' and 'for the sake of helping people and keeping them safe.' You'll find it there, Bud, if you want to research your archives. You will have been the Bishop in the chess game, who was used by the King to spin the message."

None of the men knew how Bud would react to that indictment, but Weir had said it in such an un-accusative and almost sympathetic way, they figured somehow it was okay. As a group, they seemed to be reminding themselves what Mikolas had said about this young man.

"One of the things I had to learn playing chess was that there was always an opponent. Seems silly. But most of us look at things from our own point of view, and not the opponent's. So, I had to look at my moves, and theirs, and ask what they were trying to do with theirs. What were they setting me up for? Yes, I had to learn to lay out my own moves to win, but if I didn't pay attention—and assume they were a really good chess opponent—I would miss what they were doing, and at the very least I would walk myself into trouble and a slow game. At worst, I walked into defeat."

The men chuckled, nodding. They hadn't risen to their positions either it seemed without some of that going on. One asked, "Did that happen often?"

"Only once actually." That jolted them a bit. Andy's eyes twinkled as he added, "I don't like to lose." That produced a much-needed release of laughter. It was late, however, and they quickly braced themselves with fill-ups in their coffee cups, and settled back into the meeting.

"So, here it is. Hidden amongst all the finance activities, legislation, policies, transactions—you name it—hidden amongst different countries and their currencies, separated by time durations wherein you would likely not make the connection, were some key dots. When we connect the dots, gentlemen, your picture emerges. There is a lot of what I call white noise in and around all of this camouflaging it further, but basically, there are two players in this game. We'll be White, and we'll let the opponent be Black. Keep in mind each of our moves was reactive to theirs. We have not forced them into *any* moves as of yet. It appears we have been playing defense. And my friend Brian, back there, doesn't like being on defense any more than I do."

Encouraging each man to take notes now, Andy quickly laid out key dates, marking some turning points in the world of banking and finance. Each one had been accepted or ignored by most, but each one was meticulously put in place to insure the checkmate move, and accomplish a coup in the future.

"In 1987, the Chairman of The Bank of the United States deregulated financial services and lowered interest rates. Our response to that 'move' was to create debt." He stopped to see if they were following his thought process. They were.

"In 1988, an agreement out of the Repository of International Transactions in Basel, Switzerland set how much capital banks had to have in reserve to protect themselves and depositors. Seemed desirable. But wait for another move a ways in the future."

"In 1994, the same Chairman persuaded the United States Congress to pass the Local Reinvestment Act, which allowed loans to a variety of people not normally qualified for home loans. Our response was to set aside lending criteria. That move made us quite vulnerable. As a chess player, I can tell you that one gave me the heebiejeebies. It's early in the game, and it exposes the King's flank, right out of the gate."

"In 1999, a New York bank lobby succeeded in getting the repeal of a 1933 law put in place to prevent commercial banks from speculating. It also made it possible for commercial banks to merge with investment banks, and the bundling of the sub-prime loans—from the earlier chess moves—with normal loans began. Those loans, which were all supposed to be 'mortgaged-backed,' were fraudulent to the point of being almost a Ponzi scheme. There was no real value there, unless the mortgage was paid. And remember, loans were now being made to unqualified people who likely couldn't pay, and they were bundled with other more appealing loans."

Andy was less than twenty minutes into this, but he could see the timeline was clarifying the matter for the men at the table. The Treasury Secretary for Montana looked the most ashamed. Now that he was catching a glimpse of the picture, he seemed embarrassed not to have seen it. But Andy had no time to worry about hurt feelings or ruffled egos. *Get the picture painted,* he coached himself.

"Then in April 2004, five mortgage bankers persuaded the Securities and Exchange Commission to waive the requirement for a certain level of reserves at the banks. That freed up capital that normally would be held in reserve, and the banks bought more of these loan bundles. They kept some but began selling most of them around the world.

"October 2007, the world stock markets crash and most have lost half their value. Trillions are lost. Now, guys, this is bad, but we wouldn't be losing the game if it had just been this. The White player is able; he would have figured out what to do to correct this, except for a move the Black player made back in 2004. And this began what you are experiencing now. Keep in mind this next move occurs while no one is looking. The banking world is busy with its newly freed up capital, buying and bundling and selling. However, the RIT issued a second agreement—an accounting rule basically. And that accounting rule collided with a masterfully executed Public Relations campaign aided by our media as they spread the word about the questionable loans, and they did it in such a way as to promote fear and doubt. Our move? A move to sell. And that's when this new rule out of Basel became a 'check' move. In chess, you can survive a 'check move,' but you sure as heck need to understand that your King was just threatened. It worked this way. The second rule says basically that if one security is downgraded in price with a bank selling it cheap, all other securities in the world had to be marked down to the new lower price set by the bank who sold cheap."

"Mark to market," the sheriff from Lincoln Country muttered under his breath. Andy heard it and jumped on it.

"Yes, Sheriff, it's called Mark to Market. And if my layman's analysis is correct, it basically wiped out the assets of almost every bank, on an accounting rule. One minute they were worth hundreds of billions of dollars, and the next minute a rule from RIT has forced everybody to mark it down."

The tension in the room was palpable now. Walker got up and opened an air vent to let in more air. Mark to Market was tantamount to forcing all homeowners in a neighborhood to lower the price of their home just because a neighbor sold his cheap to get out from under it. It was a ridiculous equation, which would lower the value of all owners' assets. The room was full of winners, and they all smelled defeat—along with something else: betrayal.

"Insane, right?" Andy asked. "But I warned you this was going to be difficult. Just hang in there. We have to see the whole picture."

"Damn, it gets worse?" the Governor challenged. He shut up immediately, knowing the answer to his own question.

"Now, basically that froze all credit. With the first rule in place, the banks had to use all available cash to protect themselves, even having to use the bail out money—which was our next chess move—to keep from going under. With no cash available for lending, due to the first rule about reserve requirements that forced them to keep what little cash they still had; and a near wipe-out due to the Mark to Market rule, which forced them to lose the value of their assets; and with the Media hammering away at them, banks don't have any money to lend, even if they wanted to."

"And that ground the economies of the world to a halt," added the Treasury Sec who had truly gotten the picture. "I see it now. Fewer loans could be made because reserves had to back up the loans in a certain ratio. With reserves reduced, the banks couldn't lend, and then the credit markets froze."

"Yeah, but even more, sir, is this. The media blamed just about everybody and his brother for this. To the degree that, after the 2008 collapse, in April of 2009, the RIT created a monetary authority—the Financial Responsibility Board—giving it planetary financial control so that, allegedly, such a debacle as this wouldn't happen again. The Public Relations machine made us all believe they were acting in our best interests, and apparently needed to protect us from our own banks and governments."

"Jesus, Bud, I am beginning to understand now why you were hiding out up here for three years. Did you know all this?" the question was asked jokingly by Bud's hunting buddy.

"No, I'm hearing this with you," he said. "I'm sober as a judge, and this is very sobering." The rest nodded.

After a while, Bud asked, "So, Andy, is this the checkmate move?"

He shook his head. "No, this is just connecting the dots to show you how we got to the point where they could set their checkmate move. And that has to do with money in general. I've had a 'crash course' in finance concepts in the last few days, so I am no expert. But I've been looking at what they changed, and what *we* did on the same time line." He paused for a moment to see who was still tracking. They all seemed to be, so he continued. "If you'll allow me...this was something I didn't really understand. You probably do, but I didn't. That's this. The money is not really real. There is no gold backing it, no tangible thing that it is linked to. The Bank of the United States can just print money, but they don't even print it any more. When the government needs money, they borrow in essence now a computer transaction. They just make it up and transfer it. Not only is there nothing backing it, but there is not even any money printed."

Brian seemed stunned by this. Shifting in his seat, but trying not to attract attention, it was all he could do to refrain from jumping in. In deference to his friend, he quieted the anger that was building, but which was oddly coupled with an almost hysterical sense of irony. *Keep your mouth shut*, he thought.

Brian was listening, but Andy seemed to be far away from him, talking in almost a disembodied voice. He could barely connect with what Andy was articulating.

"The more a government, any government, is in debt, the more it can be controlled by the Central Banks that have lent it money. It doesn't matter whether the deficit and resultant debt is to wage war—which seems inevitable in war—or to spend on widgets. If the country is not producing goods and services that people want and selling them, the country will turn to other means to get money in order to cover its debt payment.

"All you have to do is look at Argentina, for example. In October of 2008, they seized all private pension accounts in order to handle the deficit. Up until now, the United States has just kept raising its debt ceiling and borrowing to handle its deficit. But something changed recently. So here are the moves leading to checkmate."

Each man leaned in now. They were tired, and to the man, they were frightened. But, with a few exceptions, they were also Montanans, and more rugged than most emotionally. Brian, too, strained to focus. He felt like he was submerged, groping to reach the surface where he could breathe and hear.

"As long as the RIT continues to direct the Central Banks to 'print money' and lend to the government, there will be a host of inflation problems, etc., but the game keeps going. However, if their goal is the destruction of the United States and its dollar as the world's most stable currency, in order to accomplish a larger goal of world domination, then, at some point they will stop lending and/or call in the existing notes—nation by nation. When there is no more money coming in, where do you turn, what do you do? And that is the chess move we are in now.

"When Stoddard and Wipps downgraded the U.S. credit rating, not for fiscal irresponsibility but for failing to behave properly as a Congress, and when that justified raising interest rates, earning the banks even more money, it was a direct interference in the politics of a sovereign nation. We took it without resistance, and they knew they could set their last moves.

"They either have already, or will very soon, cut off the money supply and call up existing loans from nations. Personally, I believe that has already happened given what we hear in the news." He gestured toward the TV monitors, which permanently displayed the cable news networks. The men nodded. "And when the stock markets collapse, unemployment soars, riots begin, governments are overthrown, cities are burning, then the Black King's Queen—some select group who moves around in any direction, and who has the most power on that team—will step up and lay out their demands, which will have to be met in order for them to turn the money supply back on and begin lending again. To save their countries, nations will yield."

Andy paused before saying, "I gave some thought though to what the President might do. I asked myself what I would do if I were faced with this scenario. Here's what I think. In a desperate attempt to solve the problem, the President of the United States will invoke a power from the Roosevelt era, which can be used to freeze private assets like gold. Our government will predictably first try every possible way to raise the money to pay the note being called in. But in failing to do that, and being unable to borrow anything more, checkmate is at hand.

"The final move, the checkmate move, gentlemen, was set in place on April 2, 2009. It has twelve points, with three—it seems to me—being the most devastating of the twelve: their specification of the structure and functions of government; data gathering from ministries of education, health, finance, and other agencies; and their oversight of matters dealing with personal savings accounts and retirement incomes." He paused to give them the time to digest these revelations.

Still in charge, he concluded with, "And there it is. Frankly, I can see why they had to have the Psychiatric/ Medical terrorists in there numbing us and dumbing us first. That caused us to play a lousy chess game against a masterful chess player. So, you have Islamist terrorists, you have Medical terrorists, and now Economic terrorists, with 'all roads leading to Rome,' so to speak. And they intend to change the nature of our society. We do what they want, or we perish. *That* is checkmate."

Setting down his notes, Andy needed to see whether his analysis was resonating with this team. He looked each of them in the eye and calmly said, "Now, you are the Secretaries of the Treasury and Commerce, and Finance experts. Does that make sense to you? I may have said it very plain now, in homely 'kindergarten language,' but does it connect the dots that you know something about? Does it seem real?"

Slowly, and somewhat reluctantly, they nodded.

No one spoke. They had no idea why Walker had summoned them. Somehow, they felt more trapped than before, albeit much more aware. This picture, laid out in layman's terms, did seem real. In shock, their minds were as paralyzed as their emotions and bodies.

Bud Walker broke the silence. "Andy spoke about *who* might be doing this. I brought you here because I know who is doing this—at least one of them—and James knew Andy could figure this part out so I could see what this guy is doing. What we have to do is create a solution, or we're going to have about 300 million people fleeing up into Montana for sanctuary, followed by millions more marauders."

The Governor was the first to stutter, "But, Bud, we don't have legal authority over the United States, let alone international agencies and banks. The rules leave us out. We have few people and little money. What on earth…?"

He never completed that existential question, because Brian Washington Carver cut in. Without any warning, he rose, moved toward Andy, and said, "Well, that was the most amazing thing I've ever heard. I have to tell you law-abiding Montana folk that, if any of the *brothers* ever did anything like what Andy just described, they'd be doing twenty-five to life in Folsom prison. In fact, if I weren't such an upstanding person myself, I'd take this tale back to Compton and tell them they are wasting their time on the type of crimes they're running. They need to start doing this finance-banking-securities-capitalization scam. They'd make a fortune!"

He was bouncing right to left like he always did before he made his final move to catch the ball Andy would throw. James couldn't help but smile, because he had no idea where Brian was going with this, but he knew he wouldn't be up and moving unless he was about to change the game.

"Here's the deal. Andy, what you described in that chess game—and you gentlemen seem to have been adhering to—has a few other names that could be used for it—from my perspective. Basically, you've all been playing business games with people who may be white and brilliant, but they are guilty of racketeering, extortion, counterfeiting, loan sharking, bookmaking, fraud—and I'm just getting started here. Bottom line, they are criminals who have been allowed to operate legally. And what's ironic is that we have whole departments of law enforcement and justice who chase organized crime, and various other cartels, hoping to lock those bums up—for the very crimes I just mentioned. And we call those guys criminals! What a joke."

"Brian…" Andy tried to admonish his partner to be cool, but it was too late.

"So, what do you say we all agree we have been engaged in a lot of smoke and mirrors—pretend money, phony debt—you name it—with a bunch of "civilized" thugs who are basically coming to repo the car."

Andy couldn't help it. He burst out laughing at that analogy. "Yeah, that's it, Brian. It is a 'repo the car' move." Then he, too, was gone with laugher.

Picking up on it, enjoying the heck out of his homely analogy, Brian added, "But the real game, Andy, is not chess. I appreciate you setting it out that way, I really do, 'cause I could follow you. But, gentlemen, the game you were playing is poker. And the SOBs have been bluffing you. So I'm going to chill out and blow off some steam, and tomorrow we are going to figure out how to get those folks in Switzerland to play poker with us, under *our* terms."

He turned abruptly and marched toward the door. Before leaving the room, however, he stopped and tossed one last Brianism into the mix: "Andy and I were over in Garrison at this cool saloon earlier, and we learned something real interesting about Montana. We learned that Montanans are really good poker players. And that it better be a fair game, or there's hell to pay."

CHAPTER 25

*T*he sound of gunfire was steady for a few minutes, rousing James' curiosity. *Who the hell is shooting at this time of night?* Grabbing the keys to the four-wheeler Walker had loaned him, he headed toward the shots, realizing they were coming from the shooting range Brian and Walker had used earlier.

By the time James pulled up at the range, the firing had tapered off, and then it ceased. There was a light on the target area, but no one else around except one lone person who was slumped onto a barrel, facing the range.

James couldn't tell for sure whether the man was reloading, or just worn out, as the slumped shoulders and the drooping head indicated in silhouette. "Hey, what's up?" James asked, hoping to get the person's attention. As he stepped in a little closer, Brian lifted his head and then nodded ever so slightly. "Brian? What the hell…?"

Brian didn't answer at first; he just continued to stare at the ground. He was idly kicking some dust up with the toe of his right boot. James remembered the night the three of them had uncovered the Trojan Horse, which was taking down the United States. It seemed like an eternity ago, yet at the same time, it felt like just yesterday. He'd found Brian sitting alone in the living room, staring at the coffee table.

Like that night, James just respectfully settled in next to his friend. "So, what's troubling you, Pal?" The term of endearment caused Brian to smile ever so slightly, and James hoped that was a good sign.

"Are they all in on it, you think?"

"Who, all the central bankers?" James realized now just how enormous this must seem to Brian. It had been difficult to face the reality of a single profession almost single-handedly taking down the people of the United States. Now, to be staring at the possibility that the source profession, which had sent others to wreak havoc, was now in a position to literally change the political landscape of the entire planet, was almost too much to comprehend.

James tried to be light. "Well, it's a good thing you are a gamer, Brian. Just keep your head in the game, and treat it like one."

Brian scoffed. "Yeah, well, I didn't realize how big this is."

"I know, son. But, it's not all of them—probably just a few." He ruminated on that himself for a moment, and then affirmed his own conclusion. "These things are usually done by just a few. But the others get caught up in it, not even knowing what they are doing. They have been propagandized to believe they are doing the right thing. That's how this usually plays out—no matter the game."

Brian sighed, still unable to shed the morose mood that blanketed him. Properly, but without any enthusiasm, he placed the handgun he'd been using back in its holster and set it back on the gun table he'd been using. He stood for a moment as if to shake something off, and then said, "Yeah, well, these are *real* criminals, James. They make the psychs look like pikers."

"I know. The psychs are just the lackeys."

"You know, while I was out here, I could see a few things clearly, James. One of them is that what these men, however many there are of them, have been doing may be criminal to our way of thinking, but it is *legal*. And that ain't right."

The silence was punctuated momentarily by the bugle of an elk, and both James and Brian couldn't help but turn in the direction of that distinctive sound. "Wow…" Then Brian came back to the subject. "I meant what I said in there. What Andy laid out would be called loansharking, racketeering, counterfeiting, and extortion if the Brothers were doing it. And their butt would be in jail for a very long time, on any one of those counts."

James nodded. It was true. Hearing Brian put it that way, James realized it was like a legal version of organized crime.

"And James, a lot of money and time gets spent locking up the mob bosses and the gang leaders, but these guys, they get a pass. It ain't right, brother. It ain't right." Brian shivered suddenly, and James couldn't tell whether it was the cool Montana evening air, or Brian's reflex emotional response to injustice.

"Yeah, I know."

"They're probably into drugs as well—one way or another they are linked to the Trojan Horse they encouraged and sent." He took a deep breath, held it for a moment, and let it out slowly. "And that cannot stand. I fought my whole life to stay away from the gangbangers and criminals in my neighborhood. My good mother, may she rest in peace, worked so hard to show me the way. She and Pappy were a light for me, and I'll be damned if I am going to let some sanctimonious, self-righteous foreigners trash my neighborhood now that we finally got it cleaned up."

It had been said without vehemence. His shivering stopped, and there was a resolve in Brian's voice that caught James' attention. He had heard that same resolve once before when Brian pledged to handle the people whose drugs had resulted in the violent death of every member of his family. He swore he'd handle the psychiatric/pharmaceutical cartels, and the game he had created had done that.

The bugle sound penetrated the blackness once again. It seemed even nature was out of sync, with an elk doing its mating call a month earlier than normal. They stood together now, looking out into the blackness past the range. Above, the night was so clear, the Milky Way seemed to almost envelope them in its haze.

"What are you two talking about?" Andy startled them, as he joined on foot. He was carrying a flashlight, but neither had heard him approaching.

"Oh, I was just asking Brian if he was up to creating another game," James said, trying to tease Brian a bit.

Having missed the rest of the conversation, Andy nonetheless challenged Brian. "Well, I sure hope so, because we don't want to play the game these guys have cooked up."

Brian snorted. "And this is going to take a real collaboration, Andy. You know that, don't you?"

Andy nodded. Turning to James he said, "Before we come to them in the morning, I need to make sure I am crystal clear on the theory, James. If I am, then we—and I mean all the men in that room, too—can figure out what can be done about it. Something can always be done. I want us to remember that."

"Okay," James said. "Let's review the theory. First, we all agree this is an enemy attack, and it is linked somehow to the drug mess we've found ourselves in. The perpetrators of this are involved. But, the primary attack is economic."

Andy stopped him. "So, James, the Money game in my first analysis, that's not just money in the hands of companies and drug cartels, or terrorists. That's the whole range of economics, and the ability of people to live at all?"

James answered, "Yeah, it's a financial takedown. That's the theory." Seeing that Andy agreed, he added, "And, it has begun."

"All right, so the primary attack is economic, and it has begun, and it's being engineered in all likelihood out of Basel, you say?" Brian was making sure he was tracking and that all three of them were on exactly the same page Andy had already laid out.

"Exactly," James said. "We have been devastated by this, even if the country doesn't fully know that yet. But what we are doing and experiencing right now, and the rest of the world's reactions as well—all were anticipated by the enemy. Our reactions are setting us up for their real attack."

Both boys were waiting for James to continue. Instead, he rather abruptly asked Andy a question. "What will they do? What will their *real* attack be?"

Andy thought for a moment. Brian and James waited, knowing he'd eventually answer. Finally, stifling the impulse to laugh, he said, "Well, Brian put it very eloquently when he said 'they'll repo the car.'"

"That's it? They'll repo the car?" James said, with some consternation. "All right. So, they want their money back, and all the interest, or they want all that we own. Jesus!"

Undaunted, James continued. "So, under my theory, we know what the enemy will do next. But what will *our* government do? Or maybe what are they already doing?"

"James, I hate to tell you this, but you're the one who is supposed to answer that question. You've got to put that into the equation of your theory, being that this is an economic takedown emanating from the Bank in Basel, Switzerland, man. Unless you feel Brian and I have time to enroll at Harvard and take a graduate course in this stuff."

James hesitated for a long time, chewing on his lower lip, mulling over an idea. "We are going to have to ask the Secretary of the Treasury in there if I'm even close on this, but my guess is that our government will attempt to pay the interest—even if it is raised—until the money runs out. Following that they will cut services and anything they can to reduce the outflow of cash, so they have more to give to Basel. Then they'll follow Argentina's lead and seize Social Security funds. Failing to end it there, they will then start into the hard assets of the citizen base."

"Hard assets?" Brian asked.

"Gold. Silver. Seized in an attempt to pay the debt."

"Right, repo the car!" Brian stepped away in agitation for a moment, as if clearing his head, then, taking a deep breath of fresh, cold air, he reentered their little huddle. "Okay, these are criminals. What you are talking about here is plain old extortion. Do as we demand or we do…"

"But, Brian, that's what is mystifying me. They already did it. It appears they have already triggered something. So, their real demand is for something else. What?" James was at a loss.

"To stop it." Andy said it so quietly they almost missed it.

"What did you say?" James asked.

"You just described the moves we will make. Their next move is to say, 'We can help you. To stop this, you have to…'"

"Ahh. I get it," James was turning it over in his mind, while Brian was just hanging there, waiting for the picture to emerge.

Continuing, James said, "And our next move is that we reluctantly agree to whatever they demand in order to stop the chaos and devastation…" He looked at it again, and nodded his agreement with his own premise. "That's your twelve points thing you laid out in there."

"Checkmate." There, Andy had said it. Brian and James could hardly breathe. As dry as the Montana night was, they had difficulty inhaling, as if they were in the humid South.

Each man lingered over that idea of checkmate for a long time.

"Our government walks into the checkmate move, am I right, Andy?"

"Yeah," Andy said, nodding. "The loser always moves into the checkmate move with either his offensive move, or his defensive move. In your theory, it will be a defensive move that our government thinks will protect us. Instead, we walk into the checkmate."

"Guys, I think I got this figured!" Brian sounded excited, as if he had spotted an opening that a football player could dart through to finish the play.

Explaining himself, he said, "Maybe, just maybe I got this." Seeing that they were both all ears, he jumped into it. "You said 'our government' will make this move and that move."

"Yeah, the government," James affirmed.

"Then all we have to do is figure out what *our* move is going to be. What is the White King's move, Andy? What do the people do, not the government?"

"Okay. Yes. I got it. They won't be looking for the White King to move. There's too much distance between them and us. They've only cal-

culated on what the government will do. Good stuff, Brian, good stuff."
Andy gave him a thumbs-up.

James wasn't exactly sure he followed where these two partners had just gone, but their behavior suggested they had landed somewhere, and that somewhere held some hope.

"I got just one question, James." Brian spun around.

"Yeah, what?"

"Can the men in that room—in there—scheme up something for Montana? Not for our government, but just for Montana? Can they save Montana?"

James honestly didn't know. "I don't know, Brian. They're bright. Most of them are Montanans, and it seems they are clearly motivated."

"That's good enough, James," Andy said, interrupting. "We just have to make some smart, completely unexpected moves to throw the enemy off its game."

Now they were cooking. Just as they had appeared to be of one mind when Andy quarterbacked and Brian received in what seemed like a century ago, and just as they had repeated that by figuring out the masterful game "White King Rising," they were starting to play off of one another.

Brian nodded. "Yep. If they can figure it out—a way for Montana to win and survive, even with all that's going on elsewhere in the country, then I can create a game that reveals that solution and we can get it out to the other states and countries, before the checkmate move occurs." Then, suddenly, Brian's spirit dipped a bit and he reluctantly said, "The only thing is, Andy, I don't know international finance. I am going to need a lot of help on the intricacies of that."

"No problem, Brian. You're going to be working in *concepts*. I'll see to that. With concepts, you won't get hung up in confusing intricacies and insider vocabulary. Nobody could play that game anyway. We'll leave that to the guys who are already drowning in their finance game. Theirs is complex. Ours will be simple."

"Yeah? You think?" Brian was genuinely hoping Andy could do that for him. *I know I can do a game. I just don't know if I can do a finance game.*

Almost reading his mind, Andy assured him, "Brian, look at me. Just like you figured out the criminal activities these men in Switzerland have been perpetrating legally, and compared it to the type of crime you and just about all of us have seen on the street, we'll lay it out like that. I know you can. We are going to do a finance game people can actually understand and play."

He didn't have to say any more. "Hmmm." Brian started to roll with an idea. "Yeah, it's what that guy in the saloon was wailing about. It's like credit card debt—just on a bigger scale and camouflaged behind status. You get credit. There is your funny money like the 'Boys from Basel.' It's not really money. It's funny money that doesn't exist, which they loan you and it appears on your card. You use the card, buy stuff, or make stuff. You get too many credit cards, so the bank lowers the limit, making you look like you are irresponsible and running too close to the new ceiling. When you are too close to the ceiling, they can lower your credit rating—too much debt, too close to maximum. When they lower your credit rating, they can now raise the interest rates from 9% to 29%. Your payments go up; you can't make them; and they come for the stuff. Basically, they get stuff that is real from money that didn't exist."

Something about his spiel struck Brian as humorous. Andy was impressed. It seemed to be a pretty good analogy—good enough at least to run past some of the big boys Walker was assembling. Then Andy got the humor of it, too. The picture of Brian explaining that to the men in the room was truly incongruous. He could hardly wait to watch their reactions.

"Now that's a paradigm shifter, if I ever saw one. International Finance and the global debt crisis reduced to 'your mama's credit card debt' situation," James mused.

"Well, at least it's a start," Brian joked. "I can at least think with that. And I bet the White King can, too. You know if the ideas are too complicated, I get a headache!"

Andy returned the joke. "So how's your head now?"

"Much better. Much better. But I'm going to need a visual aid." Brian pulled out his phone and immediately started texting someone.

James rounded them up suggesting they take this all into the lodge and get some sleep. Apparently the elk agreed, because he let out another piercing bugle just as they turned to leave.

Chapter 26

J ames could tell as soon as he entered the great room that Walker really needed to talk to him. Jerking his head in the direction of the veranda, signaling where he'd like to rendezvous, Bud started walking out.

Following dutifully, James wondered, *Wonder what has him all riled up?*

Looking at the men who were assembled and helping themselves to the buffet breakfast Walker and his rehired kitchen staff had put together seemingly overnight, James felt the unmistakable pall of their somber mood. No one spoke. They seemed isolated in their own worlds, as if in the total grip of fear. It was pervasive and contagious, and James was grateful frankly just to grab a roll on his way by the bar, and slip out from under the weight of the pall.

"Mikolas, are you sure your boys can deliver?" Bud wasted no time—his voice husky from lack of sleep.

"Yeah, sure. Why?"

"Look!" Bud pointed out into the manicured lawn area where Andy and Brian were playing football—running, tossing, huddling up, then separating yet again to work on a variety of pass plays. James didn't see anything unusual, since he was accustomed to seeing these two occasionally toss some balls.

"That's good, Bud. It's a good thing," he said, reassuring him.

"Really? To me it looks like they are goofing off. Look at how they're dressed even."

"Bud, listen to me now." James lowered his voice and raised his intensity. "They're dressed in warm-up clothes, and that is exactly what they are doing. They're getting in gear for a game, practicing some moves and synchronizing their timing."

Walker frowned momentarily, but did look back out at the two who were now scuffling with each other, swatting each other, and slapping each other on the back. Their laughter carried all the way to the veranda. Neither seemed aware they were being watched.

"Well, now that you mention it, it is quite a field they've set up out there." Bud was referring to a series of barrels the boys had apparently liberated from one of the barns and placed in locations and proximities to one another to simulate opponents, and the hole Brian would have to find—the hole Andy would have to penetrate in order to reach his wide receiver.

Both were still so agile, and talented, that from a distance, it looked like more of a ballet. With Brian running and darting in and out of the various barrel obstacles—sometimes jumping them, sometimes rolling around them, eventually reaching a clear spot to receive the incoming ball—it was obvious their timing was improving and the grace and harmony was almost fun to watch. Like their time together as high school football champions, Andy was pointing to direct Brian to certain locations, and loudly shouting at him as well. James laughed, as that shouting had been a bone of contention in their first apartment in Los Angeles. The neighbors didn't seem to like the raucous interaction between the boys as they created the game called "White King Rising."

Bud almost found it enjoyable, too, but he couldn't manage to relax into it. Judging by the frown on his forehead, Bud Walker was still worried.

I got to help this guy through this, James said to himself. "Bud, the fact that those boys still have a spirit of play, and are readying themselves for the biggest game of their lives, is how I know we got a fighting chance here!"

Walker looked questioningly at him. James took that as an invitation and continued. "Yeah, contrast that to your guys inside. Go ahead; take a look, Bud. They are so somber and serious they're almost solid. Atwater and Governor Fitzerman there look like they're made of granite. Hell, I almost had to have you put chains on me and pull me through the room, it's so dense in there."

Suddenly Walker laughed. It was true. Looking at "his guys," as James called them, from the perspective of the veranda, they were a pretty serious crew he had to admit. Looking back out at the boys just in time to see Brian literally leap over two barrels on top of each other, see him disappear as the ball went over and behind the barrels, and to see Brian suddenly emerge—ball in hand, having caught a pass totally blind—Bud did have to admit that "the boys" certainly seemed to inspire confidence. Their skills, implemented so playfully, made him feel lighter somehow.

"You see?" James asked.

"Yeah, I see." He paused for a moment, looked at the men inside who also were going to have to be at the top of their game, and said, "All our lives, it's been our skills in our professions, James. From here forward, it's going to be how *well* we play a new game."

"Right. And that's good news." Then, playfully, James cuffed Walker on the head mimicking what he'd seen Brian do to Andy. Walker loosened up a little bit, just a little, and then shot James a warning look.

He'll get it. Probably be a real nice guy if he had just a bit more sense of humor, James mused.

They were all assembled back in the conference room, which was almost bulging with men and computers, when Brian and Andy entered—dressed now in jeans and polo shirts. One could almost taste the fear and anxiety in the room, and James was so grateful that the boys looked totally refreshed. *I guess there's something to my doctor telling me I'd think better if I exercised more,* he chastised himself, making a mental note that if they got through this thing, and there was still such a place as the United States of America, he'd definitely get some kind of gym contract, and stick to it.

The men may have been a little shell-shocked and afraid after Andy's briefing from the previous evening, but each one knew he was in a fight, and that alone would prove devastating to a handful of men a continent and an ocean away.

Just as Bud rose to convene the morning summit, what sounded like a pickup with a broken muffler could be heard outside. It was loud enough to grab everyone's attention. Sure enough, outside, a white Ford pickup with a gigantic brush guard on the front, a battered cab and bed, spewing a bit of black smoke and sounding like a freight train, pulled up and parked right outside.

"Great, he's here!" Brian jumped up, left the room, and approached the young man who was sliding out of the truck. He was about thirty, clean-shaven, sporting jeans, a pressed Western-style sport shirt, and wearing a Stetson-shaped straw hat that was worn enough to reveal it as the man's favorite.

The rest of the men, who had arrived in private jets, Hummers, limos, or expensive SUVs didn't know who the man was, let alone what to make of him. The mystery was soon over when Brian brought him in and introduced him as Dusty Owens from Deer Lodge.

Offering Dusty a seat, he then explained. "We haven't had a lot of time for formalities, you know. Mr. Walker here brought us all together, and we've all found ourselves in a pretty important game. Problem is, most of us have never played together before. Well, I'm a pretty fair football player, as you may know." He was interrupted by laughter, as each man did indeed know the wide receiver who had played brilliantly for four years at Los Angeles Western University before partnering with Andy Weir.

Feeling the atmosphere warming up a bit, he continued. "Well, gentlemen, it's kind of like an All-Stars game, the way I see it. A bunch of guys—all superstars in their own town—are put together to play together, instead of opposing one another. Tough, actually, since everybody knows everybody else's strengths and weaknesses and are usually roughing each other up. Yet now, they got to play as a team—a new team. The way I see it, that's what Mr. Walker, and my man James here, have put together. In my mind you are all All-Stars."

The analogy wasn't lost on the men, and they relaxed, warming up to the idea of having Brian and Andy walking point, as team captains. Truth be told, each almost welcomed someone else being captain. Especially since they had no idea what game they were actually going to be playing. All the rules seemed to have been trashed as well, and they were in fact confused.

"Well, Andy laid out James' theory last night, and what conclusion his research had led him to. That was pretty gruesome, to be sure, but at least we now know the fight we're in. Right?" They nodded. "So, since I'm the guy who likes to have things simple, I thought we'd strip away some of the confusion about the game the opponent has been running against us. Okay with you?"

They were starting to warm up to him even more, sensing that this Dusty Owens had something to do with some kind of "show and tell" they were about to receive. Brian added, "The way I look at it, if you can't understand the words, you can't really get the picture. I mean just look: 'securities, mortgage-backed securities, bonds, treasury bills, notes, margin calls, derivatives, credit swap defaults, reserve capital, ratios, mark to market'—who the hell knows what those things mean?"

Playfully he turned to and singled out the Secretary of the Treasury, Commerce Secretary, and Bud, pointing his finger at each. "Okay, well you guys probably do. But not the average guy. His head probably hurts, like mine does, and he probably wants to run the other direction. You know, get the heck out of the finance world and leave all that 'complicated stuff' to the experts."

They were smiling, even the ones he'd poked fun at. "So, we're going to just simplify this, for simple folks like me."

"Dusty, if you don't mind coming up here with me, I want you to tell these men your story."

Owens somewhat abashedly complied and made his way to the front of a group of men whose faces he'd seen in newspapers, but who had never run in the same circles as he and his buddies. Though he ran a service station in Deerlodge, none of these men had ever patronized it, or if they did, they had not noticed the owner.

Setting him up, Brian simply said, "I asked Dusty here because when I listened to Andy last night, I realized Dusty's story, which he told me at the Frontier Saloon yesterday, was pretty much the world's story, and I wanted to draw a comparison between it and what's playing out around the world right now. But frankly, when I hear talking heads on the news trying to explain this and that and using vocabulary that you guys who went to Wharton may be familiar with, it makes my head hurt. I have to have this in layman's terms." Brian's self-effacing style was raising the trust of the men in the room.

"We're with you, Brian," the Assembly Majority Leader volunteered. "Truth be told, I suspect we're all in this pickle because none of us any-where understood the words, let alone the message. So, Mr. Owens, what did you tell Brian?"

"Sir, thank you. I don't really know why I'm here with you all, and I don't know what you are working on, but I can guess it has something to do with what I been seeing on the news. I'm Dusty Owens, thirty years old, married with three children, and I have owned my service station for almost ten years now." He stopped suddenly, lowered his head, and cleared his throat. "And, two months ago my wife's SUV was repossessed, and last week the bank foreclosed on my business."

It only took Dusty Owens ten minutes to explain the scenario of how, like other small businessmen who maybe didn't qualify for standard busi-ness loans, or who maybe had, but also needed additional credit lines that they could pick up through credit cards, he'd gotten a lot of credit going. Unbeknownst to Dusty, his story mirrored that of millions of Americans who had lots of debt, were paying their payments, but who suddenly had a bank reduce the limits on their cards, making it appear they were running now too close to the limit.

Not knowing what that would lead to, he'd found suddenly that his credit rating had dropped due to running too close to the maximum, and although he had not missed a payment, it wasn't long before he received notice that since his rating had dropped, he was no longer eligible for the lower interest rates he had enjoyed, and he was now being charged a rate 20 percentage points higher than he began the debt with.

Reluctantly, he shared how he'd not been able to make the payments since the adjusted payment exceeded his income, and that of course the bank had come for the auto. They also then came for the business assets to pay his business loan. With credit card companies suing him for what he owed them, and not wanting to declare bankruptcy, he felt he had no choice but to divert money from his business loan payment to the credit cards, expecting that the local bank would work with him on that debt. In the end, no one had worked with him. Late on all fronts now, the bank decided to cut its losses by taking the collateral he had offered—the business itself. And with the credit card companies now garnishing his wife's salary, a once stable middle class family was facing bankruptcy.

When he finished telling the simple tale, which certainly had less drama and fewer expletives in it than the other night in the saloon, he looked to Brian to see if that was all right. Brian stepped forward and said, "Thank you, Dusty. That was very helpful." Placing his right arm around Owen's shoulder, he indicated that he wanted him to stay there a little longer.

With his arm still there, holding the depleted man close to him, Brian turned to the men and said, "You know, Andy and I had nothing most of our lives. His mom was a widow, and I came from the ghetto. When we started making money, we paid off our investor, and to be honest with you, we don't owe anybody anything." Then, so as to not sound like a braggart, he hastily added, "Of course, we don't have much either compared to you folks. But, we do own homes and cars. So, this mess was pretty much off our radar screen. But I suspect that the rest of you are in the same boat as Dusty here, just on a larger scale." He paused to let that sink in, and to observe which of the men momentarily averted their eyes. To the man, they flinched.

"Thought so. A great equalizer, isn't it? Debt." The room was silent. Each seemed painfully aware that it is a trait of human nature to deceive oneself into believing one is immune somehow to the tragedies of life. Humility was entering the room.

"Well, here's what struck me about Dusty's story. It's the story of our government, too, and the governments of all the other countries who are now under attack. You see, Dusty wasn't squandering money and recklessly going into debt. He was building something. And when he couldn't handle it, somebody who used money that didn't exist to allow him to make something tangible, which does exist, came and took it."

Before anybody could react, he continued. "You may say that was the risk. You bet. In good times, Dusty Owens would not have fallen behind, and ultimately would not have lost his investment and his dream. But I have a problem with this 'layman's' story, and I think I have the same problem with America's story."

He turned for a moment and looked at Dusty. As he did so, Andy couldn't help but reflect on the irony of this seeming "redneck" and "boy from the hood," standing there giving a lesson to some pretty wealthy and fine people. *I don't think I'll be so quick to use labels for folks,* he told himself.

"Here it is, gentlemen. Fair investment, fair price, fair interest, fair risk, fair remedies—I have no problem with these things. But, the game was rigged from the get-go. And that's what I was giving you such a hard time about last night before I had to leave and go to the shooting range. Sorry about that, by the way. It just hit me hard what Andy was explaining, and I had to get my wits around it."

Bud responded for all of them. "It's okay, Brian."

"Yeah, well, a rigged game is being played globally, and a lot of people are getting hurt. While I don't condone a single thing the gangs do on their turf, one thing they do understand is you don't play a rigged game. You cheat a gang, you will pay."

The Attorney General was squirming in his seat now, not knowing where Brian was headed. Seeing that, Brian reassured him. "Don't worry, man, all I'm saying is we're not bound by those rules anymore. Only a fool plays by the rules of a rigged game. And I'm no fool. And neither are any of you. I don't see that as a Montana trait especially." That produced genuine guffaws of agreement. "So, you tell me, will the U.S. still try to play by the enemy's rules?"

"I believe so, yes, Brian," the Secretary of the Treasury answered. "It's a long engrained mindset, and I think our government will follow a predictable path. Maybe not even knowing the game was rigged—surely remaining in denial if they do recognize the possibility."

"Well, then, are we all in agreement that what the U.S. and other countries face is pretty much what our neighbor Dusty faced?" It seemed to be. He got no obvious dissenters. "Good analogy then?" It was.

At that point, he hugged Owens, thanked him for sharing his story, and walked him to the truck. When he returned, the Governor was ready to engage. As the executive of a state within the United States, any governor carries tremendous authority and natural rights. If the governor was experienced and strong-willed, he knew those rights and exercised them. If weak, he had pretty much toed the party line with regard to the central government in Washington, DC.

Governor Fitzerman had ridden in the middle. He knew gubernatorial authority but had rarely exercised it, having been content to govern one of the sanest of the fifty states that made up the nation. Frankly, he enjoyed the Montana lifestyle and relished his hunting and fishing and local festivals that dotted the map of Montana year round. He was a native Montanan, however, and today, he knew he would need to step up.

"Anyone here know what the government will do?"

CHAPTER 27

*I*f they thought Andy's briefing was frightening, the Secretary of the Treasury, and the Secretary of Commerce were about to step up the gradient. Seasoned professionals, as well as politicians, they knew exactly what the government would do.

They also knew that no one else in the room probably had any idea the role Montana was about to play in the national and global drama now unfolding. *This guy, Mikolas, must have known,* Secretary of Commerce, J. Craig Hodgson thought. *Wonder why he picked Bud Walker?* Making a note to ask James that question at a more appropriate time, he knew it was imperative that he answer the question the Governor had posed.

"After they exhaust normal processes of paying the interest, and the notes that are being called up, they will have to deplete the Social Security reserves. They will take President Roosevelt's path of declaring a national emergency, which will allow them to freeze bank assets, and the assets of private citizens as well. You're seeing some of that now."

The men nodded, and one asked, "That means the earlier efforts have failed, or at least failed to stop the bleeding, right?"

Hodgson nodded. "My colleague, the Secretary of the Treasury, will likely confirm what I am about to say next. Brace yourselves, this will not be pleasant." He looked around the room, grateful to see all eyes on him. "Since the U.S. dollar has nothing tangible backing it, with our gold reserves long gone, the Federal Government will logically attempt to bolster the dollar, looking for ways to back it with something tangible in the hopes of forestalling others dumping dollars, calling in notes, and every other panicky thing you've been watching on the news."

Knowing that he was at the very core now of America's economic foundation, he explained, "This sets up the quintessential battle between the private sector and the government." Over the next five minutes, he elaborated on the anticipated move by the government of the United States to take control of the tangible assets of gold, silver, copper, diamonds, sapphires, as well as gas and oil—for the "security" of its citizens—wherever those assets might be found.

Simon Atwater had decades of experience reporting on the financial machinations of every nation, and he knew in his gut that the United States Government would make exactly that move, justifying it in the sincere belief that the only way to save the country now was to strengthen its dollar by backing it with a hard asset, trying to appease the RIT into ceasing the sale of dollars, the calling in of loans, and the freezing of credit.

"Oh my God!" The Governor was the first to realize. Turning toward Walker, with almost a look of gratitude, albeit tempered with desperation, he said, "They will come for Montana! Our assets…" His voice weakened at the magnitude of it all, and trailed off.

There, he's said it, Bud thought. Every man there was suffering from an anxiety emanating from something they knew to be true, but which was hidden from view. It was gnawing away at their confidence. In that one simple statement by a governor who was often criticized for being too dull for the job, the deceptive veil was pulled back, and there stood the naked truth.

Montana held huge silver, copper, and gold mines. Its sapphires, mined in the Phillipsburg area, were regarded as the finest in the world. Oil was abundant, and what no one in its citizenry knew, aside from the government of Montana and the Federal Government, was that there was enough natural gas under Montana to supply all of America's energy needs for 200 years.

And in the face of a global societal meltdown and possible collapse of the infrastructure, the very survival of the American people might rest on the issue of energy. Bud Walker knew that was a story he could not write about, but he knew now there were two dangers here. One, the government would want the tangible assets in its defense against the Central Banks, and two, pending the failure of that strategy and the ensuing poverty and depression, it would want the energy to at least keep people alive. *Jesus, I wonder if Harley is counting on me to use my influence, in order to preserve the assets of my beloved Montana, to get Washington to agree to RIT's terms. Better they save us with their strings attached, than for us to plunder our own country.*

The enormity of the anticipated checkmate move was now totally real to Bud Walker. Moving from theory laid out last night to a real, physical possibility, he was stunned, but unwilling to be a punching bag anymore. Helped or not by Harley Grantham-Jones, Bud Walker was a decisive man with a lot of power and a sense of himself, and what he was capable of if he put his mind to it. Dismissing any sense of inadequacy, he stepped forward boldly to break the pall in the room.

"Governor, you need to call an emergency session of the full Legislature. Get everyone in!" Bud barked.

As if shaken out of a momentary reverie, the Governor signaled that was appropriate, and then, realizing that there was a very real chance this would materialize, he knew he had to call upon the constitutionally-provided, yet monumentally-controversial Militia. Until now, it was some shadowy institution that Montanans knew existed, had heard rumors about, but had never actually encountered.

Well, I guess I blow everybody's cover now, he thought, bracing himself. "And I need to call up the Militia."

There was silence in the room. No one wanted to be the first to speak. So, hoping to forestall any discussion, the Governor immediately added, "And the National Guard."

"They're all deployed in Afghanistan." Bud turned to see who had spoken. The Majority Leader of the Senate looked a little embarrassed to have had to point that out to the Governor, knowing it left the Governor only one alternative.

"Right," Governor Fitzerman said. "We'll call them up nonetheless. But, it looks like this will fall to the Militia."

Brian's reaction to the idea of the Militia had provided some much-needed levity and laughter. The look on his face had prompted Andy to warn Brian never to play poker, and it had prompted the Attorney General to jokingly explain to him, "Brian, we're the Militia, not the Ku Klux Klan."

That had prompted Brian to inquire into who was the "we" in "we"— only to be shocked when the Attorney General, the University Provost, the businessman from Kalispell, the Sheriff of Lincoln County, and the Senate Majority Leader stood up.

What had truly settled him down, however, was their assurance that this fight was going to have to be won without weapons, as clearly a population of less than 1 million people couldn't stand up very well to the rest of the country.

The matter was resolved for Andy when James leaned into both boys and quietly said, "Andy, Brian, this is not the CIA." No matter the myths about Montana, Brian and Andy both recognized they were dealing with some pretty rational people in this room, and they were going to have to table their discussions about militias for another day.

"Governor, I believe you should get your Chief of Staff to bring in the Chief. I think we're going to need him," the man from Treasury recommended.

Everyone could see the Governor had some reservations about this recommendation, mulled them over quickly, and then issued the order to his Chief of Staff. "I have no control over them, you realize, they are in another state. But, let's see if he'll come. No doubt they have gone down a road we may need to contemplate, and his experience would be welcome, as far as I'm concerned." The others murmured their agreement.

It had been a very long time since the Decatur Indian Nation had had any traffic with the territory they once controlled, and it was the first time anyone in authority in Montana had had any interest in what they knew or what they had done after the tribe's victory at Little Big Horn, followed by their subsequent defeat. It was all ancient history—taught in the school system of Montana perhaps, but nowhere else in the country.

None of the men from the East had any interest in this, except Bud. He was a bit of a history buff, and frankly, he welcomed the idea of the Chief on his ranch. Moving on, however, he abruptly changed the subject. "Governor, my helicopter is ready to shuttle you and the Senate and Assembly leaders back and forth from the Capitol. The Legislature is going to need to know what we are working on here, and I don't want you guys driving over that McDonald Pass into Helena any more than necessary."

Not even waiting for an acknowledgement from the Governor and his staff, Bud then turned to Ray and said, "Get all the trucks and crews you can get your hands on, Ray. Move them into Montana, and get Satellite feeds going into every city in the state—especially Billings, Missoula, Helena, Butte, Kalispell, and Bozeman. We've got to make sure the people of Montana can be reached, and that they get our news."

"You said *our* news?" Ray queried.

"Yep, I did, my friend." Looking Ray directly in the eye, he moved a step closer, almost knocking over one of the computer tables in the now-crowded war room. "We are going to let the other guys—Fox, CNN, whoever—be the mouthpiece for our enemy, spreading the PR, scaring and threatening folks. They'll do exactly what we all did. But, by God

WNG fell for this once, and I am not going to get caught promoting the agenda of our enemy in *this* fight. From this point forward, WNG becomes the Network of Solutions."

"But...." Ray never got the sentence out.

Bud interrupted him. "No buts, Ray. This is my God-damned empire, and I can use its resources any way I want. We'll let the other guys do their ingrained type of journalism. We are going to bring people one thing, and one thing only—solutions." Turning to the group who were standing quietly as he seemed to be upbraiding his own company president, he said, "You bring them, I'll broadcast them!"

Bud stopped, looked over at James, and suddenly laughed. "Guess we'd all better get some solutions then, right James?"

"Seems like a good plan." Having no idea what those solutions might be, however, or what they would do with them, James turned to Brian and Andy, hoping they could carry the ball.

Andy easily slid into the conversation. His quiet voice, perfect posture, and searing intellect seemed to calm the others. "Gentlemen," turning to Brian he added, "and Brian, you weigh in here any time." Brian gave him a thumbs-up that he was listening, and would.

Continuing, Andy said, "You need to do two things—whatever it takes. Brian and I will take it from there." Seeing that they were all leaning forward now, some taking notes on a pad, others preferring their iPads, he said, "You need to get a solution that allows us to survive, and be free. Make no mistake, Brian and I need you for that. You're the ones who hold the key there. It has to be two-fold. One part ends the game they are playing right now, and the other presents the new game in the form of the new solution. From there you create a pilot program."

Out of the corner of his eye, Andy could see that Brian was smiling now. They were in sync, and Brian knew where he was headed. "Once you have that, we will create a computer game that anyone can understand. The game is about survival, and it will be based on your pilot. We'll adjust it as we go, just as you will adjust the live program in Montana."

You'd be proud, Kelly, James thought. Pulling himself out of that momentary reverie, he turned his attention back to *what* Andy was saying, not just *how* he was saying it.

"The good news, gentlemen, is that bad guys always make mistakes, and in any game there is always a move you can make. In this case, the infrastructure of the Internet is still there, and likely to remain there. This isn't a nuclear Armageddon, or a biological one. I want you to remember that. With the Internet, and with the reputation of Carver & Weir, we'll spread that game throughout the United States and around the world, and we will stop the enemy cold."

To the man, energy returned. Still seated, they sat taller in their seats, a questioning hope in their eyes, but a hope nonetheless. They had a task. *Action cures fear,* Andy mused, remembering his early years in the chess world. *All people on defense are full of fear. On offense, there is action, and potential for victory.*

James hesitated to intervene, but he felt the target had to be exactly identified here if they were going to affect the best solution. Reluctantly, he asked the necessary question. "Do we know who we are fighting here, exactly? Momentarily, it's the U.S. Government, but who are all of us fighting, precisely?"

Andy, Brian, and James had done devastating damage to Terrorism, and to the enemies of the young people of the United States, in the past few years by knowing who they were fighting, and the likely channels those people would use to execute their war strategies.

Picking up on James' clue, Andy said, "Yes, thank you, James. It will be just a person, or a few people. We're not fighting entire communities or governments here. And we are not fighting every Central Bank. They, too, are victims of our actual enemy. Regrettably they are just low-level knights on the Black King's chessboard—doing exactly what he needs and wants."

"All right, so do we know for sure which men?" Fitzerman asked.

"One is Sir Harley Grantham-Jones." Bud's voice cut the silence. He knew the others were stunned now to hear his own friend's name, one they knew as a media mogul, banking expert, and humanitarian. Bud wisely let that sink in. Then, quietly he said, "And before you ask me if I'm sure, I am."

James knew there were *others,* however, and they'd need to know who they were. *Once CIA, always CIA,* he reminded himself. "I can find the others." James Mikolas had a new theory germinating.

"Ari, I need a favor." James hadn't spoken to his counterpart in the Mossad since Ari's report that the man who had killed Kelly had himself been killed. Yet he knew Ari would respond. With Israel's economy in ruins, and the hysterical stimulus-response violence that was coming up from all sectors, he knew Ari would welcome another shoulder at the wheel.

"Tell me."

They never change, the Mossad, men of few words. James smiled. "I need to know which commercial banks are being given money by the Central Banks. Then check the Board of Directors of those commercial banks and correlate the names to the Board of Directors of Central Banks."

"I'm not sure where you are going with this, James." Ari sounded a bit skeptical.

"We're going to find out who is creating this mess, Ari, to the man. Trust me on this. The list of names that emerges will be very helpful to your government, and to me." Before Ari could hang up he added, "Also, Ari, those banks still receiving money from the Central Banks—you know, still receiving loans—will be where Al Qaeda is banking now. Good hunting!"

"Yeah, we were just thinking they'd be where the money was still flowing, so your timing is good. We've got some of this research done. Not enough. It'll take me a few days."

"Make that hours, please. We don't have much time, Ari." Knowing he was demanding a lot, and yet knowing that the best way to handle a seemingly insurmountable problem was to take on yet another one, he said almost as an afterthought, "Also, check which banks are still lending to the pharmaceutical companies, or who have resumed lending, even in the midst of this chaos. Check their Board of Directors, and then cross-reference to the Central Banks' Boards of Directors and to the Board of Directors of the pharmaceutical companies. The Directors' names that appear on that triangulation are the real bad guys. Those are the ones I want."

There it was—the demand for data, which theoretically might link Al Qaeda, terrorism, drugs, pharmaceuticals, and banks—all together.

Ari said nothing for a moment; neither man did. Then, appreciatively, Ari said, "Thank you, James. I see something even in what you are asking for that we missed. This becomes a top priority here today. Where do I reach you?"

"At Bud Walker's ranch in Montana." Realizing that was probably startling news to Ari, he clarified it with his own style of humor. "Yes, sir, Ari. He really appreciated your 'Unwitting List!' Never saw such a change in a man. Almost a religious conversion I've witnessed in the last few weeks."

CHAPTER 28

*A*licia was not alarmed when she arrived at Guadalajara International Airport, just a bit aggravated that her plane was arriving ninety minutes late. Departures out of El Paso had been interrupted, as people were frantically trying to get flights out of the border city.

With the situation in Latin America deteriorating, and concerns spreading in the U.S. that there might be a wholesale incursion into the United States, many El Paso people were escaping to relatives in other states less affected by the progressive reduction in services occurring in the United States, and by the closure of banks. Her flight was to a city in Mexico, and had no such rush of people trying to get aboard. But, she'd been caught in the general delays at the airport, and a squall that had come through that held every plane down until it cleared the airspace.

Expecting to have arrived in time to meet Reagan and Edith at their gate for their flight in from Mexico City, she now speculated they'd be waiting for her at hers. Stretching to retrieve her carry-on, she was jostled repeatedly by passengers eager to get off and on to their next flight or into the baggage claim area.

This airport wasn't known for its great efficiency anyway, and arriving at siesta time always made the afternoon interesting. Once she disembarked, she found herself standing at the gate looking around, but unsuccessful in spotting either woman in the gate area.

Having checked to see if perhaps their flight, too, had been delayed, she was informed when she walked to that arrival gate that the plane had landed on time, about sixty minutes ago. Still no sign of Reagan and Edith. *Frankly, I'm surprised they didn't stick to the plan and wait for me here.* She chastised them in absentia.

All of them were carrying on, with no one checking bags, but she decided to check that area as well, just in case security had discouraged them from waiting in a gate area. Texting them while coming down the escalator, no one responded. Nor did they answer when she dialed their cells. *Damn it! I wonder if they even thought to upgrade their service to include international calls.*

Alicia's instincts now told her that something had happened to Reagan and Edith, but she did not know what or where it had happened. Trying to quash the fear that was rising, she checked her emails and her voicemail, just in case they'd left a message. She truly hoped they had just missed their connection in Mexico City, and for whatever reason, were not able to inform her.

She waited another two hours for the arrival of the next flight from Mexico City, and when neither woman was aboard, she knew something had intervened. *But where? After the El Paso check in? In Mexico City? Or here in Guadalajara?* She could barely suppress the mounting anxiety. *If only I'd been on time, I could have at least ruled out Guadalajara.*

Using some airline contacts she had at the El Paso airport, she was informed that both women had boarded the flight to Mexico City. That ruled out El Paso, and now squarely placed their disappearance in a foreign country. Whether it was in Mexico City, or Guadalajara, this was no longer a domestic issue.

They regained consciousness at almost the same time, though Edith seemed groggier. Her attackers had administered the same dose of the drug to both women, but with Edith having a much smaller frame, and being somewhat frailer, the medication had a stronger, more deleterious effect on her. She clearly seemed to be struggling.

Reagan was bound at the feet, with her hands also bound behind her back, and her mouth was taped. Nearly gagging from the effect of the tape across her mouth, and smelling the distinct scent of urine, she could tell by how wet she felt that she must have urinated while unconscious.

Though her instinct was to squirm and try to cry out, however muffled, she too was still drugged enough to be unable to move. Edith was seated opposite her in the back of a small, single engine plane, and seemed now to just be staring at her.

Dear God, please don't let her be suffocating! Watching her more closely through the fog of her own semi-unconsciousness, she finally concluded

Edith was not under extreme duress, just still under the effect of whatever their assailants had used on them. The restoration of her muscle activity was taking longer than Reagan's, and she did not seem to be focusing well. But, her breathing was normalizing.

Mercifully, Reagan fell into unconsciousness again just as the plane descended, skimming the top of a heavy rain forest, and landed in an open meadow. Neither woman would recollect the hasty hand-off from the plane's pilot to Hyena and his men, and the equally hasty departure of the plane to its point of origin.

Given that this was the second of several expected shipments of American women, Hyena himself still wanted to inspect the merchandise. Somewhat surprised at the age of the smaller woman, he nonetheless reminded himself that Samir had specifically said any woman, any type, any age, as long as she was American. A quick check of the two women's passports confirmed they were United States citizens.

At that point, Hyena tied a red scarf around the ankle of each woman, and had them moved to the hut higher on the hillside. Four other women were already inside, fearful and cowering. Wanting to maintain, if not elevate, that fear—to keep them in line—he rather brutally dropped Edith and Reagan to the ground. Knowing they might be bruised from this "transport," as he would call it, he was very certain they would have no serious or lasting damage.

The point was to further unnerve the other girls who were now awake, and terrified by the sudden change in their circumstances.

Alicia had waited at her hotel as long as she could. She had hoped for a miracle that the women may have remembered where they would be staying, and gone on by themselves. But her gut told her they would not be there. She checked her email and text messages every half hour for another ninety minutes, and then went to the U.S. Consulate in Guadalajara. When asked why she needed to see someone, she told them simply, "I need to make a missing persons report."

That did rouse interest, especially when they learned she was a journalist from WNG. She had lied a little about that, given that she had officially resigned following the discovery that her lover, Samir Taghavi, was Al Qaeda's propaganda chief. But she knew that a journalist covering a missing person report could be helpful or harmful to the political types who would be assigned the case, and she was determined to make certain they acted on this quickly, with the resources she knew the United States Government had.

It worked. Not more than thirty minutes following her filing the report, and giving her verbal statement to Consul Caesar Espinosa himself, he summoned her into his office and explained that he had confirmed the two women did in fact make the flight to Mexico City, but had not been aboard the flight that arrived in Guadalajara.

That ruled out Guadalajara. Whatever happened, it had happened in Mexico City. Fearing the possibility of kidnapping, he told Alicia to return to her hotel, and to wait there until he could engage the Mexican and U.S. officials in Mexico City and get them to launch an official investigation.

Seeing that she was about to become hysterical—probably fearful that she was being given some kind of bureaucratic run around—he reassured her that the United States took the kidnapping of its citizens very seriously, and that the Mexico authorities were diligent and cooperative. Mexico clearly needed every bit of support they could garner from the United States to handle its drug war problem, and part of the tit for tat was rapid, and Mexico-style investigations into missing persons.

Alicia relaxed a bit. Then he asked if by any chance these two were journalists. She said no. His response was, "Too bad. They perform even better when journalists are involved." Seeing her spirits sink, he tried to cheer her up with, "That's on the good guy side. On the bad guy side, they perform worse. So, in the long run, your girls stand a better chance, not being journalists."

All Alicia could do was shake her head, try to breathe, and show him on her smart phone, hands trembling, a photo of the three of them, taken earlier at a picnic with some of her local friends. He downloaded and printed the photo, very neatly printed the names of each woman under their respective picture, and handed it to his assistant for copy and release.

"I'll get this scanned and over to the Mexico City office right away. And I'll call you, I promise. He wrote his cell phone number on the back of his Consulate card, and told her to call if she got anxious."

Alicia believed him. *A few hours, I'll give it a few hours,* she planned. *I must think, though, what else can I do?*

Shortly after leaving, however, it was gnawing at her that she had not told the Consul the whole story. Sensing that the real purpose of their trip to Mexico might be very relevant to finding Edith and Reagan, she pulled out his card, tapped it a few times; then, turning it over, she dialed Consul Espinoza's number.

"I thought of something that might be important." She paused, still weighing whether or not to tell him.

"Ms. Quixote, if you have something to tell me, please do." He sounded impatient.

"Yes. Well, they are not journalists…that is true, but they were coming to Guadalajara to meet someone who could give them information on the routes and destinations slave traders are using in Latin America. I don't know if it makes any difference, but I thought you should know that."

There was a long silence. After what seemed like an hour, he succinctly responded, "It makes a great deal of difference. Thank you for telling me." He hung up unceremoniously.

What Alicia had no way of knowing was that the Consul was well aware of a drug cartel out of Colombia that was diversifying and adding human trafficking into its portfolio in recent months. Guessing there might be a connection, that bit of information allowed him to reach the DEA and its Mexico counterpart, asking for assistance.

It was no longer a simple missing persons, probable kidnapping case. It was most likely human trafficking through a drug ring—or at least that is how he would present it—and both governments had a great many resources available to them to track and monitor cartels, and their suspected hideouts.

He prayed now that his DEA colleagues might already be tracking the activities of the drug cartel whose bragging rights now included slave trafficking. He was hoping also that the cartel would house both its drug business and its new subsidiary human trafficking business in one location, especially since the human trafficking industry was new to them. With any luck, they would not yet have set up separate compounds and transit lines.

Wishing Alicia had provided that information from the get-go, he closed out his tab at the Cantina quickly, returned to his office, and began to interrupt friends just as they were settling in for dinner. *This just may make a difference,* he thought.

CHAPTER 29

*T*he arrival of Chief Soaring Eagle of the Decatur Nation, his grandson, and staff had been quite an event that morning. They flew in on their private Beechcraft King Air 350 and were greeted by Governor Fitzerman and Bud Walker personally. Given one of the prime suites in Bud's main house as their quarters, it was less than an hour before they were prepared to meet in the War Room.

Introductions were in order as the Attorney General and Secretary of Commerce had never met the Chief, let alone his Wharton-educated grandson. It was William Graywolf Monroe who was reputed to have brought the Decaturs onto the silver standard, revolutionizing how they did business, with each other, and with anyone who traversed their reservation.

There was a distinct family resemblance, and he and the older Chief were obviously close. Two generations were educating each other: one in heritage and the other in business and commerce. It was a powerful partnership, which had attracted the attention of their neighbors Montana and Wyoming, but was little known in other states.

Bud made certain his Chief of Staff spent time with the two men, and that Simon Atwater was introduced as well. Montana's Secretary of the Treasury hailed from Eastern Montana, and was probably the most familiar with the new business model and new nation model this early Montana tribe had created in recent years.

What struck all the men in the room, as the elderly Chief entered—dressed in business attire—was a quiet confidence the man exuded. William Graywolf manifested the same poise, and neither seemed to be jockeying for position amongst the other political and business leaders. Rather they both seemed reserved, following the lead of their host.

Andy, Brian, and James had met the two in the hallway, as the Chief and William Graywolf were being escorted into the room. Simon Atwater explained the role these three were playing here, which caused the Chief to stop, and without speaking, look each one over almost from top to bottom. He spent an extra amount of time looking at Brian, then gently patted Brian on the upper arm and said, "You remind me of someone I knew long ago." That was all. He then turned and entered the War Room.

James peered into the room ten minutes later, noticing that everyone was at the conference table. They seemed comfortable; but there was no discussion going on. It was almost as if they were waiting for someone to say "start."

Motioning for Andy and Brian to casually look in, he said, "What do you think, Kid? Should we prime the pump?"

Andy chuckled. "I think so, James, or we'll be serving them lunch soon!"

"Yeah, we're burning daylight here," Brian tossed in. James and Andy both suppressed a smile, impressed at the rural lingo Brian was picking up. Then, as abruptly as he had used a Montana phrase, he switched to the Brian of Los Angeles. "Let's get that crew working!"

Andy motioned for the two to wait a moment while he went into Walker's study. Having seen a chessboard in there, he retrieved it for use within the War Room.

All right, it's game on! James thought, as he eyed the familiar chessboard and what that portended in the hands of Andrew Weir. With no hesitation whatsoever, Andy dove in front of Brian, wanting to engage the men first. Signaling to Bud that he wanted to speak, Bud seemed tremendously relieved to have him break the stalemate of silence. It was not tension, just the silence of men who are stymied—not knowing where to begin.

Guessing that this chess set held a high monetary value—given the intricate carving in dark white mahogany—and was more of an office decoration than it was a tool or game for Bud Walker, Andy gingerly set it down on the conference table, positioning it in front of him as he stood to Bud's right. That got everyone's attention.

"Would it help you gentlemen if we took a look strategically at how to stop the checkmate move?"

There was a chorus of "yes," "yeah," and a sense of relief. Andy had correctly spotted that the men's minds were confined by their very expertise. Conditioned to thinking patterns and solving problems according to the rules they had learned and used through the years, all of them were stuck. He'd seen it before with chess champions he'd beaten. They had a routine, and could win handily—as long as the opponent conformed to that routine and conventional chess moves. *Guess this is why they say I'm a natural chess player,* Andy realized. He had never thought in routines and predictable chess moves, and he was renowned for doing the unexpected. That had made him the Grandmaster he had become by age eighteen.

"Okay. We're in a game, gentlemen. That's the first thing you need to remember. It is a game." He could see by some of the recalcitrant looks that the end of the United States and the world as they knew it didn't seem like a game to them. *I have to help them here. Got to keep this simple,* he thought.

Looking at the chessboard, set for the checkmate move he expected the RIT to set up, he experienced a flash of an idea. He stopped, forcing the men to wait, as he examined the idea. Before any doubt about the boldness of the move could creep in, Andy Weir did what he had done thousands of times before in his career—he trusted his instinct. *Make the move, Andy, just make the move,* he coached himself.

"To end this game and stop the opponent, there could be many possible moves. In a perfect world, you'd all have the time to figure it out. But time is short. Let me show you what I think you need to do. This one is the one I would recommend. Just when the enemy expects you to step into the checkmate move, do this." Then very deliberately, he took the board and spun it 180 degrees so that the Black team was *facing* its own chess pieces. In short, *they* would step into their own checkmate move. Having gambled everything on the position of the pieces on the board, when the White player balked by turning the table around, figuratively speaking, Black had no move to make. That would lead to the chess phenomenon called "a draw." The White *player* would now be holding the black pieces set in the configuration to checkmate. And the Black *player* would now be holding the white pieces, with their next move being the one that would defeat them. Obviously, the Black player would not make the move. He would not step into a defeat he had orchestrated for the other guy.

Well, it seemed obvious to Andy at least. To him, the demonstration was nothing more than somebody switching sides in a debate—advocating one thing one minute and then the opposing side the next. Regrettably none of the men today, however, seemed to have the foggiest understanding of the demonstration he had just provided. It appeared they had even less understanding of the overarching strategy of a player simply refusing to move, and turning the game back to the opponent.

They may have been impressed with the visual of turning the table, but had no idea of how to do that in a real life situation. So, they were still stuck, trying to puzzle through Andy's illustration. Brian was the first to get it. "Hah!" He walked to Andy's side, knowing he could help here.

"Uh, guys, my head is starting to hurt again!" That produced laughter, since it allowed them all to escape from the awful feeling they had that they were a little dull. "I'm just a guy with an ordinary background. Most of you know this. As you might know, Andy and I were never partnered in chess, just football. I could understand *that* game. So, if you don't mind, I'd like you to look at this through the game *you* have a greater familiarity with.

"Gentlemen, do you play poker?" he asked, looking pointedly at Andy, who got the hint immediately and stepped aside. He could tell by their faces that they all did, even the Chief, who was laughing now. It seems they all had something in common.

"All right then. What Andy just did in chess terms is what I would label calling their bluff. Black was bluffing, and Andy called them on it. Understand I don't play poker, but do you understand what I just said?" They did.

Bolstered by that, Brian continued to think on his feet. "Okay then. They are bluffing, expecting you to pay or accept their terms. They are all in on the game as it appears right now, given what's going on around the world. So, help me here, guys; what happens in poker if you spot that the dealer is crooked, and you all decide to fold your hand—at the same time?"

"That hand is done," Bud answered. "In high stakes poker, the pot stays there, for the next hand. In the kind of poker the Governor plays, the house takes the pot if you fold." They all laughed at that joke at the Governor's expense, but he didn't seem to mind.

"Yeah, right!" he retorted.

"And, if there is not another hand? If all the players walk away?"

"The house keeps what's in the pot," Walker responded. It was clear he was still thinking this through.

"Andy said the other day we would need smart, unexpected moves. Well, how is walking away from the game entirely, refusing to play *or* pay?"

It had almost seemed too easy. Decades of mental programming and playing by rules put in place by an actual enemy, carefully disguised as a friend, had been blocking any kind of flexible thinking. For the moment, the men around this table were just playing, shooting the breeze, tossing out an almost preposterous idea. Yet, to the man, they were stopped and stunned.

"Doesn't that end the game of International Finance as we have known it for decades—all at once—forcing every player, and I do mean *every player* into a new game?" Brian said it the way Brian usually expressed an insight. He looked around, and added, "You know I don't know finance; I know games. In theory, as a game strategy, is that feasible?"

The men were still stunned, their minds valiantly preparing to offer up any and every objection and "yeah, but it's not possible" that could be imagined. As those calcified concepts were working themselves forward for discussion, one voice quietly said, "Yes, it is." William Graywolf Monroe looked Brian directly in the eye and repeated, "Yes, it is."

Now it was between the two of them. "But every player has to walk away from the dirty game at once, no hangers on, right?"

William nodded, joined now by the Chief.

Knowing there were going to be some fireworks on this, Brian decided to play by the rule of "he who speaks first wins." He'd used it before in talking himself out of a scrape or two in Southeast Washington. He could run fast, but he could also talk an opponent into submission. That had been the genesis of his marketing genius, where he could see and present almost any point of view.

"Call their bluff. The United States should have called the bluff of the Central Banks, but didn't...so we have to teach people to call the bluff now, if we are to survive."

His first ally appeared immediately, as the Secretary of Commerce said to Simon Atwater, "You know, he's right. It's a little crude, the poker analogy, but basically, the U.S. did not call the bluff. It *is* a bluff. Stunning!" Hodgson inspected that idea for a moment, almost relishing the realization that in addition to deception, there had been a masterful bluff. "And we've all been looking inward so much we would have missed their 'tell.'"

He continued. "We've got this paradigm that these banks are friends, acting on our behalf, and we needed their expertise and their apolitical ideas."

"Apolitical my ass," the Governor responded in language he used regularly in his Helena State Office, but rarely around constituents. "This is total global politics."

Atwater agreed. "Yes, Bruce, all he's saying is we had decades of acceptance of that idea. We surrendered our autonomy in a manner of speaking."

"The lie told often enough becomes the truth," James inserted, and then added, "It's an old propaganda technique, which our enemies have always used. It appears this one, too."

"Remember as we go forward that we must replace the old game with a new game for this to work," Andy said. "We are talking about games here. If you knock out one that has been the stable game for all countries, and you put nothing in its place, you have confusion and anarchy. But, if you replace it with something new that becomes the stable game, then stability can occur." He stopped for a moment, and then decided to prove the point. "You saw that happen with what Brian and I did just now. I ended a game suddenly, and you didn't like it. Ending the chess game, you didn't like. But when Brian came up and inserted the poker analogy, you grasped the poker game and ran with it."

Letting that sink in for a moment, he then asked the Chief, "Is that what you did, sir?"

Nodding, the Chief responded, "Yes. We ended the game of U.S. currency, and simultaneously began the game of Decatur silver, tapping our resource and creating coins."

A year earlier, each of the men at this table would have perhaps scoffed at, or at best ignored the somewhat unorthodox financial dealings of the Decatur Nation. Today, though, it seemed they were facing the same type of circumstances now that must have caused a people they had long ago conquered to take action.

Without a hint of resentment or make-wrong, the Chief finished with, "It was the right thing to do."

"Where's Andy?" James asked, as everyone was reconvening after a bathroom break.

"He's outside trying to reach Reagan."

"Oh. Okay."

"She didn't call last night, and he's a little worked up about it."

James laughed. "Yeah, well we do get attached to them, don't we?"

Andy returned, still seeming distracted. "I gather mission not accomplished?" Brian joked.

Trying to shake it off, Andy said, "Right. Still didn't get her. Went straight to voicemail. I'll try her later."

Brian resumed exactly where they had left off. Figuring he was a good one to cover this, he said, "You have to get that they are creating a slave society. You know I had a Pappy who fought in World War II, who endured a lot, frankly. But he taught me not to think like a slave and not to act like one, just because other people had problems with blacks."

Andy scanned the room. They were listening, especially the Chief. "Anyway, he taught me what the definition of a slave was. It's someone who is forced to work, through fraud or threat of violence, for no pay beyond subsistence."

"That pretty much covers all of us here—if those points Andy showed us were to be implemented. Basically we work for subsistence to pay off a lifelong debt." Bud Walker was looking at that. He'd always enjoyed history, but he had not looked at the situation from this angle.

"Matter of fact," Simon Atwater added, "You just described my ancestors. I'm an eighth generation descendant of an American Revolutionary War patriot. He was an indentured servant who fought with Washington to gain freedom, and a piece of land."

Looking around the room now, each man seemed to carry a subtle bond one to the next. In their heritage was slavery, and eventual freedom. That faint voice, which lives within most free men who have come from bondage, whispered to each of them now. They had a common denominator, and unmistakably, a responsibility to fulfill. Each man looked down for a moment, as if gathering his strength and wits. It seems each of them had had a "Pappy."

"These new age slave masters also finance terror and war. And, if you take Brian's logic, they have created a world of indentured servants who have a debt to pay off, and who have the character to adhere to it as a point of honor." James summed it up for them. Ironic laughter permeated the room.

"My fiancé, Reagan, works in human rights and has told me about millions around the world who are in debt and must slave to work it off. She doesn't know the half of it, I'm afraid," Andy reflected.

Before everyone could go into agreement about simply ending the game, the Attorney General put his "legal hat" back on and stated the obvious. "A debt is a debt, is it not? Would you have us dishonor ourselves by shrugging? Good men try, don't we?"

Surprisingly, Andy responded immediately and decisively. "Yes, Mr. Attorney General, they do, but you fell for a propaganda trick in there. A debt is a debt, but it's implicit it's an honest debt. Let me ask you all something: would you have played chess, football, or poker if the game was rigged?"

To the man, the response was, "No."

"And that's the move you need to see. The game was criminal, and it was rigged. These men—whoever they all are—gambled that the U.S. Government and the good people it represents would play fair, would try, would do anything to avoid a default. They preyed upon your goodness and the rest of the world's as well. Change the game."

"You all can make it 'right' later," Brian added. "That's part of the new game you put in, but right now, we have to survive."

Andy weighed in, uniting their message just as they had done so often while speaking to their generation on college campuses and community centers around the country.

"To create a new game, which replaces the game RIT put in place, all we have to do now is play a little game of *what if?*"

It was early evening in Basel, Switzerland, and Sir Harley Grantham-Jones had convened a summit of the five conspirators to determine exactly when they would make the call to the President of the United States, informing him of the offer to save the U.S. economy, and its attendant stipulations.

Across the ocean on a very humid Washington, D.C. afternoon, the President and his advisors had convened their own summit, anticipating the "offer" that would be forthcoming, knowing that accepting it to save the country could very well change its form of government. Throughout the centuries, men of power and influence had faced such moments, such impending defeats, and such hard decisions. No one in that summit had ever really contemplated that such a moment would occur in their time.

But back in Montana, a group of men with almost no influence and power said, "We *were* the New World once. We just remembered who we were, and what we did. We prospered, and we will again."

CHAPTER 30

*I*t had been simpler than expected, this "what if?" game upon which Andy had them embark. He had simply said, "What if there had been a catastrophe globally, and you were left with no currency supply—no money—and no government to support you? What would you do?"

Once they had mentally cleared their minds and truly gotten the idea of a world where the people had no U.S. dollars, no currency, and no one to help them, they took to the game as executives do when companies send them into the woods for survival and team building exercises. This, though, looked like it was the real thing.

Hard as it was to imagine that their country could come to this point, the end of the "we will borrow whatever you will print and will pay it back at whatever cost" game seemed imminent. Either the game would end in the violence they were already watching engulf the world, or in the surrendering of their form of government and decisions relevant to the nature of their government to a handful of elite bankers on another continent—reversing two hundred years of sovereignty, freedom, prosperity, and power—or they would just walk away, and create a new game and build America back somehow.

Inclusive in their deliberations was the understanding that the Central Banks were not part of our original Constitution. That had been pointed out by Attorney General Troy Davis. The banks inserted themselves into the landscape of government and politics, and were embraced along the way. They ostensibly worked on behalf of the countries whose currencies and monetary policies they were set up to monitor and protect.

It was quite an epiphany for the group of men when they realized that the countries themselves were still there—even if their economies were imploding in a domino effect—and they were able to function and probably willing to continue to do business with each other. All the nations had to do was figure out a way for that to happen, without the meddling of the middlemen bankers they had set in place. Once a good idea, it was now a cancer eating away at the society.

What men create and set up, they can change. Bud Walker summed it up with, "The Central Banks are not part of the Natural Order! They are a man-made phenomenon. And they have been paid handsomely for what they have done."

"Damn right on that, Bud," Atwater chimed in. "They hold huge gold reserves, which they earn interest on." He let that sink in and added, "That's commission enough. I say it's time for *them* to negotiate."

And there it was—the realization that the debt was from country to country—no matter what type of financial instrument had been used. If the countries could work out a way to deal with one another in a new and better game, the stranglehold of the bankers would be over, and a long, arduous recovery could occur.

What was true for one nation to another nation held state to state, county to county, town to town, and person to person. That additional, stunning realization opened the door and moved the men in Montana ever closer to exploiting the tiny windows the RIT had left open.

The Sheriff of Lincoln County said it best, his words reminiscent of some sheriff from long ago who was raising a posse in advance of a mission. "It's obvious to me, men, that what we need to do is draw from our heritage. We did it before, a few centuries ago. We came from nothing, and built something from nothing. We can do it again. All we have to do is ask ourselves, 'What did we do?'"

That was the release point. Ideas flowed, turning into a cascade of remembrances from forgotten history classes and civic lessons, and especially remembrances from stories told by grandfathers to their grandsons. They began to remember.

Sir Harley Grantham-Jones, and the drug cartels he had unleashed over time to sedate and subdue great people, had never expected one of his greatest prophesies to be fulfilled. Years earlier, he had coached Antonio Braghelli and the others on something he had learned from the great American Abolitionist, Frederick Douglas—only he had twisted it to suit his goals. He told them, "A sober slave is a dangerous slave. He will try to get free." That had become the justification for the drugging of an entire planet. They were to be kept "drunk"—never being allowed to have a clear enough day thought-wise to contemplate escaping from the plantation called planet Earth.

The game "White King Rising" had in fact started to sober the slaves, awakening the intelligence and strength of the American people—most especially its youth. Those same young people would soon be called upon again, using a new computer game.

Meanwhile, the game's designers napped in the bunkhouse, knowing that within hours it would be their turn. They had asked for a prototype solution. They were about to receive it.

CHAPTER 31

" **T**hank you, Harley, for the information. I wondered why you had not called, as you had promised in Basel. Seems like CNN and FOX got quite a heads up though." Bud was feigning a degree of disapproval, trying not to give away his awareness of his friend's duplicity. *Fool me once, shame on you. Fool me twice, shame on me,* he thought.

Judging by the lag on the line, Bud could almost see Harley mulling this curt, borderline critical response over in his mind, deciding whether to engage. Apparently, he felt he needed to get a true assessment of where his protégé was with this.

"I know I promised you—what is it you Americans call it?—'first dibs' on the information, but frankly, Bud, I was somewhat at a loss to discuss this with you. You know how I feel about the United States and its role in the world."

"Yes, I do." Bud had again answered curtly, leaving Grantham-Jones in mystery as to the chilliness in the conversation.

"Well, my dear fellow, I assure you I personally have spoken to no one. The information you have been watching was regrettably given out by colleagues. It most decidedly, and most regrettably I might add, has contributed to the hysteria."

Well, that's the first true thing he's said, Bud thought. *That means his next statement is likely to be false.*

And it was. Harley Grantham-Jones made the mistake of telling Bud Walker that this whole affair could have been avoided, had it not been for the United States Government, most specifically its Congress—acting on behalf of a very uninformed and self-centered public. Though he regretted having to be the bearer of that news to his friend, he hoped that at least one network in the U.S. was prepared to lay the responsibility where it properly rested.

Trying not to be too overbearing and obvious in his indictment, or too fawning in his apparent appreciation of the Executive Branch of the U.S. government, he nonetheless was carefully planting a seed of a story—if WNG chose to grab it.

What Harley Grantham-Jones could not see, however, was Bud Walker slowly smile. He had had a fairly thorough indoctrination recently in Divide and Conquer strategies, and he spotted the makings of just such an attack in Harley's desire to estrange the American public from its Congress, and attach themselves to their Executive Branch.

The chess move, as described by Andy Weir, was confirmed at that moment. Had he had any doubts, he no longer did. The RIT was getting ready to make its offer, and Harley Grantham-Jones was the Public Relations guy who was once again working to get the media to foster the division in America, allowing the President of the United States to take extraordinary measures without even so much as a whimper from the people.

Looking across the room to the chess set Andy had returned to its table, Bud nodded his head up and down, thinking, *Gotcha!*

"Well, Harley, as I said, I thank you for that consideration, and we will give it some attention at our next editorial staff meeting. I have to rejoin some people right now, but good luck to you in this mess. I trust you are staying out of the line of fire. And please give my best to Sylvia," he ended, pretending he did not know Harley's whereabouts.

That truly left Sir Harley in mystery as to what Bud Walker had or had not guessed—which was exactly what Bud wanted.

"I see you have a bit of a mean streak in you, Bud," James joked, as he placed one of his now-famous tuna fish sandwiches in front of Bud. He had caught the cat and mouse game Walker was playing with his mentor.

"You think so, Boy Scout?" Eying the sandwich, he added, "Let's take this outside and enjoy some fresh air."

He was reluctant to end his stay in the port city of Porto Alegre. The climate, fragrances, flowers, and freedom of motion he experienced had truly relaxed Samir. Knowing that no one was really looking for him, save that rabid Mossad agent who had been blood-hounding him for the better part of a decade, he had begun to enjoy the kind of lifestyle to which he had grown accustomed in Paris and Los Angeles.

Deciding that he would return to this bit of paradise on some future trip, when he had some layover time before connecting with Hyena's men for the transport into the camp, he saved the phone number of the café and hotel he had visited in his contact lists.

Next trip, though, I'll suggest Cuba, he planned. *Just in case they can offer us a more direct and less costly route.* Plus, the idea of spending time in the city of Havana was pleasing to Samir. He'd seen movies and heard tales of the once-splendid and deliciously decadent city, but had never had an assignment there. Quite the opposite. Al Qaeda would deal with Cuba, but there was no love lost between them. *Probably the politics,* he concluded. *Castro has some; Zawahiri is the chameleon who has no true politics, save the politics of Ayman Al-Zawahiri.*

Inhaling deeply, as if to take the fragrance with him, Samir Taghavi paid his bill, rose, and headed for the rendezvous point in Pelotas, a few hours to the South. From there, he would follow the route used before, and should be at the camp in a few days. He was planning on checking the "merchandise," and assessing the value of the first shipment of women he would be delivering to the Doctor, to satisfy the Doctor's unique thirst for vengeance.

Let's see what the Hyena has in his lair. What has he caught, I wonder?

"Want a sandwich, Governor?" James offered, as Fitzerman approached Bud and James, sinking into one of the dozen or so Adirondack chairs that decorated the veranda.

"No, thank you, James." Then, thinking twice about it, he added, "Sure, come to think of it."

Gulping the sandwich down, Governor Bruce Fitzerman informed them he'd summoned the Secretary of State as well, making it a full complement of his Executive Branch once she arrived. Clarissa Cameron had had to arrange for her parents to sit for her two children. As a single mom from Haver, she was the only woman on the Montana Cabinet. Newly appointed following the death in a skiing accident of the man the

Governor had initially selected, he viewed her as competent, but just a little bit distracted and tentative.

He was appreciative then that she had sensed the magnitude of being summoned to Walker's ranch, and had taken measures to free herself, and to be ready for whatever might be needed. Once her childcare arrived, she would be on the road to Ovando.

"You know that was quite a bomb shell, wasn't it?" Fitzerman commented, in relation to the exposing by the Lincoln County Sheriff of the secret trust fund holding $2 billion in it. Though the Trust was not technically a secret, almost no one in Montana was aware of it, and never bothered to get to page 18 of the audited State Budget. Taken from tax revenues, and invested into, of all things, Fannie Mae and Freddie Mac and other such "stable" investments, a peculiar law made it unusable by the people of Montana for anything much. Thus, it had just been accumulating money.

Sensing that the Sheriff was a very shrewd finance man, and investment advisor, he had nearly lost his breakfast when he realized the entire fund might have evaporated in the wake of the burst of the housing bubble, the discrediting of those mortgage giants, downgrading of their stock, and takeover by the government.

What would prove to have been a stroke of foresighted genius on the part of the Secretary of the Treasury came to light only when the man almost timidly explained he had pulled Montana's investment out of those funds—on his own authority—and that, for now, the money was just sitting on account. Its use was limited by State law, but it was *there*.

Laws are written, and laws can be changed, the Governor was thinking. If Sheriff Peters' idea proved workable, there was truly the possibility of Montana seeing some daylight, and leading the counter attack in what they hoped would eventually be known as one of the most effective surprise attacks ever put together in the annals of military or business history.

"What are you looking at, Bruce?" Bud asked, seeing the politician just looking into the distance, almost unconsciously eating the sandwich.

"I don't know. What am I looking at here?" he asked, coming out of his reverie and pointing to some mountains on the Continental Divide.

"That's the Scapegoat Wilderness, Bruce."

"Ah, yes," the Governor joked. "That's where the President is going to send our Congress, the poor dumb politicians."

All three found that irresistibly funny, and took a little time to relish it as they returned their gaze to the unforgiving wilderness known as the Scapegoat.

"What I was really looking at though, Bud, was the irony of all this."

"How so?"

"Well, the fight is coming to Montana—probably the least significant state in the country in the eyes of those folks in Washington, relative to high finance, seat of power—you know, all the barometers they use to determine who's on whose guest list. Not too many pollsters or media types interested in this state. I doubt anyone there really knows the electoral vote count from this state."

"Yeah, I know," Bud responded, almost embarrassed.

"Hey, Bud, that's the way we wanted it. We just wanted to be left alone, to enjoy our beautiful country, and to live our lives. The less truck we had with those 'kingmakers' the better. Yet, here we are." He paused, looked it over, and continued. "The fight is coming to us." Smiling now, he turned to James and Bud, looking them square in the eye and raising himself up to his full 6'4" height. "And, friend, we are ready. I guess this is the last time in history where people won't know anything about Montana. We're about to become famous, boys!"

James wasn't exactly certain what all had been discussed in that other room all morning, but he knew something was in the works. He wasn't at all surprised to see the Governor turn back into the rancher he was, right in from of them.

"Bud, would it be okay with you if I took one of your horses, saddled up, and took a ride in that direction? Be good to clear my head before those boys in there start making me make a whole boatload of decisions and phone calls."

Bud nodded, waiting until his political ally had left before saying, "James, I think we are about to get an earful!"

CHAPTER 32

*B*rian couldn't contain it any longer. The drive back from some quick grocery shopping in Seeley Lake, and a steak sandwich at the local landmark restaurant, Lucky's, was no different from the ride over. Every time he and Andy passed a vehicle going the opposite direction, the driver of the other vehicle brought his hand up off the steering wheel and waved.

And Andy obliged by mirroring the gesture—smiling and waving.

"All right, that's it," Brian said with consternation. "Have we not been together every day since we got here?"

"Yeah, sure..." Andy's voice trailed off. He'd been thinking about Reagan wondering why he still hadn't heard from her, not knowing whether this was normal when her team was out working on this kind of project. Bringing himself around, he put his attention on Brian. "Why?"

"How did you meet all these people who are waving at you? Who ARE they?"

"I don't know." Seeing that Brian was confused by that, he said, "They just wave, and I wave back."

Brian looked startled by that, his head jerking back slightly. "Seriously? They just wave at a total stranger?"

"Apparently," Andy responded, laughing.

Brian looked that over for a moment; then started to laugh, too. "Well, that's better than the one finger wave you get in Los Angeles!"

They mutually enjoyed the moment, thinking of the startling differences between the cities they had inhabited and the world of Montana. Still a tad doubtful, Brian asked again, "Just because we're here?"

"I guess... Bud mentioned that where men are scarce, men are valuable. I guess they just notice..." Andy answered, his voice trailing off as he made the turn onto the property. Now familiar residents to the guard at the gate, they were waived through without stopping. But Brian and

Andy both waved without even thinking about it, having unconsciously picked up the trait as well.

That trait—unique to Montana or not—signaled something about America. Though neither Andy nor Brian knew it then, it would make a difference in their game plan for victory.

No one in the Oval Office dared look to the Mall, where the Washington Monument rose into the evening sky, lit so magnificently. They were grateful not to be able to see the Lincoln Memorial, which stood behind trees to the right, resting on the Potomac.

The meeting of the President and his Cabinet, along with Homeland Security and the NSA, had lasted eight hours and was explosive at times, counter-balanced by long moments of solemnity. The tone at the end of the meeting was one of a barely concealed anger. There was not a man or woman among them who was not visibly shaken by their discussion, and ultimately the President's decision.

Centering on the options available after all "cash" accounts would be liquidated to answer up the call for the United States to repay its loans, all roads had led to Eminent Domain. Considered one of the most controversial and potentially dangerous decisions ever handed down by the Supreme Court, the Government and its citizens had muddled along never expecting it would or could be used in a confiscation, by the Government, of State or citizen assets en masse.

It was considered to be something that reasonable men would use with discretion, and rationality, and in a limited fashion. But these were not reasonable times.

For the last four hours, the occupants of that office had been pouring over reports, graphs, and a map of the United States. So extreme was the jeopardy to the country that it appeared—for the sake of national security—that they were going to have to federalize some assets and utilize them to stop the bleeding produced by the unexpected actions of the RIT.

They needed to find a state with many resources that could be used, either for the stabilization of the U.S. dollar, for the debt, or for the security of the nation in the event of a collapse of its social structure into rioting, like the contagion that was rolling across Europe, and which was metastasizing into portions of Brazil, Argentina, and the Pacific Rim.

Further criteria required that those assets be easily accessible. That ruled out Alaska, just on sheer distance and weather, notwithstanding its hefty resources. Selecting something closer would make it easier to justify the use of Eminent Domain on a large scale to the media and to the public.

One state already had a huge percentage of its land and forest under national jurisdiction. As the day wore on, the men and women in the Oval Office concluded reluctantly that the people of the United States probably wouldn't care about taking what was under that already federally- controlled land away from the state and the private sector, and using it for the national good.

And to the nausea of some, it was also concluded that no one would really care about the state at all. Unlike the high population states, with the major cities and industries, there were no big law firms in this state, no big advocacy groups. Though the state was running in the black, it was also assessed that the state would have no big war chest.

By the time the lights were coming on in the District of Columbia, they had settled on the state of Montana. Unable to look at each other, exhausted from an afternoon of fist slamming, tears, obscenity shouting, and restless pacing, they had surrendered to what they felt was their best option.

Looking down at the otherwise uncluttered desk, the President of the United States gave the order to assess the value of the land they were about to seize—in order to compensate the owners of the land, under the law—and he specifically ordered the Dept. of Homeland Security to prepare to execute Eminent Domain papers against thirty-four different holdings in Montana, and to prepare a national security brief justifying the action.

The Director of Homeland Security's response was barely audible, and it was obvious he wanted to escape that room as quickly as possible. Gathering papers into his valise, he exited abruptly.

There was a long silence. Finally, the President, with his forehead resting in his hand, dismissed his Cabinet. In the background, citizens of the District of Columbia ventured out to walk along the pathways in the National Mall and enjoy the evening air and a much-needed respite from the intense humidity that afflicted the Capital in the summer.

For a fleeting moment, catching the breeze from the Potomac River, it seemed as if tensions had eased ever so slightly.

CHAPTER 33

*A*ndy and Brian could feel a shift in the mood in the lodge as soon as they entered. Guessing that meant they were about to be brought into the game, they were glad they'd stocked up on some foods they liked. Each had decided there was only so much of James' tuna sandwiches that they could take—in one week at least.

Reluctantly, Andy had picked up a jar of homemade hot salsa, wishing his girl was with him, and there to mix it up herself. He was grateful they were about to begin, as the idleness only left him worrying about her, and he had been having trouble keeping his head in the game. It felt like his days at Arlington High, when he'd be on the bench, waiting for his defense to get that ball back into his hands so he could get out there, lead, and score.

So, when James approached them, with a hint of a smile, Andy knew it was time. "Kid, Pal, they are ready for you."

"Yeah, how do they look?" Brian was trying to get a little insider information before going into the briefing.

"A little red-eyed, and they are acting a little jittery, but I think that's due to the coffee Bud's been brewing. Seems he likes to do that himself, and frankly, it's enough to rouse the dead!" They all laughed at that image, and James led them into the War Room.

Indeed, the name was appropriate now. The air was stale from too many bodies in there for too long a period of time. Empty food trays had apparently been removed by Bud's staff, but the smell lingered, and the men and one woman themselves showed signs of needing a shower.

Other than that, though, the room was calm, and there was no apparent clutter on the central conference table, around which each participant had taken his seat. Rather, they were just waiting patiently.

As soon as James brought in the boys, the "Chair" of the briefing became apparent. The group had designated Governor Fitzerman to lay out their plan of attack. Whether it was out of respect for his position in the state itself, or whether he had emerged as the uniting factor amidst the business sector represented, the education sector, finance sector, media, and government sectors, was not of much concern to Andy and Brian.

They just needed to see what approach the State of Montana was going to take to ward off any erosion of its wealth, lifestyle, and heritage— and how its model could possibly provide a beacon for other entities who might be struggling to survive the global financial mayhem that was occurring.

They took their seats at the front of the conference table, with their back to the battery of screens behind them, which was still spewing disintegration and panic in various countries. Taking their clue from the Governor, who had also turned his back on the screens, they sat now to his right.

James was preparing to sit in the back row, near the door, when Andy gestured for him to sit behind them along the wall, close enough that they could lean into him if need be.

Apparently though, Bud Walker could no longer stomach the images the rest of the team were forced to see as a backdrop for the discussion. He stood and asked, "Do we need to watch those, or would you like me to turn them off for a while?"

"Speaking for myself, they're emblazoned sufficiently on my mind. I can do without them," the Attorney General responded sternly. Troy Davis dressed like a cowboy, and was slight and wiry. He was known though to be fiercely competitive from his bull-fighting days back in the day, and famously articulate. It took a strong self-image for anyone to debate him. You could put him in a suit, but you could never get him out of his cowboy boots.

The others signaled their agreement, and Walker immediately cut the feed. That factor alone had a remarkable effect on the room, and whether he was overtired, or just sensitive now, Bud Walker realized for the first time just how degrading and debilitating an effect the constant inflow of the sights and sounds of the news produced. *This is humbling,* he thought, wishing fleetingly that he had done something else with his life. Bringing himself out of it though, he fought back with, *There's still time. I can redeem myself.* Swallowing hard, he sat up straight, totally ready to hear the solution. For a moment, he wished he'd been a praying man.

The game plan was a fairly simple one. The Governor and his Secretary of Commerce were utilizing an idea the Sheriff of Lincoln County had brought to the table. They were going to create a Montana State Bank, which would not be a commercial bank but rather a bank created by the state itself, and under its control.

Though the state could not print money, as that lay within the purview of the Federal government, the Attorney General had confirmed that there was nothing prohibiting the formation of the bank, and nothing prohibiting it from coining money.

That fact would become the lynchpin in the strategy. Taking the $2 billion, which had been recovered from the endangered investment fund, the Governor was prepared to go to the Capital and have the Legislature change the law to allow that money to be invested into the state-owned bank.

Brian had interrupted for a moment to get a timeline and asked, "How long will it take to do this?"

The Governor's response was reassuring, even if a bit overoptimistic. "The Legislature is on stand-by—in session in Helena. I believe that can be accomplished within a day."

"Changing the law, or chartering a bank, or both?"

"Both." Even as he said it, one could see it was straining the credulity of anyone who had had any traffic with politics and government before. So he quickly reminded everyone, "Remember, this is an emergency. I believe a rough draft of all of this will be quick, and keep in mind we will not be dealing with Federal regulatory agencies and dictations. This is an internal matter within the state of Montana, and 'AG'—as I like to refer to my Attorney General—informs me it is constitutional. When Bud's team goes to work to get the word out to the people, it should be welcomed as well."

Brian was making notes on his laptop, and Andy, as usual, was taking handwritten notes. The rest of the details involved the opening of any closed precious metal mines, and/or expediting expansion permits for those still producing. Declaring a state of emergency, the Governor was prepared to bypass existing environmental legislation to enable the silver and gold mines to churn out as much product as possible.

Smelting operations would be immediate, and the Secretary of Commerce had already begun working with mine owners to facilitate the conversion of the raw material into coins and ingots. Having no idea how long it might take to design the coins that would become the currency of Montana, the recommendation was made to leave the "artwork" to later, and at the moment, mint something simple.

Andy and James could see the state was preparing to waive any restrictions to immediate and thorough commerce in any industry necessary to the financial and banking operations. Further, the newly formed state bank would be a principal investor—using the money retrieved from the vulnerable stock investment fund—in the mines, which would bring up gold and silver, as well as copper and sapphires.

Obviously, that would make purchase and trade within Montana possible. Game-wise, it was almost as if Montana would be seceding economically, but not physically from the country, thereby salvaging Montanans' ability to survive. Save for one thing: The question that would make or break the plan was posed by the University Chancellor.

Though Chancellor Aaron Watkins understood the plan that had swirled around in the preceding hours, he still had a nagging question about the feasibility beyond the borders of Montana, and, if this were to work, the United States itself. Daring to appear dumb, he tentatively raised his hand. The Administrator was now the student once again.

"But what if the person or a government is already wiped out? Maybe doesn't have coins…" He paused, struggling to make his point. "What if all they have is dollars, and those dollars are worthless? Or whatever their currency is becomes worthless? What do they do?" He paused for emphasis, then resumed. "I don't think we really resolved that. What if…?"

At that moment, the silence was proverbially deafening. In their haste to create a solution, the men had not looked well enough into the perspective of the individual or entity that had to make the transition from dollars and paper currency to an exchange currency backed by something. If they had "nothing," how were they to get "something?"

Both Bud and the Governor turned to the Treasury Secretary and Simon Atwater, looking for a good answer. They seemed to be stuck on it due to the fact that both had been operating from the paradigm that people would exchange their dollars in an initial period if they were to deal with the state bank. With the global assault upon the dollar's value, that appeared to be the crushing timeline. How, in fact, could they get all this up before the dollar had collapsed altogether?

He knew there was an answer, but he was having difficulty shifting the paradigm radically enough to frame an easy one.

Brian intervened. "Right, he's asking a question I have to have answered before I start designing the game, because that—though terrible—seems to be a possible scenario."

"It is," the Treasury Secretary responded, causing a fog of fear and doubt to creep into the room.

It was the Chief who intervened. "You're all forgetting a part of our heritage."

All eyes were on him now. The Governor offered for him to come forward, but the Chief signaled he was comfortable remaining at his seat. Speaking without emotion, but drawing from centuries of familiarity with his ancestry and the history of this continent, he reminded everyone of one detail they had missed, or had not articulated, when discussing solutions. Each may have thought it was implicit, but given the lag in the response time to the question posed by the Chancellor, he realized he needed to drop this into the picture. His next words would prove to be the pivotal aspect to the solution for the crisis at hand, but would also become one of the most enticing and critical game features in the game Carver & Weir would launch into the global landscape.

"You all have done a remarkable job of asking yourselves, what did we do back in the beginning when we formed this country and its economy? How did we do it? And you are right that it will work again. But you forgot one thing—the undercut to it all, gentlemen, and gentlelady," he added, in deference to the Secretary of State.

Glancing at his grandson, the young man smiled, as this was the key point in his university thesis, and one that had become foundational to the actions their Tribal Council had taken, shocking the world and rocking the boat in 2008. Given no press coverage at the time; disparaged by anyone in finance; marginalized by politicos, it answered the fundamental question, "What do you do if you have no money?"

"In the beginning, we bartered." He let that hang there for a moment, making sure that it was now indeed part of each man's thinking and equation. Continuing, he said, "What one man lacked, another had, and all of us for centuries bartered with one another to create the security we needed. It is part of the history of my people, and it is part of the history of your people—no matter where they settled this continent, and no matter when they came. We bartered. Later, we moved to the Gold Standard, coined the gold and silver we extracted from the earth to make it easier, and then finally we made paper, so as to not have to transport the gold."

There's that convenience button again! James thought, reflecting back on their discoveries of how Americans could be manipulated. *For convenience, we transitioned to paper.*

"And when it became too inconvenient to print on paper, we just started moving numbers from one computer account to another!" Andy snorted. "That is some series of chess moves!"

"Yes, and it would have worked, too, my boy," the Chief admonished, "had it not been for the separation of the value of the money—be it paper or electronic—from the value of something tangible, which was produced. We used gold and silver. That worked. But any tangible asset would be feasible—even if cumbersome."

Andy thought about it for a minute, looked it over a few times, and then turned to the Chief. "So that's the plan, basically. Recognizing that economies are in reality comprised of the worth of what is produced—measured by the total value of the movable, tangible goods, and the land and real estate, which has durability—you are going to create a new economy based on a gold or silver currency, owned by the people's state bank. And if it's not possible to do that, you are going to return to the fundamental barter system of long ago." He looked up at Brian, licked his lips, and rocked a bit in his chair. Turning back to the Governor, he asked, "Did I understand this right?"

"Yes, Andy, especially now that the Chief has been kind enough to help us past this mental constipation we had on this one point. We were assuming our bank plan would work—silver coin and all—if we could launch before the dollar became worthless. And that remains a big *If.* We'll try…" He didn't finish the sentence, rather moved in the new direction. "Anyway, we really missed the significance of the *real* undercut. Bottom line, it's barter."

"The IRS will love this!" AG almost cursed. Then suddenly, finding that funny, he reminded himself and the others, "Not really a point to worry about now. Hell, we're talking about a doomsday scenario here. I don't think anyone is going to be paying attention to tax codes for a while!"

Even with a room full of politicians—many of whom were big endorsers of hefty taxes—that comment provided a moment of much-needed levity, and they laughed. It rolled for more than a minute, and then settled down, man by man.

"We're going to have to start up the Pony Express system again, with this kind of plan," the Majority Leader of the Assembly joked. "You know, there is that Pony Express stop—hotel and all—still standing on that ranch outside of Pony!"

That caused the laughter to erupt again. Andy, James, and Brian, being outsiders, couldn't fully appreciate the inside joke, and wondered if there was really a town called Pony.

Governor Fitzerman spoke, surprisingly passionate. "There's one more thing in our heritage, gentlemen. And whether it is barter or banking we use, this activity will enable us to rebuild rapidly. Every descendant of a pioneer knows this story, and those who don't will get a lesson on how we forged the West and took this country."

His family had homesteaded Montana in the mid-19th Century, but they had filled him with the lore of how the American pioneer had moved from the shores of the Atlantic, inward and across a vast and dangerous continent, effectively colonizing each new frontier at a breathtaking speed.

It had been a team effort, and it stemmed from a fundamental American trait, and a decidedly Montana trait as well. "You all remember your history? Remember Barn Raising?"

They did. Never considered relevant to contemporary times, suddenly the underlying concept would prove pivotal to the survival of the country. "Yep, when they stopped, they would all work together to build a barn for one family in a day. Able to secure themselves and their livestock and seed from whatever would threaten its survival, they would then move on to the next homestead, building the barn for that family. And then the next and the next, until everyone had shelter, and a secure place to dwell."

Brian stopped typing, and was scrutinizing the Governor. The Governor turned to the Chief and said, "And even undercutting the barter is the Barn-raising mindset. Neighbor will help neighbor get a business up and running, or a crop in, in order for something to be created that can be bargained with."

And there it was, in stunning simplicity. Nothing more than cooperative survival efforts—the group helping members of the group to become independent, functioning, and producing—thereby providing the wherewithal to barter and trade, and so on up the line.

Each man was staring at the center of the table as if an image from the past were dancing in front of them. In their mind's eye, to the person, they all saw the legacy of our pioneering days—and that heritage and legacy was universal. Where man had been, this was endemic in man and his spirit somewhere.

That afternoon, a handful of newly humbled men understood that a once-great country was soon to be great again. It had taken only going back to its roots—a people with dreams, creativity, and the willingness to fight for those dreams.

At the root of all the barn raising, barter, trading, and production— fundamental to it all—was *people*. The ancestors of every man there had at one time been part of a New World, whether slave or master. For the moment, each remembered what we did here, how we did it, and who we were.

The moment was interrupted temporarily when Bud's Chief of Staff apologetically came in, saying there was a call coming in from Sir Harley Grantham-Jones. Bud's response was immediate. "Tell the SOB I'm in a meeting."

Bud Walker had not only a love of history, but he also had a flair for words and drama. "These New Worlders, or whatever they choose to call themselves, are about to meet the *Old* New World. They enslaved; we freed, and we will again."

Brian nudged Andy with his elbow. Both looked over their shoulder to James. He was watching them both, hoping and praying they could work with this. Brian winked.

Turning back to the Governor, Brian took his time to look around the table at each of the men and lone woman who made up what he had referred to a few days earlier as "the crew." Quite matter-of-factly, he said, "I can do that game."

CHAPTER 34

*B*rian and Andy had commenced work immediately on the game. Back at the bunkhouse, which had become their headquarters, they began planning format and strategies of the game they entitled, "The Battle of America."

Knowing the game would be launching into a tumultuous environment, where emotions and mob reactions would be a factor, each knew that the game had to immediately reflect the current economic environment, and that it had to be a game for laymen. If the vocabulary or moves in the game required the equivalent of a Harvard MBA, with a minor in Finance and Statistics, in order to participate, they knew they'd miss the people they were trying to salvage.

James had decided to stay out at the bunkhouse, too, just in case they needed him for anything, and also to keep an eye on them. Well did he remember how they'd get to shouting back and forth to each other in the heat of a creative endeavor. Neither seemed to notice that the other was shouting. So, James was glad they had originated the need to do the game's plan back at their quarters.

He couldn't sleep though. Sitting outside, he looked up at the heavens on a night when the sky appeared chock full of twinkling lights. Periodically, shooting stars would catch his attention.

By dawn, the game's key pieces were identified, and the sequence leading to victory options was on paper. The game began with the destruction the world was actually witnessing. Players encountered closed banks, un-retrievable safety deposit boxes, rioting, looting, fire-bombing, fear, and panic—and the villain in the game was the Central Banker.

Each player had to figure out how to survive and then win without stealing or exploiting anyone else. Any move in that direction forced the player back to the beginning.

At one point Andy stopped, suggesting they have the players personalize the game to themselves by entering every tangible item they owned. Once entered, it vanished, but would appear later at a higher level of the game. Both men realized that this mystery element, which brought the player's real life into the game, had worked with the first game, and that fans of the game would like that format.

Key to success was the player learning how to create a team—whether he put it together from other game characters supplied by Brian and Andy, or whether he was playing an actual person somewhere else in the world. Both had to interact, and unless they teamed up, neither could advance.

"Yesterday's Barn Raising is today's Team Work!" Brian had exclaimed. Progressing through the game, the first real victory was the Barn Raising Level. That opened the door to the Barter Level, wherein the player would figure out how to select something from his own personal tangible items list to exchange with someone else.

"You know, this is all individuals, Brian," Andy was pointing out. "It's one person to another here. Do we need to make this about state to state and nation to nation?" The question was a valid one, given that nations were being pitted against each other and were pressuring each other due to the treacherous financial bondage they had created with one another.

Looking it over, Brian decisively said, "No, not at this time. We can make that Version 2 or 3, if need be. But right now, let's hold to the idea that the solution to this whole thing lies with the individual. We're going for the White King here. If he makes the right moves, he'll figure out in real life how to reach his government."

There it was—a game for the average man that wrenched control of finances from the hands of the Central Bankers and put it in the hands of that individual. Once the player advanced through the Barter Level, his confidence was climbing and he next had to figure out how to create money. That level could not be successfully navigated unless the player figured out that any type of money he created had to be backed by something, and near the top of the game, that it had to be tied to production.

The more production the player could figure out for his team in the game, the more money they could have. Any attempt to advance without production, or to confiscate another team's production, carried huge penalties in points and position. Back down at the entry level where they learned not to steal, the players would have to advance again.

Brian decided also to introduce near the top of the game the idea of investment and lending, but there could be no usury involved in the return on the investment. Tying modern day elements of loan sharking into the mix, the players at the very top of the game had the option to bring up on criminal charges anyone or any team that insisted on interest so high it jeopardized people, and their freedom of movement.

With their characteristic humor, the upper game level was known as Global Repo. In there, any player—one person or, in later versions, nations—would encounter the vicious cycle where debt and credit rules would cause a person to tumble from managing their debt to being managed into default and repossession.

What would later be regarded as one of the strokes of genius of the game was the element that allowed the player to make bad financial decisions and still think he was climbing and moving to a higher level. Later, however, those bad decisions brought him into the Global Repo area. If he had made healthier choices earlier, he might never see that layer of the game. But, if not, he would now have to learn some very hard lessons, or be expelled from the game.

In order to escape from the most treacherous aspects of someone modifying a loan or doing credit counseling—if they had run into trouble in their game choices—whereby the downward spiral began of lowered credit limits, lowered credit scores, raised interest rates, higher payments, can't pay, to repossession and default, the player had to ascend out of it by learning about "funny money." Receiving something that didn't really exist, he would discover that he got or created something tangible with it, and that he had to pay back the loan with something tangible—a produced tangible. If he spotted that the non-producer printed the funny money, and repossessed tangibles from the producers, making him feel guilty "to boot"—he was at the point of having to face default, *or* the creation of a new game.

There, at the toughest juncture by far, the player—whether he was an underprivileged youth in the inner city, a university student, businessman, farmer, politician, housewife, grandmother, or minister—had to figure out how to end the Global Repo game and start the Producing Game. They also had to figure out the need to further call the opponent's bluff.

Andy and Brian recognized that the key had to be everybody simultaneously abandoning one game and beginning the other. Otherwise, the enemy in the game could pick off opponents one person at a time, or, in real life, one nation at a time. For the game to be won, the players had to figure out that their actions had to be joint, and provide for the survival of everyone. Anything less and they were demoted in the game.

Players forming up from different parts of the country, playing with each other, had to make the same moves at the same time in order for their real-life team to win.

Near dawn, Andy sat back in the chair, looking over the game's concept. Knowing that all the "poker players"—as he thought of them—would have to call the villain's bluff at the same time, he was certain the game could deliver that message. His attention now was on how to reach enough people quickly enough to make a difference. "How do we do that, Brian?"

Surprisingly, Brian was confident. "Ah, that's just a marketing problem, Andy." Then, reassuring him further, he added, "We've done the tough stuff."

"You think so?" Andy was a tad skeptical.

"Sure, you'll put this all to code, and we'll get this out over the Internet. We'll launch a campaign right now through Facebook and Twitter and our blogs. I'll start on that tomorrow morning."

Looking out the window though, he realized it was already morning. "All right, correction, I'll start on that right now—even before I shower."

"Yeah, you don't want to miss showering," Andy jabbed at him lightheartedly.

"Right, it's simple. We'll let them know there's a new game coming from Carver & Weir called 'The Battle of America' and the word should go viral by tomorrow night."

It didn't take long for them to make the calls to the sales department of Carver & Weir, telling them to get a purchase link set and ready, and assuring them they would launch without any hot cover design, snazzy boxes for stores, or advance deals with retail stores. There was in fact no time for that. It would get picked up later.

"Push it out when Andy delivers the file," Brian ordered their production manager and marketing manager. "We'll fix in place; add versions, upgrades, all that good stuff. You can work on it, but you push this out as soon as it comes in, understood?"

It was.

"The goal is to win, guys. And we have a lot of real life bad guys to outrun. Right now they are picking people off one at a time, and one country at a time."

Back in Los Angeles, his staff was somewhat bewildered—first to have been awakened at dawn, and second to hear Brian rattling on about Montana and this place where people protect and help their neighbors. Having no idea what he meant by "people call and alert their neighbor about grizzlies headed onto his property," or his phrase, "where men are scarce, men are valuable," or phrases like, "self-reliant, yet cooperative," they nonetheless understood that something big was coming their way, and that whatever else was going on up there in Montana, it sounded like Carver & Weir were about to make a big impression with something. It sounded like it was coming on fast—whatever it was—and they began to rally the troops, calling in everyone in marketing and production.

Brian hung up abruptly, asleep before the connection was even severed.

It was mid-afternoon in Basel and Sir Harley Grantham-Jones had been resting after lunch. A strange case of indigestion and heartburn had overtaken him during the morning, continuing through lunch, so he had retired to his chamber to nap.

Suddenly, he was stricken with a terrible sense of dread. He sat up, his stomach churning with anxiety, and his emotional level at a high pitch. Hoping he could get an anti-anxiety pill from the in-compound pharmacy, he called downstairs. *Something has happened,* he told himself, trying to identify the source of his fear.

Chapter 35

"They get it done?" Bud asked quietly, as he came up onto the porch behind James. He had seen from the 4-wheeler that both boys were apparently passed out—Andy in the hammock, and Brian sitting almost upright in an Adirondack chair.

"Yeah, I assume so. That's Andy's computer on his chest. My guess, he fell asleep writing code for it." James smiled affectionately at his two sleeping wards.

"Well, Boy Scout, I got to hand it to you."

James turned to face Bud, taking his arm and guiding him away from the porch. "Yeah? How so?"

Without hesitation Walker responded, eager to get this off his chest. "This whole thing has been a pretty humbling experience for me, James, and I have a hunch we're just getting started."

James didn't know what to do with that, having no idea how that remark was responsive to his question. So, he just waited, figuring Bud would get around to the answer in his own way. He did.

"You were right about those two. They're an almost seamless team. Never seen anything quite like it, frankly." He paused, looking at James even more closely, and added, "My world...puh...it's dog eat dog."

James appreciated that and nodded his head in agreement. "Thing of beauty, isn't it?" Remembering their football career, he said, "They've been like that since I first met them. When they are in sync, you almost can't tell one from the other. And on the football field, miracles happened."

"Well, let's hope that applies here, too, James. We need a Hail Mary pass for sure!"

Neither man said anything for a while. Nearby, a flock of turkeys was raising a ruckus about something, and that was enough to wake the dead. James watched the strident birds protect their young from some threat he couldn't even see; then said, "They're like sons to me, you know?"

"Yeah, I can surely see that. You're an unusual family, no question, Boy Scout, but a family for sure."

"Do you have kids, Bud?"

"No, I don't. And seeing these two, it's one regret I have…" His voice trailed off. Choking for a moment, and swallowing hard to clear his throat, he softly added, "I was like a son to him, you know?"

James knew full well Bud was referring to Sir Harley Grantham-Jones, and that it had cost Walker to face this enemy. It hurt to face betrayal. Not knowing what to say, he said nothing.

The moment was thankfully interrupted when Walker's personal aide rode up quickly, kicking up a cloud of dust that was sure to settle on them. Handing Walker a satellite phone, he said, "Sir, there's a call coming in from Alicia Quixote. She says it's urgent."

"Alicia, I am having trouble hearing you!" Bud was shouting into the phone. The crackling and the mention of her name must have awakened Andy. Reagan was never far from his mind, not even when he was immersed in this huge national security issue. Worry had never departed.

Hearing Walker talking to Alicia, he was fully awake, getting out of the hammock, and shaking Brian into consciousness as well.

"Brian, get up. Walker's on the phone with Alicia Quixote!"

"What are they talking about?"

"I don't know, Brian, but Reagan is with Alicia Quixote, and I have a bad feeling about this!"

By then both had joined James, telling him about Reagan while trying to eavesdrop on Bud's conversation. Andy's heart sank when he heard Walker say, "All right, sweetie, calm down. We'll figure this out. When did they disappear?"

CHAPTER 36

Unaware yet of the relevance of the two women to his own world, Bud Walker firmly took control of the conversation with Alicia. He had noticed the stricken look on Andy's face, pushing it aside until he could finish with Alicia. Part father-figure and part boss, he ordered her to Montana.

"Alicia, we'll solve this from here."

She had apparently started to protest because he sternly overrode her. "I have friends, and they owe me favors. But I need you here, and not stuck in El Paso. It's getting dangerous there, my dear. You must get out before that border collapses and we're overrun by desperate people."

She had no disagreement with that, since part of her tears and hysteria was coming from the disintegrating airport situation she had experienced just getting back to El Paso. The Consul had ordered her home, and reassured her that they would pursue this but that he would not assume responsibility for yet another American woman.

Reluctantly, yet still relieved, she had returned home, reaching out to the only man she had ever trusted with judgment calls about stories and human nature.

Alicia Quixote had no idea the journey Bud Walker had been making recently, nor the ever-increasing danger into which the world was racing, but she knew him well enough to know that if he said come to Montana, he meant it. What he said next, though said with composure, alarmed her.

"Do not attempt to fly out commercially. I need you here immediately. There is an airstrip twenty miles west of you on Coyote Canyon Road. Be there in three hours; leave your car, and one of my planes will transport you to the ranch."

Almost forgetting, he caught her just before she hung up and asked, "I am going to call the Ambassador myself, and the State Department. What are their names?"

"Reagan Lynch and Edith Church," Andy shouted at him, his face red with emotion, his chest heaving.

"What the hell?" Bud said, to no one in particular. Hearing Alicia on the phone answering him simultaneously, he said, "I've got that. I'll see you this evening."

Trying to put this together, James spared him the time. Andy and Brian stood next to each other, Brian's hand on Andy's shoulder. James moved close in to Walker and said, "You're going to need to call the DEA, too."

"The DEA? I...I... James, what's the connection here, and why the DEA?"

"Reagan Lynch and her boss, Edith Church, are human rights activists, and they were working with Alicia Quixote on a human trafficking issue."

"Human *slavery*, issue, James!" Brian interrupted passionately. "You have to get this right. It is slavery, and the government needs to be told *that way*. My field is marketing, remember that!"

"Oh my God!" Bud turned away momentarily to catch his breath. Somehow looking at the space in front of him, seeing the glitter of the creek back at the end of the property, he calmed down a bit. Then he asked, "So, is this kidnapping for ransom, or *slave trading?*"

James shook his head, indicating he had no idea. Bud then asked the question he almost didn't want to know the answer to. "And what's the connection to the Kid and his Pal, Boy Scout?"

Brian had taken Andy off the porch and was "taking him for a walk." They needed to blow off steam and clear their heads. James was relieved to have them a bit of a distance from him when he answered, "Reagan Lynch is Andy's fiancé."

Bud just stood there. For a moment, all he could do was shake his head in disbelief. He had the urge to cuss, but somehow the words wouldn't come out. It was almost too much to fathom. One thing he did know though was that he needed Andy Weir, and the game he was about to create from Brian Washington Carver's design. The *world* needed those boys "in the game."

Gazing out again, taking a deep breath, he started the plan. "All right, I'll call my friend in the State Department. He's got a lot of influence over there. But, James, I'm not particularly connected with Law Enforcement." Almost ashamedly, he explained, "My network hasn't always exactly been supportive of them—especially related to Latin America."

"I understand." And James did understand. There had not been one time in his career with the CIA, or his experience with crises amongst nations, where the issue of "politics" had not intervened, sometimes wholly wrecking an otherwise wholesome progression of events. He held no expectation that this would be any different. What he prayed for now was that his skill could supersede the gnarly political entanglements and save these women. The alternative was unthinkable.

The day Kelly Weir had died, there was nothing he could have done. But, today, there was a chance. There was something he could do. That thought alone empowered him, and carried him past the emotional upheaval he was experiencing at the reminder of his own fiancé's murder at the hands of thugs.

"First, Bud, we have to find out whether this was a kidnapping for ransom, or whether it was slave trading. I know a guy at the DEA who can probably ask a few questions."

"Good. But, tell me, why the DEA? I'm lost on that one."

"Bud, if they are in the hands of a drug cartel, it is slave trading, and they have been taken to be sold. If they are in the hands of a Latin American gang, or revolutionary group, it's likely kidnapping for ransom."

Bud signaled that he understood. James finished with, "All right, you and I have calls to make. Either scenario we need the State Department, so be persuasive. It's not like they don't have a few things on their minds right now."

The sheer magnitude of that statement put the whole issue into perspective. These two women were very important to everyone on this ranch, but to the State Department, under global financial attack, it would be a low priority. Bud wanted to cry, but he knew that wouldn't help anyone. Instead, he looked to James for his expertise. "Do you have a hunch about which one it is?"

"Yeah, I do." He paused a second and then said, "Kidnapping for ransom is a pretty stupid thing to do with the value of the dollar dropping, and the whole world's financial situation in upheaval."

"So, you think it's slave trading?"

"I do." Waiting a moment, he added, "And, Bud, for the girls, either one is bad. But for us—slave trading is much better. I personally know what to do with that."

James had been right. First calling Ari Ben Gurion—who was still working on the coordination of banking lists, to cull the culprits—he explained the situation briefly. Andy and Brian were both listening in.

Ben Gurion confirmed immediately that Mossad was tracking Al Qaeda and Hezbollah involvement with the Latin American drug cartels, particularly the Cali Cartel and the FARC.

As frightening as that was, the field needed to be narrowed. James' contact with the DEA was able to confirm that one of those drug cartels was believed to have branched out recently into human trafficking, as he euphemistically put it. With the callousness that sometimes accompanies law enforcement discussions, he referred to that as the FARC expanding its portfolio.

James had no problem listening to this type of rhetoric, but he could see that Andy was biting his tongue. Signaling him to be cool, James in fact was somewhat optimistic. His contact had said the FARC. That would likely mean Colombia, drugs, terrorism, and it was consistent with the kidnapping industry the FARC had pioneered back in the 1990s. Initially they did it for ransom; then they graduated up into the big-time drug world and arms trading with terrorists.

Very pointedly, he asked his contact, "What will it take to find out if it was the FARC, and where they might be?" Knowing that Bud Walker would strike out with the State Department, he was already developing a plan. If these women were coming home, it would be up to him to figure out how.

———————

Brian had persuaded Andy to keep his head in the game. Andy, knowing that they needed more information before anything could be done, was impatient but still alert. In the chess game of his mind, he was resolved and ready to make a move, once he knew more about his opponent.

He and Brian spent the next hours adding a few additional features into the design, before Andy could begin creating the computer version. Brian reminded him that they had to have a section where the players would access their own personal assets data—input at the beginning of the game—in order to attempt bartering.

Having discovered that Montanans had the third highest IQ in the United States, right behind Massachusetts and Wisconsin, he asked the Chancellor to have some college students who were gamers prepared to test a game in a matter of days. He had Bud's assistant go into the towns in their vicinity, locating any poker tables in the saloons and finding volunteers for a new game. They were going to need all types of players before launching it, and what little he'd seen of the Montana saloons had led him to believe there was some—as he referred to it—local color there. *More like all shapes and sizes, nice variety!* he almost joked to himself.

But the specter of Reagan in peril jerked him back, plunging his mood again.

Around dinner time, and shortly before Alicia Quixote was expected to arrive, Bud Walker's Chief of Staff came in and announced it was time for them to leave for the auction.

It was like an announcement from another planet, left over in some relic of a Franklin Planner from another century. Bud, James, Andy, Brian—they all had a look of consternation and rebellion.

But Walker's staff member was insistent and argued decisively. "It is important for you to go, Mr. Walker. You were pledged to attend. I have the saddle you are auctioning off in the Hummer. The people need to see some continuity now. Your presence will help."

That argument won the day. Bud insisted they all come, that it would show them something about Montana they would appreciate. No one had any idea why all of them attending an auction would be so important—especially in the light of the enormous issues and workload ahead of them.

They were wrong. What was about to happen there would prove to be a living example of one of the most important aspects of their game, and it would lead to a section of the game so unique only the best players—those who were totally self-reliant, yet cooperative—would tackle. Discovering that level, and electing to play it, would bring the player to the very core of our heritage, and to the very threshold of defeat for Sir Harley Grantham-Jones.

It was a hot night, with no breeze stirring, and the auction was being held inside the arena of a neighboring rancher. Judging by the number of cars, pick-ups, and campers parked throughout the pasture near the arena, it appeared that most of the area had turned out.

What on earth?! Brian wondered, as he, James, and Andy were escorted in. The Chief of Staff had wisely provided each man with an item for the auction. None were very expensive—in fact, they were ordinary things anyone could pick up at a local hardware store. The exception was Bud's saddle. It was nothing special either, just more valuable than a tool set. The items were taken from each man as he came in, and a round woman whose weathered face showed no signs of skin care shook their hand, saying, "Thank you. God bless you."

What the hell kind of auction is this? Brian was still wondering.

A few minutes later, Bud Walker's guests encountered something unique to Montana, but hopefully not unique to America. It was something their enemy, who studied only the upper echelon of New York, D.C., and Los Angeles society, could never fathom.

The auction was for the benefit of a husband and wife who lived in Avon. The man had been in need of a kidney transplant. His wife's kidney was finally determined to be the only match close enough to potentially save him. She had been totally willing to give her kidney.

The boys learned from asking someone sitting next to them that the surgery had gone well, and it looked like the man would survive. But, both husband and wife would now be out of work for months. Between the huge medical costs, a portion of which were covered by insurance, and the lost income with both of them out of work, the auction was to benefit them.

In what could best be described as a modern-day example of "barn-raising," every person from the town had brought something to auction off. What was startling was how high the bidding was. When a man paid $75 for an Alaskan King Salmon, Andy smiled. He knew generosity when he saw it.

That was true of every item auctioned. It went for a price far above its actual worth, and in the end, the small community of people who did not have much even for themselves, had raised $69,000—and had spared the couple from bankruptcy or eviction as they recovered. It would be enough to live on, and pay what they still owed the hospital.

James choked up a bit when he saw Brian's new friend, Dusty Owens, arrive in that noisy pickup he now shared with his in-laws. He bid for the tool box Brian had brought, which could be purchased new at any Ace

Hardware for around $50. He kept topping the bid, and ultimately this young man who had lost his business paid $120.

Brian, Andy, and James placed polite and appropriate bids as well, in order to contribute. As did Bud Walker. No one gave too excessively. They all gave something.

In the end, Brian passed Andy a note that they had to design a scene called "The Auction," to be placed near the top of the game. If selected, since it would appear like a diversion or distraction to an ambitious player, the player would be rewarded with a huge additional score. He would rise in rank, too, if he helped every other player select Auction. The reward was for self-reliance, yet cooperation.

Returning to the ranch, Andy leaned over to Brian and said something that had been on all their minds. "This place never ceases to amaze me!"

Alicia had arrived and explained what little she knew. She looked worn out from worry and travel. So, Bud had her escorted to her room, with instructions for her dinner to be delivered there. "I suggest you rest, Alicia, as we'll have information, God willing, in the morning."

Whether James' contact had been lucky, or just pissed off enough to scare someone else, James would never know. All he knew was that at 6AM the next morning, dozing in the great room with the others, he got a call.

"Yeah?" he said, clearing his throat.

Andy and Brian were hovering above him, with Walker as well, trying not to speak as James was listening. Reaching across the footstool to the end table, James grabbed a pen and paper. His only words were a periodic, "Uh, huh. I see. Okay."

These CIA guys with their poker faces! Andy thought. *Wait, Andy, just wait. You're next move is coming!* he thought, valiantly stemming a rising fear.

"All right, my friend, I thank you. I don't even know how to tell you I 'owe you' on this one. But, you let me know." His DEA counterpart must have laughed, as whatever he said made James smile ever so slightly. "And call with anything else."

"My man leaned on one of his confidential informants pretty hard last night. They had to risk exposing someone who has been tracking the FARC's drug trafficking activity in Mexico, giving them information. Seems the man went soft when he heard about the two women. Edith's picture, which they'd apparently gotten from Alicia somehow, reminded the man of his favorite aunt."

The man had confirmed of course that the FARC were dealing drugs, moving them up through Mexico into the U.S. But more importantly, he confirmed that it was the FARC, not the Cali Cartel, that was slave trading. That led them to a man at the airport in Mexico City, who, in exchange for information, was given immunity and an offer of deportation to the country of his choice. He had confirmed that those two women in the photo had been taken by men who paid him monthly to send any American women who were by themselves down a deserted corridor.

Regrettably, though that confirmed Reagan and Edith were in the hands of the FARC, the man did not know what route or destination was involved. He was paid just to direct unsuspecting women into the corridor. He did not know for sure where they went, but he was pretty sure it was Colombia.

"Bud," James said, "my bet is they are in Colombia at the main base for the FARC. They are moving drugs up through Mexico, but there's no reason to hold people you plan to sell in Mexico."

"Maybe they would, to sell in Mexico or the U.S.," Bud debated.

"No, I don't think so. They are not going to capture American women to sell back to America. These women are headed someplace else. Most of the buyers are in Africa, India, the Mid-East, and Europe." Looking at the boys, he said directly to Andy, "You are going to have to trust me on this, Kid. Years in the field tells me they will take them to their main staging area, and that is Colombia for the FARC, still. The route out is South America. The slaves are brought in and out through various South American countries."

More than anyone else, Andy accepted James' analysis right away.

"How much time do we have?"

"Not much, Andy. We're going to have to locate them inside Colombia. We're going to have to find a way to get them out before they are moved. It gets a lot harder after that."

"Well, how fast can the State Department move on this, and the Colombian authorities?" Bud asked. "I understand they are very cooperative with us."

"They are, but that would take far too long, and require too much politics, diplomacy, and approvals through channels."

"So what are you suggesting?" Bud asked, knowing the answer.

"We're going to have to do this ourselves."

There was silence in the room. Alicia, who had rushed down as soon as she had heard them talking, was in the mix.

Bud Walker broke the stalemate. "James, you find where they are—where the camp is—and I'll put together the rescue operation." It was said as if this was something Walker had done before.

Wonder what else I don't know about him, James reflected momentarily. Then, he said, "I will find them. Now that I know it's the FARC, the Mossad can help. They are on top of them due to the terrorism, arms dealing, and drug connection. I will find them."

"Good, I have a call to make." Bud rose, walked to the phone on the counter, pressed a speed dial number, and waited. After three rings, the phone was apparently answered. "Hi, it's me." He paused; then said, "I need your help with something. I need you in Montana. My jet or yours?"

Returning to the others, he said simply, "We may need more men. Any ideas?"

One man in the room did. Years of growing up in Southeast Washington, D.C.—even when he'd tried to avoid and separate himself from it—had taught him one thing: the "brothers" stick together.

Ironically, Brian Washington Carver was about to come full circle with a "brother." On a dark street in Compton, that man's life had changed four years ago. Brian had a hunch the man would feel a sense of "debt."

Chapter 37

*B*ud Walker stood gazing out onto the manicured lawn. It had been just a few days since he'd watched Brian and Andy tossing balls, preparing themselves for their opportunity to help solve the country's crisis.

Now, he was staring at James, Andy, and Brian who stood in what looked like a huddle—all upright—and talking earnestly with one another. The wind was strong enough to be kicking up some dust, but they seemed unaware of it.

A strange sense of sadness swept over him. He'd had impulses to weep now for several days, each time suppressing them in order to continue the work, and appear strong for everyone.

Somehow, he felt responsible for all that was happening, and he wondered just how much one person could be expected to withstand. *Isn't it enough that those two have to somehow come up with a solution for this whole damned mess?! Do they also have to be saddled with this terrible news about the girl?*

Even before the thought was complete in his mind, a part of him started to pull himself back. Proceeding along that line was leading to an abyss, and Bud Walker knew somehow not to let his mind wander to the edge of it.

Hell, if I hadn't reluctantly played their game to satisfy my nephew, I'd probably be reaching for one of those meds Harley's psychiatrist gave me! The irony of having already been rescued from the abyss once by those two partners did not escape him. His clarity of vision following the insights he'd gained by playing that game had transformed Bud's life.

True, his fortunes were reduced; his influence waning; his marriage over; but for the first time in a long time his conscience was clear. And he hadn't even known it was muddied.

Wondering what they were talking about, he decided to hang back and stay near the phone.

She had said she'd be bringing someone with her when her plane landed.

Andy had protested initially, but was just standing there now, listening to first Brian and then James. Deciding not to be the quarterback today, but rather to listen to his coach, he was eyeing James at the moment.

"I will find Reagan, Andy. And I will bring her home."

"But, Andy, you have to stay *here*. You can't come with James and me," Brian said, stepping in. "Hell, I don't even want James to come, but you know him, he insists, so I'm just going to have to put up with it."

That did bring a hint of a smile to Andy, so Brian continued. "You have got to stay and finish that game software, test it, and get it out. Bud needs you, you know that."

"He needs all of us!" Andy responded a bit defiantly.

"Yeah, well, that's true, brother, but we are now fighting on two fronts, and we are going to have to divide up. James and I will head on down to L.A. I got somebody I need to see."

Andy, resigned, nodded his agreement.

"I told you, brother, we are not losing any more family. No more dying. I promise."

"Thank you." Andy could barely get it out.

"Yeah." Brian broke out of the huddle, signaling they should get back to Walker, who seemed to be standing like a wooden statue on the veranda. Then, apparently getting another idea, he turned to Andy and added, "And, I changed my mind on something. I'm going to want you to add in a Global Barn Raising section after all, near the top. Given the kind of unsolicited International help we just experienced in about 24 hours, it would be good to have the gamers figure out how to cooperate, coordinate, and create the final solution on a nation to nation level—you know, make it global."

"Okay, okay, I can think with that. Good place to put the 'everyone folds his poker hand at once' move. Let each nation coordinate the move; then do it simultaneously. A kind of reverse barn-raising."

Brian laughed as all three returned to the veranda. "That's a good one. First, we have a global barn destruction; then a global barn raising with a new financial game. That's good stuff."

"Should I put in a capitulation level, you know, where the RIT capitulates?"

Brian stopped dead in his tracks, looked at that, and, in what would prove to be a pivotal decision, created a part of the game that would make history. "Let's leave that level open, see what the gamers do with it, what solution they bring. They might have the RIT start negotiating, you know, cow-towing to the people once they know the world has abandoned their game; they might put them on trial. Hopefully they don't kill them. Let's see what the players feel is a solution for the bad guys. More creative, don't you think?"

"I do. That's good, Brian." Andy smiled.

"What?" Brian queried.

"Well, I was just salivating a bit over what the 'intended victims' will create here."

"Yeah, well, payback's a bitch! Just be sure to reward for the rational solutions, not the violent ones. Violent solution, player goes back down and comes up again. Without that penalty in the game, we have a world in anarchy and war."

Suddenly Andy started to laugh at the irony of that given how scary things were already. The three of them passed Walker just in time for him to overhear Andy say, "Remember that line in *Butch Cassidy and the Sundance Kid*? The one where Redford is afraid to jump off the cliff into the river, and Paul Newman says, 'Can't swim?! Hell, the fall will probably kill you!'"

"Yeah, sweet, man, that is one of my all-time favorite lines!"

There it was—that odd playfulness again. It wrenched Walker out of his sympathy bout over Andy and his Reagan. *I just really don't get this generation!*

CHAPTER 38

Whole sections of Los Angeles were condoned off—under a quasi, undeclared martial law—protected by National Guard, armed and backed up by tanks. Long lines were outside every bank, and the tanks with water guns and military presence were there to clear the area at night so the armored trucks could get in; and to prevent a swarming, overrun, and destruction of the commercial banks throughout all the major cities.

Closed since the crash and credit freeze, no one was allowed in, but Washington had decided that citizens could take a small, regulated amount of cash from ATMs attached to banks on a daily basis. It was a stop gap move designed to quash fear, and present an appearance of business as usual—despite the tanks. No one liked the tanks, and no one wanted to ask the obvious—what happens when the money runs out, and there is no more to be brought in?

James' credentials got them through the checkpoint and into Compton. The last time Brian and James had come into this neighborhood, he'd been driving an old car, not his current BMW, and it had been in the dead of night. It was that night he had first met DeShawn Williams and his gang.

Once again, James was literally riding shotgun in case they ran into trouble. Even today, the picture of a white man riding around with a black man was incongruous for the neighborhood. The night they had first come here, Brian was hell bent on testing his game with under-privileged and compromised youth in a dangerous section of Compton. Andy and James had insisted on accompanying him.

They had in fact found a choice gang to run the test on; the gang leader had refrained from killing them outright for daring to come onto his turf that late at night—largely because he recognized Brian Washington Carver as the star wide-receiver for his favorite local football team, LA Western University.

Giving Brian a pass of his own for bringing two white dude's into the neighborhood, one of them armed even, DeShawn Williams had agreed to let one of his homeboys test the game. Their best player was oddly enough a Hispanic youth named Hector Sanchez, whose sister had married into DeShawn's neighborhood, hooking up with one of the gang. Hector had come along with his sister, as he had no other place to live except a shed at the back of one of the houses in his own neighborhood.

Alone, hungry, abused by the neighborhood gangs, he didn't care what color his companions were—he wanted to be with his sister. So, he'd appeared one day, wondering if he could at least sleep in the house with her and her husband. He'd stayed. Not hungry anymore, and not sleeping on cardboard in a shed, he nonetheless had been bloodhounded by guys in Williams' gang. Until one day, now weighing in excess of 225 pounds, strong from weight lifting in the safety of her backyard, covered in tattoos, he had soundly trounced the worst of his offenders.

DeShawn had observed him that day and made an executive decision that Hector was one of them—in size and spirit—and should be invited into the gang rather than hounded by it. It took a while for the others to accept DeShawn's decision, but as it turned out Hector Sanchez was also a really good gamer, and he taught everyone a lot about games, strategy, weapons, winning—all the skills needed in reality for them to survive in one of Los Angeles's most dangerous areas.

Today, Brian was looking for DeShawn Williams and Hector Sanchez. Starting where he had last located them, the neighborhood looked so different in daylight, he really had a hard time orienting.

"Geez, man, you'd never know there was ever any trouble here. Just a little run down, is all," he commented to James.

James nodded. Other than a few panes of broken windows in a store front here or there, and more abandoned shops than one would have expected, the area was not menacing. It merely appeared impoverished—and it was deserted. No one was on the streets, and there seemed to be no commerce going on. Though broad daylight on what would normally be a business day, it was eerily quiet.

Finally, they'd pulled up in front of a corner convenience store whose owner must have been optimistic about *selling* product rather than having it *stolen*. The only one open in a four-block radius, he appeared to be the lone optimist. They inquired into the whereabouts of Williams. The store owner did know him, but chuckled when they asked. "You know, you two ain't going to be buying anything from him these days," he admonished, assuming they had come to buy drugs. "He's straight now—has been for four years at least."

James lowered his head, masking a smile. *I smelled that something has changed here.*

"Well, do you know where he is?"

"Sure, I expect he's at his shop. He owns an automotive restoration shop over on Hawthorne and 118th."

James grabbed a couple of bags of chips and a six-pack of soda, paying the man as a thank you for the information. "You two have a good day now," the man called after them.

The reunion was sweet. DeShawn recognized both men as soon as they pulled up outside one of the bay doors, which was open to increase ventilation. "It's my man, Brian!" They exchanged a type of handshake James couldn't fully duplicate. But it wasn't necessary, as DeShawn just grinned at him, extended his hand—which James took comfortably—and said, "You still packin,' old man?"

"Always," James answered, lifting his pant leg to reveal the same weapon he'd worn there as a backup for more than a decade now.

"Well, some things don't change." DeShawn smiled, turned back to Brian, looked outside, and asked, "Where's your white brother? I never seen one of you without the other."

It hadn't taken long for Brian to explain that Andy's fiancé had been seized by slavers, and that Andy was working on a game to stop the financial debacle that was occurring. Both things were important to DeShawn because after he'd played their first game, there had been a shift in his reality so severe that he had disbanded his gang, quit the drug dealing and crime scene, and purchased a business of his own—which employed other members of the gang who had turned their back on the violent and pointless games they had once played.

So, DeShawn Williams had an unexpressed, but significant, appreciation and affection for Andrew Weir, whose game had opened the door to a different life for him. Having dealt with the main drug suppliers for Los Angeles County, he could only imagine the peril Andy's girl must be in, if she were in the hands of the source cartels themselves.

DeShawn Williams had an innate sense of justice. Once, he exercised it within a criminal street gang, but recently he had exercised it in sincere attempts at rehabilitation, both physically and financially, of those hurt by his previous actions. No jail cell had ever housed him, and he had initiated his own rehabilitation program, making him now a bit of a hero to the people in his neighborhood. Once afraid of him and his boys, they now turned to him for help in guiding their young ones through the harsh Compton school system, street gangs, and drug dealers.

What Brian didn't know was that DeShawn Williams had made amends for his transgressions, and then some, in the eyes of his community. And so had Hector Sanchez, who had appeared from underneath one of the cars they were working on. Hulking as ever, and resplendent with even more tattoos, his demeanor, too, suggested a transformation.

"So, how many of these places do you own?" James asked, sensing the two were actually better off financially than one might guess.

"Eight of them throughout the Southland. Figured we'd stripped enough cars in our day, maybe we should restore some! We're Williams and Sanchez, Automotive Restoration Specialists, and we're known for a fair deal and an honest job, Mr. Mikolas," Hector answered respectfully. For Hector, that was all he had to say. He had never made apologies for himself—not when he lived in crime, and not now that he was a successful businessman.

"Congratulations, Hector, DeShawn." James was surprised to find that his eyes were misting up. He regretted it, but couldn't suppress the emotion. In his line of work, he had never had the opportunity to see the final and end result of his actions. But today, he was experiencing what was possible when people get some truth. In his heart, he was praying that somehow these two former gangbangers could help them.

"Hey, old man," Williams broke James' reverie. "You'll have us all bawling here in a minute!" He smiled briefly, directed everyone into his office, telling the body guys still on the floor to wrap up their work, go home, and close up shop.

"I know how rough those drug traffickers are, James. Word is they're in tight with Al Qaeda. 'Course, I'm long gone from that scene, but I hear things, you know."

James nodded that he did. DeShawn continued. "You know, this neighborhood was really coming around. Prosperity returning. Now, everything's come to a screeching halt—not because of drugs but because of whatever the hell is going on with the banks and money. And now the tanks...! James, no one likes being surrounded by tanks, especially when we smell criminal actions here, and no one in government seeming to even give a damn. Hector here is worried for the safety of his niece. Good folks are barricaded up at night, barely on the street during the day, and businesses are failing." He stopped for a moment to scrutinize James and then continued. "But it's not just Compton, though, is it? It's everywhere, right?"

"Yeah, son, it is."

In that moment, there were no dividing lines between the races, educations, or incomes. Shared fear and impending shared misery were looming, and DeShawn Williams was a natural leader. Never afraid of a fight, he asked quietly, having closed the door so no one else would hear, "Do I gather, Brian, that you and the White Brother have a plan to reverse this?"

"We do."

"Is it a game?"

"It is. Andy's working on it right now, to release in a matter of weeks."

The very idea of another game sat well with Hector. He was truly one of those "gamers" that people joked about—addicted to the challenge, and really good at it. He couldn't resist. "Any chance you'll let me try it out?"

Brian was pretty cool about it, but his heart jumped. "Hector, I think there is a pretty darn good chance of that." Hector grinned and Brian added, "But you'll have to come to Montana."

Though Hector didn't grasp the full impact of that, DeShawn did. He mulled it over for a moment. "You know, business is down. Hector and I and a few of the boys can take a leave for a while. Hell, it'd improve the payroll if we did. My best men are really expensive employees, you know. Had to offset their pretty handsome drug income!"

That made all of them laugh. It felt good. Then DeShawn sobered. "What do you need?"

"Well, James believes he can locate where the two women have been taken, and Bud Walker says he'll set up and finance a rescue operation. James and I need somebody who can speak Spanish," he said pointedly in the direction of Hector, who grinned once again. "And we'll need some men. They'll be trained in Montana."

"And I gather you need someone who can handle automatic weapons and maybe even assault weapons, right?"

"Yeah, although we'll handle that in Montana, if they are totally green." Brian was negotiating a mercenary force, right there in broad daylight, in the middle of a global financial meltdown. James observed that same kind of steely calm he'd had in his voice years ago when he started communicating following the death, and burial, of his family.

Brian hadn't spoken much back then, had stuck to playing his computer games. But with resolve and skill, he had engineered the game that had turned an enemy tide. James saw that same look, and heard the same determination as before.

It must have been recognizable to DeShawn as well. Knowing that his legitimate enterprises would ultimately collapse under the weight of the financial meltdown, currency collapses, bank closures, and the inevitable anarchy that would sweep his neighborhood, he recognized that his old skill set and connections could be of help now. DeShawn Williams had never been the kind of leader who liked to wait for trouble to come to him. He preferred to go to the fight.

"All right, friend. You tell Andy Weir to finish that game, and I'm personally counting on you two to save us all. Meanwhile, we'll go save this girl. Count me, Hector, and three others who can handle a pretty steep learning curve on assaulting a location. I'll call them now."

Just as James and Brian were finishing the directions to the inland airstrip Walker was using for his Citation, James got a text. It came in from Ari Ben Gurion's number. It was apparent he'd finished his analysis, and had located the common denominator men who formed a nexus between the Central Banks, commercial banks funding terror, and the pharmaceutical giants. The text read simply, "U R looking for 5. Details follow Ncryptd."

James smiled. "Son of a gun. It's only five men!" He expected the message to confirm the one they already suspected. Now all he had to do was lure out the other four from the sixty or so who were involved in this whole mess, albeit ignorantly. "Sixty countries, sixty banks, twenty major banks, eight major bank players, five bad guys." He must have been humming without realizing it because Brian jabbed him in the shoulder blade on the way to the car. "What the heck are you singing about?"

CHAPTER 39

*I*n what could only be described as a true example of global departmental cooperation, governed by the valiant and optimistic philosophy that something can be done about it, Bud Walker, with Alicia's help, had confirmed through Mexico authorities that it was indeed a kidnapping for slave traders within the FARC's command structure.

Through a coordination of surveillance and investigative data, which James had secured through the DEA, the FBI, the NSA, and Israel's Mossad, steps were in motion to pinpoint the likely location of the FARC's headquarters in Colombia. Colombia itself agreed that, if they were branching out into slave trading, they would likely set up their initial slave facilities there, in conjunction with the training camps they were already using, and where they could be near the central command.

The Colombians had also expressed concern about the FARC having crossed into Venezuela for sanctuary and training. Whether they soft-pedaled it, or no one wanted to confront that possibility, the red flag went unheeded.

It was overshadowed by a most unlikely additional bit of information coming out of France, whose government was already embarrassed by the revelation that numerous of the French Foreign Legion were involved in the slave trading industry worldwide. Armed, trained, and very militant, they had become a force to be reckoned with. The Foreign Legion's intelligence agency had received credible Intel that a buyer was moving from Yemen to Somalia, then to a port in Brazil, and from there into Colombia, inside the jungle areas controlled by the FARC and their military force. No one knew his name, however. Just that such a man existed.

Bin Laden's computer had revealed discourse regarding the establishment of, and payment for, relocation of Al Qaeda's training camps to a location not far from Bogota.

Why all these agencies were willing to give up this information, all at the same time, James would never know. He could only assume that the good men and women who otherwise would have been hamstrung by the politics of one agency versus another, or one country versus another, recognized that the world was facing a much greater threat with the daily renting of the fabric of the society into violence and chaos, and that perhaps one of the last good deeds they could do would be to provide what little assistance or information they might have in the matter of the disappearance of two American women.

Or perhaps they had justified it in their minds that if the link between terrorists, drug cartels, and slave traders could be made, and if their operations could be compromised at a primary base of activity, that action alone would wreck part of the evil financial game. It is said there is honor among thieves. James reflected, *There is honor among men of good will, too.*

CHAPTER 40

*B*y the end of the day, the lights in the Montana State Capitol were burning in almost every wing. Cots had been brought into the Legislative chambers, catering trucks were summoned, and both branches of government were fully operational in a special session convened by the Governor. All supporting staff members were available as Governor Fitzerman and his team prepared to re-create their economy, in order to make Montana independence possible.

A new game, with a new type of bank, would offer a prototype for other states and Governors, which would lead them through the maze and enable them to begin afresh, if the world situation worsened.

Meanwhile, the AG walked into the Governor's office without so much as a "is he available?" query to the governor's assistant.

Both men had known this would be coming if Washington failed in its attempts to stopgap the economic free-fall. It didn't make what had arrived by currier late in the afternoon any easier to take, however. Placing the document on Governor Fitzerman's desk, the AG said, "This arrived about three hours ago."

The Governor hesitated before opening the folder, placing his hand gingerly on it, holding it on the desk for a moment, and asked, "Is it pretty much what you expected?"

"Yes, Governor, it is." The AG waited for a moment to let the Governor shake his head in disappointment, then open the document folder to scan the contents. "You'll see they want the Bakken oil fields. Given that it's the biggest oil find in modern U.S. history, I wasn't surprised. They want all the coal bed natural gas in the Miles City field. Pretty much all that Fallon, Phillips, Hill, Blain, and Richland counties have. And they want the Marysville Gold Mine." He paused, knowing this was excruciating for the Governor, and that the gold mine was necessary to their plan. He added,

"It's the richest vein found anywhere in a century, sir, and it was too much for us to expect they'd overlook it."

Fitzerman simply nodded. "The list includes the Libby silver mine, Troy and Anaconda copper, the Yugo sapphire mine, and, it appears from the Addendum, a certain number of private land holdings, under which lie natural resources that are also deemed essential to the national security of the U.S., and thereby subject to Eminent Domain as land needed for the public good."

"And what are they offering Montana for the assets you have listed?"

"$10 billion total, and the promise of keeping the jobs inside Montana that are related to the utilization of the resources—no imported workers."

The Governor laughed at this idea. "Let me guess. Some kind of treasury note, or cash?"

"Cash."

"They think we're pikers, don't they? That we're so small that would seem like a fortune to us! And that we would want the cash no one else wants."

"Well, sir, I don't presume to understand their thought process, or what they think, but it's clear they aren't very good at asset evaluation—certainly not on the long-term!" He had said it satirically, and Bruce took it as such. Something in the AG's tone calmed Fitzerman's temper a bit, and he felt the flush of rage diminish.

Wanting to take advantage of the calm, the AG immediately said, "We're preparing the legal briefs right now, along with notification that the State of Montana is refusing to relinquish State holdings, and that we will move to defend the holdings of the citizens of Montana, as they are a vital part of our economy, and intrinsic to our natural resource development."

"Good." Then, looking at the AG, he could tell there was more. "And...?"

"And I'm going to need more money, Governor, as this will be a full-court press by the Government on all of our holdings. Likely to turn into the most massive coordinated legal activity the State has ever undertaken. I'm going to need to hire every available lawyer in Montana, and most of the law school students at the University of Montana in Missoula."

"Ouch! And you'll have to pay them?"

"The lawyers, yes, unless they do it pro-bono—which I expect I can make a good case for. Nonetheless, we'll have staff costs, printing costs, research costs—you name it. As for the students, I may be able to negotiate internships that count toward class credit, and the Montana Bar."

"Can you do that, legally?" Bruce asked.

"At this point, sir, I believe I can pretty much do what I please, under my own authority—which my staff has researched—if it is accompanied by a declaration of a state emergency by the Governor."

The Governor was indeed laughing now. The idiocy of this whole scene, and the almost ludicrous jeopardy involved, would certainly be an emergency in anyone's mind. *I cannot even imagine what the political fallout from this could be!* he thought.

Knowing, however, that there was something more fundamental here, that survival of the government transcended politics, Governor Bruce Fitzerman signaled to his AG—a man from the opposite party, whom he had campaigned against, and disrespected for years—to proceed as he thought fit.

"So, just so I'm clear here, you are planning to tell the Justice Department to shove it?"

"That's about it," the AG responded. Turning at the door before he exited, he added, "Of course, I'll be a bit more diplomatic than that, and rest assured it will be in the legal language they understand."

He was about to leave and then decided to add, "Don't worry about the Eminent Domain attack. I'll counter them and go to the Supreme Court on a State's Rights issue. I'll protect that new bank. It may be a bit crude, but we'll tweak it, and if we have evaluated this right, once we defeat the RIT's intention to force Washington to steal our state, most of the other issues will go away."

"Jesus, I hope you are right."

"Yeah. Knowing my country, if we win on any of these issues the RIT is precipitating, the Feds will yield and start looking for another way. By then we'll be more influential than we are now. And we have one advantage," the AG added, somewhat smugly.

"What's that?"

"I'm a good poker player, Governor. I can 'bluff' and I can 'call.'" On that note, he winked and hurried out, leaving the folder.

Guys got balls, I'll give him that!

At the same moment, two jets landed within five minutes of each other at Walker's airstrip. Earlier that day, he, too, had received a currier pack with notification that the U.S. Government was proceeding under Eminent Domain to take his entire ranch. Seems there was something under it, which was needed by his country.

His response had been to simply call his NY attorney, who advised him this would be better handled by Montana legal counsel, and that alone would delay the proceedings considerably if this involved two different court districts. The Feds would file in the District, and the case would end up at the 9th Circuit Court of Appeals before heading to the Supreme Court.

Frankly, Bud had very little attention on it. He had the financial resources to wage a lengthy legal battle, and he had the business acumen to immediately prioritize this disturbing, but not earth-shattering, intrusion. His top priority right now was figuring out how to rescue these women, and help his Governor and Andy Weir launch their respective projects.

Waiting at the foot of the stairs of the silver Citation that had just landed, he looked merely determined. The stairs swung down, and Brian and James popped out immediately. Shaking hands at the bottom, they turned to introduce Bud to the team they had recruited.

Filling the entire doorway, and then some, was Hector Sanchez. He was massive, and the startling array of tattoos adorning his body caught Walker's eye immediately. *Thank God the man isn't armed; otherwise, I'd think James had recruited Rambo!*

The analogy wasn't all that far off. Save for the absent criss-crossed ammo belts Rambo wore across his chest, Hector did resemble a Latino version of that screen hero. Deciding to expose his tattoos in order to intimidate anybody he met up here, so as to create a level playing ground, Hector would be in for a surprise in the coming days when he discovered that almost all Montanans—male and female—had tattoos. Seems it was quite an industry.

Inconsistent with Hector's formidable physical presentation however was his totally ingenuous response to the views to the Scapegoat Range. "Wow, oh, wow!" He stopped, mesmerized, blocking the door. Recovering himself, he jumped to the ground.

Behind him, looking like a Los Angeles businessman, was DeShawn Williams. Bud Walker had no idea what type of business DeShawn was in, or had been in, but it was clear to Bud the guy walked in confidence.

Shaking hands with Walker, DeShawn then said, "The rest of my team—Willie, we call him 'God'; Richard; and Jon-Jon." Each man shook hands appropriately, keeping a very stern and intimidating face.

As the other plane taxied up, Bud leaned into James and Brian and said, "This looks like an African-American gang, with one outside recruit."

Brian responded, "Absolutely, Bud! One of the toughest bunch of guys in L.A., all of them straight now. And they have one real advantage here."

"Yeah, what's that?" Bud asked sincerely.

"They really like Andy Weir. And they possess some really fine skill sets!"

Before Bud could respond, the sound of the newly arrived plane revving its engines just before they were cut, made it hard to hear anyway. Bud signaled for the blocks to be hastily put under the wheels, and to receive the private jet he'd invited to his ranch.

Just as they were pulling down the stairs, Andy raced up in one of the ranch's jeeps, leaping out. "DeShawn, Hector, man am I glad to see you! I *really* need your help!"

Confirming what Brian had said to Bud, the five gangbangers embraced Andy as one of them, and the handshake normally reserved only for one of their race or their group was exchanged all the way around with Andy.

Their attention then went to the arriving jet, whose passengers were disembarking. Andy was the first to see her as she stepped out of the plane in a St. John pantsuit in banana yellow. "Oh my God!" He was speechless, jaw hanging open.

Their Investor—the woman who had bankrolled "White King Rising," and who was one of the most successful venture capitalists in the Southwest—briskly deplaned, walked straight to Bud for a handshake and then a more personal hug; then walked directly to Andy and Brian. "Hello, Andy. Brian. You, too, James. I wish we were meeting again under better circumstances."

They had no idea what to say except to nod. Not knowing whether to shake hands or hug her, she solved the problem with a handshake and the eerily mysterious words, "I'm here on a different mission today—one of my other *endeavors* you aren't aware of."

They remained speechless, wondering how on earth she was involved in Bud's promised rescue mission. Before they could even frame a question, however, another man emerged from her jet. Blue-eyed, with blond hair peppered by a touch of gray, he wore khaki trousers with a stark crease, a royal blue sport shirt and navy blazer, and carried a small duffle bag.

Walking toward the crowd that had now coalesced, she introduced him to Bud. "Bud, meet Vince McCoy." The two shook hands. Then, one by one, eyes on each man as he was introduced, he shook hands with them, politely and cheerfully saying, "Vince McCoy. Good to meet you. I look forward to working with you."

Bud tried to whisper the question to the woman Andy, James, and Brian knew as their Investor, but it came out louder than he anticipated. "Is he a negotiator?" It was said as if this were an alternate strategy in the event this turned out to be a kidnapping for ransom.

"No, I'm an extraction man, Mr. Walker."

"And that's part of the rescue mission?" Bud was trying to get his mind around this.

Vince's answer would stun them all, and set the stage for one of Al Qaeda's worst defeats. "From what I understand the facts to be, this will not be a typical rescue or payback mission. It will be strictly insertion, location, and extraction. In and out—stealth—nobody knows we were there."

James had to suppress the smile over this irony. *Son of a gun! She brought a mercenary to the party!*

CHAPTER 41

"Why do you think they've been holding us separate from the others?" Edith whispered to Reagan. "They must be planning something different for us. Perhaps a different type of ransom."

"I do not honestly know, Edith. I have picked up nothing from them. But, I do know Alicia will come for us. She will get us ransomed. I'm sure of it." Reagan was indeed so self-convincing that Edith tabled her own doubts. She was grateful to have her young, optimistic companion with her. Between her street smarts and Reagan's certainty, she believed somehow that they would come out of this. The two had stayed tightly together since they awoke inside the hut.

The four other women seemed strangers to one another—their only common ground being they found themselves unharmed, but incarcerated, inside some kind of compound in Venezuela, Colombia, or Mexico. None of them spoke Spanish, so subtleties of Hispanic dialects were wasted on them. They could not discern anything from the muted interchanges of their captors.

Over the next few days, the captive women began tentative conversations—each woman interested in learning where the others had been snatched, hoping to understand why they were being spared the obvious abuses other prisoners were experiencing in a section of the camp they could hear but not see.

Food was regularly delivered. It was palatable, and the women were allowed to go to a stream downhill every three days to wash. Their guards treated them with disdain or indifference, but not with brutality. That mystery was what aroused fear.

One of the girls was menstruating, and the guard, with disgust, found a few shirts that he allowed her to tear up and use. Under his breath, he was murmuring something, and they assumed he would be glad to be rid of them. Clearly women hostages were a burden to these men.

Each of the other women had been by herself, exiting the airport. What seemed to be common to their stories—as Edith made them painstakingly repeat the exact sequence of events leading up to their kidnapping—was the location and circumstance.

Traveling alone, landing in Mexico City Airport, there was an apparently innocuous exchange that each woman had had. Needing directions to find their way out of the airport and to the taxi, each had stopped at an information kiosk to seek assistance. By description, the same man was posted at the kiosk, and had been most helpful in directing them down a corridor towards their desired destination. Only, no one made it out of that corridor.

Surmising that all of them were victims of the same kidnap ring, which must be operating out of the airport, waiting for prey, and delivering their catch to this location, Edith noted that all the women here were American, traveling under American passports, and none spoke Spanish. What her kidnappers did not know, however, was that Edith's years in Los Angeles pursuing human rights abusers had brought her into frequent contact with Hispanics.

Though she did not speak Spanish, she understood a fair amount. Deducing that would prove helpful—if not possibly life-saving—she pretended she knew no more than the others. It was something she had withheld even from Reagan.

It had become obvious to all in the hut that the lot of the other prisoners was much worse, that their lives had somehow been changed forever. What went unspoken was an underlying, debilitating fear that theirs had too—but in a different, and perhaps more sinister, way.

And so they had minimal conversation, except as drawn out by Edith. Reagan followed her lead, speaking only if Edith did. Tonight, however, Edith had decided to change that dynamic, and lead the women into the natural type of bonding and sharing that is characteristic of American women.

What Edith knew, and her enemies did not, was that American women have a trait of almost immediately creating relationships with other women, and that they would create a team and work as a team almost instinctively. Given the fact that they could work at more than one task at a time, a group of American women could be easily organized for a project.

Knowing that it was just fear gripping them, and how effective a weapon fear is against the mind, Edith had concluded someone needed to step up and suggest they form a group—other than become a group of victims by default.

She was just about to share that with Reagan when men's voices could be heard outside the door.

"Si," was uttered by the guard they knew was posted there. A moment later, the bolt was thrown and the door swung open into the room. Stepping into the room was a handsome young man dressed in very neatly pressed jungle camouflage. Though he was in the attire of the others in order to maintain the security of the location, it was obvious by the man's pressed and creased trousers that he was not one of their captors.

"I want to inspect the condition of the six, while we wait for word on the remaining five," he said in rough Spanish to the guard. In response, the guard yielded access to the room, stepping aside.

Samir Taghavi did not speak to any of the women, as he did not want them to know he spoke English fluently. Expecting he'd learn more from them by appearing to speak only Spanish, he simply stepped into the room, walking to the women in their various locations, looking them over, and observing the conditions of the room.

Never let them hear Arabic! he reminded himself. If that were to occur, the women would likely realize where they were headed and whose hands they were in. That would make the entire journey and its outcome far more unpredictable. *Better they think this is a kidnap for ransom. Probably the only thing the American media has allowed into their consciousness,* he thought, smirking.

Satisfied that they were in decent shape, and totally submissive, given they were sitting separate from one another, in terror of him and what his intentions might be, he turned and exited.

Just five more and this first premium lot will be delivered! With any good fortune at all, this will get the Doctor off my back!

Waiting until she was certain he was gone, and that the guard had resumed his normal position, Reagan leaned into Edith with a shocking observation. "Edith, I recognize that man."

It was said so matter-of-factly that Edith for a moment failed to grasp it. Then, without blinking, she asked, "You do? From where?"

"From television. I saw him a few times on WNG. He's Samir Taghavi!"

Edith could hardly put it together. "The Al Qaeda propaganda chief operating inside Walker News Group? The reason Alicia vanished from cable news?"

"The same." Then, wanting to make sure Edith knew how certain Reagan was, she added, "I'm certain of it, Edith. I remember thinking at the time how smooth he was, and that it didn't surprise me at all he could have infiltrated the media at its highest level."

Edith thought for a moment and quietly ordered Reagan, "Do not tell the others. It will frighten them to hear the words Al Qaeda."

Reagan nodded agreement, sitting silently, reflecting on something.

But for Edith, her mind was thrown into a terrible turmoil. Edith Church did not believe in coincidences, and the probabilities that Alicia Quixote would have arranged flights for them, which resulted in them being imprisoned, and that the man whose care they were in was her former lover and exposed enemy infiltrator, and that this would be a coincidence, were just too incredible.

She rose, ostensibly to stretch her legs, but more to walk a bit and catch her breath. *Is Alicia in on this?* For the first time, Edith felt real terror.

CHAPTER 42

*T*he rain running down the glass windows in rivulets was almost hypnotic. Harley Grantham-Jones had decided to watch the summer storms, which were approaching Basel from France. He liked the drama of thunder, lightning, torrential rain, and winds. And he welcomed some time away from his cabal of finance colleagues. The top floor restaurant was glass all the way around, enabling him to look through the rain in any direction. For some reason, though, he was fixated on the West.

The news had been coming in from around the world that the U.S. government was exerting Eminent Domain claims in Montana, and was preparing to expand the reach into other sectors as well. No matter what channel one was watching, the world's news media had been relentlessly focusing the eyes of the world on the U.S. That is, all but one. WNG was apparently missing in action, with not a single comment on the historic maneuver.

Harley was experiencing a mix of emotions. *It won't be long now,* he reassured himself. *The U.S. is doing just what we programmed them to do. Once they've plundered their people, it still won't be enough, and they will be forced to ask us to intervene and help.* He smiled at the irony of just how ready the Financial Responsibility Board was to take the assets the government would offer towards its debt, and then implement its program to restore calm and assure the world that this kind of devastation would not occur again.

Suddenly he experienced a surge of anxiety, which prompted him to pour a glass of water and take one of the tablets their doctor had recommended. Grateful now that Braghelli had moved the attack up a few years, it was clear to him that, although there was some sporadic rioting in America's metropolitan areas, it was nothing compared to the plundering, riots, and fire-bombings that were spreading throughout Europe, parts of South America, and now into Asia.

It was not as he had predicted. The U.S. had not been the first to stagger. *It's only a matter of time—a few weeks at most,* he told himself, trying to dismiss the nagging doubt. *Sane or not, the Americans are soft on the issue of inconvenience. After thirty years, they're weak now. When they start to really feel the lack, they'll expect their government to make the pain go away.* "And in we will come, like the knight on the white horse, to save them," he said out loud to no one.

The medication was taking effect, and he felt calmer now. He thought of Bud Walker and WNG and their complete failure to engage at this momentous time in world history. *He must have really lost it. What a pity to have him hiding, wherever he is. He's missing all the fun.* Sneering, he dismissed his once-powerful protégé with, *What a disappointment he has turned out to be!*

Sir Harley concluded his reverie just as the rain ceased. It had left the city shrouded in fog. *Well, the other media are performing exactly as we knew they would. No harm in losing one player.* As he entered the elevator to return to his quarters, however, the doubt crept back and he couldn't help but ask himself, "Still, I wonder what he's up to?"

Had it not been for the distinctive sound of the helicopter blades rotating, no one at the ranch would have known what was transpiring on the north end of Walker's property, which bordered the Bob Marshall Wilderness.

McCoy's regular team was on a lucrative security assignment in North Africa, where things were heating up. That left him with the stand-ins Brian had recruited. The inexperience of this volunteer crew presented a unique challenge to him, to be sure. So, McCoy had insisted on training the men in the forest—as its density would approximate the type of overhead cover, and undergrowth, at least in terms of quantity and difficulty of passage, that they would encounter in the portions of Colombia the FARC were reported to inhabit. The Governor had supplied a National Guard helicopter comparable to the type of machine that could fly in low, hopefully undetected, set down in a small clearing, and lift off.

Since the pilot's skill for that type of mission would be far beyond the capabilities of this mercenary crew, a retired Special Forces Major nicknamed "Blacky" had volunteered to participate. His wife's cousin had married into the Governor's family. He had made it a habit since his retirement of weighing in on every issue he felt important to national security and to the State of Montana. Given that he was usually loud, and of a contrary opinion to Bruce Fitzerman, he was oddly the first man the Governor thought of.

Partisan politics had indeed evaporated in deference to the broader definition of politics as the government and affairs of men. The survival of the country and its government was bringing many odd bedfellows together in this unknown sector of Montana.

McCoy was impressed with Blacky and his ability to thread that machine down through trees and into almost invisible landing zones. *Man, this really helps,* he told himself, knowing that even if they found the women, and got out of the camp alive, the helicopter rescue presented their most dangerous moments. "I'm grateful for the help, Blacky," he said sincerely, giving him a thumbs up as they returned to base.

Blacky just grinned. It was obvious he was happy to be included, and to be taking some kind of action. Though he did not know his orders, or where he would be embarking from or returning, he had been told he was going into jungle terrain. For the former Viet Nam vet, it was like returning to a comfort zone.

McCoy then hopped onto the ATV he rode, and disappeared into the forest at the head of a trail. There were six young men up this trail, whose skills were improving, but he needed to verify that the last week's work had been sufficient. Normally for an operation this urgent, an already assembled and trained team would be deployed. Asking a bunch of former gang bangers and a famous computer gamer to pull this off was the stuff legends are made of—also the stuff that horror stories are made of.

Hanging just outside the training area, he watched the drill commence again. Having no idea where the women would be, or how many armed men would have to be bypassed, each drill he created changed up the location and number of adversaries in order to keep the six-man squad thinking.

Each man carried multiple weapons. All assault weapons had silencers, since their only real hope lay in stealth. Vince McCoy was no fool, and he knew he was walking in greatly outnumbered. To their credit, these guys did know how to use a knife, and they had no back-off whatsoever on the handguns and rifles.

Hand-to-hand combat training had been a bit touchier, as it seemed these guys would have just shot someone in their neighborhood, not bothering to get into a one-on-one fight. But, each knew that scenario could appear, and none wanted to be left behind in an as yet to be identified jungle location in some foreign land. *Motivated men,* he thought. Smiling, he said to himself, "And 'God' can really handle that M16 sniper rifle!"

Willie was the last man down, and there was no doubt in McCoy's mind that, should he want another career, the U.S. military would put him to good use. "Glad you're on our side, son." Willie grinned as he moved past McCoy into the jeep and headed on to the next location and its drill.

Even tougher than dropping in, rescuing, and successfully extracting all personnel was figuring out how to find the exact location of Edith Church and Reagan Lynch. The Mexico government had offered assistance there. Promising protection to the airport employee who had been sending American women down that corridor, the man remained on post. He had no problem switching sides for his own self-preservation. The officials were quite certain he had not been compromised, and that the channel would work—if not for the women, perhaps for a contact message.

They were aided almost serendipitously by the reluctance of any American now to fly anywhere out of the country. With most of Europe embroiled in meltdowns, and South America appearing less appealing by the minute, American women were not coming through the Mexico City Airport. That fact alone was holding Samir Taghavi in a camp in Venezuela, and delaying his delivery to the Doctor of the women he had promised. He had six, and needed five more.

In normal times, that quota would have already been filled, but these were anything but normal days. The delay, and the jeopardy it posed for Samir, opened a door for a bold and ingenious strategy to develop in Ovando, Montana.

Bud Walker was shocked to the point of being speechless, and literally needing to sit down. "Shut the damned door!" he barked.

James obliged, leaving the Investor, McCoy, himself, Alicia, and Walker sequestered in the War Room.

Her name was Jessica Ranger. In all the years the boys had dealt with her, she was known to them only as their Investor. Looking back on their first meeting now, James saw very clearly the image of her extending her hand to Brian and Andy, introducing herself with, "I am your Investor." He'd been in the spy game a long time, and the intelligence game even longer. How this had escaped his notice was humbling. *She never told me her name!*

"Bud, for Pete's sake, stop acting so shocked. You've known for some time that I have connections into mercenaries and a network of people who can help in delicate situations."

"Sure, Jessica, I have known that. But to hear you tell me now that you are a slave trader is...." He stopped, seemingly at a loss.

"Well, it was something I could do. Women were being brought into this country, or enslaved here, and unless I bought them, they would have ended up in prostitution or captive in some upscale neighborhood, right under our noses."

Bud was listening, clearly trying to get his mind around this new identity of his long-time friend. McCoy seemed to know this about Jessica, so James concluded this was not their first rodeo regarding women in duress.

"So, I set myself up as a wealthy buyer, and whenever I could, I would purchase the slave—and then free her of course."

It was said so matter-of-factly that Bud did not have anything to add. Logically, it was the humanitarian thing to do, and he'd heard of people who would receive phone calls when journalists would stumble onto some human rights issue that they personally could not resolve, but where a private citizen could. It had just never occurred to him that one of his own friends was one of them. For a moment, they just stared at each other. Bud broke the stalemate with, "Jessica Ranger, I had no idea. Now, that's a *story!*"

"Which you are never going to tell," she said, completing his sentence for him.

"Jessica, I presume you have an idea, here," Vince said, interrupting.

"Yes. Just send word through that airport weasel that an American wants to sell some American women. Surely his contacts will get word to 'whomever' that there are additional American women for sale. Didn't the man tell us they were pressuring him recently, wondering why he wasn't sending anyone down the corridor?"

James nodded.

"Well, there you have it. That tells me there is a demand for the product—a very specific type of product—and they are likely to need someone who can supply what they need."

That was sobering enough. Even discussing this was disturbing to Bud, and he was gaining a newfound appreciation for those who can stare evil in the face and not flinch.

McCoy was the first to develop the idea. "All right, so the man at the airport gets word that Jessica wants to negotiate. If they want to talk, she may be able to find the location of the destination. If they just want to buy, we will need to send someone down that corridor with a well-concealed transponder—probably inserted through the navel, and activated remotely once she has been picked up and scanned."

"But who?" Bud was struggling with this. The idea of sending in a rescue team was chivalrous and familiar to him. But sending some woman to be grabbed by the FARC—which was only a guess—and landing her in some location, hopefully within range of their helicopter and rescue team, was hard for him to stomach. There were no women on the team, and the risks seemed enormous. *What if they take her to some other location? And we end up with two women in one place and one in another?*

"Bud," James took over for a moment. "This is within our purview here. Assuming the FARC have our girls, then it is likely the same feeder line will deposit the next victim into the same location. We have to assume that. Otherwise we're all screwed. So, assuming that, the unknown for us is how to find the damned location once they do take our decoy. A GPS locater would confirm that. And, if our theory is correct, we would already be 'in country.' Colombia has agreed to cooperate. Is that right, Vince?"

"Yes. They just want the coordinates, once we have extracted. Frankly, they are happy we're willing to do some work for them our 'officials' weren't, if you know what I mean."

"But who?" Bud reiterated. By the look on his face, they could see this was really fixating him.

"It should be me, Bud," Alicia said firmly. "I know Edith and Reagan and can easily spot them."

"Oh, no! No! You're just doing this out of some perverted sense of guilt over having sent them to Mexico in the first place. I know you, Alicia!" Bud was vehement and determined on this point.

But Alicia Quixote also knew her former boss. He had always had a passionate loyalty to his team, and a huge commitment to his enterprises. She came around the table and sat down next to him. "Bud, that may be part of it," she said. "But, you know I am an investigative journalist, and I can think on my feet. And I am more observant than most. It goes with the territory. You trained me well."

She knew she'd won when Walker just let out a huge exhale and shook his head. That had always been his signal for capitulating on something against his better judgment. Smiling, she patted him on the hand. "Remember, they'll be tracking me. Vince, Brian, and the boys will be flying into Colombia, ready to deploy in the helicopter. If the location seems logical, they go. If not, they wait a bit to see if I am moved. Am I right, guys?"

Surprised at her perception and her professionalism, Vince responded immediately, "Yes, ma'am. We would take those factors into account. If you stop in the middle of a crowded mall in Bogota, we will assume you are not at the final destination. That judgment call is mine."

"And that's good enough for me." Looking to Jessica to see if she agreed, Alicia asked, "Jessica?"

"I have always trusted Vince's judgment." There was not even a fraction of a second delay in Jessica Ranger's response.

And that was good enough for James.

CHAPTER 43

*K*nowing that the longer the training took, the greater the risk to Reagan, James was eager to get to Andy with their plan. While Brian and the others were playing "war games," as Andy referred to it, Andy had been holed up in his room placing the design elements into the computer game.

From time to time James had checked in on him. Though he looked tired from the obviously long hours he was putting in, Andy seemed focused and intent upon his own mission. James experienced an aching as he watched this young man once again tackle an almost insurmountable problem for the sake of a government that seemed hell bent on destroying itself.

Andy's probably got it right, James told himself. *He seems to know this is for country, and he seems able to avoid the distraction of the news and the hysterical comments that are appearing daily. Hell, I ought to turn off the damn news feed!*

Each night a sliver of light would illuminate the Indian rug in front of Andy's door. That was the only sign he was up and working, as he had always been quiet. It was still light out, even though it was 9 PM, and James was certain Andy would still be up.

Knocking respectfully, he heard Andy's voice. "Come in, James."

"How'd you know it was me, Kid?"

"Well, James, after all these years, I am actually used to your foot-steps." Andy smiled slightly without taking his eyes off the computer monitor. "What's up?"

"Good news, Andy." At that moment, Andy turned to him with such hope in his eyes that it unnerved James. From Andy's perspective, the good news would mean Reagan had been found. From James' point of view, just knowing the mission was about to commence was sufficient. *Man, I can be a thoughtless SOB sometimes,* James thought, chastising himself.

"The mission is planned. One piece needs to fall into place, and it's a go."

Andy's interest waned instantly once he realized the news was not about Reagan, and he returned to his work with, "Humph. Okay, thanks for letting me know." Then, as if he felt he needed to encourage James, he added, "I'm progressing well here, too. I should be ready for Brian tomorrow or the next day."

James placed his hand gently on Andy's shoulder and squeezed. "That's great news, son."

"You bet. We're going to lick this thing, James, you have my word."

James squeezed Andy's shoulder again and left him to continue. At the door, he added, "There's a campfire tonight. Bud wants everyone there."

At first, Andy didn't respond, but then he quietly said, "Sure."

James waited until he was not only outside the door but also into his own room before letting himself address his feelings. There was something in Andy's resolute demeanor that had unnerved him. True, Andy had faced world-changing challenges before in the times they had worked on these analyses. But this was the first time Andy was trying to work, still having to deal with the threatened loss of his fiancé. This made the game personal. In all the others, there had been a natural detachment—a problem to be solved. But, in this one, Andy had to do something few can do: have enough altitude to observe the game field, choose winning strategies and tactics, and at the same time play one of the roles in the game himself. He had not had to do that before.

Exterior to the game, he could remain objective. But inside the very game itself, surely there were unbearable subjective pressures on Andy. *Can he do it?*

Without intending to, he found himself whispering, "Oh, Kelly, if only you could tell me whether our boy's okay. You know him. You would know; I'm sure of it. I never had a son. Help me now, girl, if you can!"

Wiping the tears from his eyes with the heels of his hands, James inhaled deeply, pulled himself together, and began calling everyone Bud wanted to see at the campfire.

The whole scene was déjà vu to Walker. Except, this time all the personnel around the campfire were different. The last time he'd found a lot of men sitting around the fire enjoying the night air, it had been with all the Conservative Talk Radio hosts he had invited to his ranch. They had come, had a great party, and were enjoying drinks and cigars around the fire when Bud Walker had introduced them to his protégé, Samir Taghavi.

And it was there that Samir had slipped like a viper into the debate, altering it forever, precipitating the downfall of a President. Looking back on it now, that night stood out more than almost any other in Bud Walker's career. For, at his own home, with his own guests, an enemy agent had infiltrated and inserted a brilliant propaganda line that seasoned and respected journalists had embraced and carried forward. The "amnesty" question had created quite a diversion, and further divided America—and it had started here.

Divide and conquer, he reflected. It had been a simple maneuver made possible by Bud's advancing the credibility of Samir. Shaking it off, he reminded himself, *Well, I may get a chance to redeem myself yet. Set this straight when it really counts.*

He'd arranged for an elegant and robust barbecue for all the men and women who'd been involved in this project. Those staying at the ranch arrived at least showered after their day's responsibilities. Those coming in from the State Capital arrived early in a caravan of SUVs and vans. It seemed the whole front pasture was filled with vehicles. Every person looked haggard and exhausted, but there was pride in their step. Grim-faced, they still held their heads high, shoulders back. Though worried, it was clear Montana was reporting for duty.

Andy and Brian were the last to arrive. Standing slightly away from the large circle of guests, they seemed to be watching them closely. Andy was more subdued, obviously unable to shake the thoughts of Reagan that were crowding into his mind, once he took a break from his game. But, for Brian, something was stirring. He saw something tonight he had never really seen before. And just like that moment when he'd "awakened" and began the sojourn to Florida to try to save Mrs. Schiavo—a woman he'd never met and of whom he'd had no real awareness—Brian was seeing something for the first time. As he thought about it now, his entire relationship with Andy had been a series of awakenings.

"How's the training going?" Andy said, interrupting his reflection.

"Great! Or so they tell me." He laughed, self-deprecatingly. "Man, I'd rather be playing computer games, I got to tell you!"

Andy couldn't help but smile. Until recent years when Brian had more or less come out of a shell, he'd been this somewhat recalcitrant kid who said almost nothing, but who played computer games obsessively, and spent what other time he had playing football. "I bet you would," he said admiringly.

Then Brian returned his attention to the collection of people who had joined the circle. The atmosphere was lively, yet hanging over it was a sense of impending battle. And this odd group was about to commence it.

The more he looked at the group and the folks talking with one another comfortably, the more surreal the whole scene seemed to him. Most had never met one another before, and certainly not worked together. Some had been political opponents. Natural tensions between disparate personalities had flowed during the week, and doubts about each other had obviously surfaced, as the urgency of the situation strained every man and woman to the limits. Yet, this new group they had formed over the summer had created a different kind of comradeship.

He couldn't quite put his finger on it, but a memory was stirring in Brian. The scene was evocative of something. To his right were the Chief and his grandson, William Graywolf, in conversation with Hector Sanchez, Willie, and the other two gang members, Richard and Jon-Jon. Like two different tribes meeting, he could not even fathom what they might be talking about.

Even stranger was DeShawn forking another steak onto the Sheriff's plate. *I wonder whether he knows the man's Militia?* Vince McCoy, too, seemed a little out of place, and not too certain why he had been included, until James brought the Governor up and introduced them. Then the three had their heads together over something.

Understandably, the three women were sitting together, sipping the draft beers that were being served. He couldn't help but wonder what Jessica Ranger and Alicia Quixote would have in common with the single mom Secretary of State, but they were chatting like sorority sisters. He looked closely to see what held their attention, and, of all things, they were deeply interested in some kind of lip gloss with a light on it that the Montana woman seemed to be bragging about.

Predictably, Bud was with Simon Atwater, Ray, and his Chief of Staff, for a few moments. Then each seemed to want to talk with the businessmen who were going to have to carry a heavy load in the near future. Bud caught sight of Blacky and personally served him a plate, with the requested extra helping of potato salad.

His observations were interrupted by oohs and ahhs from the entire party, as their attention universally went to the sky. *What the hell?* he asked himself, as the ephemeral green and whitish lights appeared over the mountains. The boys from Compton were equally stunned by the phenomenon, and tried to act nonchalant—all the while wondering whether there was some kind of extra-terrestrial activity going on.

The dancing lights, and their unpredictable movements over their heads, spooked Brian. "Those are the Northern Lights," Bud Walker said, stepping out of the group and standing next to Brian. "We don't get to see them too often. Nice that they made an appearance tonight."

"Wow, I had no idea, Bud. Wow! Thought for a minute there we were under invasion."

Bud laughed. "Yeah, they sure are a bit spooky. To me they look like ladies in gossamer gowns."

For some reason that wasn't comforting to Brian. The images and shapes were just too much like a ghost story for his liking. But, looking around, he could see that the movements of the feathery shapes were delighting everyone else. Glancing over at Andy, even he was out of his introverted mode, and grinning.

It was then Brian realized what had been surfacing, effecting his emotions. Turning to Bud, he quietly said, "Almost humbling, isn't it?"

"The lights?"

"No, sir, this group." Knowing he needed to explain his comment, he continued. "I mean, look at 'em. What a mixed bag. I would never put this selection of people together."

Bud nodded.

"You know, my Pappy fought in World War II. He was my great-grandfather, and next to my mama, he was the most influential person in my life. I just remembered something he told me."

"What was that?" Bud asked sincerely.

"'Take men one at a time, son, not as a group or category, and you'll get through.' I see now he had to do that, you know—not see 'white men,' but individuals. He had that gift. And he was a very wise man." Unexpectedly, Brian's eyes misted up.

He paused, cleared his throat, and then confessed, "I had no idea how prejudiced I was until this." He could see the agreement in Bud's eyes and in the modest nod of his head. "Thank you, Mr. Walker."

Bud was uncomfortable now, as it was he who felt his life was changing due to his time with James and the boys. "Thanks, Brian, but you are the ones doing it. It's your game, and your rescue."

"But you really made it happen. It's your money, your practice area, staging, helicopter—all that. Honestly, me and the home boys there would not have been able to do this."

Warmth flushed through Bud, as he realized he really had made a contribution here. Looking at the group with all its diversity, it seemed a tapestry to him. He felt grateful to have been put in this position. Yet he experienced a twinge of embarrassment. For he well knew now the length and breadth of the manipulation Sir Harley Grantham-Jones had engaged in. Bud Walker had many flaws, and had done many things, but betrayal was not one of them.

He reached out and patted Brian on the back. It was a bit awkward, but heartfelt, and Brian seemed to understand. Everyone at this party was "playing wounded"; everyone seemed to have faced some demons along the way. For whatever reason, they had convened in this small berg in Montana.

"We'll get them back, Bud."

"And we'll get your game out." Bud turned to face Brian directly, meeting him eye to eye. "And God willing, we all win."

CHAPTER 44

They had all known their counter attack was imminent. The daily news feeds from competing networks were not only showing rioting throughout Europe, but also "experts" were now rattling the sabers of war, warning that if the economies did not turn around, the European Union would implode and nations would go to war.

Though that undoubtedly was coming from the Public Relations machine of the men in Switzerland in order to force governments to reach for their solution, and accept the heinous terms of their "assistance," it nonetheless was programming the populations of the planet to live in fear, and to oust governments. People were beginning to expect the worst, rather than expect a solution or turn-around.

Even the once-mighty Chinese Yuan was under attack, and the robust Chinese economy was slowing to the point of a stall. And that would affect all other economies. All of it had been produced by the inability to conduct business as usual. Bud had concluded the United States would hold only as long as there was food on grocery shelves in the major cities. Once gone, they would erupt and deteriorate, but he felt the rest of the country would hold—for a while.

Knowing that things were getting more precarious, Andy had been struggling with something in the game. The State of Montana was in fact setting up its own bank, and had invested in silver and gold to provide something to back up its "currency." That currency was silver coin, and crudely designed at that. But they were ready.

However, the game broke down when the university students who were testing the game, before it would launch into general testing, came to the point of exchanging their dollars for gold and silver. It stopped altogether when random Montana citizens who lived ordinary lives came to that juncture. Men and women who were already accustomed to running households hit a stone wall.

Andy had agonized over this since the previous night, when he had refrained from wrecking everyone's barbecue. But now he knew he had to point this out. They could not risk delaying the game's launch, and he had just arrived at what he felt was a bold solution for the problem.

James, Bud, Brian, Atwater, and the Secretary of the Treasury were all assembled. Brian was the last one to run in just as Andy entered the room. He'd been hauled from his last dry run on the rescue mission, gear and all, into this meeting. After all, it was his design, and he needed to be involved.

They all listened attentively as Andy exposed a weak link. Gamers were choosing to go with their State Bank, and were willing to switch to gold and silver coins, but the bank itself could not accept it. The reason was that the dollar had in fact been so devalued that the bank—even though it could issue coin in exchange for dollars—had nowhere to go to exchange the dollars for themselves. It left them with worthless money. The test players balked right there.

"It might as well be Confederate money!" Andy explained.

All of them could see the problem, once he pointed it out. It confirmed their earlier fear. They knew they were racing against a clock. It was a gargantuan task to attempt what they were, and complete it before the enemy's run on the dollar made the point moot. They asked almost in unison, "What do you suggest?"

"Two things, gentlemen. First, we set the game, but with the supposition that you will have to go to barter immediately. Independent state banks, with gold backing them, is a great solution, but it's too far down the road in the evolution."

Brian was leaning in now, reminiscent of his leaning into a huddle. "What's your play, Andy?"

Andy also characteristically leaned in, preparing to call an audible. James smiled, while the others sat there with quizzical looks. "Punt."

"Punt? What the hell is punt?" The Governor immediately realized they all knew what the word meant, so he rushed to clarify. "I mean, what does that mean to the game?"

Andy's explanation took their breath away for a moment. He told Brian he would recommend they leave that particular solution to the gamers themselves—task them to solve it for the next iteration of the game. And that the solutions chosen would not only be incorporated, but that the gamers who brought the solutions would be published with the game, and therefore would receive part of the profits.

There was silence for a moment, as all eyes turned to Brian. He looked it over, tilting his head a couple of times as if viewing it from different angles, then said simply, "That will work, as long as you tell them the solutions have to be within the guidelines and principles already established in the game. Don't want some fool screwing up the whole rest of the game!"

"Got it. I can do that," Andy assured him. "Now, the current game will go to Barter as the way to return following a cataclysmic event. That's our first version." He seemed happy with that, but knew he would have to explain this to the men from Montana who were trying to implement the real life prototype.

"Governor, with the Feds closing banks in order to prevent a run, and with the dollar already devalued, even with your new bank, the people can't exchange their money. We could have forced the players to do it in the game, but you will be unable to sync your real life model with the game's."

It took a moment for the magnitude of that statement to sink in. The Governor looked over at his Treasury Secretary, hoping for some bright idea from him, but all he saw was resignation. His own examination of the banking project had exposed the same potential weakness. He was just grateful Andy was bringing it up first. Atwater also grasped the scene right about then, and looked to Bud.

"So, we're too late? *Our* project is doomed?"

No one answered.

Andy finally broke the silence. "Governor, the project is not doomed, but you *will* have to tell your people that they have already been wiped out. The cataclysmic event has already happened. Regrettably, money in the banks is near worthless to them. The erosion of the dollar value was too great and too swift. Their gold, silver, and gems that are in banks are embargoed for now, too. Pretty basically, they are going to have to start again. That is the reality of it, and the game will help them figure out how."

Bruce Fitzerman nodded; then broke down and wept, exhaustion and fear overtaking him. The others waited respectfully. No one spoke. Every man there had carried burdens in their time, so all understood the enormity of his burden. The population of Montana was expected to crest at 1 million in a few months. How does one tell 1 million people they have lost everything and must start again?

Bud Walker was the first to speak, and there was a true sense of understanding in his voice, and a clarity in his communication. "Governor, it will be all right. We all chose Montana, because we knew America had its best chance here. You are going to write a talk, and you are going to tell every citizen of this state the whole, unvarnished truth—no political correctness, no politicking, none of the usual spin. You are going to respect them enough to tell them the magnitude of what they face, and guide them toward the solution the game has already identified."

The Governor seemed resigned to the idea of the speech and willing to do it, but he was concerned with, "How do we reach everyone?"

"WNG will help with that, Governor. I've already had all vans, reporters, cameramen, and equipment from around the country moved into the state. You can go 'live' from your Helena Office, and we'll get it fed into every hamlet in this state. We'll reach them. We'll reach them..." His voice trailed off.

"All right then, I'll complete the game emphasizing 'Barter,' and we'll task gamers to solve the rest. I should be ready to launch the next test within a few days," Andy said, clearly interested in getting on with the last of his work.

Brian had only one question. "Have you announced on the Internet that our company is launching a new game—one designed to solve the global economic crises, and that we are looking for people to test it?"

Andy smiled. "Yeah, and before you even ask, Brother, 10,000 people responded. Biggest problem they have in our offices in L.A. is getting that set up. Looks like they *will* be set, though. Additional servers are in. We load the game from our end here; they get it out; the 'serious gamers' start playing; and we'll see the results very quickly. Once I see the win percentages, paths chosen, and we survey for their feedback on the game, I'll adjust, and launch."

"And your Public Relations?" James asked.

"I'd say the game is highly anticipated!" That brought a grin to Andy's face as well as Brian's. "We'll deliver on that, no problem." Andy said the last very pointedly to the other three men, as if admonishing them to make sure they delivered in the coming weeks. To the man—now that they knew the state was in fact going to be starting its people from scratch in real life, real time—the path actually seemed clearer.

"And did I tell you the game, for now, is free?" Andy added.

That was a stunner for a moment, but Brian broke any tension with his wholehearted agreement. "Absolutely! The fewer barriers we have to this going viral globally the better. We'll pick up the revenue on the back side, and with the next versions. Now, if you all will excuse me, that guy

McCoy will skin me alive if I'm not aboard that chopper when it departs the LZ."

"How's he justifying your absence from the drill right now?" James joked.

"Simple, James," Brian quipped. "For this drill, I'm a casualty! Still need to be extracted though."

And with nothing more than that on it, both Andy and Brian darted out to resume their war games.

CHAPTER 45

"**Y**our Americans are less emotional than I would have liked," Harley said to the Director of the Bank of the United States. Not waiting for any kind of answer, he added, "Nonetheless, the media is performing as expected. We are perceived as White Hats. No one seems to have any questions whatsoever about all of us being sequestered here. It seems they have 'bought' that we are working feverishly to save the day. Perhaps our stay in this fortress will not be as long as we feared. With luck, my friend, no one will even know what we did." Again, he continued the conversation with himself. "In fact, my fears that we would be pariahs, estranged from our lives from this point forward, appear to be unfounded. And by George, that is a welcome possibility."

Harley was just adding a second sugar cube to his afternoon tea, continuing to reflect on the success of their recent maneuvers. His attention however kept rubber-banding to the United States and China, abbreviating his self-congratulatory mood. Absence of demonstrable violence in China was to be expected, given the restrictions they placed on media coverage.

Indeed, he knew he would only know what their government was in need of by virtue of its communication to their Central Bank Director, and that Director's subsequent delivery of information to those he trusted and worked with at the RIT. Having been kept out of the loop, every move China's Director made, he believed to be in the best interest of the central government in Beijing.

The United States was more of a puzzle though. *Surely after all the dire warnings and images of collapse the Americans are seeing, they should be doing something by now.* He was uneasy and angry about this, yet tried to reassure himself. "Well, Braghelli was right. They are tougher than they were. If we had waited, they would be sober for sure."

Rather than dwell on it though, Harley turned his attention to the Director of the Bank of the United States, who had joined him more for the cakes and sandwiches than for the tea. Harley's companion and fellow conspirator had recovered from his heart episode, and chosen to stay in Basel, rather than return to New York. But, he was cautious in his activities, and from Harley's perspective seemed somewhat detached. Truth be told, Harley didn't know what to expect from the man. He seemed different following his collapse.

One thing that disturbed Harley was the man's lag in answering questions. There were interminable pauses, which Harley concluded must have had to do with lack of oxygen to the brain. For that reason, the delay in his response to Harley's observations seemed just further confirmation of the fact that the man was not at the top of his game. *Probably just as well,* Harley concluded. *Easier to keep in line.*

"I expect you'll see what you are looking for when the food runs out in the grocery stores. When the warehouses are depleted, violence will begin—at least in the cities."

Harley had already concluded that days earlier, and had also concluded that in a couple of months, he'd have the U.S. exactly where he wanted. He would find America on her knees, begging for him to turn the credit spigot back on—even if it were accompanied by the heinous conditions of the Financial Responsibility Board. *Then they are ours; we own them—whether they know it or not.*

Relishing his imminent conquest, he turned his attention back to his colleague. "Any rioting elsewhere, you think?" he asked the Director.

"Don't know, Harley. My perspective of my country has always been the perspective of the major cities, since that's the only place people of quality will be found. I can assure you though, that they will react when the food supply runs out. Quality or not, educated or not, when men are hungry, you can count on them to do what any other animal will do."

That was enough to reassure Harley. "Good, so just a little longer then."

"Did I or did I not make myself clear that the order is for eleven American women?" Samir hissed at Hyena. His patience had been tried to the breaking point, waiting in this steam bath of a jungle camp, with hundreds of men with whom he had very little in common. Given that he was willing to pay a premium for these next women, Samir felt that Hyena should be prioritizing completing his contract.

Every day Samir was receiving news of the increased civil war and violence in Yemen, and he knew that Al-Awlaki's remaining in control of their movement in Yemen was imperative to other military operations for Al Qaeda in the future. Furthermore, he was plagued by fears of trying to bring these eleven in through Somalia. Personally he regarded everyone there as too unreliable, and he had concluded they were drugged up enough that they might in fact kill him, steal the women, and retain the profit themselves.

That—and the fact that the Doctor was not a man to disappoint— were causing Samir to have trouble sleeping. His relationship with the Doctor needed to be enhanced, with Bin Laden out of the picture. In fact, Samir knew he had to prove himself with Al Qaeda's new head. The longer it took for him to deliver what the Doctor wanted, the more Samir knew Zawahiri might doubt either his loyalty or his competence. And he knew that doubt, when it festered too long with the Doctor, had always led to sudden and brutal changes.

Determined not to end up a casualty of Hyena's incompetence, he had decided to ratchet up the pressure on the man to deliver.

"Señor, it has become difficult. The Americans are not traveling so much as before, and my man has to wait for someone to come down unattended. Be patient, my friend. We will get the remaining women. After all, I want my money, too, you know."

"Patience, I am out of, my *friend*." Samir's tone made it very clear to Hyena that he was not regarded as a friend. Quite the opposite. He was turning now into a distrusted business partner, and that was enough for Hyena to change his plan.

Until that moment, greed had been driving his actions, and he had been willing to wait until the man in Mexico City could pick women off one at a time, allowing him to pocket the bonus money Samir was willing to pay for Americans. But realizing now that the entire arrangement was in jeopardy, he decided to reduce his profit margin a bit by bringing in another middle man—a partner in the United States who could guarantee American captives, but who would want a cut.

Ever desirous of lucrative deals, he decided to make a phone call, and make an offer. "I will handle this, Samir. You will have someone very soon. I assure you."

Once Samir had turned, never lessening the menacing glare, Hyena placed a phone call to a Mexico City cell phone. "¡Hola! You told me you had someone in the United States who wished to sell?" Apparently the man's answer was affirmative, as he continued with, "Well, contact them and tell them I wish to negotiate a purchase. And tell them, it must come down our normal business lines."

Hyena had no way of knowing then that the ensuing phone call was headed to a cell phone with a 323 area code. Nor could he have known that the owner of that cell phone was just finishing lunch on the veranda of a sprawling ranch home in a remote area on the Continental Divide in Montana.

"Yes?"

"Señora, they have made contact. They are ready to buy." Jessica Ranger listened a little longer to the terms of the purchase; then she smiled, snapping her finger to get Vince McCoy's attention. She said only, "Tell them I will send only one person the first time. Once I am assured of their good faith, then I will send the remaining four. They will understand I am not risking my best inventory on people I have never dealt with before." Then she ended the call.

McCoy was at her side, really hoping this was the call they had been expecting. Knowing his anxiety to get going, she nodded, without saying anything, and he immediately walked into the War Room to inform Bud and James. "Green light."

Hyena was resentful enough about bringing any other players into his game, but he saw no alternative. The amount the woman from the United States was asking as her cut really nauseated him, but he knew she was clearly taking the greater risk, and the businessman in him decided he could stomach it. *I'll renegotiate this later. Right now, I want that mad dog off my back.*

Feeling better having just made a decision, he looked it over and realized it wasn't so bad. After all, no one could compromise his situation, since the woman would be handled like any of the others: picked up in Mexico City and flown into camp. Clearly, the American slave trader was taking the risk. They were sending somebody across the border and into the hands of another business machine, with no guarantee of payment.

So, he approved the deal. The U.S. slave trader would transport the person personally into Mexico, and once the money transfer lines were established and confirmed, she would escort a woman down the corridor for the hand-off. From that point on, it was the FARC's operation, and the American would fly home—all of this done on private aircraft, not commercial. *Gotta hand it to those Gringos. They have ingenuity. If Americans can't fly commercially out of the country, they'll use their wealth to fly their private craft.* Smiling once again, he concluded, *This might not be so bad an arrangement after all. These times require changes, and bold leadership.*

And with that self-aggrandizing thought, Hyena congratulated himself for being a bold and flexible businessman. Then he went to Samir's quarters to inform him of the newly-acquired supply line, and that one additional woman would be arriving soon. Before Samir could even respond, he then added, "And once this new arrangement proves acceptable to both parties, the remaining four will be delivered immediately. Acceptable?"

It was. Samir's only thought was, *Another bullet dodged!*

After weeks of preparation and agonizing waiting in between, the plan had gelled. Adrenalin was flowing profusely, as the timeline was tight. Only Vince McCoy and James had been through the fever pitch of activity once a Special Forces operation is given the go ahead.

Less than six hours later, Bud, James, and Andy stood on the tarmac as the equipment was loaded aboard Jessica's jet. Hector went aboard first, followed by Willie, Jon-Jon, and Richard. DeShawn had started to step into the plane, but had changed his mind and took a position next to McCoy, acting as if he had something he wanted to say.

They helped Jessica, Alicia, and Blacky re-board unceremoniously. Then DeShawn leaned over to Brian, speaking into his ear. They turned to McCoy, indicating they'd come aboard, but that they wanted to speak with Andy.

McCoy nodded, and ducked into the plane, while Blacky slid into the co-pilot's seat. Bud was speechless. Frankly, the whole scenario was almost surreal. When the plan was devised, it was just another story, like some fiction plot for a film. Though he knew it would have to turn real in order to save the girls, he was having trouble grasping it all. He was gripped with fear. James sensed that and leaned into him. "Breathe, Bud."

"Yeah. Right." Bud laughed nervously.

"I still don't know why you have to go, Brian," Andy said plaintively, as Brian and DeShawn approached him.

"Because I'm the only one of this bunch who knows what she looks like, bro. We don't know what we'll encounter down there, but I don't want anyone missing her because she doesn't look like her picture. You get me?"

"Yeah. But I should go, too."

"Hell no! You have your job. You deliver that game. You were always meant to save the world, Andy. Right, James?" He looked at James, asking for support.

"That's right, Kid. You have your job. Brian's got his. He can run, and he can maneuver."

"And no offense meant, but his color works better," DeShawn said facetiously. "This is no job for a white boy."

"Tell that to Vince," Andy retorted.

"Ohhh, you got me!" DeShawn flinched, pretending to be shot. "Andy, seriously, Vince has a nickname you know. He's called 'the Ghost' in his circles. Seems the man disappears in the jungle." De Shawn said confidently, "I would never have wanted to face him, even on my own turf, man. The guy's a menace."

Brian motioned for DeShawn to board. Taking the hint, DeShawn very uncharacteristically embraced both James and Andy, shook hands with Bud, and darted away. Sensing that Brian needed a moment, James shook hands with Brian, saying only, "Good luck, Pal." Bud followed his lead, and they both pulled back a bit to give the boys a moment of privacy.

"Andy, just keep your head in the game. You are the best there is. Our fans will follow you now."

Andy nodded that he understood. So Brian continued. "I told you, we'll bring her back. No one else in this family dies, you understand?"

After a moment, Andy grinned. "Remember this family includes you, Brian. You remember that down there. Now huddle up." They did, as they had done since high school. James would never know the last words that Andy spoke to Brian, but when they broke from their huddle, both were ready for the play.

"I'll see you when I see you!" Brian tossed the words to Andy, and disappeared into the jet.

Later the next day, a private jet from the United States was cleared to land at the International airport in Mexico City. It was on the ground for approximately one hour, during which time two women exited and were taxied to an adjacent hotel. The plane was then cleared for take-off with a flight plan filed for Bogota, Colombia. The interface between the U.S. government and the Colombian government had gone seamlessly, and waiting in Bogota, as promised, was a retired Huey—a U.S. Army helicopter that became famous in Viet Nam, but which was dwarfed in later years by the infamous Blackhawk. The Governor of Montana had supplied Blacky with a Huey, and now Colombia was obliging as well.

Eight men disembarked with full gear. They were escorted to an abandoned barracks, and the plane returned to Mexico City where it was secured in a hangar, scheduled for pickup at a later date by its owner, an American named Ranger.

Now, everyone had only to wait. Brian took Vince McCoy aside and worriedly asked, "What if we're wrong? You know, about the location?"

Without hesitation, Vince assured him, "Well, better to be on the ground here than Mexico, if that turns out to be the case. At least we'll be in friendly airspace if we have to redeploy rapidly."

Seeing that Brian was still uncertain, he added, "We just have to wait, Brian. Once Ms. Quixote is taken, then we'll know for sure. Until then, don't drive yourself nuts over it."

"Right. You're right, Vince." Brian concluded with, "I think I'm going to be taking a lot of walks."

Vince smiled.

The counter-attack had begun.

CHAPTER 46

The next counter attack began almost immediately. And just as no one noticed the comings and goings of private aircraft in Mexico or Colombia, and assigned no significance to it, no one paid any attention to the rather eccentric activities going on in Montana.

Dubbed "the last best place" and thought of as more of a quaint reminiscence of early America, no person of "quality" had even the remotest idea of the earthquake that was coming. That was a secret Bud Walker was determined to keep. The stealth launch was cemented by a brilliant strategic decision. Realizing that Sir Harley Grantham-Jones was likely suspicious of him and WNG by now, at the very least mystified by the fact that the network was missing in action during the most dire situation of our times, Bud had ordered Ray and Simon Atwater to ignore the growing global deterioration. And he was sticking to that strategy.

It made the network a source of ridicule, and an easy target for Fox, CNN, MSNBC—all of them. Ever eager for viewers, they had all welcomed this as yet another opportunity to seize their share of WNG's viewers. They had done the expected and missed no opportunity to spew the propaganda of the RIT, The Global Monetary Fund, and the Central Banks' Directors, and had relentlessly pummeled their audiences with doom and gloom, with fear and threats. In that, they were all consistent, and fighting it out in their own ratings wars.

Shadowed behind all that, and off the radar screen of Sir Harley Grantham-Jones—to the point of having sunk to just an object of disdain in his eyes—was Bud Walker.

"What have you done, you old fox?" James unexpectedly chided Walker late one evening.

Bud laughed abruptly, just once. Then sobering, he said, "Well, James, hard as it was to face, once I accepted it was him, I knew what would come next would not be good. He was expecting to use me to further the propaganda line. I had to make it appear I had truly taken leave of my senses. And I had to remove WNG from his and others' radar screens."

"You went covert on them."

"Yes. For this to work, we have to give the people of Montana time to make some things happen, and we have to give your boys time for their game to work. So, I want no national attention on us."

Wondering how long that could last, Bud seemed to anticipate the question because he picked up the phone and dialed an in-house extension. "Hey, Simon, Ray, can you join James and me? I have something I want you to do."

The plan was simple, and it appeared to work. Throughout Montana, while the major news networks were covering the "bad news" and instilling ever-increasing fear and uncertainty into the populace, WNG vans were appearing in every town and city in the state, readying to broadcast a live message from their Governor.

In Helena, before they launched the counter attack involving their state bank, and the new financial model they hoped the citizens themselves would figure out, the Governor had called his Cabinet together, as well as the Legislature. Most had been working non-stop for two months, and had barely seen their families.

Bringing them into the legislative joint chamber, he thanked them for their service and told them to take their seats, so that he could broadcast to their constituents. Before they could actually sit though, he asked them to remain standing. "Ladies and Gentlemen," he said, "as we begin this, let us pray."

The prayer had been short, but it had calmed everyone, and the broadcast began. In towns scattered throughout the state, the men, women, and children of Montana crowded around the WNG vans to hear and watch the address.

James and Andy were struck by something, as they too joined some folks in Seeley Lake. There was something characteristic of Montanans that James observed for the first time. Clearly the speech, which laid out the severity of the situation nationally, and which revealed to all of them the likelihood that their savings and money were gone, with expected high unemployment, and an already nearly-worthless dollar, gave them all a radical adjustment in the reality of their lives. Hopes were dashed. Emotions welled up. But, Montanans could take a blow.

James noticed it first. To the man, no matter what emotion was welling inside them, they suppressed its surfacing into raw emotion, or unmanly conduct, and seemed to straighten up, stiffen their backs, and focus more intently with emotionless faces. Silent for a while, they were nonetheless listening to the description of the new bank, calculating already how they were going to use it, or not.

"James, is that what they mean by 'stiff upper lip?'" Andy whispered to him. "Because if this is how the rest of the country takes this bad news, we are going to win this thing."

Having accepted the truth of what their state government was laying out, the people of Montana listened as the Governor explained to them about the $2 billion in gold and silver reserves backing the bank, and assured them that the gems and precious metals mines—along with oil and natural gas deposits—would be protected. He told them that the Attorney General would use all resources necessary to protect them from any misguided Eminent Domain issues, and he gave his pledge to use the full resources of the state to help build an economy. By the time he concluded with his assurance that he had the complete agreement of all the major industries within the state—and that regulatory changes were already occurring to free up those businesses to redefine themselves— most of the citizens were already out in front of the Governor.

Even with that Herculean effort coming from Helena, each under- stood somehow that, really, they were on their own, and they would have to figure out how to survive. The Governor's words carried logic and sin- cerity. But the subtext beneath was clearly understood. Because they were all in groups, huddled around the WNG vans and not isolated at home, none seemed afraid. All were cognizant that they were in this together. No shoulders were slumped, no heads were drooping, no crying was heard. To the person, they looked each other in the eye in complete agreement.

Brilliant, James thought. *That sly old fox. He knows his people.*

"What'd you think, Boy Scout?" Bud asked eagerly, as Andy and James returned from the meeting.

"I think Sir Harley Grantham-Jones is about to get bushwhacked, is what I think. He has no idea what you have done."

Noticing Simon Atwater and Ray in the room, both looking somewhat Cheshire cat-like themselves, James nudged Andy and asked Bud, "What *have* you done?"

Bud Walker had immediately ordered that the vans and crews redeploy as soon as the Governor was finished. Ray's direction as acting head of the network had been for them to head into localities throughout not only Montana, but also throughout the United States—border to border, coast to coast—to look for human interest stories. Most especially, they were to find any of those actions taken by U.S. citizens under duress where they refused to lose, and where they had figured out a way to help each other, or accomplish any other component of the game.

"They'll be specifically looking for impromptu barn raising type activities, and barter situations that the folks figure out; and they will film that. Once your boys' game hits, and starts impacting, WNG is set to change its coverage. As the 'Network of Solutions'—which Ray and the New York boys are promoting PR-wise in all markets as we speak—WNG is about to switch from broadcasting "cooking shows" to broadcasting true stories of ordinary Americans in ordinary towns solving the problems that the Boys from Basel dropped on them. We're about to raise a new standard and create new heroes."

James just stood there, shaking his head. After all his years in public service, one thing he and his counterparts knew their government did not understand was other people, and human behavior. Viewing all through the lens of their own realities, the men who sent James Mikolas on missions had made that mistake. They never really understood who they were dealing with.

Tonight, he had seen Bud Walker demonstrate that he knew Montanans and how they would react, and he saw him gambling now that that characteristic would be universal throughout America.

"How did you know, Bud?"

"Well, I'll tell you a secret, Boy Scout. When you decide to live in Montana, there's one thing you'd better learn real quick." He paused for effect. It worked. Andy and James both were at attention. "Alone, you succumb. But united, you can survive."

With that strategy, on the eve of "The Battle of America" game rolling out, the stealth counter attack against a handful of financial despots had begun. Picked by his adversary, groomed by his adversary, and trained by his adversary—reluctant or not—Bud Walker would prove himself to be a mighty opponent.

"Okay, Kid, looks like it's on you now," James joked.

And for a brief moment, Andy looked away to his left and smiled.

CHAPTER 47

*H*aving never produced anything in his career in finance, but rather just having made money by an ever-increasing complexity of financial maneuvers, Harley Grantham-Jones was trained to monitor the successes of his plans and attacks by watching the numbers he and the handful of co-conspirators controlled.

Compounding that was the problem that he was British, and had never bothered to study the Americans particularly. In his mind, passed down through the family heritage, was a healthy disdain for the rabble that had been allowed to go there, and who had eventually struck out on their own. But, he did not discriminate only against Americans. Holding pretty much the same view of any Canadian west of Quebec, and anyone who went down under to Australia, he had no idea how sturdy the stock, which had sprung from British seed, was.

In his mind, he was now ready to call the President of the United States and explain to him his options, and had so informed the Directors of the U.S., German, and Swiss banks—and Braghelli himself—at their secret weekly dinner meeting atop the tower. Careful scrutiny of all data regarding every financial transaction occurring globally, paralleled by monitoring of the TV coverage of the human suffering angle, had brought him to the conclusion that it was time.

They may resist for a while longer, flailing around with some new attempted solution, but in the end they will submit, and it is time to plant the seed.

An ocean away, the President of the United States and his Cabinet and Congressional finance committees were monitoring those same metrics. Why wouldn't they? After all, it had been their *friends* in banking who had taught them about finance, what to watch, and what to do to control economies.

Sir Harley Grantham-Jones was supremely confident, and eager to end this first part of the game. Unbeknownst to him, his confidence camouflaged a blind spot.

The message had gone to all private and state-owned enterprises at the same time. Delivered in both digital document and by certified mail, the letterhead of the Governor of Montana caught everyone's immediate attention.

It was a simple statement, but one that cemented his commitment. It read simply that the resources of the state were being directed to defend any and all encroachments upon land or property in the State of Montana, which might emanate from the Federal level, resultant from legal matters pertaining to Eminent Domain—whether those encroachments were against private citizens or land already held by the state.

Sitting at his desk, looking out the window, he noticed a few trees were turning an early yellow. Slowly he got up and walked into the office of his Attorney General, signaling to his assistant that he was going in. "So, it's on its way."

"Excellent," was the only remark the AG could muster. He was thinking about something apparently, which made him laugh, and then decided to share it with the Governor. "Reminds me of that WWII general who was surrounded at Bastogne, I think. The one who was told to surrender, and his answer was, 'nuts!'"

Bruce laughed, too, enjoying the levity for a moment. "So, we're surrounded you think?"

"Yeah, but we can fight for a long time." He paused as if chewing on something; then he decided to say it. "It'd be great though if some kind of miracle occurred here."

Curious as to what would constitute a miracle, Bruce asked, "And what are you thinking we need?"

The answer was immediate. "Either reinforcements, or something to negotiate with—you know, get them to back off."

Neither man knew it, but both would happen. The surprise would be the direction from which it came.

Two other things happened that day. Back at the ranch in Ovando, Andy had completed his review of the game testers, as much as was possible. The response had been immediate, with more than 10,000 starting to test the game. With 2,000 successful completions, and terrific feedback coming in from those who had played "White King Rising," he looked at the speed and success of those players compared to players who were attempting "The Battle of America" without the first game under their belt. That data confirmed his decision to require the gamer to play "White King Rising" first, in order to get rational enough to play the second.

Without that failsafe, the solution attempts always led to angry, violent choices, and the gamer being thrown out, only to have to start again.

He called his staff in Los Angeles, to confirm they were prepared to handle the hits that would come, and for the downloads to be free and seamless. Still grumbling a bit over lost revenues, his Marketing Department nonetheless confirmed that the Production Department was ready, and all engineers were on stand-by for any traffic jams at the "front door."

Andrew Weir, with his friend James Mikolas watching, pressed "Enter"—officially launching "The Battle of America" onto the Internet, using every social media and commercial tool available to Carver & Weir. Sir Harley Grantham-Jones had no idea that a counter attack had launched. The only thing he experienced just before retiring was that nagging feeling of indigestion that had plagued him periodically.

His only thought, however, was, *Something's wrong.*

The second miracle would be a surprise to them all.

CHAPTER 48

"What the hell am I supposed to do with this?" forty-eight-year-old veteran miner, Charles Sanger, exclaimed.

First in line with the paymaster at the Yugo Sapphire Mine, having worked skillfully and diligently for his first two weeks back in the mine, which had been closed for some time, he was staring at a small cotton sack the company cashier had handed him, instead of a paycheck.

"Open it," the paymaster said, with more than just a little trepidation in his voice.

The executives of the mine had met through the night to figure out how to pay these men. With the dollar devalued, and with them having no credit lines open anyway, they knew paying the men with checks or cash would not provide what the men needed—something to exchange reasonably for the things they required, like food, fuel, etc.

Boldly, they examined their assets, getting the bright idea that if they took a portion of what the miners mined, and returned it to them in sapphires, whose worth they estimated to match the value of the service the miner had provided, the miner would then have something tangible, not something worthless, for his efforts.

On their own, they hoped the men would figure out they could barter with sapphires, but not dollars. It was a hope anyway, and it was all they could think of to do.

Charles Sanger was a 6th generation Montanan, and had been a working man his whole adult life. Labor was his field, and he had raised a family of four and managed to send all three sons and one daughter off to college in the East and Midwest. He was an uneducated man himself, having dropped out of Haver High School when he was seventeen to help his grandfather on a small horse ranch.

But, educated or not, Charles Sanger was a smart man. He turned the stones over once or twice, looked at them closely to ascertain whether they would cut to a good stone, looked up at the cashier, and said, "That's fair. Tell the boss men, I'll see them Monday." Pocketing the pouch, he signed off and left.

While the paymaster continued to pay the men in sapphires instead of cash, hoping they, too, would find it to be a fair exchange, he had no idea, nor did the mine owners, that Charles had a bright idea of his own.

The new state bank was in Helena, close enough to the mine for Sanger to reach it before closing. Walking in just in time, he walked up to the teller—who had barely gotten it together to even have a window open. The bank had only been accepting deposits of people's gold and silver for the last couple of weeks. That provided them with something they could draw against to get hold of the newly minted Montana silver coins, which were small enough in denomination to give to merchants and landlords. He began a revolution with, "I want to make a deposit."

Dropping the pouch in front of the teller, he waited.

"What the hell am I supposed to do with this?" the teller shouted to no one in particular. Hearing the commotion, the bank's CEO came out of his office and approached the window.

"Man wants to deposit sapphires…"

"I see that." This was coming sooner to the bank than they had anticipated. Sensing that this was not only inevitable but likely to turn epidemic, he informed Charles Sanger that they would accept the deposit, and issue coin in exchange, but that he would have to wait for a few hours while they determined relative value. "Is that acceptable to you, sir?"

Sanger grinned. "You bet your ass, it is. We're doing some business, and I will be happy to wait while you smart guys figure something out."

Seeing the coffee, he settled into an overstuffed chair, munching on early Halloween cookies, calling his wife to let her know he might be, "real late for dinner tonight."

Four hours later, a gem assessor had been hired by the bank and hastily put into place on the premises. All Board of Directors had convened using Skype, and had conferenced into the Secretary of Treasury's office, the Governor, the Secretary of Commerce, and the Secretary of State, who was at home holding her littlest one on her left thigh while stirring a buffalo stew with the other.

The exchange of gold or silver, for a substance of relative value, such as a gem, was fairly easy to accomplish. But what they needed to do, before Sanger walked out that door and notified the rumor mill, was determine what other types of assets they could take in and store. Policy needed to be created quickly.

"What the hell are we going to do if the Troy Copper Mine decides to pay its people with vans of copper?"

That question, posed by the Governor, stumped them for a while. Finally, they determined they could take in gold, silver, sapphires, and any other precious metal or stone, as equivalency was fairly easy to ascertain, and storage was feasible.

For those whose pay might be in oil, gas, or, Lord forbid, even wheat, two options were created: persuade your company to issue you a "security-type" paper pledging a specific amount of the commodity—a form of percentage share of the known asset—for the bank to take, and which would be redeemable by the company upon demand of the bank. Everyone knew that option just kicked the can down the road a little further, since it did not solve the problem of where the bank would store the "asset" if they did in fact redeem the share.

The second choice was for the citizen to exchange the "pay" himself—either with a private exchanger, if he could find such a person, or with a fellow citizen for something the fellow citizen had.

Charles Sanger accepted the coins, and his deposit slip, and read and signed the hastily drawn-up legal document. Turning at the door, he said, "Okay for me to tell others about this?"

The CEO nodded, thinking, *God knows where this will end up!*

It ended well. The Barter option had begun, and it wasn't long before Montanans figured out what to do with fellow citizens who didn't yet have anything to trade. Some relied on the charitable spirit Bud Walker had allowed James, Andy, and Brian to experience at the auction. And some used a unique type of "Barn Raising," where people helped others get a small, one-man-band business going—whereby the owner could provide a service that was needed to a neighbor, in exchange for coin, food, or rent.

Basically, there was no limit. Given the extremity of the fear and end of the world messages with which they had been pummeled for so long, taking matters into their own hands was somehow empowering to most folks. In one small berg, when interviewed by a WNG field reporter, a blacksmith said, "We're just taking care of each other, you know. We're making it go right. We're sticking together."

Watching that on the News, Governor Fitzerman buzzed his Chief of Staff, telling him to get the Attorney General on the line, the Secretary of Commerce, and to join him in his office. Thirty minutes later, plans had been laid, and the Secretary of Commerce commenced the invitations.

The Governor of Montana was convening a Summit of Governors, requesting their presence in Billings in order to discuss workable options to restore and maintain their economies. At the suggestion of the Lieutenant Governor, who had never before been known to have any real ideas, all Commerce Secretaries were also invited, and all Attorney Generals, if their Governors felt it appropriate.

All did feel it appropriate; and only the New England states—including New York—plus the District of Colombia, Washington, and Oregon declined the invitation. To his surprise, the Governor of California called Bruce personally, hoping to get some inside scoop on the summit. Holding the mystery in place, but with the caveat that solutions had been found, Bruce Fitzerman smiled when his California counterpart capitulated and said, "Oh, what the hell! Count me in. And I expect you to buy me a steak dinner in that cow town of yours, for all the bragging you do about your beef."

"You can count on it!"

CHAPTER 49

*T*hey had no way of knowing for sure whether their summit and its actions might push the President of the United States closer to the checkmate move set by Sir Harley Grantham-Jones. It was discussed, and each Governor had concluded that his state and its people were in jeopardy, it was a risk that they had to take, and that more of the same "think" from Washington wasn't going to work.

What had turned the tide for the Governors and their Cabinet members in attendance had been the first day of the summit, when Andy Weir had been introduced, and had brought them all two games to play. He had had to help some of the baby boom generation get the hang of playing a game, and not quitting, and he certainly had had to help them past some embarrassingly wrong choices. But each governor had done it.

Once Governor Fitzerman had explained the state bank, but, more importantly, the almost instinctive barter mode his citizens had resorted to, the other governors were full of questions. Most came from states that did not have gold, silver, and sapphire mines. It took them a while to identify just what resources they did have that could be used as a tangible means of exchange with another state that did have precious metals.

Oddly enough, when Andy returned from a break, there was an unexpected lightness in the room. Many were laughing for the first time in many months. Somehow they had realized that the "people" themselves were about to remove the burden from them, by doing what they were all capable of doing in the first place. Dependency upon government and its institutions was not in the DNA of the United States citizen. It had been an acquired taste, and a repugnant one at that. They knew the release from that burden was imminent, and the prospect of it was quite liberating.

And they were prepared to make their case to just fold the game with the Central Banks; fold the hand and let the banks keep the pot, and let

America start again from the ground up. Somehow, construction seemed like a much better option than destruction to them.

In a separate room, the Attorney Generals had arrived at an agreement. They would all coordinate through the Attorney General of Montana any matters of legal defense.

The AG of Wisconsin had summed it up when he commented, "If the Federal Government moves on any of us, they will know they are facing united states, who will be bringing separate but coordinated cases against them to the Supreme Court."

Once frightened by potential future actions of their own government, they were no longer. In poker terms, they had all agreed to call the bluff. Just knowing they were of like mind bolstered their spirits and their resolve.

What they did not know was that this move alone would close the door on what was probably the last move their President might have, if he held any hope of paying the usurious debt. To the person they had concluded such a move was destructive, and they were prepared to applaud his backing down from any action against state assets. It was, however, the one move Sir Harley Grantham-Jones would welcome, even if he had not anticipated this economic rebellion. It would bring his ultimatum, and the acquiescence of the United States to his "rescue," even closer.

Internet chatter was explosive regarding the new game from Carver & Weir. With so many people in the world hammered by the current economic affairs, millions of gamers were poised to interact, gaining some control over the matter—even if only in a game.

Skilled "gamers" who accepted the task of introducing their own solutions were hard at work. But it was the popular movement that went viral. The game was fun; it was challenging; and it was important. More than anything, it validated the individual player's worth in an area of global concern.

Like before, it began with the kids. Playing it, they then Tweeted, chatted, blogged, and Facebooked about it. Downloads topped 10 million in a matter of days, which was not only meteoric but also historic. And then, the kids began to help their beleaguered and embattled parents

play the game. Before long, it was appearing in ministers' offices, with local leaders, then state officials, and whether they were ready or not, more
than one Senator or Congresswoman arrived in his offices on Capital Hill
to discover their top aides immersed in a computer game.

Aided by translation units at the Los Angeles offices, the game was
spreading around the world. Banks might have closed, businesses might
have shut down, riots may have begun as food supplies became critical,
but no one shut down the Internet.

Historians have long referred to the "fog of war." No matter how well
laid the battle plans are, once the battle commences, the chaos created
generates a fog, thereby making the outcome not so certain. The RIT had
created global chaos, and no one inside the "Keep" walls of the RIT had
any idea about the game. Fixated on the real life game they were monitoring or creating, "entertainment of the masses" was outside their ken. That
elitist mindset would make all the difference. Knowing it or not, a fog was
enshrouding the Repository of International Transactions.

There was also a little known fact about China, and its system of
government, which would tip the scales.

It was common knowledge of course that China's economy had been
booming, that they were buying up huge sections of America, and engaging in as much commerce as possible with the United States. Their
currency had been strong, though slipping recently.

Their central government in Beijing recognized that China was linked
to the economy of the United States like Siamese twins, and they fully
recognized that whatever was happening to their old enemy, and no matter how appealing that might have been under other circumstances in
another time, China could not afford for the United States to implode.
They held too much of the United States debt to risk America default-
ing. Counting on the revenue from that debt, "You go, we go," was the
mentality dominating their behind-closed-door economic meetings.

For that reason, the Central Government was exerting pressure on
the President of the United States to seek out, secure, and agree to some
kind of rescue by the Repository of International Transactions. China's
leaders could care less if fundamental changes in the structure of the U.S.

government could accrue, let alone that those changes threatened the liberty and security of the country the world still regarded as the guarantor of freedom. Beijing could care less about liberty. After all, they were still a Communist nation, with the oddity of a free market economy that was developing at a breathtaking pace. So, the totalitarian government mindset had no qualms about the United States turning into a totalitarian regime if need be. What mattered to them was that the United States survived, regardless of what form of government it acquired in the process. Sir Harley Grantham-Jones was betting on that very attitude from the Chinese, and felt that they were his "ace."

But one group within China held quite a different view of things. China's provinces all had Governors who were responsible for the affairs of that province. What Westerners either failed to understand or observe, or what they had never been educated about, was the fact that these governors were autonomous.

Though appearing to defer to what they referred to as "those people in Beijing"—their affectionate name for the Communist Party's central leaders—in reality, they made economic decisions for their province independently, and fiercely independently at that. Knowing that their people always needed to save face, and never wanting to embarrass themselves or their country, it was a secret type of independence—never spoken about or bragged about publicly.

Long ago, when China's pilot had downed the American spy plane, providing President Bush with his first international incident within weeks of his taking office, his National Security Director discovered this reality, and used it to bring about a successful resolution of the crisis. She had had to wait for the Governor of the province to travel to Beijing to meet face to face with a central leader and explain that his province was not interested in enduring a U.S. embargo or boycott over the grandstanding of a pilot, and that they wanted the Central Government to work out a solution.

Less than a month after James and Andy had sent Brian and DeShawn off on the rescue mission, the summit of U.S. governors had commenced. The incipient barter system had taken hold in just two weeks of employment, and the summit was called quietly and urgently. Unbeknownst to anyone except Bud Walker, the Governor of Montana, and his chipper Secretary of State, a second summit would begin on the heels of the first.

Oddly enough, the state of Montana had extremely cordial relations with the governors of the Chinese provinces of Shandong, Guangdong, and Sichuan, as well the cities Shanghai and Guangzhou, and they in turn talked regularly with their counterparts. All had agreed to come to a summit—this time at a lodge just outside Glacier Park.

The Chinese love to travel, and they love Glacier Park—a fact the Montana Chamber of Commerce had discovered when they hired a consultant to advise them on how to enhance tourism in their state.

The urgency of the invitation, and the temptation of a junket to the U.S., sealed the deal for all Provincial Governors. They departed secretly to a meeting occurring not too far from Lake McDonald.

At the last minute, Andy had been brought in, accompanied by his Mandarin translator. He had sped from Billings to Kalispell, coming up the Swan River Valley, known as "the Swan," in order to meet these men.

As he had done for their U.S. counterparts, the Governor commenced the summit with the games—requiring all participants to play both computer games. The outcome was the same. Unlike the U.S. governors, who had a natural reluctance to present a united defiance to its government, the Chinese province governors seemed to have no such reluctance. They all agreed it was unwise for China to yield to its Central Bank, since they were naturally suspicious of the men who had suckered them into buying the toxic mortgage-backed securities that had started this whole slide. Noting that most of those men were now in prominent positions within Central Banks, and currently hiding inside the main bank in Switzerland, they weren't in the mood for giving anyone the benefit of the doubt.

"We'll explain this to 'those people in Beijing,'" they assured Governor Fitzerman. "China will stand with the United States—providing the United States stands with its Governors." Supremely confident that nothing more needed to be said than this simple understated demand, they asked whether it would not be possible to perhaps take a ride up the "Going to the Sun Road." Like the Great Wall of China for the Western tourist, this "Going to the Sun Road" held an equal fascination for those from the Far East.

Andy suppressed a smile at the surrealistic request, but he was heartened by the almost child-like playfulness these men exuded. *Here we are handling the world's greatest crisis, and they just whipped up a solution and want to do some sightseeing! Man, I wish Carver & Weir could hire some of these guys.*

"By all means," Bud interjected graciously. "My cars are at your disposal."

Twenty minutes later, a caravan of over-sized Hummers was winding its way up the precarious and famous highway to the sun, prompting locals to wonder what on earth was going on.

Hours later, even as the flight of happy "tourists" was returning to China, the "people in Beijing" were already commencing phone calls through channels to ratchet up the pressure on the President of the United States to do "whatever it takes" to get the money flowing again, and credit going. It seemed the right hand did not know what the left hand was doing—in either country.

Sir Harley Grantham-Jones, sitting alone in his palatial quarters, drinking his Bristol Cream Sherry, had no way of knowing how this would affect the outcome.

CHAPTER 50

*T*he mixed signals from China were confusing to the President, and they were equally confusing to the men in Basel. On the one hand, the Central Government in Beijing was diplomatically pressuring the President to stop the free-fall.

On the other hand they were offering what appeared to be a gesture of good faith, which probably also revealed China's dependence on the United States. China was holding back, not calling in any of the debt markers it held under a variety of financial labels, and was not selling dollars. Though China undoubtedly held leverage over the President, and was pushing him into a corner, he sensed there was something below the surface there—and his instinct was that whatever China's agenda was, it was not menacing.

The President had no way of knowing that a number of visits had been paid, one after the other, to the "people in Beijing," by their Governors, who were adamant about standing with the United States now. The case was being made that the rest of the world was teetering, but that they were watching what the U.S. and China did—most specifically, what China would do to the United States. Would it behave like an enemy, or a friend?

Despite decades of fantasies about taking the United States down, the old men who were now "the people in Beijing" knew their time was nearing its end. They recognized that every economic choice they had made in recent decades had really been patterned after the unique free market approach the United States took. Viscerally, they would have loved to ascend to supremacy now, but they had made errors along the way. They had partnered with the U.S. to such a degree that if they endangered the U.S. economy further, they would endanger their own survival. The situation cut with a double-edged sword.

So, while Beijing's Central Government leaders continued to pressure the President and his Administration, the men who secretly held the most power in their country had been playing some mysterious game on the Internet. To the man, they had come to Beijing to exhort them to "stand fast," not listen to the media hysteria and dire warnings from the banks, and to cooperate with the Governors of the United States.

One had even gone so far as to recommend they recall the Director of their Central Bank, and have him withdraw from the meetings in Switzerland. He had argued it would send a bold signal to the rest of the world's embattled countries that not everyone was listening to or under the control of the men from Basel.

His disarming display of passion, and his high level of enthusiasm, was disconcerting to the Chairman of the Party when the two met in private. "You see, I won the game, comrade! I won the game!" Recognizing the man had no idea what he was talking about, he elaborated, "And, I accepted the 'task' of putting in additional solutions. One worked."

"And what was that?"

"Let the Governors of China deal directly with the Governors of the United States. The debt and vulnerabilities to us vary throughout our dealings with the U.S. A single solution on our part, or the government of that country, cannot resolve all the issues." He paused for a moment to choose his next words carefully. "But each of the states has a governor who can work out solutions for us, on an individual basis."

"And you know this, how?" his senior asked, with some skepticism.

"We looked at Montana, and realized we had already done a type of barter that bypassed bank loans to some degree, when we pledged to increase their mining technologies using an infusion of technology and money, enabling them to once again mine. They planned to make us a partner in the mine."

"I fail to see how that solves anything. If the United States cannot produce and does not have a valuable currency, what on earth do you hope to gain by owning a share of what could turn out to be nothing?" The question had been asked assertively, but the Governor from Guangzhou knew it would not have been asked at all, if his man were not looking for a solution, too.

Smiling respectfully, he said, "Because, they have something we would take in exchange—sapphires."

"Ooh, I have heard Montana mines the finest sapphire in the world."

"True, comrade, and, unlike Sierra Leone and other lesser developed and extremely criminal nations, I do not have any concern about Montana honoring a deal. The deal is: sapphires for technology investment."

The old man sat back in his chair for a moment, then got up and walked to the French-door style window that opened onto an elaborate rock garden. The building in which they were all headquartered was an ironic blend of ancient China and 19th Century Colonialism. Rich with history, the building nonetheless represented the conflict that existed within the regime. He opened the window and looked down into the garden, staring at nothing in particular. But he was tapping his left foot, and his long-term colleague knew that meant he was thinking.

If he contributes now, I have him, the Governor thought, holding his breath a bit. His wait was short.

"And we have a tangible good in the bargain, not imaginary money or an eroding dollar."

"Exactly."

The old fox knew he had an opportunity for a Public Relations victory here, and he turned quickly back to his Governor. "So, we will be demonstrating to the world the ancient barter system that made us a trading giant in centuries past, and *we* are seen as a force for solutions, capable of leading other countries out of a morass."

The Governor did not care who took the credit here. No one other than the Central Government had ever been credited with any foresight or breakthroughs anyway. As far as he was concerned, the light of adoration and acclamation could shine on Beijing 'til the end of time. He merely wanted his deal, so that the people of his province would not lose jobs, or be set back.

The people of China have come a long way. And we are not going backwards.

He had a keen sense of irony, and he recognized the magnificence of a truth, and workable business model from the past, emerging like a sword of salvation.

At that moment, he knew to wait for the head of the Party to make the proclamation himself. He did.

"All right. I will speak to the others. Present to me the list of U.S. governors you believe will deal with us, and what they will barter with us in exchange for what we have already loaned them, or committed to them. Make it all goods, and not money with interest. And insure please that the goods are desirable in our society." What he thought, but would not express to his younger colleague, whose political ambitions were unknown to him, was, *So, it is the end of an old game, and the beginning of a new one.*

Then he chuckled as he thought, *The old is now new!*

Chuckling with him respectfully, the Governor agreed, saying, "Of course." He rose to leave, bowed courteously, and said, "Thank you for your time, and your wise counsel."

The old man returned the bow, less deeply of course.

Just as the Governor was about to leave the room, he called after him. "You must teach me that computer game someday."

Chapter 51

Samir was watching the storm status reports, hoping to get out of the wretched, mosquito-infested camp and over to Somalia with the captives in the first two buildings. Aggravated beyond belief at having to delay the "special shipment" to the Doctor, he nonetheless had concluded there would be time to deliver another shipment of regular captives, get paid, and return for the remaining eleven women—that was until the storms, which ravaged all of Central and South America, prevented any safe travel by air, land, or sea. Weeks of downpours and flash flooding had delayed everything.

"Do you want to speak with her?" Hyena approached Samir in the mess tent, holding out the satellite phone.

"Who?" Samir barked. *The fool is using that phone more than he should!*

"Our new supplier. She is confirming the receipt of our money, and said she's sending the first package through as we speak."

"Then there is no need for me to speak with her is there? The deal is done."

"Tell her—" Samir had to waive off Hyena once again as he presented the phone. "I will inspect the package when it arrives, and if it is satisfactory, we will then complete the next four. It must be within the month, however."

In order to avoid any other involvement in this, he turned his back and walked away, relieved not to have had to get into personal negotiations with whomever this slave trader was. *What a hypocrite! An American selling her own people!*

Had Samir taken the phone, he would have likely recognized the voice of the Supplier, for on the other end of the phone was Jessica Ranger herself. She was known to Samir as a friend of Bud Walker's, and he had met and spoken with her on numerous occasions. Each would have recognized the other. But Samir's distaste for detailed negotiation, and his resentment of the demeaning role he was now playing with the current Al Qaeda leadership, caused him to elevate himself by allowing the *riff-raff* to do the dirty work.

He had other matters on his mind as well. The uprisings throughout the Mid-East and recent revolutions in Egypt and Libya were unsettling the whole region. Silent in all this was Zawahiri, and Samir wondered now just exactly what the condition of the Head of Al Qaeda was.

Though he had initially thought Yemen, and an association with Al-Awlaki, would be his safest choice, with the greatest chance of returning to prominence once again in his specialized field of propaganda, he sensed now a rift between Zawahiri and Al-Awlaki. And with the mysterious silence of the Doctor, Samir had no idea if he himself was in good standing, or whether he would be walking into an execution by returning to Yemen.

All doubts and debates became moot, however, as reports came into the camp that the United States had successfully killed the Yemeni Al Qaeda chief and others. Drenched in sweat, and smelling now like his FARC counterparts, he sat down on the cot and leaned forward into his hands. *So, it's just you and me now, old man. Where are you? And what are you planning?*

The weeks of delay had taken their toll on Alicia as well. She was desperately concerned that, even if Reagan and Edith were in the location in which she would end up, they would already have been transported to their final slave masters. All she could do was wait for the negotiations to be complete, and for the storms—which seemed to hit the area in staggered waves—to subside sufficiently for planes to fly. She spent her days looking out the window, and ultimately praying that her friends would still be there and that she would not, in fact, be too late.

Finally, word came. The deal was done. Jessica escorted her to the Kiosk inside the airport, staying an appropriate distance behind Alicia, so as not to arouse any suspicion that the girl was not, in fact, traveling alone. At the same time, she sent a message to Vince McCoy that the "parcel" was on its way, and called for her plane to be brought out of the hangar.

Alicia Quixote walked to the information kiosk in a distant wing of the airport and approached a man who was waiting for her. Pointing her toward a corridor on the right, he made a phone call. She entered alone, and about 100 feet into the corridor, two men appeared and captured her, just as they had done the others before.

Just as Ranger's plane was cleared to land in Bogota, the transport plane for captured slaves took off, headed, with a bogus flight plan, for its destination. Only one passenger was aboard in the rear, drugged and unconscious.

"Señor, the latest package *is* being delivered. We just confirmed she was captured at the airport, even as I was speaking with the Señora. The plane lands in three hours. Do you wish to inspect her?"

Another chance; another choice. Normally, Samir would have accepted readily, as he was keenly interested in this new "middle man" and the quality of what she could deliver. But, disheartened by the news out of Yemen, and uncertain now as to *his* next move, he decided to remain behind.

After all, he thought, *if she is not acceptable, it is on Hyena, not me.*

"No, that will not be necessary. It is your deal, Hyena. You are the one who called in another partner, not I. So, you satisfy yourself, and I will see her when she is returned to the camp."

"Suit yourself, Samir." Hyena spoke succinctly. "Once she is conscious, we will notify you."

"Gracias."

"I gather you are not leaving with the others today?" Hyena was sniffing around now. He had a bad feeling about the solidity of his dealings with Samir. The Doctor he could trust—if he delivered. This man, he was not so sure of. He smelled a double-cross.

"No, the weather and circumstances in the Africa zone are too unstable. I will leave with *all* of them—within the month."

"And my final payments?" Hyena asked menacingly, his hand on his holster.

"All in one, when the last four are delivered to me. That's an incentive for you, don't you think?" Then, wanting to stay in good graces with Hyena until he was out of here with the full load, he added, "And there will be a bonus for you, for your patience."

With Hyena gone to pick up the girl, Samir turned to coded email communications, needing to inform his buyers in Somalia and Yemen, and wherever the hell the Doctor was, that delivery had been delayed, but that it was imminent.

"Any word?" Andy asked anxiously, as he walked into the great room, dropping his gear gingerly by the door.

James and Bud were in front of the fire in some kind of discussion. He could not tell whether they were in agreement or disagreement, just that they were scrutinizing a piece of paper.

"Yeah," Bud said. "They just went in. Alicia's on her way."

"Thanks," Andy said, almost inaudibly.

He was reaching for his bag when Bud interrupted. "Actually, Kid, James and you are now in the main house with me. We moved you in while you were over with the Chinese."

Knowing that Andy would want to be alone, and knowing also that it would be better for him to remain with them, James said, "Hey, Kid, I know you are tired and all, but—"

Andy interrupted him before he could ask. "You have some puzzle you'd like me to put my mind on, right?"

James grinned sheepishly. "Yeah, well, you know. Idle minds, all that. Makes the clock stop, doesn't it?"

Whether it was accumulated fatigue or tension, Andy started to laugh at the idiocy of that remark, and the typically James-type awkward attempts at comfort. Still laughing, he flopped down on the huge square footstool and said, "All right. I'll wait with you. Seems you guys need some company."

It was late afternoon when the plane landed in the clearing. Alicia's unconscious body was dropped off, looked over by Hyena, and her citizenship authenticated—though under a bogus passport supplied by one of James' undercover friends at the DEA. Hyena was new to the slave trading business. No one had ever come for any of the hapless people he had purchased in the past. For that reason, it never occurred to him to search Alicia, let alone scan her.

Satisfied that she fit the bill, he waived the pilot for takeoff and Alicia was transported to the camp, where she was dumped unceremoniously in front of the six existing captives. The other women remained passive, going out of their way not to engage Hyena or his men, avoiding looking at them directly. Edith had coached them on how to prevent inciting anything with the men—by feigning submission if need be, but by signaling it for sure through lack of eye contact and looking down.

The men left, throwing the bolt behind them. In whispered discussion, the six women decided to leave the new girl alone until she came around. They could tell by her breathing that she was all right, and though her face was covered by the disheveled mop of dark hair, which had cascaded over it, hiding her features, Reagan decided to at least un-tie her hands and feet. That done, she opened the bag that had been dropped beside the girl and looked for identification.

"Her name is Mary Ciprianni. She's from Chicago." Then she returned the document to the bag, looking no further. "We'll learn more when she wakes up."

Just then, the girl moaned, twisted her body, and rolled over, revealing her face. Reagan gasped and looked to Edith for help. Before the word "Alicia" could spill out of her mouth, Edith grabbed Reagan, jerking her away from the girl quickly before the others noticed anything unusual and said, "There, now, Reagan, let's just let her wake up on her own. No need to worry!"

"But?" Before Reagan could get any other words out, Edith placed her finger over her lips, signaling for her to be quiet. By then Reagan knew something was wrong. Edith's behavior was uncharacteristic and there was alarm in her voice and actions—and a warning.

What is going on here? Reagan wondered.

Less than a minute later, a microchip GPS transponder inserted into Alicia's navel was turned on remotely.

CHAPTER 52

"You got to get me to the President, right away!" Andy shouted, as he barged into Bud's office, brandishing his smart phone. He'd been outside taking a walk, trying not to introvert and obsess about Reagan and the rescue mission, when the key report came in.

"What the hell?" Bud and James said simultaneously. James had heard the door slam and Andy shouting, and had dashed downstairs, knowing by the tone in Andy's voice that something significant had happened.

"Bud, the Kid never shouts like that unless it is important."

Turning to Andy, he said, "What has happened?"

"James, you remember how once before I told you I had to reach the President?"

James did. In fact, he could never forget the night Andy realized the U.S. was walking into a trap regarding the invasion of Iraq. Spotting that the WMD was a complete set-up to discredit British, U.S., and Israeli intelligence, Andy had tried desperately to get the CIA director to take it up channels.

James had tried; Andy had tried; but they ran into a phenomenon of war that has to do with the tipping point. There is a point of no return in the readiness for war. The United States went ahead with its invasion. The fact that Andrew Weir, an eighteen-year-old Grandmaster chess champion, had tried to warn them of a potential public relations debacle, had only gone hard for Andrew Weir.

The feverishness of Andy's communication made James wary. *Are we once again at such a precipice?*

The painful memory caused James to hesitate. Andy, though, was in no mood for any lag in response. "James, you got to get me to the President. There is a move he can make, and I can prove it. He doesn't need to step into the checkmate move. Please, get me to him!"

The urgency in Andy's voice, and the trust he had earned from Bud Walker through the summer, urged Bud to take immediate action. While James had no access to the White House, never had, and certainly not recently in view of how the Agency viewed him, Bud Walker still had a marker or two he could call in.

Before Andy had even finished his plea, Walker was speed-dialing someone.

Jesus, how many people does that man have on speed dial? James pondered fleetingly. Holding his breath, he prayed Bud knew what to do.

"Hi, it's me. You know that favor you owe me? Well, much as I am reluctant to do this, I am calling it in. I need to meet with the President in…" He looked to Andy for a timeline. Andy mouthed tomorrow morning. "The morning. It is urgent. And I need his Chief of Staff there beforehand. I want to brief him myself. Just tell them it involves national security, and that I am bringing two people with me." Bud paused for a moment, listening to the other person. Then he added, "Yes, this clears the deck with us. Much as I admire you, and all you do, this handles it for Bud Walker."

The pause seemed interminable, especially given James and Andy had no idea who Bud had just called.

"All right then. We'll be wheels up within the hour and ready to meet by 7AM." Before hanging up, he very sincerely added, "And thank you. You do not know yet what you have done for your country."

Hanging up, he turned with the same resoluteness to James and Andy. "Okay, we're in for 7AM. This had better be good, Kid."

Andy signaled it was, and then said, "Thank you."

James was both relieved to have the meeting, and taken aback by what had just unfolded. "Bud, if you don't mind my asking, who did you just call?"

"The First Lady. Now, get yourself, and whatever is on that device you are holding, together. We are going to Washington. She's clearing us for a landing at Andrews Air Force Base. Apparently something has happened in Washington."

Indeed, something *had* happened. With food supplies gone in city grocery stores, and the warehouses that supplied those stores just days away from depletion—and with no funds to purchase additional goods—the White House knew they were about five days away from a societal Armageddon. The first major disturbances had already begun. Not limited to income strata, surprisingly, disturbances requiring police presence in riot gear had broken out in Roswell, Va.; Southeast D.C.; lower Manhattan; multiple locations in Broward County, Fl.; and Flushing, Queens.

With the Chairman of the Joint Chiefs in his office, the President of the United States was being informed that in the opinion of the military, there would be a contagion of this insanity throughout the United States, as the food supply became more and more scarce. Not surprisingly, their advice to the President in order to secure the safety of American citizens was to declare Martial Law, giving the Government time to override Congress and seize the resources necessary to secure the people.

"Mr. President," Chief of Staff Gabe Levine interjected, "the bulk of the United States is holding steady. This action is a slippery slope."

"Slippery slope?!" The President jumped on him. "It's a God-damned avalanche. What I need to do here is declare a state of national emergency and invoke every Executive power this office holds. I will not have our cities burn!"

The vehemence with which he spoke raised the hair on the back of the neck of the Chairman of the Joint Chiefs. He had given his military advice, and he would stand behind it, but there was some other agenda going on here he did not understand.

Before he could inquire, however, Gabe Levine said, "Thank you, Admiral, the President will take this under advisement." With that, he shuffled the Admiral out the door.

"I can declare a state of emergency, suspend national elections, and override Congressional oversight to implement asset seizure. I can't just let our cities burn. Americans are going to have to ante up on this one, by God!"

Smelling the fear and desperation of the man in charge, with Levine himself also feeling the weight of the situation, he still needed to hold the formality of their offices. Levine said, "Sir, yes, you could do that. And I understand why you might feel you need to. But, let's look at the whole picture here."

The President sat down on one of the two couches in the Oval Office that faced each other. Each was yellow and stood in a bold contrast to the royal blue carpet that connected them.

Letting him cool down, the President's Chief of Staff attempted to normalize the situation with an amenity. "Would you like a scotch?"

"I would, but do not even think of getting me one! The least the people can expect is for me to be stone-cold sober as I decide this."

That brought a smile to both men. Feeling the coast was clear, and that he could talk candidly, without any military or Cabinet people around, Levine, who was known for being a small man with a huge mind and extraordinary ability to assess a situation, simply said, "It's called the 'fog of war,' sir."

"I beg your pardon!" the President shot back.

"In any war situation, there is a confusion that creates a fog, and an inability to see clearly…"

The President interrupted him impatiently. "I know what the hell the fog of war is. But what war are you talking about?"

"The Economic War, Mr. President. We may not have identified precisely why the RIT has been attacking, instead of helping, but it seems to me the whole world is under attack economically; and there is a 'fog' preventing us from seeing clearly."

The President sat back. He was looking at this. So his friend continued delicately. "So, I suggest there is something we are not seeing here. And we should not respond in haste."

"Humph!"

"If you attempt to override Congress in this matter, and strip them of their *Constitutionally*-protected oversight and checks and balances, they will file suit and take it directly to the Supreme Court."

"My Party? You think so?"

"I do, sir. You need to understand that this issue transcends party alliances. It is harbored in the guardianship of our very form of government. Long before you or I came on the scene, this nation decided to have three branches of government. And if you, for whatever reason, decide to reduce it to two, or even one, the interests of the larger group prevail, and they will fight you."

"Well, let them. I am just trying to respond to RIT's demands and save the country from sinking into depression and poverty."

"Frankly, my friend, that does not matter." Levine removed his signature wire-rimmed glasses, set them on the coffee table, and looked directly at his colleague. "One can always justify despotism. It's been done throughout Man's history. But, in this case, you will meet massive internal resistance, and then the RIT wins for sure." He paused before presenting some evidence for his argument.

"I need to tell you the Justice Department has been on the phone with me for what seems like every minute today. Montana is pushing back hard. The AG out there—who by the way I lost a national debate championship to years ago—is filing briefs as we speak. They are challenging all claims we made for their state's assets necessary for the public good, including filing legal briefs defending the rights of the private citizens whose holdings we wanted to procure."

"Circling the wagons..." the President's voice trailed off.

"The point is they are not giving ground, sir. They are challenging on issues other than Eminent Domain. Could be in the courts for years." Levine paused; then added, "Unless you suspend the Judicial System as well."

By now, the President's head was in his left hand, his fingers desperately scratching his forehead.

With caution, Levine proceeded. He felt the Commander-in-Chief needed all the data he had to hand, in order to truly evaluate the momentous action he was considering taking. "And more than that, sir, is the fact that we are not getting return calls from anybody."

"Who? Be specific, Gabe."

"Well, that's just it, Mr. President. There is no *one* person. We can't reach anyone in authority at any State Capital."

That news seemed to shock the President. He had grown accustomed to the prestige associated with the title of President of the United States, and was stunned to hear that anyone would dare to ignore a communication. Doubting that he had heard his friend correctly, he challenged, "And you are sure they know the White House is calling?"

Levine nodded. "It's like we are invisible to them."

The President's next question penetrated to the very core of the issue, even if he himself did not fully grasp it. "Invisible...or irrelevant?"

Gabe Levine had no real answer for that. Truth be told, the President felt more isolated now, in this Oval Office, than he had ever felt in his life. Having risen to a position of power and influence that should have put him at the very pinnacle of awareness of what was going on, he felt like a man blind-folded, who was being led somewhere he did not want to go, by people whose real identity reeked of treason. All he could do was shrug.

The President had no idea how to handle the communication that had just transpired either. Normally he would have treated it as insubordination, and had the man fired, but this was his best friend. They had met at Harvard long ago, taken law degrees together, participated in politics in the same party, and worked as a team to get the President into a position to influence the direction of his country. Now, here the man was, sitting opposite him talking like a political opponent, and an inept one at that.

Heading off the expected tongue-lashing he might receive, his Chief of Staff spoke calmly. "I know what you are thinking. You know I do. But this is government, sir, not politics. And we have to find another way."

That disarmed the President. Frankly, he was too exhausted from the suspense of this nightmare unfolding over the last few months to have the strength to attack the man he had personally chosen to advise him. He dropped his head, sighed, and asked, "What?"

"Well it isn't seizing Social Security funds, confiscating IRAs, safety deposit boxes, and declaring Martial Law—or deconstructing our own form of government. We may have only one choice here..."

"You mean, make the call to Sir Harley?"

Levine said nothing, merely breathing deeply. Both men sat silent, the only sound in a room dimming with the twilight outside, was the clock given to the President by the President of Russia during his State visit earlier that year. Finally, Chief of Staff Gabe Levine said the words no one in Washington wanted to even face, let alone speak. He felt he owed that at least to his friend. "Either we do it to ourselves, or they do it to us. If *they* do it, we are at least still intact, and we live to fight another day."

"Oh, man, what on earth possessed me to want this job!" the President lamented, laughing even as he said it.

Okay, he's stepping back from the abyss. Levine congratulated himself. *He's himself again.*

Deciding now was the time to change the subject, Gabe said, "Let's get some food into you, sir." The two friends then adjourned to the Residence kitchen, telling the chef they would make their own sandwiches, and encouraging him to go home to his family.

"This is tough." The President spoke first.

Without looking up, continuing to spread an obscene amount of mayonnaise on the turkey, tomato, and avocado sandwich that they both liked, the Chief said, "I know. But, you are up to it. We'll figure something out."

A moment later, the First Lady charged into the room in sweats and running shoes, obviously concluding her day with an aggressive workout. Seeing them eating, she said, "Fix me one, too. And let me tell you about a meeting I set for you two tomorrow at 7AM."

Chapter 53

The President was in the Oval Office, receiving his morning National Security Briefing, all the while closely monitoring the continued downward trajectory of the U.S. dollar, and any news on the metropolitan disturbances. Having no idea why his wife had agreed to Bud Walker's insistence on a meeting, he had decided to have his Chief of Staff take the meeting, and, if necessary, involve him later. He had slept poorly, choosing to remain alone in the President's bedroom. The morning wake-up call brought little relief, as he had an unshakable sense of dread. As far as he was concerned, the day ahead of him could well turn out to be the worst day of his life, and a turning point in history.

The meeting with Gabe Levine had commenced promptly at seven, in the office adjacent to the President's. Though it began with the usual amenities, Gabe Levine was a man with a lot on his plate at the moment, and a great deal weighing on his mind. As Chief of Staff, and the President's sounding board, he had a full and stressful day, every day.

So, within thirty seconds he had dispensed with the small talk. Looking at James Mikolas and Andy Weir, who were seated to Walker's right, he made the opening move. "Is this about our notification that we want to acquire the copper mines in the Anaconda area, or any of your own personal holdings in that vicinity? Because, if it is, the Attorney General is already handling that, and it is not really up for discussion."

Bud smiled. "No, Mr. Levine, it's not about that. I expect by now you all are hearing from a whole lot of people from Montana—you know, Governor, Attorney General, Militia, you name it. I'm here with something that can make this whole mess go away."

Levine said nothing, but gestured for him to go ahead. In his mind he was planning on hearing them out as quickly as possible, discharging whatever obligation the First Lady had to Bud Walker, and getting back into the crisis evaluation going on through the door to his right.

"Mr. Mikolas is a retired CIA analyst, and Mr. Weir is the co-owner of Carver & Weir. And Andy, in particular, requires a thorough hearing."

Thirty minutes later, Gabriel Levine walked assertively into the Oval Office, escorting his guests and indicating that they should sit in the sofa area.

The President was seated at his desk, hand poised to receive a call. He said, "Gabe, I can't meet anyone right now! There is a call coming in from Sir Harley Grantham-Jones, who says he is calling on behalf of the RIT. This is *the call.*" His voice cracked just a hint. Distracted too much to notice the protocol breach of having civilians in his office while discussing national emergencies, he continued. "Only *he* made it. The SOB has drawn enough blood, now he's the shark circling in the water!"

Authoritatively, Gabe Levine advanced to the President, signaling by his hand gesture that the President should wave off the call. "I know what I recommended last night, but do *not* take the call, Mr. President—not until after you have heard from these men!" Though not shouting, his voice conveyed the urgency.

"What the hell are you talking about? This is it, Gabe; this is ultimatum time." He reached for the extension button, only to find Levine's hand on his, firmly pushing it aside.

"No, Mr. President. Sir Harley Grantham-Jones can wait." Nodding his head in the direction of Andy, he added, "Sir, you are most definitely going to want to speak with Mr. Weir."

The President moved his hand away from the phone, walked to his outer office, and informed his personal secretary that he would have to get back to the RIT, and that he would be in another meeting, which was not on her schedule.

Gabe took a seat opposite the threesome, and the President pulled the rocking chair once used by his hero John Kennedy into position at the head of the coffee table so that he could engage the men on his left easily.

Andy was quite articulate at explaining succinctly to the President the goings on in Montana, and what he and Brian Washington Carver had been tasked to do. Knowing that it was unlikely this President was much in tune with the computer gaming world, he emphasized that the game had been created to unmask unethical activity on the part of the banks, and to challenge the player to create solutions that would enable him to survive—ending one finance game, beginning a new one. He had been careful to add that they were looking to empower *individuals,* but hoped that there might be solutions evident to larger groups like states or governments as well.

Bringing his tablet out, he very confidently said, "And you, sir, are going to want to see the initial 'Game Winners Analysis.'"

You gotta love this kid, James was thinking. *He's not at all impressed by his surroundings. Just knows what he knows, and won't back down!*

Bringing up a screen that showed a bar graph for U.S. gamers, and a side screen that showed another bar graph for the International game players, the graphs revealed a stunning truth—and with that truth, hope.

"What we were tracking, Mr. President, were the various routes gamers took to create financial solutions, and even what solutions they entered into the game. The game has been out only a few days, sir, but it has gone global, as you can see by the International graph, and the number of countries already using it."

"It looks like a God-damned list of the United Nations!"

Andy didn't quite know what the man meant by that exclamation, but he took it as positive, and said, "Yes, anything coming out of Carver & Weir is pretty highly anticipated in the marketplace. And, we had done advance marketing to alert gamers. But the point, sir, is that, as you can see, some chose more conventional routes of renegotiating interest rates, and lowering principle amounts; some chose to bring our currency back onto the gold standard; some chose to abolish the currency altogether and create a new one backed by tangible goods; a lot of ideas you have probably entertained yourself."

The President said nothing, but Andy could see his eye was fixated on one area on both graphs where the bar spiked dramatically. "As you can see, however, most of the gamers picked one particular path as their route to personal survival, and that was bartering. Stunningly, it was almost automatically chosen as the best path, and it clearly enabled the gamers to reach the game's top."

The President pulled his chair a little closer now, looking at Andy for interpretation. "At first, we considered that might be just an American trait, albeit one certainly that could save the day right now, with the effects the country is experiencing with money supplies shut down."

"But, the graph is the same with the International gamers!" The President himself was thinking with the data.

"Yes, sir, and that is why I am here."

"Do you have this identified by country, or is this just the aggregate?"

With a smooth movement, Andy brought up a sub-screen with the graph laid out country by country.

"Ahhhhh." The President's reaction was immediate and involuntary. The stunning reality was that in every country represented, the largest number of gamers who had completed the game had created paths involving Barter.

"My God…" The President turned to Levine—the look on his face almost one of hope.

Levine nodded.

"And there is one more analysis I want to show you." On a second pad, Andy brought up the breakdown on how many had chosen to select "Auction" and play through that section of the game. It was almost identical to the other graphs.

"What is this 'Auction' thing?"

"We isolated a fundamental American activity known as barn-raising, and when you come to Montana, you see that factor still in existence today. We called it the Auction to see which players would stop to help someone else, and not just proceed hell bent on saving their own hides." Andy stopped for a moment and looked calmly at the man who was holding the burden of this crisis, and on whose decisions so much rested.

Their eyes met briefly, and while the President's were somewhat questioning, Andy's revealed a serenity and certainty.

"You see, nearly everyone who selected Barter as the best solution, and one they could implement simply and easily, also selected the Auction, and went through it, rather than bailing out of it. The key, sir, is that this is not just an American trait."

"Mikolas, are you tracking with this?" the President suddenly asked James.

"Yes, most definitely. If I were here in an official CIA capacity briefing you on any matter, with a graph like this, I would be saying, 'Mr. President, *there* is your window.'"

The President rose and walked back to behind his desk, looking out the bay window area across to the Mall, and its monuments. "This is a universal trait." He was trying to digest the reality of it. "It's apparently part of the culture of every country, at some point?"

"Yes." Andy grinned now.

"With that being the case, Mr. Weir, what would you have me do?"

CHAPTER 54

"What is bloody going on in the White House?" Harley Grantham-Jones shouted to a near-empty War Room. Only the Director of the New York Bank of the United States was with him. Sir Harley had felt the man's presence might be helpful, but now he was flushed from the sudden termination of his much-anticipated phone call with the President of the United States. He knew that America's cities were on the verge of full-blown rioting, thereby creating a scenario in the United States that would mirror the devastation occurring elsewhere around the world. He also knew that the President would be looking for an offer, and a way to resolve this—even if it were heavy-handed and smelled like extortion. Sir Harley was reeling from the refused call.

The man's a pragmatist. He's got to know when he's beaten. Harley was reviewing in his mind his own thought process. *He can't turn to any countries for help; he can't turn to any banks. He's got no place to go, but into my arms. He'll make his move, and then I'll have him.*

Except for the fact that the President of the United States had just refused to take the call. It didn't matter that the President's Secretary had diplomatically cloaked it in the usual "something has detained him, and he'll have to get back to you" jargon. He could *feel* something was wrong.

Regrettably, the Director of the New York Bank of the United States was of no help. He either knew nothing, or he was pretending he knew nothing. That made Sir Harley even more alarmed. *Has he turned? Is that why he has not rebounded after his heart episode?* Looking at the man suspiciously, he asked himself, *Do we have a mole here?*

Concluding that trying to probe that any further right now was pointless, he dismissed the man rather rudely and descended to the infirmary to see if perhaps he could have another tablet for his anxiety.

"Look to China first," Andy said simply.

Out of the corner of his eye, the President saw Bud and Mikolas nod agreement. This was confusing to him. After all, it had been just yesterday that the Chairman of the Party had been on the phone from Beijing, exhorting him to reach some kind of agreement with the RIT that would turn the money back on.

"The Central Government has been applying pressure to you, have they not, to continue to play the old finance game with the Central Banks? You know, capitulate somehow and get the money flowing again, for the sake of all? Find some way to do business as usual?" It was Bud who had spoken.

Gabe Levine signaled the President that it would be appropriate for him to answer. "Bud, are you here on your own, or as a representative of the Governor of Montana?"

"You could say I represent the Governor."

"Gabe?" Once again, the President checked.

Levine indicated he had spoken with Governor Bruce Fitzerman and that, while he wished he could be with these three, they did in fact speak for him, as well as for themselves.

With that reassurance, the President decided to answer. "Yes, they have. And they have mysteriously refrained from calling in any of our debt. Their only demand has been to resolve this with the RIT. Frankly, I don't know what to make of it. In their shoes, I would have..." He was searching for a good word when Andy finished his sentence for him.

"Repo'd the car?"

That non-sequitur stopped the President, causing him to scrunch his forehead as if trying to grasp the meaning. Then, getting it, he suddenly laughed. It sounded more like a bark, but it was sincere.

"Yeah, that is one way to put it." Then he laughed again. "But where are you going with this?"

"Have you checked to see what their Governors are doing?"

To the shock of nearly everyone in the room, the President's answer was, "No, why should I?"

Bud chose to walk point on this. Under the guise of a billionaire who had had business dealings in China, and who had run across the little-known or little-understood autonomy of the Provincial Governors, and whose bureau chief had a better understanding of this than most diplomats, he graciously skated past this glaring omission in the foreign affairs arena.

"You are saying it is China's governors, taking some kind of alternative action, that are causing China to appear to be sitting on the fence—equivocating?"

Bud nodded.

"How on earth do we prove that? You know, find out what they are up to?" The President was clearly hamstrung by his own authority at this point. His dealings were with Beijing, and protocol had limited them to that.

Though the news was startling that the Governor of Montana had held a summit of China's governors, and commenced barter relationships with them to handle his entanglements with China; and though it was equally surprising to learn that the same governor had called a Governors' Summit, with most U.S. governors in attendance, which subsequently led to barter programs going on state to state and internally in each state vis-a-vis their own citizens, it was well-received by the President.

"I suppose you had all these people play this game?" he joked.

"I did."

At that, the President just shook his head.

"Mr. President, you asked what I would have you do. We will win the United States with this. The people will make it. The game will win the world. Give it time, and then call their bluff."

"Their bluff?" the President challenged. "Does what's going on out there look like a bluff to you?!"

Andy responded without any hesitation, "Oh, yes, sir. What's going on out there is what we are doing to *ourselves*. They have no power to enforce unless we agree they have the power. Call their bluff." He waited only a beat before adding, "They have been bluffing you for years."

The President decided to move past that for a moment. "How long do you think?" This was the real question. How much time did the United States have, and how much time would it take for other nations to reach the same conclusion?

The mood in the room dampened as soon as the President asked the question—all except for Andy. "Judging by these analyses, I think you can have your people start calling the leaders of the main countries…"

Levine supplied the correct name for the target countries, the ones whose financial decisions would influence the rest of the world. "The G20."

"Yes, those. The ones that matter the most. Call them and see if they are starting to see people in government playing a game?"

The President winced at the absurdity of that type of call, but Andy sailed right on, uninhibited. "See if maybe their grandkids aren't already chattering about a new finance game. If, maybe, their 'governors' or people are resorting to fledgling bartering. You know, see if that thing, which appears to be part of the heritage of every nation that grew into economic power, has been resurrected and is making a comeback."

More than twenty minutes ago, while listening to and learning from Andrew Weir, the President of the United States had abandoned any considerations he had had about a citizen coming to him with an offer of help. He had dropped his idea that some twenty-something young man, with a boyish face, could not possibly outweigh experts in this area. Despite all that had happened in the course of his political career, the President had aspired to that office not for power but for service. The spirit of that desire to serve was humbly rekindled now.

"And, if I find they have been?"

"Then, Mr. President, I am going to teach you a chess move."

CHAPTER 55

*A*ll had confirmed, and all had agreed. What had taken decades to develop, fester, and turn toxic in an entanglement of complexities and corruption, unraveled with breathtaking speed and simplicity.

The President had called through the night. His first call was to "the people in Beijing," as he had recently been taught to think of them. Their response was immediate and totally along his lines. Japan, France, Germany, the Netherlands—all had gone well. By morning of the next day, with smoke appearing in the distance from some fire bombs and increasing tension, and with police in riot control gear working to stop the looting, the President looked disheveled and physically exhausted, but mentally invigorated.

While he changed his shirt in the small pantry area connecting a dining room with his office, and splashed cold water on his face, Andy approached the door. Astonishingly, all of them had waited it out through the night in the Oval Office. That had taken some doing with the Secret Service, but they had finally agreed.

Andy had been keeping stats, growing calmer by the minute. "Are you ready to see the chess move?"

Drying his face, and putting on his reading glasses, the President laughed. "What do you call this one?"

"This one is simple. It's the 'turn the tables' move."

"Can't wait."

Neither could the Heads of State of the rest of the G20. Summoned to an urgent video conference with the President of the United States, each of the President's counterparts had been informed the call would start with them, and then would expand to include the Director from the Bank of the United Kingdom and that, "Ladies and Gentlemen, it is *show time!*"

The President of the United States had decided to introduce the leaders to Andrew Weir, who was seated to the President's right at the table in the Situation Room. The lights in the room were dimmed so that he could see the faces of his counterparts clearly. Small table lamps illuminated the space in front of each participant in the event he needed to take notes. From this room, communications could come and go securely.

Gabe Levine, James, and Bud were in the room as well, but seated along the wall.

Like fans of a celebrity, there had been a spontaneous burst of applause and enthusiastic greetings for Andy when he was introduced, and he smiled somewhat uncomfortably. Normally not shy, this was a bit more than expected. All pro, however, he directly informed them that the next move in the game for them would be to turn the tables on the RIT and their own Central Banks.

"They are expecting you to fold—to acquiesce to their demands in order to avoid your nations slipping into an abyss, and ushering in darkness. You are going to fold, but not before you turn the table. Just picture in your mind that you spin the board 180 degrees and the move which was facing you is now facing Sir Harley Grantham-Jones."

He waited for a moment, as some members were languishing over that image. Then he continued. "Now you are going to fold the whole game—all of you at once. Like a poker game, you are all folding like you don't like your cards, and you don't want to play poker anymore. The 'House' gets to keep the pot…"

The President couldn't resist interjecting, "Which by the way is worthless now. They drove the value of all our currencies down after extracting every ounce of money from us they could in interest on our loans, so what they hold is valueless to them now." He was salivating over this, however professionally he was presenting it.

"And you are going to go play another game—one set up amongst yourselves, and agreed to by you for mutual benefit. You can barter. You can do many things. If you like, I will have our best gamers tasked to create games that nations can play one nation to another, without the middle man in there controlling you, and taking a cut."

"Hear, hear!" the Prime Minister of Great Britain shouted. "I expect we'll get word of the Americans printing their Lincoln Greenbacks before you know it!"

Andy could see on the multiple screens that they all liked this. *Seems I'm not the only game player in the crowd,* Andy thought. "Sir Harley will recognize the checkmate move, so to speak. You are calling their bluff by all folding at once. Game over."

There was silence, as each head of state contemplated this—and the adventure they would be beginning. The road back would not be easy, but at least they felt they had an option. It was the French President who asked the question most had on their minds. "What do you think *he* will do?"

"He will likely, once he recognizes the game is over, start to negotiate a new game. But, it is important to remember, it will be your game, on your terms now," Andy answered.

"Any advice?" the Prime Minister queried.

Characteristically, Andy had no hesitation in responding. "Just remember your heritage, is all. That's something my mother instilled in me always. Trust your people. They are good, and they are smart."

And with that parting thought, the President of the United States placed the call to the Repository of International Transactions, stating the representatives of the G20 were all on the line and wished to speak with Sir Harley Grantham-Jones.

CHAPTER 56

Sir Harley was walking rapidly to the War Room, having been informed there was a call coming in from the President of the United States. He therefore put very little attention on his longtime aide who had caught up with him and was breathlessly trying to get some instruction from his employer. An urgent email had come through from Ayman Al-Zawahiri.

Through the years, Zawahiri had used an encrypted email to request personal funds, new identities, escape routes—basically anything he needed to accomplish his Hide in Plain Sight strategies. Knowing he was dealing with the same bank that had aided some of Hitler's top brass as they fled Germany following the surrender, the Doctor nonetheless had never known who, actually, he was dealing with. Frankly, he did not care. All Ayman Al-Zawahiri had cared about was getting the resources he needed to continue his missions.

"What is it? What is it?" Sir Harley almost spat it at his aide. "Can't you see I am in a hurry?"

Suppliant, the man answered, "Yes, I can, sir, but this came in on urgent flash traffic, and I thought you would want to see his request and advise me what to do with it."

"Very well," Harley said, stopping long enough to cursorily look over the paper. Then, with no hesitation whatsoever, he handed it back to his man with, "Ignore it."

The man just stood there, fumbling for words before daring to advance an argument. "But, but…we have always provided what he requested—"

Sir Harley interrupted before he could finish his argument. "Yes, well, there is no need now. The man has played his part." Dismissing Zawahiri with the flick of a piece of paper, he then added, "Understood, my dear fellow?"

The man nodded.

"Now, if that is all, I have a very important call to take."

Finally, he thought, as he sped down the remainder of the corridor, *we will end this game and get on with our lives. None too soon, if I may say!*

Sir Harley Grantham-Jones literally had the wind knocked out of him. What made matters worse was that the video conference revealed that to all the other participants. In shock, his mind offered the nagging reminder that the whole world is a stage. And there he was, in the center of it. Without a moment to regain his composure—after the immediate and decisive statement by the G20 members that they were terminating their relationship with RIT, and preparing to abandon their Central Banks—his long-awaited coup d'etat evaporated, and he found himself in total confusion.

What happened? I was attacking. Now I am being attacked? How could this happen?

He had no way of knowing he had just faced off with a gamer whose initial game had turned the tables on all the pharmaceutical cartels in recent years. Even if told, Harley's own arrogance would likely have discounted it. All he could think about was that his head was spinning, making his body unstable. He was conscious enough to realize all this would be visible to everyone on the teleconference with him. But it was all he could do to remain upright in his chair.

Sipping water to give himself time, he thought, *What went wrong?*

Sir Harley would never know the answer to that, however, since he possessed the same fatal flaw that all totalitarians possess. The nature of totalitarianism and despotism is that they do not comprehend autonomy, and he thought like a totalitarian. He was therefore totally certain that the Central U.S. government, and the Central Chinese government, would do what he'd predicted in order to save lives, and that he could therefore control them.

But the pesky thing about autonomy, which he never had discovered, was its tendency to maintain creativity and flexibility, and to be as hard to restrain and control as the people who created autonomies.

Facing a true unity created by the governors, making their own brand of united states, and facing a true unity of these heads of state, making their own brand of united nations, he was absolutely stymied. To make matters worse, he knew it would only be a matter of time before his colleagues within the Central Bank community would discover what he and the other four had attempted to do, right under their noses, and would exile them—most likely attempting to negotiate on their own in order to save their fortunes, and stay in some kind of finance game.

"Sir Harley?" the President of France interjected. "You do not look well. Perhaps we should cut this call short."

"Yes, yes, I am not breathing well. This turn of events is not what I was expecting. And I seem to need to take a break."

"By all means," the man said unctuously. "Take your time. We will just go on about our business, and you may get back to us as you choose."

Then each, on their own, disconnected the feed to Basel, Switzerland. Still on conference with each other, their attention turned back to the President of the United States, who simply said, "Well, I suggest we adjourn and address our nations. The people need to hear from us."

"Indeed! Hear, hear! Absolutely! Understood!" The sound lingered as the pictures evaporated from the screen.

As Andy rose, James put his arm around him and said, "You did great, Kid." Not wanting to speak of Kelly, he swallowed hard and simply repeated, "You did great. Brian will be relieved, I know."

With that, one counter attack was completed. Andy could now do what his heart had been screaming for—turn his attention to the second attack, which he prayed had launched.

Chapter 57

" All right, boys, we have a green light!" Vince's normally quiet voice penetrated the room in the Quonset hut at the far end of the Colombian air base. "We have a green light. This is not a drill. I repeat. This is not a drill."

Like coiled springs released, there was an explosion of activity in the bunk room, as the seven-man team grabbed weapons and gear and headed for the chopper, whose rotating blades were already churning up dust.

"Hey Pal, you are riding with me," Vince ordered Brian. "Get your buddy DeShawn. I want one of you on my right and one on my left as we go in."

"Roger." Brian had no idea why he had said that. *I've been watching too many war movies, man!*

"And get everybody huddled up for the final briefing. There's something I need to explain to you all."

Knowing that amateurs could introvert and get themselves tangled up into all kinds of thinking relative to a mission like this, he had delayed informing them of the precise and limited activity they were tasked to accomplish. One by one, they headed into the huddle, in their jungle camouflage and painted faces—all of which further enhanced the stealth operation.

Then he explained that this was an extraction only, not a rescue of everyone in the camp. "We don't know what the hell we are going to find there, but you all need to understand—totally—that we are there for one purpose only: to locate and extract Reagan Lynch, Edith Church, and Alicia Quixote. Is that understood?"

They all affirmed, but he knew by their expressions they didn't quite get it. "Now, I know you *softies...*" He was interrupted by their laughter. "And I know you are going to want to save every other person we find there. Especially you, Hector. I know your type."

That produced some jeers in jest, and back slapping. So Vince McCoy continued. "But the plain truth is, there is no room for anyone but those three, and I promised your mamas I would bring you all back in once piece. So I want you all to be crystal clear that I am not exchanging one of your dead bodies for another captive. Is that understood?"

It was—sobering as it was.

Brian, however, seemed to have a question he needed to ask. "What happens to everybody else there?"

Vince smiled. "Now this is where you Boy Scouts will be tickled pink. The Colombian military will enter immediately upon our evacuation from the area. Once we confirm the coordinates, and get the hell out of Dodge without alerting the whole camp, they will take up the operation of Rescue and Clear."

They all understood then. His explanation impinged immensely now as to why they were to just get in and get out. Allowed by a foreign ally to come for these three women, they were being used by the Colombian forces as "scouts" to locate the camp.

And the Colombians were smartly using Jessica Ranger's "assets" to accomplish the hard part of finding these ghosts in the dense and vast area.

The location was surprisingly close to the town of Cejal in the Southeast corner of Colombia. *Hide in plain sight, man! These guys are something else!* Vince was admiring his opponents, and secretly happy to be delivering them to hell at the hands of a now well-armed and well-trained Colombian Special Forces team.

Not wanting the sound of the approaching helicopter to be heard by the suspected camp in the late afternoon quieting of jungle sounds, Blacky had selected a primary landing zone from satellite photos he'd procured. It would require a hike along a ridge beginning near some waterfalls whose water noise was significant. But he knew also that the sound of the water would provide a natural guide in the event these newbies got lost in their escape.

His second, and back-up LZ, was about one half mile further up the mountain, right at the edge of the forest. Though more exposed, the men could remain concealed until they broke cover and headed to the chopper.

He preferred, however, the first one, and made that abundantly clear in typical Ranger pilot language to Vince.

Equipped with night vision gear, and GPS instruments, the plan was to go in near sundown, identify the location of Alicia Quixote and the others, extract them, and escape under cover of darkness. Time from boots down to boots off the ground was planned at two hours, twenty minutes.

But like many war plans, something had changed even before they took off. Vince and Blacky had yelled, cajoled, and begged for the better part of an hour. Once the Colombian commander saw the location of the transmission, he realized the FARC base was inside Venezuela, and that the FARC were ensconced in the bosom of a sovereign nation providing them sanctuary.

Waving the map at Vince in the heated exchange, pointing repeatedly to the base location, he had then flatly refused to go in and clean up the camp. Normally quiet, if not jovial, Vince had let loose his best Marine language—only to have it fall on deaf ears.

"I am telling you, señor, we cannot go there. You are forgetting the International incident we Colombians caused last year when we crossed the border into Venezuela in pursuit of a drug cartel."

That stopped Vince in his tracks. He well remembered the shouting and posturing at the United Nations when the thug nation of Venezuela sent its Ambassador to whip up support in the International community.

What a charade, Vince thought. *Pretended irate rantings and a bunch of pussies who should have been grateful for Colombia shellacking a cartel.*

The other nations, however, were not supportive and had sanctioned Colombia, warning them severely. It was that wall Vince McCoy ran into. With the world slipping into chaos, he had hoped the man would have the balls to do the right thing. But he did not. Vince knew not to berate him further, lest he cancel the mission altogether.

Putting on a stone face of resignation, he told only Blacky, who, to his credit, only shrugged and walked away, muttering something under his breath. They mounted up, and thirty minutes later had crossed into Venezuela.

"Wow! That is gorgeous!" Hector exclaimed unexpectedly, as he looked down into the lush green canopy, the waterfall, and the rainbow that was arcing across the ravine.

DeShawn was quick to shoot him an "are you out of your mind?" glance, when Vince gave him a nudge.

"He's okay, DeShawn. I'd rather hear that any day than, 'oh, shit!'"

DeShawn took a deep breath and relaxed a bit. As the chopper landed, Vince said, "From this point, no talking. Exactly like we drilled it. Pass the word." Then his right foot became the first boot on the ground, and the clock was ticking.

Edith had been debating what her first actions should be when Alicia became conscious. Knowing that Reagan didn't understand why Edith had warned her off, and that she would just automatically want to acknowledge that they knew each other, Edith had been forced to take Reagan aside and explain that it could be dangerous—that they did not know whether this was all a ruse, and that Alicia was reconnecting in a plausible way with her lover, planning an escape with Samir. That would make her an Al Qaeda operative—driven by love—to forsake her country.

Or, in the event that this *was* some monstrous coincidence with Alicia and Samir colliding in yet another Al Qaeda operation, thereby placing Alicia at huge risk should she be recognized by Samir, it required that she and Reagan find some way to alert Alicia, and disguise her somehow. A plan had to be created.

The additional risk was that if the other four women knew of the connection of the three, and the true identity of this newest arrival, one of them might try to gain an advantage and save herself by giving Alicia up.

Reagan had her firm opinion about Alicia's non-complicity in anything with Samir, but she knew immediately there was considerable jeopardy all the way around. So, as Alicia was starting to move more and more, and beginning to open her eyes, Edith told the other women she would see to the girl, and get her cleaned up.

They agreed readily, not wanting to share any of what water or food they did have anyway. So, Edith dragged Alicia into the corner of the hut farthest from the other girls, where there was the least light coming through the window to the right of the door.

Then, to a barely conscious Alicia, she whispered, "Shhh, Alicia, do not let on who you are, or that we know each other. It is not safe."

Alicia's smile, which had started when she recognized her friend, and realized that she had indeed found the right location, vanished upon hearing the urgency in Edith's communication. She nodded her head, indicating she understood, and pulled herself up further out of the drug stupor. Other than a headache, she was feeling all right. There was a residual weakness, but her mind was fairly clear—clear enough to engage some of her investigative journalist skills, and to play along.

"Thank you. What happened to me? Who are you?"

"You were kidnapped, as were all of us here," Edith said, loudly enough for the other four women to overhear. "We don't know where we are, but no one has harmed us. And my name is Edith Church. This is Reagan Lynch."

CHAPTER 58

Getting to the FARC camp proved uneventful, but what Vince and Willie, whom Vince had nicknamed "God," found as they scouted the area, was challenging. Though it was clear from their transmitter that Alicia Quixote was in a hut set up the hill, and guarded by one man primarily who was about thirty yards below the hut, they could tell the other two buildings housed many more people, and had a much greater security level around them.

Praying that Church and Lynch were in fact in the same building as Alicia, Vince hoped he was only going to have to breach the one, and not have to go from hut to hut. The risk was much greater if more than one building was involved. Not to mention he could see farther down the hill to what appeared to be a large camp and fortification about 1,000 yards away.

Not enough breathing room if this turns into a shooting match, he reminded himself.

Picking the God spot for Willie, he waited until Willie was in position to be able to fire into the entire area around the target hut. Then he returned to the others, pantomiming the plan and route to use for each person.

Within minutes, Brian, Hector, DeShawn, and he were close in and flanking the hut. The remaining two were between the guard and the other buildings—all under the watchful eye of "God." Vince was assessing how to get into the hut, without being seen by the guard, and without having to take him down. Knowing that might just require some patience and waiting, he was prepared to settle in when a window of opportunity appeared.

A second man was walking up the path, having emerged from a tent midway between the huts and the main camp below. Though he was of a similar complexion to the men in the camp, he nonetheless dressed differently. *Wonder where the laundry is that pressed his fatigues?* Vince joked with himself. He'd seen all kinds of things, but the meticulous grooming of this man, and his attire, not only struck Vince as humorous but it also raised suspicion in his mind as to who this man was.

Even stranger was the fact that the man was using a satellite phone, talking to someone in…he strained to hear the language, but could not quite get it. As the man passed the guard, the guard nodded as if he'd been relieved of duty for a few minutes, and started down the path, probably to relieve himself and take a break.

The man with the satellite phone then continued up the path toward the hut.

All right, this is it! Vince signaled the others that he was going in behind the man. That scenario had been drilled, in the unlikely event they found themselves in a position to enter an almost unprotected structure. Given the man was seemingly distracted by his conversation, Vince was about to engage in a stealth entry.

Brian, DeShawn, and Hector were to stand fast, until needed.

Edith and Reagan heard Samir's voice first, as he approached the door; unbolted it; and stepped into the darkened room, saying to the other person on the phone, "This is the seventh package. The remaining four are within days, and the entire shipment will be…"

His speaking in Arabic startled and frightened the four women to his left, and for a moment, it distracted him. He did not notice a "ghost" enter right behind him and slip into the corner to his right, disappearing into the shadow. Edith, Reagan, and Alicia had not seen it either, because the suppressed shrieking of the other four drew their attention as well.

Then, in English, the man told Reagan to push the new arrival forward, as he could not see her in the shadows at the rear of the room. Still holding the phone, as if preparing to describe something to the partner in his conversation, he returned his attention to the woman stepping forward.

She had fully raised her head, and at the same moment, they recognized each other. Samir exclaimed, "Alicia!" and she cried out, "Samir!"

Samir Taghavi had no time to think. Trained, and expert in his craft, he knew that somehow he had been compromised, and standing in front of him was the one woman who could expose him. Knowing also her presence in this unlikely environment meant danger to him, without letting go of the phone he drew his weapon and raised it directly at Alicia.

Before he could pull the trigger, however, two sudden and unidentifiable thumping sounds occurred, and Samir fell lifeless to the floor, gun in hand. He would never know who had shot him, but Vince McCoy emerged quickly from the shadows before any screaming could occur and indicated to the women not to speak—not one word.

Reaching for the phone to disconnect the call, the line was already dead. He would never know that Ayman Al-Zawahiri recognized those two thumps, had heard his man drop, and had hurriedly hung up to save himself.

Comparing their pictures to the women themselves—having learned long ago not to trust desperate hostages—Vince confirmed the three he was there to extract and started to push them toward the door. Unfortunately, Reagan refused to leave without the other four.

They were in shock from the sudden and brutal change in their apparent fortunes, but they seemed calm enough to know this man was not a slave purchaser, or poacher, but rather some kind of rescue operation. Their relief turned to fear when it became apparent they were going to be left behind. Vince explained to them that he was taking the three but leaving them, and that in a few hours they, too, would be rescued. He felt a twinge of remorse in having to lie to them, knowing that thanks to "diplomacy" no rescue would occur. He justified it by reminding himself that his mission was very clear.

By then Brian, DeShawn, and Hector had entered the room, frightening everyone. Then Reagan recognized Brian. "Hey, girl!" That was all he said, realizing only urgent talking was possible. Seeing immediately that the plan had been compromised by the necessity of killing whoever this guy was, Brian had taken a look at him.

Totally stunned, he recognized Samir Taghavi, having met the man when Taghavi's PR firm pitched to Carver & Weir about handling the marketing campaign for their first game, and from the subsequent revelation about Taghavi.

"Hey man," he said to Vince softly. "This dude is Al Qaeda, and you just killed him." Vince was startled by the news of the man's affiliation, and looked to Alicia for confirmation. It had been his plan to merely slip in while the man was there, remain in the room until he left, and then evacuate the three women. Clearly, he would have to re-evaluate, as the guard would be returning.

"Okay, we'll take the girls and barricade the door. Hopefully the guard will just assume he missed this joker when he returns and sees the barricaded door." That seemed feasible, except for the fact that Reagan inserted herself between Brian and Vince with a defiant, "You take all of us, or none of us."

"Ma'am, that is not possible. Our mission is you three. The others are later," he whispered. Getting nowhere with her, he turned to Brian for support. "You know her. Explain it."

"No use, Boss. I do know her. She's like my partner. When her mind is made up, it is made up. They're perfect for each other."

"Jesus!" Vince McCoy knew when he was licked. He'd have to take them all, and figure out the evacuation on the way. There was no way they were all going to fit on the helo." Before they could get to the door, however, "God" notified Vince that the guard was returning. With the door open slightly, surely he would notice that Samir must still be inside.

"Señor, is everything all right in there?" the guard asked, more with leering intent than any concern for Samir's safety. He'd been asked to guard, and knew it would go hard on him if *he* "damaged the goods," as Hyena had put it. Nonetheless, he envied Samir, who seemed to be the real man in charge.

Hector immediately called out in a somewhat hoarse voice, "Si, si, take your post!"

Thinking Samir was engaged in a little tasting of the goods, the man snorted his agreement and said, "Okay." Then he resumed his position.

"All right." Vince put a new plan in place. All of the team heard it through their ear pieces. "God, where did this man come from? Can you see his quarters?"

"Yes, definitely."

"DeShawn, I'm sorry, man, but you are going to have to change clothes with Taghavi here. Leave now that it's dark and go to the man's tent. With any luck, the guard will recognize the *wardrobe* and not think anything of it. Double back, and meet us at the LZ."

"Got it."

"Hector, we have night vision equipment only for the three, so you're going to have to carry these two right here, and keep them awfully close."

Vince pushed two women forward, having selected the two heavier ones, knowing Hector's upper body strength was significant. Hector nodded.

"Brian, you and I will carry Edith and Reagan, who are petite, and the other women get the gear." He looked at the women and pointedly said, "Understood?" It was.

"DeShawn, fake the bolt, and God, you tell us when that man has opened a window for us to slip out."

"Roger."

Then, more kindly, he spoke to the seven women in hushed tones. "This has turned more dangerous now, ladies, but we are going to get you out of here. But you must, and I mean *must*, exit exactly when we tell you, in tow of one of these guys, and you are to disappear off that step into the night as if you were a ghost. Do you understand?"

He could see they did, doubts and all. Reassuring them, he added, "These boys are trained, and, if you just let them whisk you away, this will be total stealth. I can promise you your feet are going to hurt, and your bodies are going to hurt before we are out of this. But no words, no cries, no gasps, nothing. Our lives depend on it. Can you do it?"

He knew their answer of course, so he patted the one who looked the most terrified on the arm and said, "You stay right behind me."

We're going to be late! Vince thought. *Good news is these bad guys are complacent. I guess outsmarting their own people for so long has made them think they are immune to discovery.*

It was now dark. DeShawn was dressed in the blood-soaked uniform Samir had been wearing, and Samir's naked body had been dragged back into the shadows, covered with Alicia's skirt. She had donned DeShawn's fatigues. They were ready.

The first part went easily enough. DeShawn exited, phone in hand, and appeared to bolt the door. From a distance and in the dark, the guard would not see that the door was still ajar unless he came close. But the night's shadows would disrupt anyone's depth perception enough to carry it off.

DeShawn walked easily down the path, slipping around the back of Samir's tent rather than entering it.

A short time later, predictably, the guard turned to relieve himself. "God" gave the signal, and they all vanished into the darkness. Arriving thirty minutes later than planned, Blacky scowled at them and started to pitch a fit when he saw there were seven women instead of three. And he noticed immediately that DeShawn was missing.

"Please tell me what the hell happened." He was in Vince's face as much as he could be still sitting at the controls.

"Nothing. It's fine. Just a little change of plans, that's all. You're taking seven women out. And before you explain physics and aerodynamics to me, I know you can't hold this many. DeShawn, once he gets his ass back up here, and Hector are staying with me."

Brian was not in agreement with that, and started to protest. As he looked at the women, however, he knew they had to get them out. He wanted to substitute himself for DeShawn or Vince—anybody. But Hector knew exactly what he was thinking and intervened. "You got cajones, bro, I know that. But you also know that you never were on the street. You came from the Hood, but you ain't no Homeboy. Do you understand me?"

Brian did, and he knew Hector and DeShawn had fought together before. He nodded that it was okay. Vince was staying, and he could help them handle anything. A few interminable minutes later, DeShawn appeared.

Everyone was aboard who was going aboard, and Vince had pushed Hector and DeShawn back into the brush. "Blacky, see if there's some way to get that Colombian commander to reconsider. I don't want any crazed drug crew following us here. Tell the Colombians they need to take out everybody right now while their guard is down." Jerking his head in the direction of DeShawn and Hector, he leaned in and whispered, "These boys deserve a long life."

"Roger." Then Blacky added, "And I'll be back for you myself. LZ 2."

CHAPTER 59

*T*he mood was more one of relief than jubilation aboard Walker's private jet. He, James, and Andy had been intent on leaving Washington as soon as it was clear the President didn't need them anymore. The man was already in behind-closed-door meetings with Congressional Committee Heads, and his Cabinet—and the Secretary of the Treasury had already tendered his resignation.

As they headed West to the ranch, for the first time Andy could let down enough to allow thoughts of Reagan to crowd in. No longer feeling guilty about stealing time away from his own mission, he experienced the questionable luxury of worrying. He was looking out the window at the lights of Omaha when the call came in.

"Sir, you have a call coming in from Jessica Ranger on your secure line." His pilot had delivered that personally, trying to keep his voice down. But in a small jet, Bud knew that was pointless. Besides, the Kid *knew* everything. So, he turned to James and Andy, who were sitting beside each other on the sofa in the lounge quarters of the jet. His recliner was opposite them.

"Okay with you if I put this on speaker?"

"Please."

Jessica came on first, and Bud alerted her to the fact that James and Andy were both listening. Her response was, "Good. Andy, there is someone here with me on the plane who wants to speak with you."

"Andy?" Reagan spoke tearfully into the phone. "I'm okay, sweetie. We're okay."

"Oh, thank God, Reagan. It is soooo good to hear your voice. Thank God."

James was speechless, but his eyes welled with tears. For a long moment, there was absolute silence on both ends. Words were not needed.

Bud, however, had to ask. He had such a knot in his stomach, and needed to know who all was aboard. "Alicia? Is Alicia there?"

"You bet I am," she said, "and they're going to get this damned thing out of my navel before we land in Ovando, or there will be hell to pay!" That made Bud laugh, as that was so typical of his girl. She really had balls, he had to hand it to her.

"Well, there's no mistaking it's you, Alicia. Thank God. And thank you!"

The silence that followed revealed the question all wanted asked, but whose answer, all feared. Jessica was the first to speak. "Bud, Andy, I know you want to ask, so before you do, I'll just answer. They weren't harmed." She paused, then added, "Not beaten, not molested, not starved." There was silence on both ends of the line. She finished with, "No one knows *why.*"

Hearing that, James knew they would never know, and Andy didn't care.

Mercifully, Bud asked, "So, Jessica, do I gather that a slave trading ring bit the dust tonight?"

"Bud, there was a complication. Damned Colombians wouldn't fly into or invade Venezuela for fear of diplomatic sanctions. They refused to back our boys up."

"No..." Bud went numb, and started to lose his voice.

"Yep, but hang on, Bud. Breathe." She knew him well, and he followed her instruction. Sensing he was doing better, she continued. "But your girl Alicia fixed that. According to her, our old friend, Samir Taghavi, was there and became a casualty of his own war."

"My God!"

"Yep. The Colombians were of the same sentiment. Once they heard Al Qaeda was on the scene—and a high value target at that—they invoked the Bush Doctrine that if you harbor a terrorist, you are a terrorist. Cloaking themselves in that mantra, they sent their boys in. You should have seen that commander. The prospect of bringing in the dead body of one of the world's most wanted men...and the visions of promotions for years to come...well, he unleashed himself! Didn't even wait for it to clear channels."

The picture of that, and the relief of it all, made everyone laugh. Sobering just a bit, Bud asked, "Were they in time?"

"Yes. They got them all—the slave traders, their captives, and the entire senior command of the drug cartel. It was a haul, let me tell you!"

Bud knew the details on that were better handled once everyone had landed, but Jessica was on a roll. "It was a wipe-out, and there's a lot of backslapping going on between Colombia, Mexico, Texas, and D.C. It was a good night, a really good night." Jessica remembered then the extraordinary mission her friend had been on, and in a far more subdued voice asked, "Good night for you boys?"

"Yeah. We're back from the brink! And we'll exchange war stories when you land." Relieved about what he'd heard so far, Bud still sensed something was being withheld. The old newspaperman smelled it. He was about to take the phone off speaker when James shook his head, "no," so he left it on. "Jessica, is everyone aboard?"

The momentary lag didn't really compute with Andy. His fatigue, coupled with his gut-wrenching joy about Reagan, fogged him a bit. But James picked up on it. "Jessica, it's James Mikolas. Who all is aboard? Is Brian there?"

"Yeah, James, my man, I'm here!" Brian shouted from what James guessed was the back of the plane.

James sighed, then persisted. "Who else?"

"Everybody but Vince, Hector, and DeShawn," Jessica said, resuming control of the conversation. "They had to stay behind, since there were seven women, not three."

"I see. Are they coming in on another flight?"

"We don't know, James. They haven't returned to the base yet, according to the Colombians. Blacky went back in, but no one's heard from him yet either."

The only thing James could say was, "I see."

"Yeah, I know, James." Jessica full-well understood his anxiety. Vince McCoy was her friend, and she was trying valiantly to suppress the sense of foreboding she had. "We just have to wait, that's all. The boys are with the best in the business, and I'm sure Vince and Blacky will bring them out. My second plane is landing even as we speak, and will stand by to bring them home. I will call you as soon as I know anything."

Though the mood on Walker's jet was now subdued rather than jubilant, they knew it was good news overall, and that Brian had kept his promise.

Blacky was on the ground refueling, preparing to take off again in his search for Vince and the other two. He'd stayed at LZ 2 as long as he could. But once the Colombians had engaged, they waived him out of the area, saying there was just too much air activity going on from their end to confuse the matter with his bird flying around. Despite his colorful protests, the Colombian commander had been firm on it, insisting he did not want to see Blacky go down as "friendly fire."

Seeming to acquiesce, Blacky had turned around and come back. But he was determined to get back in there. *Hell, if there's that much confusion, how do I know those Colombians, jacked up on adrenalin, won't mistake my boys on the ground for the riff raff and shoot them anyway!* So, approved or not, he was going to risk it and go back in.

Just as he came around the nose of the bird to climb in the pilot's side, he saw something out of the corner of his eye. Directing his attention to the edge of the forest, it appeared that a piece of the forest moved slightly. What happened next made his spine tingle. Coming out from under the canopy of forestation at the edge of the base were three figures, covered in foliage themselves. It didn't take him long to know for sure that this was not the FARC just suddenly deciding to walk into an enemy air base.

He raced out to the middle of the clearing to intercept the three, in case anyone was injured. Seeing the grin on Vince's face—those white teeth gleaming through what otherwise looked like an indigenous plant he was using for camouflage—he knew they were all right.

"You picked a hell of a day for a stroll, old man! And you're a couple of months early on Halloween!"

"True, but it was a bit dicey there, and we couldn't hang around for *you.* Talk about your *hot zone!*" Tilting his head in the direction of Hector, he said, "And Hector here thought for a moment he was actually going to have to kill someone, right DeShawn?"

DeShawn laughed, and between gulps of water from the canteen Blacky had taken from his belt and handed to him, he said, "Yeah. Those Colombians came in like a bolt of lightning, with a lot of firepower, and, frankly, the bad guys started scrambling out in our direction. Probably trying to get back to their own turf. Anyway, Vince here managed to get this 'big guy' to hide, rather than engage. There were hundreds headed up that hill!"

Seeing the picture very quickly, Blacky understood Vince had immediately deployed an evade and escape tactic. Surely the walk back under cover had taken longer, and drained them physically, but going the opposite direction of their pursuers had kept them out of harm's way.

As it turned out, the one who had been in the greatest danger had been Blacky, circling around up there looking like he was trying to evacuate someone. *No wonder that commander about took my head off,* he thought. Glad now that he hadn't yet gone back in, he called Jessica and gave her the good news, and said it might be a few days though before they got out of the area. He could smell bureaucracy coming his direction with the Colombian military wanting a debriefing from the "commander of the extraction team."

"You boys got your story straight?" he pointedly asked all three of them.

"You bet," DeShawn responded. "Vince never shut up the whole way back. So we are well practiced. Frankly, we'd even be able to withstand an LAPD interrogation, after Vince's drilling!" he joked, and winked at Vince. Vince just shook his head, relieved the mission was over, and accomplished.

"I see we missed the sunrise," Vince commented. "I was really looking forward to seeing that, you know. My tour book said the sunrise over Cejal was especially impressive, eclipsing even the one over Bogota."

Blacky started laughing. This was just the kind of attitude he was accustomed to from hot dogs like Vince McCoy. It was a game to these guys. *Damn,* he thought, as he looked appreciatively at McCoy.

CHAPTER 60

Governor Fitzerman knew Bud Walker's mysterious flight to Washington must have been a success because before sunrise even, his office, and every other office at the State Capitol had jammed phone lines. The United States government, which had nearly been entrapped into abrogating its own structure and function—turning into an enemy of its own people—seemed to have mysteriously "stood down."

Governors from every state were reporting two things. They were overrun with young people who were figuring out solutions in this finance game, and who were almost forcing parents and grandparents to play. Then whole families were phoning, faxing, calling, and even walking into public offices demanding to speak to their Representatives.

The revolt of the governors, and their populations, had gotten the message through. All Attorney Generals were reporting the same. The Justice Department indicated they were withdrawing their legal actions.

The entire crisis seemed almost to evaporate, leaving people wondering if this had just been a nightmare, from which they were waking up. The "nightmare" was real, however, and it would leave quite an aftermath.

Though the economic depression caused by the deliberate calling in of loans, freezing of credit, and deliberate erosion of the value of all currency through various manipulations was leaving the United States' population pretty much wiped out financially, the tangible assets were there—untouched for now, due to the hastily-put-together, but effective, revolt of all the states.

With assets to trade, and a game which was virtually teaching people—and their government—how to identify which of their assets were "barterable," and rewarding them for ever-increasing flexibility and creativity, *fear* had evaporated.

What no enemy of free people had ever understood, but what *was* a characteristic of free people, started to take hold. The people had been pushed to the brink of capitulation under threat of starvation. They were unwittingly propagandized to choose slavery in order to eat, thereby placing themselves and their descendants, their currency and control of that currency, into the clutches of a handful of men whose goal was to inherit all the wealth of the world—and whose game had been a masterful charade going on for a long time.

But once unmasked by the game "White King and the Battle of America," the "bluff" was viewed for what it was. People smiled at the simplicity of the "magic trick." Just as the audience falls for the distractions while watching a magic trick, what seems impenetrable and unfathomable to the audience becomes mundane and artfully simple, and obvious, once the "trick" is exposed. The audience gets bored and moves on to another entertainment. Governor Fitzerman guessed it would be that way now.

Just as Jessica Ranger's plane landed and pulled forward for deplaning, Bud Walker thanked the Governor and acknowledged him, knowing the man was exhausted going into the fight, but was even more tired now. Bud knew much would be demanded of the man still, since the state of Montana would now become the model for others to follow. Montana businesses were open; men and women were working; they were being paid; and property—privately owned—was secured by the American "Barn Raising" and "Bartering" ideas Montanans had learned from generations past.

"I know we all have some hard times ahead of us, Governor, as we rebuild. But if history is any indicator, we will roar back stronger. And WNG's resources are at your disposal. We remain the Network of Solutions. And we will let our competitors remain the Networks of Chaos and Fear." Then, ever the competitor, he added, "And may the best man win!"

Chapter 61

*B*rian bounded down the plane's stairway, dancing from right foot to left foot, and turning at the base of the stairs to help Jessica down. She walked with composure and purpose to Bud, Andy, and James, shaking hands with each of them. Jessica Ranger showed no excessive emotion—just the quiet professionalism that had likely characterized her whole career.

Stepping to the side, however, she couldn't wait to watch as the others emerged. First through the door was Edith Church, whose body had clearly been the most impacted by her captivity. Already weakened by osteoporosis, her structure was a little rickety, but otherwise she was in fine spirits.

So that's Edith, Andy mused. *She looks like she's a handful!*

Alicia and Reagan exited next, almost simultaneously, with Alicia waving jubilantly to them all. She ran ahead and quickly hugged everyone like a high school cheerleader hugging the varsity line after a victory. Bud was almost speechless, because in his heart he had feared he would never see Alicia again. There were so many risks and unknowns in this plan, he was still stunned it had all worked.

"I gather by your high spirits that they got the transponder out!"

Alicia squealed with laughter and responded like the old Alicia. "You bet your ass they did, Bud. And man, have I got a story for you!"

For a moment, Reagan just stood there, looking at Andy. Both seemed frozen in position. Ever one to insert himself into the conversation, Brian unabashedly gave her a gentle shove and whispered into her ear, "For Pete's sake, girl, put him out of his misery!"

Then she was off like a shot, racing to Andy. Their embrace was long and tender. Brian just stood there, until James signaled to let Andy and Reagan have their privacy. Brian, however, was still clueless. He was perfectly content just to stand there with his two friends.

I wonder if my Pal is planning on going on the honeymoon with the Kid and his bride! James mused.

Reagan leaned back, looked up at Andy, and said, "And what were you and James doing while I was *detained?* Saving the world?"

"As a matter of fact, we were," Andy said, without a hint of bragging. He simply smiled at her.

Reagan looked over to James, and moved to him and Bud to thank them for what they had done. That left Brian and Andy, standing together. Their handshake immediately turned into the embrace of brothers who had gone out separately to win—and had both come back victorious. There was no sentimentality between these two, just a mutual respect that was impossible to verbalize. They did not even try.

Finally, Andy broke the silence. His quiet words spoke volumes. "Thank you."

Brian smiled, nodding repeatedly and swaying back and forth in place. Slapping Andy on the butt, as he often had, coming out of a huddle with his quarterback, he said, "Told ya..."

Chapter 62

"**Y**ou might want to take a look at this one—maybe forward it on to the White House. Might be a slick move for somebody to make," Andy said, as he and Brian walked into the breakfast area at the ranch. Handing James and Bud each a report, with one section highlighted in yellow, they just stood and watched.

Over the weeks, every nation was slowly rebounding, learning to function independent of any ties with their former dictator, the Central Banks. It had been 100 years since they had last been free of a Central Bank. The governments of the G20 had cancelled the charters of all Central Banks, effectively putting them out of business. They were each now working on their own, and in cooperation with other nations, to re-establish trade, economies, get people back to work, and clean up the physical devastation brought about by the riots and sabotage of infrastructure that had occurred as the world approached the outer shadows of an intended Dark Age.

Back in the light, the pioneer spirit that lives in man was rekindled, and work progressed. The United States temporarily reissued the old Abraham Lincoln Greenbacks, realizing that if they could print bonds without anyone's permission, they could print currency. Confidence was returning.

WNG devoted its journalism to human interest stories of success. Everywhere some municipality or citizen tried something that worked, and benefited himself and his community, they covered it and sent it out as national news. Those watching were picking up ideas from the successful actions of their peers.

But the gamers were just beginning. Every day the top gamers were going interactive with Carver & Weir, and with each other, to bring up solutions and options in the game. Every choice a gamer created provided potential real-world options to governments, as well as individuals. Every new option removed them further and further from the mind and hands of the evil that had tried to seize them.

In fact, the Greenback idea had been submitted by a gamer, hoping it would create a whole new game for governments to play. The ideas had ranged from seizing the vaults of the RIT, recovering the gold and returning it to the countries from which it had been taken so that the monopoly of that scarce metal would end; to keeping the RIT and Central Banks but putting them under oversight by elected officials of the nation, so they would be accountable for the decisions they made and could be fired; to each nation printing its own currency, but tying the currency to the actual production of goods, to land, and to real estate, so it was equated to the true wealth of the country.

Then there was the idea that Andy had highlighted in golden yellow. Lips sealed, not wanting to influence James or Bud, they merely stood there, watching Bud's reaction. Had it not been for the fact that he immediately reached for the phone and dialed a number, they would have had no idea what he was thinking.

"Get me the First Lady, please."

As he waited, he looked at Brian very directly, asking pointedly, "Did you create this one yourself, Brian?"

Brian laughed. "No, sir, I swear. But I do admit it sounds like me. Point of fact, this was submitted by a law student at the University of Montana."

"You expect me to believe that the idea of 'arrest the main conspirators; try them in the World Court for fraud, extortion, and crimes against humanity' did not come out of your noggin?"

Andy came to Brian's rescue. "I swear, Bud, this is one of the submissions. Brian did not make this up. Kind of makes me feel good to know though that there are other kids out there who think like him."

Turning his attention back to the phone, Bud suddenly said, "Hello, my dear. No. No. No more favors. Actually, I was about to do you one."

———

Plagued nightly now by the nightmare of the white horse hunting him down, Ayman Al-Zawahiri lay on a mattress in a dark, somewhat rancid room in one of the safe houses in Pakistan.

Knowing that Samir had been killed in Venezuela, and seeing the news of the massive and brutal take-down of the drug cartel, he knew Al

Qaeda's drugs-for-weapons business, and its hopefully life-infusing entrance into the slave trading business, not to mention its investment into the training camps for future Al Qaeda operations throughout Central and South America, were now all hopelessly compromised.

Always a pragmatist, he listed in his mind the loss of personnel. Bin Laden was gone; Atef was gone; Zarqawi was gone; Nanda was gone; al-Awlaki was gone; and now the superstar whose strategies had won the most decisive propaganda and Public Relations victories in the annals of war—Samir Taghavi—was gone.

I never really liked any of these men, he thought. *Still, they served their purpose.*

The final blow for the Doctor, and his obsessive desire to dominate the world by acquiring wealth, came when Reuters reported the closing of three banks in Switzerland. The banks, their funds, and all their accounts had been seized by Interpol, and the bank officers were under indictment for using their banks to fund psychiatric/pharmaceutical cartels in an attempt to subdue and enslave the populations of the world—most specifically the people of the United States—and to fund drug cartels, human traffickers, and terror networks in the game of financing both sides of any conflict.

It was rumored that one bank officer was negotiating a deal in exchange for revealing all money laundering operations he was aware of, as well as the true identities of people who, though appearing to be legitimate depositors of his bank, seemed specious to him.

At least I am still head of Al Qaeda, he thought, in a feeble attempt to reassure himself. Physically weak, and financially disempowered, he made a command decision. He would not assume yet another identity and camouflage himself once again amongst the citizenry of nations he plotted to exploit. The hide in plain sight game he had mastered was a game of the past in his mind now.

I will just wait here. Those swine will probably never find me, and my name will live in legend.

He knew it would be only a matter of time before officials figured out that it had been basically the Directors from Great Britain, the United

States, Germany, Switzerland, and a key official from Italy who had masterminded the manipulation of the entire world into a depression in order to coerce them into accepting the group's heinous demands and power grab. The rest of their G20 Central bankers had been involved, but mostly just out of their naïve view of a proper world order.

After all, in time, their constituents would forgive them, and they would turn on him and Braghelli. Of this he was certain. He had gambled everything on his perverted understanding of human nature, and the one thing he *knew* was that one will always justify his greed. Sir Harley Grantham-Jones decided it was time to leave the turret, before they found their scapegoat.

Using the disguise he had donned to come into the facility some months back, he hoped he could hastily escape, with enough gold from the vaults to disappear into the world, and live out the rest of his life in anonymity.

It was not to be the case, however. As he emerged, wheeling an obviously heavy cart of luggage loaded with gold, he was intercepted at the railroad station by Interpol—acting on a tip concerning his likely appearance. They identified him, confiscated his possessions, and informed him that he was being arrested and would be tried in The Hague for a series of crimes, which they carefully read to him. One of them was "Crimes Against Humanity."

Epilogue

*J*ames was standing at the edge of the wedding reception, dividing his attention between the mirror-like marine blue Pacific behind Brian's new home and the truly unusual collection of wedding guests.

The Governor of Montana had been too busy with his state's affairs to make it, but the Sheriff of Lincoln County and his wife were thrilled to have been invited. Never really liking the gray, cloudy Montana Thanksgivings, they had welcomed the chance to come to sunny Southern California on Thanksgiving Day to represent the men and women who had chosen victory in Montana, and who were bringing it off.

Accompanying him were Dusty Owens and his family. Brian had deposited silver coins into the Montana Bank, with the understanding that they would in fact loan this man enough money to restart his service garage, and begin again. With fair terms for both, the young man, who had never lost his pride, was grateful. He was honored to be at the wedding.

Oddly enough, the Montana crew were sitting with and dancing with the Compton gang who had invaded their turf. "God," Richard, Jon-Jon, Hector, and DeShawn—all of them were there.

"What are your plans, DeShawn? A shindig like this in your future?" James asked.

"No, sir! Don't have the lady yet. But I'm looking. I'll be back with my car restoration businesses, and I plan to work with some local ministers. I need to talk with the brothers about what I learned up there, and your boys asked me to speak on the circuit with them. You know, do some good."

He didn't need to say any more. James understood. "What about Hector?"

"He and McCoy are partnering!" Seeing that James was surprised by this, he added, "My man, seriously. He really got into that whole 'disappear into the jungle, rescue people thing,' and McCoy said he has what it takes. So, right after this, he's gone."

Bud Walker and Jessica Ranger were deep in conversation, so James decided not to interrupt them. *Hope that guy sees the obvious here,* James thought. What surprised him though was watching Brian dancing with Alicia Quixote. Always graceful, he had the odd sensation that Brian was persuading Ms. Quixote that she might just want to return to Los Angeles.

Seeing James standing there, Brian excused himself and walked over so as not to leave James alone. Clueless as Brian sometimes seemed when he was into his computer games, in reality, he was very sensitive to James and to the feelings of the man who was alone here today. "Hey, Pal," James said, calling out the familiar nickname.

"Hey."

"Magnificent house, Brian."

Brian grinned. He had kept his eye on this place, and money or not, he had been determined to get it. To his surprise, the owner had been a huge fan of Brian's, enough that he had bartered the home, in exchange for Brian committing four seasons to his son's football team—coaching and mentoring.

Brian looked around, nodding his agreement with that. As his eyes returned to Alicia, he said, "She's a hottie!"

"Yeah, you two look good together. I suggest you tell *her* though."

Brian slapped him on the arm and said, "Thanks, man. Really."

Reagan and Andy were headed into the house to change before leaving on their honeymoon, so James started to head towards his car, intending to be ready to pull out as soon as they left. He didn't realize Bud had followed him until Bud yelled, "Boy Scout..."

James laughed. Stopping, he turned to find out what Bud wanted. "I wanted to thank you for breaking and entering my house," Bud said. "No telling where we'd be if you hadn't done that."

"Yeah, well..." James was a little uncomfortable. Frankly, the truth of that statement was almost too much to comprehend. He waited a moment, and then extended his hand for the first handshake the two had given each other. Looking Bud Walker directly in the eye, he said, "Well, I enjoyed my time with you, too, up there in the 'Last Best Place.' I learned a lot."

Walker waited, sensing James had something to add. He did. "You all taught me something I'd forgotten in all my years of ferreting out rats and vermin. Maybe I never knew it in the first place." Swallowing to conceal the lump that was rising in his throat, he added quietly, "You all showed me that people are basically good."

Then, breaking the mood, once again he started toward the car. Bud strode up alongside him however. "Any chance you'll invite me down to the Cape Fear River? I'd like to do some fishing with you. Maybe kick around an idea or two."

"We'll see."

The loud applause signaled both men that the couple was leaving the reception and saying their goodbyes. The only conventional wedding activity of the day was the bouquet toss, and Edith Church caught it. "Is she even seeing anybody?" Bud asked. "I just don't quite see that. But she sure seems pleased to have caught it!"

James laughed. "Yeah. She does. Well, nothing would surprise me with that woman. She's a corker!"

Somehow, the guests knew the final moments belonged to James, Andy, and Reagan. Guided by Edith, they all crossed the lawn to the western edge of the property where they could enjoy the view and be way out of earshot, while the three went to Andy's car—which was mercifully undecorated!

It was James' turn this time to help load the trunk. As he helped Andy and Reagan load their bags into the trunk of Andy's convertible, and begin first their much-needed honeymoon, and then their lives together, the rightness of it took his breath away.

He had not been able to save Kelly, but they had saved the beautiful and brave Reagan Lynch. Her emerald green eyes, copper hair, and indomitable effervescence overwhelmed him with remembrances of Kelly. Today, he did not even try to shake it off. *Perhaps this is Kelly's way of being here to see Andy get married—in my mind's eye.*

Reagan's wedding location choice, and the festivities she had created, had graced them all, and he knew the Kid had "done good." Embracing them both, he more formally than intended congratulated them and said he expected to see a lot of photos. Cocking her head, smiling, Reagan reached up, touched his face, and kissed him affectionately on the cheek.

James turned and walked easily to his own Mustang convertible, totally looking forward to the drive from Pacific Palisades to his cabin on the Cape Fear River. Every time he had tried to retire there before, some crisis brought him out to analyze, and do battle.

But today was different. Today, he could finally leave—no scores to settle, no terrorist rats to hunt down, and no friends to rescue. The tranquility of Cape Fear beckoned. Before he had even gotten his seat belt on, however, Andy's familiar voice interrupted his reverie. "So, James, Reagan says you're really hanging it up this time."

"Yep, Kid, I'm leaving it in your capable hands."

Andy nodded, looked away into the distance, and smiled once again.

James could not hold it back any longer. "Kid, I been meaning to ask you all these years…"

"What?"

"That thing you do, you know, looking away like that and smiling? What in the hell are you looking at?"

Andy almost shrugged it off with an "aw shucks" gesture, but instead, he leaned down to James, placing his hand on James' shoulder, and answered, "What *can be*. That's all."

James ruminated on that for a moment, looked away as well, and then turned the key in the ignition. "I'll see you when I see you."

Andy slapped him on the shoulder and stepped back, making room for James to pull into reverse and leave. A moment later, the Mustang was gone.

ACKNOWLEDGMENTS

*S*ince the release of the first book in the trilogy, *White King and the Doctor*, and its sequel, *White King Rising*, friends and professional colleagues have continued to provide help in their tireless promotion of the books, and in keeping the dream alive through to the completion of the story. It has been appreciated more than words can say. I will mention you, in no particular order, as each and every one of you are simply the best.

Before I do so, however, there are three non-fiction authors whose works I feel present enormous insight into the world in which we live—Rachel Ehrenfeld, John Truman Wolfe, and E. Benjamin Skinner, writing about the funding of terrorism, financial dictators, and slave trafficking respectively. Their courageous works inspired me to "put my shoulder to the wheel."

And now to that magnificent group: Carter and Mariya Ransom, Marcia Powell, Steve and Jeannie Luckey, Ivan and Anne Passer, Rich DeVos, Jerry and Pat Molen, Paul and Muffin Vallely, Juanda Marshall, Louise and Richard Cole, Patricia Zehnder, Earl and Tina Charles, Dale and Gayle Bax, Robin and Carrie Alkins, Jon Batson, Ashton Sanders, C.J. and Sharon Johnson, "Sam" Warner, Verna Sabelle, Larry and Pam Winters, Terry and Lorri Taylor, John and Martha Stevens, Marcy Sanders, Rex and Judy Nichols, London Garcia, Vince Rush, Tara McCleskey, Jessica Phillips, Steve and Julie Ridley, Mike Walimaa, Michelle Flanagan, Phil and Joanne Moody, Laurie Anspach, Dave and Susan Cox, Charles and Tanii Carr, Paul and Pam Reeb, Jack Potter, James Kessler, Ann Good, Theresa Hafen, Liam and Shannon Leahy, and Brandon Kjar.

Last, my unending gratitude to the management and PR team: Todd Smith and Millicent Crisp, my managers and friends; Laurie Jessup and Eileen Batson, my oh-so-talented publicists; and to the creative team who produced such a quality book: Linda Gipson of www.gipsonstudio.com, who created three gorgeous and impactful covers; and Stephanee of <u>www.</u> <u>integrativeink.com</u>, whose gracious and wise editing and internal book design contributed to a stellar and consistent trilogy.

*L*ee Kessler is a television actress, screenwriter, playwright, and stage director. Her career in Hollywood and New York spans thirty-eight years, and includes dozens of guest starring roles in episodic TV, mini-series, and movies-of-the-week. She had reoccurring roles in the series *Hill Street Blues* and *Matlock*, and was submitted for Emmy nominations twice for her starring roles in the movie *Collision Course*, and the ABC special, *Which Mother Is mine?* She co-starred with Peter O'Toole in the movie *Creator*.

Lee became the first actress in the world authorized to portray the legendary diarist Anais Nin when her play, "Anais Nin—The Paris Years," was produced in New York and Los Angeles, with a subsequent tour on the West Coast. She also directed the West Coast premiere of A.R. Gurney's "Who Killed Richard Cory?"

Since the publication of her suspense novels *White King and the Doctor* and *White King Rising*, Lee has made numerous radio and TV appearances discussing the books' relevance to the events we have all witnessed and experienced in the first decade of the new Millennium, and has spoken often at book signings and private readings in New York and Los Angeles.

She has a passionate commitment to the youth of today, known as Generation Y, and speaks to them often about their role in keeping America free. Further, she challenges them to make the journey from being the "Trophy Generation," which is their current mantle, to the "Hero Generation," which she believes they are destined to become.